THE LAND OF NIGHTINGALES

In 1919 Phoebe Maynard found the old journal in the attic. It reminded her of her childhood in Spain and of her father's distress whenever she spoke of that country. Phoebe and her sister Lydia had never understood why 'the land of nightingales' was such an emotive subject within the family, but when their father dies it became clear. His will revealed that they had a half-brother—Juan Rodriguez. When Holly, Phoebe's niece by marriage, came onto the scene the two worlds met as Holly and Juan found themselves drawn into the turbulence of the Spanish Civil War.

THE LAND OF NIGHTINGALES

THE LAND OF NIGHTINGALES

by
Sally Stewart

Magna Large Print Books
Long Preston, North Yorkshire,
England.

British Library Cataloguing in Publication Data.

Stewart, Sally
    The land of nightingales.

    A catalogue record for this book is
    available from the British Library

    ISBN 0-7505-0973-2

First published in Great Britain by Bantam Press, a division of
Transworld Publishers Ltd., 1995

Published in Large Print December, 1996 by arrangement with
Transworld Publishers Limited and the copyright holder.

Magna Large Print is an imprint of
Library Magna Books Ltd.
Printed and bound in Great Britain by
T.J. Press (Padstow) Ltd., Cornwall, PL28 8RW.

For Mary,
to whom much is owed

PART ONE
1918

1

It was the year of the Armistice, though only just still 1918—the tag-end days of December that ought in any properly arranged calendar, Phoebe thought, to take themselves off the scene as soon as Christmas was over. It was true that *this* dying year had seen the ending of the most terrible war in history, but otherwise she could see no reason to think well of it. At the moment, oppressed by a severe cold, she wasn't even inclined to be optimistic about the year ahead; life looked as uniformly grey as the winter sky beyond the drawing-room's long windows. She was poking mournfully at the logs smouldering on the hearth when the door opened and her elder sister walked in. Fresh cold air came with her, and the impression Lydia always conveyed of having a thousand urgent matters to attend to.

'I've caught you moping, Phee...that won't do at all,' said Lydia briskly. 'I know Mama's illness was a dreadful strain for you, and a funeral takes getting over; but *she's* beyond the reach of any more suffering, and *you* must think about the future.'

'I *was*,' Phoebe answered hoarsely. 'I'm bound to say it didn't look particularly enticing.'

The sight of her pale face made Lydia speak more gently. 'Dearest, you're feeling tired still, perhaps a trifle bored as well. Life *will* get better, but you have to give it a push—by being positive.'

A glimmer of amusement touched Phoebe's mouth. 'I was *very* positively poking the fire, but I'm afraid it didn't respond!' Her sister's expression made her smile outright and she felt more cheerful. 'Take no notice of me...my New Year resolution shall be *not* to be glum after Christmas!'

Lydia nodded and then, her sister having been dealt with, moved on to the next matter in hand. 'Now, Phee, it's time a thorough inspection was made of the house. Mrs Jim and the maids have done their best, no doubt, but servants need proper supervision. You can leave it to me...it's too cold for *you* at the moment to wander through this barn of a house. I shan't be very long.'

She bustled away and returned a quarter of an hour later. Her face shone with such virtuous pleasure that Phoebe guessed she'd enjoyed finding error in others, being above the sin of sloppy housekeeping herself.

'I knew it, the attic rooms upstairs are a disgrace—not touched, by the look of them, since we returned from Spain, and *that's* nearly fifteen years ago.'

'Does it matter very much?' Phoebe enquired reasonably. 'There are more rooms here than Father and I ever use; why not just forget about the attics?'

'Of course it matters. Apart from the dust and cobwebs, I counted several cracked panes

14

of glass in the windows up there; they, *at least,* must be attended to.' In case she had sounded severe she allowed her voice to soften. 'Not your fault, Phoebe, and poor Mama certainly never felt well enough for the role of chatelaine.'

Phoebe reflected that, well or ill, it wasn't a role that had ever appealed to their mother. In fact, it was doubtful whether anything had appealed to her at all, except the pleasure of fancying herself an invalid. But then real illness had suddenly come, in the shape of the influenza epidemic sweeping through Europe at the end of the war. Eliza Maynard hadn't put up much of a fight against it...hadn't even seemed to want to. In Phoebe's view *that* needed thinking about more than dust-covered trunks in the attics. Lydia wouldn't think so; effects interested her, not causes, and she never felt inclined to enquire into the reasons why people often behaved so strangely. Phoebe's view was that her sister would have made an excellent barrister, but life had cast her for the part of vicar's wife instead. It was a pity in a way, having strengthened her natural preference for telling other people what to do, but Phoebe forgave her the flaw, loving her for other qualities. She knew that the rest of Hindleford forgave her sister too. Village women twice Lydia's age managed not to smile when she advised them how to raise their families on the weekly fifteen shillings brought home by farm-labouring husbands. They agreed across their washing-lines that the poor good soul meant well, and it was true enough that she never refused them help in times of trouble.

15

Phoebe halted her own train of thought, aware that it had wandered as usual from the subject in view. 'I'll do something about the attics,' she promised. 'As a matter of fact I rather like delving into the past—*our* past, I suppose some of it must be.'

Lydia frowned because, as usual, Phoebe *would* always complicate simple matters. There was no mystery contained in the littered rooms upstairs; only a great deal of antiquated lumber, and perhaps some cast-off clothes that the village women would find useful. In any case, the past was better left unconfronted. Being five years older than Phoebe, Lydia could remember more about the years they'd spent away from England. She could still recall her mother's iron determination to close that mistaken Spanish chapter in their lives, but more vividly remembered still had been her father's anguish when they sailed for home. The reason for it hadn't been understood, then or since, but she'd never discussed it with her sister, and didn't propose to do so now.

'I must go,' she said instead. 'Elfrida Bates gave birth to her seventh child yesterday evening. I shall have to call and make sure her feckless husband is coping.'

'Yet *another* daughter, I suppose?' Phoebe enquired, without the smallest hope of being contradicted.

Lydia's frown faded into a smile that made her look her true age again—twenty-three to Phoebe's eighteen. 'You won't believe it, but she and Simeon finally managed to produce a son.

16

They want to christen him "Welcome Thomas", if you please, but I doubt if Francis will feel able to announce *that* at the baptismal font.'

She bustled back to the Rectory next door, leaving Phoebe to sit idly staring at the flames that now danced among the logs on the hearth. She thought it a pity that Lydia didn't find the time to smile more often, but it had become a necessity to her sister to fill every unforgiving minute of the day. Perhaps it was to make up for the life their mother had wasted; more likely to help Lydia herself forget that her heart's true choice of husband had been a young man called Christopher Bellingham, not the Reverend Francis Fanshawe. But Christopher lay buried in a Flanders grave beside thousands of others who hadn't survived the slaughter in the first Ypres battle of the war. Lydia Maynard's fierce energy and beauty had been given instead to the gentle priest next door. Phoebe was inclined to think him, after three years of marriage, still bemused by the fact, and even more astonished by the twins, Richard and Helena, who now tumbled like puppies about his feet while he pored over some Greek translation from the Hebrew.

The New Year set in with a spell of weather so arctic that not even Lydia could expect the work of attic clearance to begin. But at last a morning in early March brought a sudden change. Bitter cold yielded to the promise of spring, and almost overnight every tiny bud suddenly visible on every branch signalled the explosion of fresh, brilliant green to come. A pair of robins in the big cedar tree argued over territorial rights, and the orchard grass, snow-hidden a week before, was now drifted with the gold of wild daffodils.

Phoebe wandered about the gardens, and the water-meadows that lay between the village and the river, registering each new miracle. It seemed more than ever necessary not to miss a single lovely thing about this spring. She was usually alone on her walks, but was accustomed by now to solitary pleasure. Lydia was too busy to 'stand and stare' with her, and although Francis Fanshawe would certainly have enjoyed the intricate marvel of a moorhen's nest found in the rushes along the river-bank, it was unfair to encourage him to dawdle. The Vicar must attend to all those duties that the Church forbade his wife to perform; she could and did do much, but the baptizing, marrying and burying of the people of Hindleford had, unfortunately, to be left to Francis.

The matter of the attic spring-clean had almost faded from Phoebe's mind when her father looked up suddenly from his breakfast one morning to watch her more carefully than usual.

'It's lonely for you here now, my dear. I should have thought of it myself, without giving Lydia the chance to point it out to me,' he said unhappily.

Mischief glinted in her face, surprising him—he'd always thought of her as being a solemn child. 'That's what we rely on her for—to see all the little things that escape our notice! But I'm *not* lonely...just under-employed until work starts again in the garden. Mrs Jim doesn't need much help from me inside the house.'

Henry Maynard picked up his coffee-cup, then put it down again. 'You could help *me*...with the village...that is, if you'd like to.'

She stared at him, with colour beginning to tinge her pale cheeks. 'Your *model* village, you mean?... Oh, I'd *love* it more than anything. I've always longed to help, but...but it didn't seem very possible while Mama was alive.'

It hadn't been possible at all; he knew better than Phoebe how much his wife had resented the one interest in his life that had enabled him to shut himself away from her. She'd made sure that she didn't allow her daughter to escape as well.

'You were needed elsewhere,' he agreed. Then, as if to put the past behind them, his hands swept a gesture in the air. 'Things are different now, but at the rate of progress I'm making alone, the model won't ever be complete. Another pair of hands would make a lot of difference.'

She smiled so ravishingly at the unexpected pleasure in store that he was surprised again. He'd seen strength and intelligence in her face, but never beauty before, because the Maynard good looks had been shared unequally between his daughters. Lydia's fair beauty was well known throughout the neighbourhood; in Phoebe it had been muted into mouse-brown hair, hazel eyes, and neat but ordinary features. All the same, she'd grown up without resentment in her sister's shadow, and endured without complaint a girlhood devoted to her ailing mother. Eliza's tyranny had been gentle, but a tyranny for all that. Remembering it, Henry felt suddenly guilty.

'You should be with friends of your own age,' he said with sharp regret, 'not helping your father to ride his hobby-horse.' He might have added that she was nearly of an age to marry and have children of her own, instead of being the willing slave of the twins next door. But there were few of her own age and kind left around Hindleford; the damnable, bloody war had cut a swathe through the young men who should have provided husbands for the girls of her generation.

Phoebe saw, almost with surprise, that his concern was for *her*. He'd been a distant, courteous figure in her life, but she'd gradually become aware that geniality was a mask he wore. Behind it grief for something lost lay hidden—grief, she'd always supposed, for the baby son between Lydia and herself who hadn't lived beyond a month or two. Henry had taken his wife and daughter to live in Spain after that and Eliza's health had seemed to improve; but after Phoebe was born she'd become sickly again and there'd been no other son to carry on the Maynard name.

'I *want* to help,' she repeated gently, 'and I'd like to start right now.'

She saw him smile, and registered almost with a sense of shock that he was a handsome man

20

still in the prime of life. He'd been tied for years to a querulous and fading invalid, but even Lydia—well versed in local gossip—had never once hinted that any local lady felt it worth pursuing him. Henry Maynard's only interest seemed to be in his estate and the model village of Hindleford that he was laboriously constructing. One day the spreading tentacles of Oxford would probably engulf them, but by then his replica in miniature would be complete—every building, clump of trees, and flowered byway faithfully represented. The work was delicate, and had to be precise, but as Phoebe began to share the peaceful hours in his studio, Henry gradually discovered with delight that his daughter's skill outshone his own. It wasn't from the Maynards—mere soldiers and minor landed gentry—that she'd inherited such remarkable artistic flair. It came, more likely, from her mother's Harkness ancestors up in Staffordshire.

One morning, instead of working in the studio, he invited her to accompany him into Oxford. She considered the invitation, but shook her head.

'Not if it's to visit old Mr Taverner again. You took me once when I was a child before the war. He smelled horribly of snuff, and cracked his finger-joints in the most off-putting way.'

'You're very severe...it's his party piece, and he can still do it at the age of eighty-one! But he only walks to the office in the Turl nowadays to drink a glass of sherry with privileged old clients like me. "Young" Archibald does the work,

21

helped by an even younger great-nephew who returned damaged from the war, poor fellow.'

'I still think I'll stay here—the church is waiting for a second coat of paint this morning.' Phoebe smiled at the idea, then the pleasure in her face faded. 'No, I've just remembered something else. Lydia says the attics upstairs require my attention and even if I could go on forgetting about them, *she* won't. She's very good at ferreting out sins of omission!'

'I know—we should never have let her become a vicar's wife,' Henry agreed wryly. He smiled at his younger daughter and then set off for Oxford alone.

An hour later, wrapped in an apron borrowed from ample Mrs Jim in the kitchen downstairs, Phoebe sneezed attic dust and admitted to herself that Lydia had been right. The trunks, still plastered with the labels of the Peninsular and Oriental Steamship Company, had lain undisturbed since the Maynard family returned from that very peninsula—Spain—where she herself had been born.

Considering that fact, something was noticeably missing from the assortment of relics that she was now sifting through. There were heaps of antiquated clothes, fashionable perhaps in the last years of Victoria's reign, but only to be smiled at by today's village women; there were well-thumbed books that had been Eliza Maynard's youthful reading, and faded daguerreotypes of people, stiffly posed in front of bottle-shaped kilns, who had surely belonged to her Harkness family at Burslem. There were a few more recent photographs—Phoebe recognized her father in the dashing regimentals of a captain in the Queen's Hussars, and a very small Lydia weighed down by the adult clothes in miniature that Victorian children had had to wear. But of Spain, where Henry had taken his frail wife to live for nearly seven years, there was no single memento at all.

After a morning's dutiful work Phoebe was on the point of abandoning her task, but one last package remained at the bottom of the trunk in front of her. Its covers of marbled board tied with green tape promised no excitement—perhaps more sepia-coloured views of Staffordshire, or someone's forgotten commonplace book; but she recognized the name inscribed inside in a flowing hand. Nathaniel Harkness had been her maternal great-grandfather.

On the next page came his first entry:

> *We are to sail from Southampton on this evening's tide. Feeling now much less intrepid than when I left dear inland Burslem a week ago, I try to believe the Captain's promise that the Bay of Biscay's villainous reputation is quite without foundation. But there is something about the smile of this wall-eyed sailorman that discourages comfort. God send us a speedy voyage and the haven of Corunna in due course.*

Phoebe smiled at the opening paragraph, eager to read on, but the date at the bottom of the page suddenly made her shiver. Nathaniel had begun his narrative on 'this 3rd day of April, 1819', and by a coincidence that seemed very strange she had stumbled on it exactly one hundred years later.

The faded ink on yellowing pages was difficult to read, but she persevered, too engrossed to put it down. After Corunna, reached safely after a crossing of the bay that had given the lie to the deceitful captain, had come Lisbon, and then Cadiz. Here, Nathaniel had returned thankfully to dry land and horse power, and begun to amble through Andalusia, surviving unseasonable weather, primitive lodgings, and even the occasional brigand with what seemed to Phoebe amazing intrepidity after all. She thought he would have made an ideal travelling companion—observant and good-humoured, but convinced of what it meant to be an English gentleman; he could not in any circumstances allow himself to be intimidated or swindled.

She closed the book at last, aware of several things at once: pangs of hunger reminded her that she had missed luncheon, but there was a more interesting discovery. Impressions from earliest childhood that she'd supposed too distant to recall were suddenly clear in her mind again, like photographic images brought into focus. Even as she thought about them, she found herself taking Nathaniel's journal to her own room before she went downstairs. There was something unpleasantly furtive about hiding it in this way, but she needed time to work out what to do with it.

She was still undecided when her father

returned from Oxford, seeming so preoccupied himself that they sat at dinner almost without speaking.

'I hope you found all the Taverners well this morning,' she ventured at last.

'Archibald and his son were out,' Henry said briefly. 'I saw the great-nephew instead, Hugo Taverner. He seems to manage very well with one hand, but I fancy that the firm will change when *he* becomes senior partner...no more friendly chats by the fire and glasses of vintage sherry.'

He lapsed into silence again, and this time Phoebe left him undisturbed, knowing that whatever matter had taken him to Oxford still entirely occupied his mind. In the candlelight his face looked drawn and sad, and suddenly she longed to know and share what made it so. As if reached by the little breath of her affection, he glanced across the table and smiled at her.

'You've had a tiring day making good your sin of omission, I'm afraid. Shall we tell dear Lydia that we like the attics as they are? There's nothing worth bothering about up there.'

'I rather enjoyed myself,' she confessed, glad to be truthful at least to that extent, since deceitfulness was proving such an unexpected strain. It was a relief to both of them, she thought, when the evening limped to an end and they could tell each other that it was time to go to bed.

The following morning Phoebe took her problem to the pleasant Georgian rectory next door, but for once her sister was still upstairs, and the Vicar seemed vague about the reason for such unusual behaviour. She found Lydia lying down on the chaise longue in her bedroom, a sight so rare that it sent Phoebe running across the room to kneel beside her.

'Lyddy dear, you *aren't* well. You must tell me what is the matter, because Francis doesn't seem to know.'

Amusement touched her sister's mouth for a moment, reminding Phoebe of their father. Lydia had inherited not only his fair colouring but his beautifully chiselled features as well. She looked too young to be a vicar's wife, and much too sophisticated.

'Francis does know my ailment,' she commented, 'but he can't forget that he was born a Victorian—his wife's pregnancy is not for discussing with an unmarried maiden like you! I'm feeling sick this morning, that's all; so you needn't look alarmed.'

Phoebe was trying to took suitably pleased, but Lydia had offered the news so flatly that it was impossible to guess her reaction to the prospect of another child.

'Well, *good,*' she said hopefully, 'I like being an aunt, and rely on you and Francis to go on providing me with new nieces and nephews.'

Her sister's expression registered another fleeting change, too brief to be identified, and Phoebe grew suddenly impatient with her.

'Look happy about it, for heaven's sake. I'm sure Francis is.'

'Oh yes, he's happy enough considering

the names of all his favourite Shakespearian heroines. The possibility of a son doesn't occur to him.' It seemed to be all she was going to say, and her visitor had just decided to leave when she spoke again.

'There's something to be thankful for—at least I can be certain this child is *his*. I doubt if the twins are.'

With just as little expression in her voice she might as well have said that the day was unlikely to stay fine.

Phoebe closed her eyes, opened them again when the room stopped whirling around her, and found herself thinking most of all of the gentle Victorian downstairs. 'Does Francis know?' she croaked.

Lydia shook her head. 'I can't think why I blurted it out just then—I never imagined I'd tell anyone.'

Phoebe swallowed the obstruction in her throat. 'Perhaps we'd better forget you've told me now. You're not yourself, Lyddy...I'll go away and leave you in peace.'

'I'm feeling sick, *not* wandering in my mind,' Lydia said sharply, 'and it's a relief to tell someone...I was getting desperate.' She pulled herself upright on the couch and gave a little shrug. 'You might as well hear the rest of it now. After Christopher was killed I wanted to die too—all I could see were the empty years ahead without him. That's why I threw myself at Francis—he was next door, and being *somebody's* wife was better than being alone. Then, just as we were about to marry something

27

else happened. Charles Harkness turned up in Hindleford. His regiment was due to sail for France but got delayed. There wasn't time for him to go home to Staffordshire so he came here instead.'

Phoebe nodded, retrieving from memory easily enough the picture of a dark-haired young man in khaki uniform, a distant cousin not seen before. 'I didn't like him,' she admitted cautiously, 'probably because he didn't bother to take any notice of me when you were around. I couldn't really blame him for that, but he was arrogant as well.'

Lydia stared out of the window, seeing nothing of the view; she looked instead down a corridor of time to the laughing face of a man who'd managed to blot out the image of dead Christopher.

'Yes, he was arrogant,' she agreed slowly, '...and I was half mad. A lifetime of church fêtes and sermons and evensong lay ahead, and the man I was on the point of marrying didn't even understand how unsuited I was to be his wife.'

There was suddenly such desolation in her face that Phoebe wrapped warm hands round her cold ones. 'Don't say it, Lyddy—you've made a wonderful vicarage lady.'

Almost as if she hadn't heard, Lydia ignored the interruption. 'I was desperate for exactly what Charles Harkness offered me—fierce young animal loving. There wasn't any tenderness in it...just my need and his; but for the few days he was here I was alive again. The past was dead, and the future could take care of itself. Then he went away and all I could do was go on with marrying Francis.'

'Charles was killed too, wasn't he?' Phoebe asked after a long pause.

'Yes, almost at the end of the war. I didn't even hear from him...didn't expect to. What had happened was complete, and almost unimportant, except that it's stood between me and Francis ever since. Oh God, Phee, I do *want* to love him, but I see him adoring the twins, and feel sick with the terror of wondering whether I'll shout one day that perhaps they aren't his. I *need* to tell him the truth.'

After a long pause Phoebe heard herself speak in a cold, remote voice that didn't sound like hers. 'By all means tell Francis what you don't even know *is* the truth. Destroy all his confidence in you and his joy in the twins, just so that *you* can feel brave and honest.'

She had to wait for an answer; even then the cry of rage or passionate denial she had expected didn't come.

'You make me feel extremely small,' Lydia muttered finally. 'How...dare you, when I'm your b...bossy elder sister?'

She tried to smile, but tears began to trickle down her face, and Phoebe offered the only comfort she could think of. 'There's the new child coming, Lyddy dear—can't that be a sign of hope?'

'It's a sign that Francis is a good churchman, that's all—procreation is needed to justify the sacrament of marriage.'

They sat in silence after that, until a little tap at the door signalled that the Reverend Fanshawe had come to enquire about his wife.

2

Francis walked in still wearing the old black cassock he used for everyday. He was a tall, thin man, now thirty-two, with a shy, sweet smile and the freckled skin that goes with reddish fair hair. The living of Hindleford had been his godfather's, and in visits to the Rectory as a student and then curate of a parish on the other side of Oxford, he'd watched Lydia Maynard grow to womanhood. It hadn't even seemed possible to dream that she might one day be his wife; it still seemed more than he deserved whenever he looked at her. But there was another cause for guilt as well. He knew that given the slightest encouragement, she would have pushed him up the clerical ladder and made of herself a bishop's wife; but overriding even what *she* wanted was God's purpose for him—the people of Hindleford were *His* care. He prayed that Lydia would understand this in time...she didn't now.

At the sight of her brother-in-law, Phoebe blushed scarlet, thinking of the story she had just heard, and then clutched at the errand that had brought her to the Rectory.

'Look...clearing out the rubbish in the attics yesterday, I found *this*—our great-grandfather's account of a journey through southern Spain. Apparently, the Harkness Pottery was in need of fresh inspiration to compete with all-conquering Wedgwoods, and Nathaniel thought he'd look for it among the ceramic traditions left behind by the Moors; but *this* reads more like an adventure story.'

She handed the volume to Francis, able to smile now at the sudden eagerness in his face. A glance at the first few pages was enough to enchant him. 'My dear Phoebe, it's the sort of treasure any antiquarian bookman would sell his soul for! Do you realize that it was written on the very heels of the Napoleonic Wars? May I borrow it, if I promise to treat it with the greatest care?'

'Of course...but I'm hoping you'll also tell me what to do with it afterwards. Father doesn't know about it yet.'

'Why not, pray?' Lydia asked immediately. 'If it belonged to Mama, it's *his* now, and valuable by the sound of it.'

'I know, it sounds easy enough...to hand it over with a gay laugh and a "look what I've found",' Phoebe muttered finally. 'If it were anywhere but Spain I could, but Father never mentions that we were ever there, and so nor do I. It's as if we'd silently agreed to pretend it had fallen off the edge of Europe while we weren't looking.'

'Well, are you surprised?' Lydia put in again. 'It was the kind of place anyone would *want* to forget—too hot, too poor, and too violent for people like us, quite apart from the fact that nobody there could ever speak below a shout!'

'England's view of Spain, in a nutshell!' Francis agreed, with the humorous dryness that still took Phoebe by surprise. Then he smiled charmingly at her. 'I suppose you were too young to take a view at all?'

She shook her head, thinking of the memories that Nathaniel's journal had brought to life in her mind. 'I *can* remember things, but not what Lydia remembers—there were colours in the garden more vivid than the ones we know here...and rainbows in the sunlit spray of a fountain...and always the sound of a girl singing—to match the *ruiseñor,* she told me. I didn't know then that it was the nightingale she was talking about. I did once ask my father who she was, and he said, "a maid called Asunción". I tried to say how lovely the name was, but he suddenly shouted at me not to mention Spain again because it upset Mama. I couldn't help remembering the maid, though, and the nightingales.'

'What *was* there to mention, except that she hated it and came home in worse health than when Father moved us there?' Lydia pointed out sharply. 'It's no wonder they wanted to forget about it ever afterwards.'

Phoebe realized that it explained why there'd been no reference to that chapter of their life among her mother's belongings; any reminder of it had been destroyed as soon as they were back in Hindleford. It seemed to increase the problem of what to do with Nathaniel's journal, but Francis finally answered the question in her mind.

'I fear there's no doubt where your great-grandfather's book belongs—with the Harkness family.' But his agonized expression doubted the wisdom, if not the morality, of what he recommended because he still remembered his one and only visit to Burslem. In the first year of their marriage he and Lydia had been invited there so that he, as a usefully related clergyman, could baptize Sir Joshua's third grandson, 'young' Josh, to distinguish him from his grandfather. Francis had come home unable to decide who he disliked most—the bullying old patriarch himself, his Fabian socialist daughter, Jane, or his forceful daughter-in-law, Cecily. None of them deserved this precious find, and they would understand nothing except perhaps its monetary value. He almost wavered, saw Phoebe's perfect faith in him, and felt obliged to be firm.

'I'll return it tomorrow, Phoebe,' he said valiantly, 'and then you must simply say that among some of your mother's old books you found a Harkness volume that belongs to Sir Joshua. There need be nothing in that to upset your father.'

He smiled guiltily at them both, knowing that he was now about to hide himself in the garden summerhouse where no parishioner would find him until he'd finished Nathaniel's story.

Lydia waited until the door had closed behind him before she swung her legs to the ground and stood up. 'I'm all right now, and if I don't go and relieve Mrs Briggs of the twins, they'll be driving her mad.'

She smoothed her bright hair at the dressing table and stared at Phoebe in the mirror. 'By the way, Mama spoke to me once about the girl called Asunción, who was *not* perhaps as lovely as her name! She was hired to look after *us,* but made such a habit of throwing herself in Father's way that it got to be very embarrassing in the end. Her parents blamed Pa, but then of course they would.'

'Was *that* why we came back here?...surely not.'

'No, she left before we did, but I dare say Mama thought a new nursemaid would present the same problem all over again. In any case, she decided it was time you and I had a decent, English upbringing.' She kissed her sister's cheek in a rare gesture of affection and led the way to the door. 'I expect you forgot to do anything about the cracked panes in the attic windows!'

Phoebe blinked at a reminder that was typical of Lydia. After the conversation they'd just had only her sister could have remembered the matter of cracked windowpanes. 'I spoke to Mrs Jim's husband this morning,' she mumbled. 'He's going to see to the windows.'

It enabled her to have the last word for once, but she walked through the Rectory garden into the grounds of her own home, grateful to remember that her father was lunching out that day, and needn't be faced for an hour or two. About her shimmered the heart-stopping

34

beauty of an English spring...surely no less vivid, after all, than the colours of Andalusia? And although there was a picture in her mind now of the whitewashed house, gorgeously splashed with pink and purple blossom, where she'd been born, what was *that* compared with the mellow Queen Anne grace of this English home in front of her? It was true that she was feeling strangely unsettled, but it had nothing to do with finding Nathaniel's journal, or the recollection of her father's face when he'd shouted at her the name of Asunción. All that belonged to the past; what mattered much more now was the family next door, balanced so precariously on the edge of disaster.

Reminded by his wife, Francis intended to return the journal the following day at a moment when his father-in-law would be safely out visiting his tenants in the village. But long before he walked over to the Manor, a peaceful April morning had already been disturbed by the arrival of another visitor.

Phoebe was outside, arrayed in her oldest clothes. Some good hard work would clear her mind, and the long herbaceous border in which she and Wilkins, Mrs Jim's husband, took such midsummer pride was overdue for weeding. But, as usual, there was something to distract her from the task in hand. This morning it was a speckle-breasted missel-thrush about to rehearse his new spring song. She waited patiently but in vain because a voice spoke unexpectedly behind her and the thrush went scurrying away.

Disappointment was so sharp that she turned to scowl at the intruder.

'I was sent out here to find Miss Phoebe Maynard,' he said apologetically. 'I'm sorry if I arrived at the wrong moment.'

At least it was something that he'd noticed. She scrambled to her feet, brushing earth off her hands. 'Well, he *was* about to sing for me, but it doesn't matter; he'll come back. I'm Phoebe Maynard, but if you came to see my father he'll be out until lunch time.'

The man in front of her, of middle height and dressed in dark clothes too formal for a country call, was a stranger...though not entirely so; when he smiled she knew what made him familiar. On top of yesterday's coincidence, it seemed doubly strange that his mop of thick, curly hair and bright, deep-set eyes should remind her of the very people she'd been looking at in her mother's faded photographs.

'I should have expected it, I suppose..."by the pricking of my thumbs"!' she muttered obscurely. Then, as his blank expression told her that she'd spoken the thought out loud, a smile lit her face, transforming its plainness. 'My sister says it's a bad habit of mine to blurt out the first quotation that comes into my mind. I seem to think you might be a distant cousin, in which case I'm very pleased to see you.'

He'd been expecting a younger version of her sister's cool beauty, and had found instead a sulky schoolgirl kneeling on the path. But that was wrong, too—she was now quaintly but charmingly self-possessed, even in her shabby clothes.

'I'm George Harkness,' he said slowly, holding out his hand. 'Your sister and brother-in-law came to Burslem for my third son's christening, but you and I have never met. I should have attended your mother's funeral, but my father chose that moment to be ill—for the first time in his life that I can remember.'

It was, by all accounts, exactly what they might have expected of Sir Joshua, but for once Phoebe managed *not* to say the thought that was in her mind. Instead, because she stared curiously at her visitor, he anticipated what he guessed would be her next frank remark. 'I'm not much like my brother—Charlie stayed here, didn't he, before he went to France?'

'Y-yes, he d-did,' she stammered, cheeks suddenly flushed with colour. 'He was d-darker than you...taller, too.'

She was younger than he'd thought, after all, George decided—uncertain how to express sympathy because Charlie had been killed. To give her time to recover he stared at the sunlit beauty all around them. A cherry tree shed snowflake petals on the grass, and a nearby clump of wallflowers scented the air. At the far limit of green lawns, the river sparkled through the bronze fringe made by a line of willow trees coming into leaf.

'It's not a bit like home,' he said wistfully. 'I'm not saying we don't have gardens in Staffordshire, but we keep them under strict control—my wife prefers things neat, you see.'

It was Phoebe's turn to feel sorry for *him,* and for his poor flowers; she could see them in her mind's eye—straight rows of vermilion tulips, with any that strayed out of line hauled up immediately. She was almost certain that she wouldn't like his wife, although she was beginning to approve of George.

'You haven't said what brought you to Hindleford,' she reminded him.

'I had work to do in Oxford. One of the colleges there wants a new dinner service to commemorate its founding. Without seeing the place I couldn't seem to get any idea at all, but as soon as I walked in, there it was in front of me—an old magnolia tree they're very proud of in the Master's garden that happened to be just coming into bloom.' He pulled a sheet of paper out of a folder under his arm and offered it shyly to Phoebe. In the centre was the College coat-of-arms, precisely and exquisitely drawn; around it the outer border was an interlacing swirl of magnolia flowers and leaves, delicately beautiful as an illuminated missal.

After a moment she handed it back, betrayed again into saying what was in her mind. 'If I'd known I was going to meet you today I'd have guessed you'd be a prosperous-looking businessman with a loud voice and a handsome gold watch-chain stretched across his waistcoat! I hope it teaches me a lesson in future.'

Her self-disgust was comical enough to make him smile, but the smile grew into a chuckle, and then into a joyous shout of laughter that surprised her into joining in. The more helpless

38

they became, the funnier it seemed, and all the time she seemed to know that his life among the Harknesses in Burslem didn't usually include such childlike merriment.

'My father is the businessman,' he said unsteadily at last, 'but you were quite right about his watch-chain! I'm also bound to say *he'd* go straight back if the work here was done, but I allowed myself two days and I might not get the chance to come to Hindleford again. Shall I be in the way if I don't go straight away?'

She shook her head, aware of the strange stab of pain; there was no reason to think this gentle, smiling man was made to feel a nuisance at home, but she could see that he might not be loud enough or arrogant enough for the formidable family he lived among.

'It will take me five minutes to change; then I'll show you the village,' she suggested. 'We can be back before Father gets home because, to be truthful, there isn't a great deal to see.'

Five minutes *was* all she took to reappear in a jacket and skirt that seemed to match the colour of the willow fronds. He smiled with pleasure at the sight of her because, unlike himself, she fitted the place exactly...there was no false note anywhere. If he'd known her a little better he would have explained how rare that was. Nothing in nature ever jarred, but human beings often did in his experience.

Phoebe was right about Hindleford; apart from its riverside setting, it wasn't very different from a hundred other country villages—a harmonious muddle of thatch, tile, whitewashed plaster, and weathered brick. There was a tree-lined green, as usual, and her brother-in-law's simple Norman church, but in the churchyard her hand touched with pride a worn stone cross that was already old before the Normans came.

'We look on Oxford as being a very *new* sort of place,' she confided with a grave air that almost set him laughing again. 'On the hills you can see behind the village there are still traces of Iron Age settlements—so even *those* ancient people must have understood when they got here that they'd stumbled on to a good thing!'

George Harkness didn't disagree; he thought he might have stayed happily in Hindleford himself if he'd stumbled on it soon enough.

'It's only lacking one thing,' he suggested. 'Having no Iron Age goatskin tent to pitch, I was hoping to see an inn! Is there anywhere I could get a room for the night?'

'There's Ada Wilkin's alehouse where the farmhands congregate, but you won't need that; Father will expect you to stay with us.' Being several inches shorter than her cousin, she tilted her chin to look up at him. 'I know we're kin, but where exactly do we meet on the family tree?'

'With our great-grandfather, Nathaniel. *We* descended through Harkness sons, you and Lydia through daughters who changed their name with marriage.'

She thought she might have guessed; it was bound to be old Nathaniel, the cause of her present embarrassment. To have told this new friend of hers about her attic treasure-trove would have been the easiest thing in the world, but she couldn't do it while her father was still ignorant of what she'd found. There was an even worse problem bothering her as well. George Harkness must reasonably be expecting to meet the members of her family that he already knew. But, with imagination beginning to run riot, her mind shied like a frightened horse from a scene in which her cousin encountered Lydia's twins. Suppose he saw a Harkness likeness so strong that he publicly identified them as his dead brother's children? She steered nervously away from the Rectory and announced that it was time they went home to luncheon.

Her reward, when she led George indoors, was to find that her father had returned earlier than usual. Open on the desk in front of him was Nathaniel's masterpiece, and she could now visualize another scene as well—poor Francis creeping in to hand her back the journal only to bump into his father-in-law instead.

George watched her expressive face, and *thought* he heard a desperate *sotto voce* mutter... 'she could not think but would not cease to speak'. Then she launched into a racy account of finding *him* in the garden—so strange, was it not, almost on top of finding that old book of Nathaniel's in the attic upstairs? But she finally ran out of steam and Henry Maynard got up to shake hands with his unexpected guest.

'Faint but pursuing, I *think* I've followed my daughter's breathless recital! At least I have the impression that you can stay with us tonight. It's years since we met, but I should certainly have recognized you, my dear George.'

Phoebe's taut nerves relaxed. There was no distress in her father's handsome face...he was his usual charming self; and even if Nathaniel's diary *had* upset him, he was more than capable of concealing the fact.

'I knew Francis would be fascinated by the journal, so I took it to him when you weren't here yesterday,' she said simply. 'Cousin George hasn't heard about it yet—we've been too busy inspecting Hindleford.' If that wasn't entirely true it was near enough the truth for her to be able to smile at their visitor. 'Did you know that our joint great-grandfather went wandering around Spain on horseback, as a little change from Staffordshire?'

'Certainly we knew,' George agreed; 'he brought back a great sheaf of drawings—Moorish patterns he wanted Harkness craftsmen to copy. Unfortunately his elder brother had become "t'Gaffer" by then, and since Benjamin wasn't impressed by "flowery Arabic nonsense", very little use was made of Nathaniel's ideas. But that was long ago; the great white queen is dead and we live in different times now.' His glance lingered thoughtfully on Phoebe's pretty ankles, clearly visible under a skirt that didn't sweep the ground. 'Victorian ideas about more than ceramics are as dead as the dodo, I'm glad to say.'

'Does that mean *you're* blowing the dust off Nathaniel's drawings after all?' Henry asked.

'Well, I'm certainly going to Spain soon myself. A wonderful pottery tradition has been handed down there and even my father—not noted for his willingness to accept new ideas—agrees that we can learn from it.'

The conversation was interesting but Phoebe allowed her attention to wander to her other problem. She had just solved it by deciding on a casual reference to her sister's condition that would rule out a call at the Rectory, when her father suggested inviting Lydia and Francis to dinner. They would be sure, he said confidently, to want to see George again. She could only nod, bearing him no grudge for a serious complication he didn't know about. But it was George himself who inadvertently spoiled the pleasant atmosphere.

'I was forgetting your long stay in Spain with poor cousin Eliza. *You* must remember it very well.'

Phoebe knew that she didn't imagine the change in her father's expression, nor the sudden lack of warmth in his voice.

'We went there twenty years ago; my recollections of the country would be of no use to you now, and I doubt if Phoebe remembers it at all—she was scarcely more than a baby when we returned to England.'

This time she didn't feel inclined to insist on Spanish memories. She would deny them thrice, even, if that would comfort her father, and pretend that the only life she could remember had begun in Hindleford. Aware of the sudden chill, George told himself that he'd been a clumsy fool; Eliza's death was still a very recent grief to them and he should never

43

have mentioned her at all. It was a relief to hear the luncheon bell in the dining-room being rung vigorously by Mrs Jim.

Conversation at the table went more easily. Henry Maynard remembered what was required of a good host, and in any case discovered that his relative-by-marriage was unexpectedly pleasant company. There was a faint resemblance to his dead wife in George—bright eyes set in a thin face and a mop of curly auburn hair seemed to be persistent Harkness characteristics; but whereas Eliza had become querulous and bored, Henry observed in their visitor a quiet relish for life and the streak of humour that must certainly be required for working closely with Sir Joshua Harkness, Bt. Henry thought he observed, too, that his daughter was pleased with their guest, but when the meal was over she announced that her afternoon was mapped out. She would go and see if Lydia felt well enough for dining out, and after that her interrupted work in the garden must be resumed.

'*Your* afternoon is mapped out as well,' she told George kindly. 'My father is longing to show you another version of Hindleford from the one you saw this morning.'

She smiled at them and went away, leaving the visitor aware of a slight feeling of disappointment. He could imagine what his wife's almost certain comment about Phoebe Maynard would be—'odd, if you ask me; few looks, and no dress sense, poor thing'. Cecily would speak with the confidence of a woman who knew that nine years of marriage and the bearing of

44

three children had done nothing to harm her prettiness. She would see no charm in an elusive smile, and the unexpected remarks that Phoebe offered in her husky voice. George had made it a habit to agree with Cecily's judgements; domestic harmony was assured that way. He probably wouldn't disagree openly with her opinion of Phoebe Maynard, but he was quite certain in his own mind that for once his wife would be wrong; Phoebe was no 'poor thing' at all.

3

On her way to the Rectory, Phoebe got waylaid. The twins enticed her into a game of hide-and-seek that might have lasted until teatime if Lydia hadn't heard the noise they were making and come out to rescue her. Helena was inclined to resent the interruption.

'Love Auntie Phee...don't love *you*,' she told her mother pointedly.

'Well, I'm sorry about that, and so will Mrs Briggs be if you don't love her either—she's in the kitchen cutting out gingerbread men for you.'

It was painful to watch as the outcome hung in the balance for a moment or two. Then Helena's resistance crumbled and she planted a farewell kiss on her aunt's cheek. By virtue of half-an-hour's seniority it was usually she who took the lead, and now she dragged her brother towards the house.

'Greed versus affection,' Phoebe remarked when they were out of earshot. 'It's a hard choice to be given when you're still not quite four!'

'She's always going to find the choice hard, being too much like me,' Lydia said honestly.

Phoebe smiled but remembered suddenly why she was there. 'I was on my way to see *you*. We've an unexpected visitor and Father thinks you and Francis ought to dine with us.' She shook her head at the enquiry in her sister's face. 'No, not the Bishop of Oxford this time, nor another peculiar College don. I'm afraid it happens to be someone you might not want to meet—our distant cousin, George Harkness.'

Lydia stared at the flowering forsythia bush beside her, without seeing its golden blaze. 'Happens to be...' she repeated after a moment or two. 'Does anything just "happen", I wonder, or was it my mad little confession about Charlie yesterday that suddenly conjured up his brother in Hindleford?'

'A divinity that shapes our ends?' Phoebe asked gravely. 'I don't know any more than you do why things happen as they do, but I haven't told you the rest of it. Almost in the moment that we find Nathaniel's book about Spain, another Harkness arrives who says that *he* is going there as well. Doesn't that strike you as verging on the uncanny?'

Her voice had dropped to a whisper so fearful that Lydia felt the flesh creep on her

46

arms; but she was elder sister and vicar's wife combined, and therefore obliged to outface the supernatural.

'Phee, we're being ridiculous. If we don't pull ourselves together we'll be dancing round each other muttering spells, like those poor mad creatures in *Macbeth*. There's nothing sinister about odd coincidences; they happen all the time. And I certainly don't mind meeting Charlie's brother if *that's* what is bothering you. In fact, I remember him as rather a pleasant man.'

Phoebe's face was transformed by a shy smile. 'Oh, he's *that,* all right. Even Father, who doesn't exactly embrace Mama's family with enthusiasm, obviously likes him. I left them together with such a happy afternoon in store that it wouldn't surprise me to find George working on Father's village when I get back. He would enjoy that. He's a true artist, by the way...someone who belongs in spirit to an age when pottery was still the work of individual craftsmen, not turned out wholesale by machines.'

Lydia stared at her sister. 'You seem to have discovered quite a lot about him since this morning. When Francis and I went to Burslem Mrs George Harkness was so much to the fore that there was scarcely any need for *him* to talk at all.'

Phoebe examined her thin fingers as if she hadn't seen them before. 'Yes, he mentioned Cecily.'

'I'm sure he did. Not being like Charlie at all,

he allowed himself to be talked into marriage before the war. Cecily is the daughter of a rich and pushy industrialist from Birmingham.'

'There is something direful in the sound of Birmingham'...the words of Jane Austen's Mrs Elton rang in Phoebe's head, but she felt obliged to do her best for Cecily Harkness. 'She's an excellent mother, George says—brings their three sons up most...most...'

'Tenderly?' Lydia interrupted. 'I'll swear he didn't say that.'

Phoebe stood up, brushing dirt off the seat of her skirt. ' "Splendidly" was the word he used. I must go now; my weeding isn't getting done at all. See you this evening, Lyddy dear.'

Lydia watched her slender, boyish figure disappear, and wondered why a thought that hadn't occurred to her before should trouble her now. She had confessed her own unhappiness, but might never know if grief visited her sister, because Phoebe would keep it locked up inside herself. It was probably ridiculous to fear for her now, but her face had never lit before as it had at the mention of George Harkness. Lydia thought of what she knew of the Harkness family, thought especially of Cecily, and gave a little sigh. Then she put the problem aside to consider a more immediate duty. Her husband must be found and warned of the evening ahead if he was to be persuaded to be ready on time.

Phoebe laboured so diligently for the rest of the afternoon that half the border was now transformed, with freshly turned earth surrounding each bright green cushion of new shoots. She could chart the progress of the year just by thinking about them—first the cool, early-summer beauty of pale peonies and blue delphiniums, then the blaze that July and August brought, and finally the brilliant, dying colours of autumn. The flowers would bloom more gloriously for the attention she gave them, but she was aware that another day or week would make no difference to their welfare; she was out there now for her own sake, not theirs. Lydia's story still filled her mind, destroying the pleasure she would otherwise have found in George Harkness's company. Obscurely but certainly, she felt guilty for liking him so much. Less obscurely, she knew that it was better to remain where she was; she was growing calm, and at least the border was benefiting. Then a commotion in the stableyard at last signalled that her father and his guest were no longer in the studio. The dogs were there, about to lead them on a pre-dinner inspection of the water-meadows; it was safe now to put her tools away.

But instead of going towards the house, she walked across the garden to the lane that led to the churchyard. The early evening light fell softly there, and the air smelled of the damp grass that old Will Tomkins would have been scything all day. It was full of peace as usual—the place she'd always brought her worries to. Perched on her favourite, lichen-padded stone, she listened to a thrush mimicking the song of a nightingale and felt agitation gradually drop away. She'd been a fool to imagine that the familiar ground of everyday life was cracking beneath her feet. Nothing significant had happened; her cousin would return to Burslem, no doubt taking Nathaniel's troublesome journal with him, and she would think no more about him. That was necessary enough, but it was even more needful that Lydia should be brave and sensible, and see that Charles Harkness need never be remembered again, either. He must be allowed to rest in peace now, like the dusty remains of old Ebenezer Bates that she was sitting on.

'Is there room enough for me?' a pleasant voice enquired, and the man who filled her thoughts was suddenly beside her.

Amid the wild greenness all about them he made an even more incongruous figure than in the gardens at home. His suit was too heavy, his collar too uncomfortably stiff; but no doubt everything about him and his sons that should be starched, *was;* Phoebe thought that in such matters as starch Cecily could certainly be relied upon.

'Your father is out with the dogs,' he explained when she didn't immediately answer. 'I wanted to see the original of the model church you've painted so beautifully. You forgot to mention that you're a rather better artist than I am.'

She left that unanswered but shuffled along the stone, making room for him. 'Better sit on a handkerchief,' she said briefly. 'Otherwise your suit will be stained bright green.'

50

'Thank you, but my trousers will have to take their chance. I look ridiculous enough here as it is...like an undertaker on his day off, I expect you're thinking.'

It was disconcerting until she turned to look at him and saw the glint of humour in his face. There was another discovery to make as well. She need fear nothing after all because, even barely acquainted, they understood each other. It had been foolish to avoid him...quite infantile, in fact. She smiled wholeheartedly at last, knowing that she was happy in his company.

'Can you always guess what people are thinking? I almost never can, because I'm expecting them to have the same idea as me. Lydia calls it arrogance, but Francis is more kind—he says it's because in general I think so well of people that I imagine they'll agree with me!'

'I prefer his version, and hope you aren't often disappointed,' her companion said gravely. A little silence fell, but there was no awkwardness in it now to disturb the tranquillity of the place they sat in. At last George gestured with his hand at the grey stone church in front of them.

'The Harknesses have always favoured Methodism at home. There's nothing wrong with that, of course, but it obliges us to worship in a red brick chapel full of dreadful Victorian stained glass. It must have strained your brother-in-law's kindness to the utmost when he came for young Josh's baptism—he even managed not to wince at the sight of it!'

51

Phoebe smiled again, but was only half aware of what he'd said. Her attention was suddenly fixed on her cousin's hand, resting now against the dark cloth of his undertaker's suit; if a man's hand could be said to be beautiful, she thought *his* was. She had a sudden vision of it coaxing, stroking wet clay...could see the shapeless splodge of material being transformed into something he judged perfect—she knew he wouldn't be satisfied with less.

'Do you ever wish your life was different?' she asked...'no huge enterprise to inherit, no Victorian chapel, no watch-chain of your own one day?'

The abrupt question didn't seem to ruffle him; in fact she had a different conviction—that his tolerance of other people's quirks and lunacies would be proof against almost anything they might choose to say or do. If she began to turn somersaults on the grass or announced that she thought of becoming a Buddhist, he'd be an interested, but not a disapproving, observer.

'I suppose the change I'd make would be to have more time for real potting,' he said finally. 'There's nothing like the joy of working clay—throwing it on the wheel and seeing it become whatever *you* decide it's going to be.'

She nodded but, so as not to look again at the hands she found disturbing, watched a shaft of sunlight instead. It was turning the church tower beautifully to gold. She would remember the golden tower as part of this moment's enchantment.

'I don't know anything about being a potter.

That strikes me as rather shameful now, but my mother never seemed proud of her family, or interested in what they did. Once she'd arrived in London to be brought out and fixed up with a husband, the Potteries were forgotten.' Phoebe drew an imaginary bowl in the air. 'I think I'd have liked the work myself.'

George watched the graceful movement she made; she was altogether graceful, he thought. He almost told her so, but explained something else instead that was unexpected enough to take her breath away. 'I had a reason for wanting to come to Hindleford: Charlie wrote and told me about *his* visit.'

She could feel a pulse beating in her throat while she waited for what he might say next, but he merely encompassed the view in front of them with another sweep of his hands and her panic seemed absurd.

'He was in a different part of the line from me in France—worse, if anything, than our sector up in the north. Now that I've seen this place for myself I'm glad he had it to remember out there. We needed such memories, you know, in order to stay sane.'

She heard remembered anguish in his voice and knew that she would never regret again the fact that Charles Harkness had had Lydia to remember as well. When it was safe to talk of it one day she would repeat to her sister what George had said; then perhaps Lydia, too, would understand, and there would be no need for the guilt or frantic regret that seemed to drive her onwards nowadays.

'I belong in Burslem,' she heard George's quiet voice saying, 'but it's a world away from this. Your mother couldn't be blamed for wanting to forget the noise and smoke she left behind. I shan't forget *this* when I go home.' His glance lingered on the old grey church, so sunk in its bed of turf and wild flowers that it might have grown out of the earth as naturally as they had done. Quite close at hand a pair of cuckoos began to sing in counterpoint, one bird's voice pitched two distinct notes lower than the other. George turned his face towards the direction of their song, and she was free to watch him unobserved. Measured beside her father, she supposed he would be judged an unimpressive man, but his face pleased her—she was certain of that now. At the moment, because it looked sad, she offered the only comfort she could find.

'It doesn't really matter...about your raw red bricks and horrid glass, I mean. You'll find the same "beauty of holiness" inside.'

He smiled, because she was funny and earnest and sweet—different from the women he knew at home. 'So I shall, if I look for it,' he agreed gently. He put out his hand to pull her to her feet, but didn't immediately release her and she was forced to look at him. His clothes didn't trouble her now...all she was aware of was the kindness in his face, and the warmth of his hand holding hers. But there was more excitement in it than comfort, setting alight a tingle in her own blood that was unfamiliar and disturbing.

'We m-must go...we'll be l-late otherwise,' she

stammered suddenly.

He let go of her at once, and they walked back along the lane together—not finding anything to say, but sharply aware of each other.

Indoors, she made a hurried inspection of the dining-room, visited the kitchen for the obligatory chat with Mrs Jim, and then bolted up the stairs to her own room. Half an hour later, bathed and dressed, she stared at herself in the cheval mirror. The green silk suited her skin and hair, but her reflection confirmed the truth; no fairy-tale transformation had taken place. Beside Lydia she would be, as usual, just Henry Maynard's younger, plainer daughter. There'd been time enough in her life to grow accustomed to the idea, but something had changed this evening; she went downstairs knowing that for the first time she was reluctant to be judged and found wanting against her sister.

Lydia and Francis were already there, talking to her friend...the words forming instantly in her mind sent colour into her pale face in a scalding flush. *Hers*...just because he'd smiled at her and touched her hand? She was behaving like an adolescent fool, and making matters worse by staring at them now without a word to say. Lydia rescued her by holding out the little package she held.

'For she whom my daughter loves! For pity's sake tell her tomorrow that I *did* deliver it safely. She was very inclined to insist on bringing it herself.'

Inside the silver paper Phoebe found a blob

of pastry, oddly shaped and a trifle overcooked but, seen with the eye of love, recognizably a gingerbread man. She felt a sudden prickle behind her eyelids, and realized that what had changed about this evening was herself. Almost between one moment and the next she'd stumbled into adulthood, and become so vulnerable to joy or hurt that even a small child's gift could touch her to the point of pain. Her eyes were bright with unshed tears when she looked up and found George Harkness watching her. His glance held a message that was clear and comforting: he'd been nineteen himself...had known and could remember just what it was like to be swinging on this see-saw of sadness and delight.

She could talk normally after that, and listen to a dinner-table conversation that found the rest of them divided on one of the burning issues of the day. Francis was optimistic about the founding of the League of Nations...it was the world's guarantee against another Armageddon. But his father-in-law, a one-time professional soldier, distrusted all politicians and was bound to disagree.

'It's all very fine on paper, my dears, but what practical hope has it got when the two giants, America and Russia, don't even belong?'

Unable to express an opinion either way, Phoebe waited to hear what their visitor would say. George smiled apologetically at his host, but spoke with the authority of a man who knew the horrors of trench warfare at first hand. 'As a very *unprofessional*, wartime soldier, I'm afraid I distrust all generals as well! For better or worse we're in the hands of the politicians now, and God send them wisdom enough to hammer out a fair peace treaty at Versailles. Otherwise not even the League will be enough to protect us against another catastrophe. Warlike nations don't voluntarily change because other nations would like them to; they still have ambitions, greeds—needs, *they*'d call them—that must be satisfied.'

Francis nodded, but judged that it was time to talk of something else. 'You won't have had time to study Nathaniel's diary yet. It's fascinating, but ominous as well, because he clearly predicts some cataclysmic end to Spain's isolation from the rest of Europe. He wrote that a hundred years ago, and if he is right we are much nearer to it now.'

The room was warm, but Phoebe shivered... aware once again of echoes that Nathaniel's book had set trembling on the air. Then Lydia spoke, more briskly than usual, as if to demolish some spectre of her own. 'What's going to happen to the journal, Father? Is George taking it back to Staffordshire?'

Henry lifted his glass as if to examine the colour of the wine. 'I know Francis thinks that it belongs in Burslem, but perhaps Sir Joshua can wait a little longer.' He smiled at their expectant faces but kept them waiting while he took a sip of wine. 'Phoebe needs a change. It occurs to me that she and I might repeat Nathaniel's tour, though not on horseback...backward as Spain still is, it does have a railway system now. If

Nathaniel is right about the troubles to come we should obviously make our journey soon, and perhaps the same goes for *you*, George, if you're thinking of a visit.' Then, as if what he'd just proposed was a casual drive to Oxford, Henry changed the conversation once again.

Phoebe scarcely heard the rest of the discussion; she had more to think about than the battle between Lloyd George and Mr Asquith for the soul of the Liberal Party. She had grown up with the conviction that Spain was a forbidden subject, but the finding of Nathaniel's journal seemed to be the key that unlocked a door into the past. They hadn't finished with that strange peninsula after all. The peaceful ground of everyday life *was* shifting beneath her feet, and she felt threatened and excited at the same time. When she looked up George Harkness was watching her across the table. No threat there...but oh, still *more* excitement.

She went downstairs the following morning aware that life suddenly looked full of promise. It would be too much to expect George to say that he needn't rush back to Burslem, but if they didn't dawdle at the breakfast table, much happiness could be crammed into the hour or two before he had to leave. There would certainly be time to climb to the Wittenham Clumps, so that she could show him the Thames valley, green and beautiful, spread out below them.

Then, even as she thought about it, he spoke to her father. 'It's been a lovely visit, but now I must take the first train back to Oxford. If I set off soon, there's a connection I should be able to catch.' He glanced at Phoebe fleetingly, then hurried on. 'No need for me to disturb you, though; I enjoyed the walk here across the meadows from Appleford.'

'Nonsense...Phoebe can take you there in the trap in half the time...she's a demon driver.'

She smiled still more brightly because it seemed to be expected of her, but ate no more of the food on her plate. Half an hour later they were turning out of the stableyard and she made a huge effort to sound composed.

'I'm afraid my father misled you. Our dear Dulcinea is inclined to sulk on the outward journey and stop to investigate every clump of clover she sees. It's only on the way home that she gets up speed.'

'Your name for her...Dulcinea?'

Phoebe stared at the mare's solid, broad rump in front of them. 'I thought it might allow her at least to *feel* more dainty.'

He thought the explanation was typical of her and it made him smile, but his next question was serious. 'Is that important...to be allowed to feel what we know we're not?'

She wanted to implore him to believe that it was crucial, but managed an almost careless shrug instead. 'We're supposed to outgrow fantasy, along with mumps and chickenpox, when we leave childhood behind; I still like to dabble in it a little myself.'

He had a sudden vision of his father, and of Cecily...no more fantasy between the two of *them* than would cover a farthing piece; they prided themselves on seeing things clear and straight.

'I think my own little fantasy might be to stay here,' he said slowly, 'throwing good pots, and going at Hindleford's lovely, slow pace.' It wasn't what he'd intended to say...couldn't be left hanging on the air, misleading her. 'The boys might enjoy it here—the river, especially—but my bright, clever Cecily doesn't care for the countryside. It wouldn't be fair to expect her to when she was born and bred in Birmingham.'

'No "green thought in a green shade" for her?' Phoebe asked coolly.

The change in her manner hurt him—tempted him; but there was *this* to be said for a Methodist upbringing...he had no excuse not to know right from wrong.

'No green thoughts for my wife, and, if I'm truthful, none for the Harknesses, either,' he said deliberately. 'Leaving charming fantasy aside, we all belong in Burslem.'

Her only answer was to give the mare a little flick of the whip that Dulcinea very properly ignored. George turned his attention to the passing hedgerow beside him, not seeing its tapestry of wild flowers. For a little while yesterday he'd almost mislaid his own hold on things as they really were. Now, after a night's painful reflection, he was himself again—a married man nearly twice the age of the girl who sat beside him...a man who had no right at all to be listening to what she probably heard so easily—the horns of elfland faintly blowing.

She pointed suddenly to a small building just ahead of them. 'There's Appleford. Excuse me if I don't stay, but the mare doesn't like engines and you won't have long to wait before the Oxford train arrives.' She sounded barely courteous, and her luminous smile had disappeared.

He climbed down, lifted out his bag, and stood for a moment staring up at her, holding his city hat in his hand.

'I doubt if I shall ever come to Hindleford again, Phoebe, but I shall remember it always. Keep a hold of fantasy as long as you can.'

She nodded, by way of agreement and goodbye, and then wheeled the trap round, leaving him standing there...a man who was going back to Burslem when he'd have fitted so beautifully into a quiet, green valley by the Thames.

They galloped home after that, just as she'd said they would, and it didn't matter that she couldn't see the road for tears—Dulcinea knew the way.

4

Their journey to Spain began to take shape, and Henry emerged from studying Baedekers and timetables to announce that they would take the short sea-crossing to Calais. It was time, he said, for Phoebe to become acquainted with Paris before they travelled on. She was grateful for his kindness, and anxious to seem excited by a prospect that Lydia envied; but instead of listening to their discussions, all her concentration was on herself. It was a strange sensation to be so self-intent and detached from the rest of them...enjoyable in a way, but she could foresee that it might become very lonely, too. Her Burslem friend would have understood the muddle she was in; but he'd made it clear that in future he would stay where he belonged, and in any case he was the cause of all her painful self-examination. The manner of their parting at Appleford still seared her memory. Wishing above all for George Harkness to think well of her, she'd left him with the petulance of a disappointed child; the picture of him standing there was vivid in her mind—the absurd hat in his hand, sadness in his face.

Then, within a day of her departure for France, his gift arrived. The carefully wrapped parcel contained a small porcelain bowl, so beautiful that she scarcely dared to touch it. Glazed on the outside the dark, shining green of a holly leaf, within it was the colour of pale jade. To add to its loveliness, a single crimson water lily filled the bottom of the bowl, scarcely painted, simply floating there. She could only guess at the skill needed to fashion something so perfect, but she was certain of its message: the sulky child had been forgotten—they were friends, and always would be now.

Twenty-four hours later Paris in early May welcomed them with chestnut trees in flower and a softer, more southerly-feeling air than the spring had so far brought to Hindleford. It was beautiful and exciting, but in her present frame of mind she felt repelled by the city's hectic post-war atmosphere. Gaiety, it seemed to say, was everybody's duty now; how else could they survive the memory of more than a million young Frenchmen lost in four years of slaughter? Everything else about the past must be considered dead as well; only the experimental, the newest thing, the latest craze, counted now. She found it a relief to leave. At least the excitement at the Gare d'Austerlitz was genuine—the excitement that always hung around long-distance trains getting up steam in night-time stations.

She slept fitfully on the journey, only half-aware of the wheels' changing rhythms and the plaintive voices that called out in the darkness names she didn't recognize. More insistent was the struggle going on inside her: did she long to see Spain again, or wish even more strongly that they were travelling towards home?

The following morning France was left behind; they were on the far side of the frontier at Irún, and everything around them altered. Melancholy-eyed officials wearing white gloves inspected their luggage while the slow ritual of a change of train was accomplished. The conversations that exploded around her now in volleys of sound stirred echoes of voices heard long ago. She thought of the discreet murmur of talk in the weekly Hindleford to Oxford bus, and suddenly smiled at a dialogue now being conducted on the platform outside their window. For Spanish women communication involved heart, hands, and lungs, apparently.

'That's better,' her father commented. 'You've been looking homesick until now. I don't think Paris agreed with you.'

She let the word 'homesick' pass, even though it didn't truly describe her state of mind. 'Perhaps I'll go back one day when it isn't trying quite so feverishly to be carefree—we shall suit each other better then.'

He smiled at a turn of phrase that was typical of her; then, as the train jerked into life, gave his own little sigh of relief. Watching him across the narrow space of the compartment, Phoebe realized that his sigh was deeper than an impatient man's reaction to the fact that the frontier delay was over. They were back on Spanish soil and because of that very fact she could sense a profound change in him.

'I always used to think you hated the memory of Spain—I was wrong, wasn't I?' she suggested suddenly.

Henry stared out of the window while he assembled an answer. 'Your mother preferred to forget a place she'd been unhappy in; I expect that's why we never talked about it.'

She let that pass too, even though it wasn't the whole truth. In recent months they'd grown to know one another quite well, but habits of privacy between them remained. Then, because she hadn't badgered him, he offered what was in his mind.

'It's true what people say—we all have two countries; our own, and one other where we feel at home. My second country happens to be Spain. You were born here...it would be nice if it turned out to be yours as well.'

However 'nice' it might seem to him, she knew she was free to make her own choice. Born in the middle of the old Queen's reign, he was still the least Victorian of men, rejecting an ordering of things in which the sons of the British Raj ruled their womenfolk as they ruled half the world—with kindness if possible, but never forgetting their natural superiority. Phoebe knew what most men of her father's class and age still believed—according to their circumstances, women were either playthings or domestic slaves, but Henry Maynard's unconventional theory was that they were equal members of the human race. She now wondered for the first time whether he'd been too unconventional altogether for the family he'd married into. But the Harkness recollection was a mistake, inevitably bringing to mind her friend so vividly that she had to speak of him.

'Do you suppose George *will* have come to Spain?'

'Bound to, I should say,' Henry answered. 'He told me of a pottery in Seville that its English owner wants to sell, and old Joshua is very keen to get his hands on. *He* might have decided to come out here and negotiate himself, but I doubt it. Being caught at a disadvantage because he doesn't know the language wouldn't appeal to him. He'll have given the job to George.'

Phoebe smiled at the landscape of Navarre sliding past the window—as green as England, but it didn't remind her of home. Perhaps more than anything else it was the high, bright sky that insisted they were in Spain. She tried to keep her mind on this discovery but it strayed back again to the man she'd shared a conversation with, in an English country churchyard.

'Strange things happen abroad—we might even bump into George in Seville, and you could help him with the language problem!'

'No chance of that, I imagine. He's probably been and gone by now; Joshua doesn't let the grass grow under his feet.'

Faint hope slain, Phoebe continued to stare at the passing landscape, unaware that her father was composing another careful comment of his own.

'There's someone else from England we might meet here,' he suggested eventually...'Archibald Taverner's great-nephew. He's in the habit of coming because his mother's related to one of the old Anglo-Spanish families that own half the sherry business in Jerez.'

'It seems even more unlikely that we shall bump into *him*—Jerez isn't on our itinerary,' Phoebe pointed out, sounding cool. 'In any case, I thought you disapproved of a man who can't wait for poor old Mr Taverner to die so that he can start changing things.'

'It's not as bad as that; in fact they think rather

highly of one another. Hugo lacks Archibald's courtly manners, but he's a good lawyer for all that.'

She let the subject lapse for lack of interest. It was the passing scenery that demanded a traveller's attention as they plunged down into the wide valley of the River Ebro and then, with the slow passing of hours, climbed out of it again on to the immense, high plateau of Castile. It was a harsh place for the people who lived there, her guidebook said cheerfully—scoured by winter winds, burned in summer by a pitiless sun; and limited only on the far horizon by the ever-present mountains she could see, changing colour as the hours of daylight waned.

Andalusia, when they finally reached it after a stay in Madrid, seemed almost a different country. It was no less desperate in its hardship and poverty, Henry explained, but more human in scale, and somehow bewitched by memories of the past. The Moorish occupation had ended long since, but there still hung on the air, faint as a sigh, a breath of the caliphate's seductive, silken glamour, and the richness of a civilization that Catholic Isabella and Ferdinand had finally destroyed.

From the moment of arriving, tired and travel-worn at the Hotel Victoria in Córdoba, Phoebe was certain of one thing. Half-measures wouldn't do for Spain; it must be either one's second country, or one's last choice on earth. She wasn't sure which it would turn out to be, but already something had changed. The fog of

67

useless regret and self-pity she'd been groping in ever since George's visit to Hindleford couldn't withstand the illumination that poured down from this high Spanish sky. The world around her was in sharp focus again, its extremes of light and dark almost too painfully visible. Beauty rubbed shoulders here with ugliness, luxury for some with bitter destitution for most, and much gentleness with cruelty.

They travelled on, to Granada and Seville, and between the ancient cities was the haunted landscape, the white villages clinging improbably to mountainsides, the flowers and the people... still able to forget the grinding hardship of their lives in music and dance and the ritual drama of the bullfight.

Phoebe thought her father the sort of companion Nathaniel Harkness would have been—knowledgeable, perceptive and unruffled. Accustomed to taking life in Hindleford for granted, she realized that she'd always taken *him* for granted as well. Now, seeing him among strangers who immediately became aware of him, she came to the conclusion that she'd been blind. Women, especially, watched and considered him, and then returned to listening to their own companions with an almost audible sigh.

The leisurely weeks of travelling southwards seemed so enjoyable that the truth dawned on Phoebe only very slowly: her father's heart and inward mind had gone ahead of them on some private pilgrimage. She was sure of it when they arrived late one evening at their hotel in Seville. Tired of travelling, of the struggle to understand what was being said around her, and of the assault on all her senses of so many different impressions, she still knew that she wasn't too dazed to be mistaken. Her father *had* accepted an envelope from the hotel receptionist, certain that it would be there. It bore no stamp, and therefore hadn't arrived from England. She waited for him to comment on it but he simply put it in his pocket without a word. At breakfast next morning she trod delicately round the subject of the mysterious message.

'Are there likely to be many people still here that you and Mama knew twenty years ago?'

'Very few, I imagine,' Henry said, concentrating on the food in front of him, 'but I know of one couple I ought to call on as a matter of courtesy, if you don't mind being left alone.'

Phoebe spoke of an overdue letter to Lydia that must be written, allowed her father a few minutes' peace, and then tried again. 'Shall we have time to revisit Santolina before our ship sails? I can just recall the house...there's a picture in my mind's eye of white walls, and wrought iron balconies delicate as stiff black lace, and flowers everywhere...is that how you remember it?'

She glanced up from her plate to see her father's eyes looking past her at a vision even more vividly recollected than her own. 'Yes, that's how it was,' he agreed slowly, 'but I remember it for the people more than anything else, and they aren't there now.' The disappointment in her face made him gentle. 'My dear, I promise you that if we went you would be sadly let down. You remember a palace and a magic wonderland that will now have become merely an ordinary house and overgrown garden...better by far to keep your childhood memory of them.'

She nodded, agreed that it might be so, and left him to make his necessary call. Later in the morning, with her letter to Lydia written, she left a message for her father that she would be visiting the Cathedral until it closed at lunch time. Its huge bulk reared up at the end of the street they were staying in—impossible to lose her way in going there alone. It was third in size after St Peter's, Rome, and St Paul's in London, her invaluable guidebook informed her, and adorned with the gold and silver that had poured into Seville from the New World. Phoebe was just deciding that the delicate grace of the Moorish tower alongside it was more to her taste when a large man stepped in front of her, raising his panama hat.

'Miss Maynard? The people at the hotel told me to look for you here...described you so accurately that I didn't think I could be mistaken.'

She stared at him from under the shadowy brim of a white straw hat, puzzled but not alarmed. 'Yes, I'm Phoebe Maynard.' On the point of adding that she had no idea who *he* might be, she was halted by the sight of the pinned-up left sleeve of his jacket. 'He seems to manage well enough with one hand', hadn't her father said of the man who was Archibald's great-nephew?

'My name is Taverner,' he said briefly. 'I expect it's familiar to you.'

'Of course, and I imagine that you've really come to see my father. He spoke of the chance of meeting you, but he's out visiting an old friend.'

'I know...that's why I'm here; there's nothing wrong, but he asked me to call on you.'

Her hazel eyes inspected him with a thoroughness he found irritating; he was more accustomed nowadays to people avoiding looking at him if they could. Certainly young girls, embarrassed by mutilation, normally did so.

'Why should my father have asked you to come?' she enquired, still sounding more curious than perturbed.

'To let you know that he'd be delayed in getting back. He hoped that you'd allow *me* to take you to luncheon.' For Hugo Taverner it was a notable effort to have to sound so courteously willing to entertain. It went for nothing because Phoebe was unaware of the favour she was receiving.

'I don't understand,' she said flatly. 'He was only going to call on an old acquaintance. Were you there too?'

'I *arranged* the meeting.' The correction sounded very curt, because he was bored with the prospect ahead of him and tired of a secrecy that seemed absurd, as well as unnecessary. 'Your father had asked me to try to trace the couple who looked after you years ago. When he knew that I'd finally found them he decided to go and see them at once. They

71

were servants that you wouldn't remember, he said, and since they spoke only Spanish there was no point in your going with him.'

'Did you write my father a note about them?' Phoebe asked, anxious to clear up one mystery at least.

He nodded, still wondering why Henry Maynard hadn't simply told his daughter the truth. 'He always felt that Lucía and Manolo Vargas had been unkindly abandoned when you returned to England. But it's not easy to keep in touch with people who can neither read nor write. The owner of the house at Santolina died and the couple had to move to another job. I tracked them down at last to an address here in Seville.'

She scarcely heard Hugo Taverner's last remark, being concerned with things she hadn't understood until now. Her mother wouldn't have allowed Spanish servants to come to England even if it had been practical to bring them, but her father's anxiety for them would have grown with the years. She saw now why he'd seized the chance to return to Spain so soon after his wife's death. Even the ill-feeling Lydia hinted at wouldn't have lessened her father's concern for the welfare of the family—he was the most generous and honourable of men.

She smiled suddenly, glad to think he had found them again even though it had required the help of this large and rather unfriendly man, but Hugo Taverner was now consulting his watch in a very pointed manner.

'Even by Spanish standards it's time for

luncheon...would you prefer to return to the hotel, or shall we be a bit more adventurous?'

'Even by Spanish standards,' she repeated coolly, 'a single lady may eat alone in the hotel where she is staying. Thank you for troubling to deliver my father's message, but there's really no need for you to do more than that.'

'I'm afraid there's every need—I *said* I would. I think it should be adventure after all.'

That, it seemed, was that; still clutching the sketchbook she hadn't even opened, she was helped into a horse-drawn carriage waiting in the shade of the Cathedral and driven away. None of old Archibald's courtly manners, she remembered her father saying of the man who sat silently by her side. The recollection made her smile and she felt more well-disposed towards him until they were seated in the coolness of the restaurant he'd chosen. Then, when their order had been taken, he irritated her all over again by picking up the sketchbook she'd placed on the empty chair beside her.

She didn't know that he was doing what he thought would please an amateur artist, even at the risk to himself of annihilating embarrassment if her efforts should turn out to be as dreadful as he feared. But the sketches that he leafed through astonished him in quite a different way. Street scenes realized in a few, sharp, thick lines leapt vividly off the pages; other drawings, more delicate in style, captured anything of beauty that had caught her eye...the tracery of a Moorish window arch...a wrought iron balcony dripping blossom...the face of an old woman absorbed in the lace she was fashioning.

'My God—you *can* draw,' he almost shouted.

'But not well enough,' she answered briefly. 'I haven't been taught, you see, so technical problems catch me out.' She closed the book and replaced it on the chair, then for good measure removed her hat and put *that* on the top of the sketchbook. It would have discouraged any other man, but not, apparently, Hugo Taverner.

'With a gift like that you *should* have had lessons if you thought you needed them.'

'I had other things to do,' she pointed out, not mentioning that it had been a full-time occupation to look after a sad and querulous invalid. She smiled at the waiter who was pouring wine into her glass, but decided that she wasn't obliged to make conversation with her host; the less they found to say, the sooner luncheon would be over. A faint qualm of pity stirred at the sight of him one-handedly forking food, but it was stifled soon enough by his next abrupt remark.

'It's clear that you see the beauties of this part of Spain, but are they all you see? Does it strike you as it does every other visitor—a paradisal place where the sun always shines, the air smells of orange blossom, and the Andalusians themselves just loll about waiting to be inspired to sing flamenco?'

To someone else she might have confessed that she'd seen all too many signs of hell as well as of heaven, that the very air seemed heavy with the weight of too much bitterness

74

and despair; but she wasn't inclined to confide in Hugo Taverner.

'We're guests here,' she said instead. 'Like any other good guest, I enjoy what I'm expected to enjoy. Is there anything wrong with that?'

'There's everything wrong with it, Miss Maynard. In just that way the legend grows...all that's needed for human contentment is here; only let the idle, pleasure-loving peasants of Andalusia work a little harder and expect a little less, and joy can be unconfined! The truth is that the music of Spain is more than the song of the nightingales and the thrumming of guitars. It's the bray of trumpets for the dance of death in the bullring, and the muffled roar of people too long cruelly oppressed.' The scathing anger in his voice would have silenced her but for the memory of something else her father had said.

'You're in a better position than most to dispute the legend, seeing that your mother's family probably employs a good many such peasants. Why don't *you* do something more than talk about their hardships—pay *them* more and allow them to work less hard?'

She had taken him by surprise for the second time, and without the obscuring hat he could see her clearly. He decided that she missed prettiness but her eyes were beautiful, and now bright with an anger that matched his own. Phoebe Maynard wasn't like any other young woman he knew, but then he should have expected that. Her father didn't conform, either, to the usual run of Archibald's clients.

'Our work people at Jerez *are* well treated,' he

said more quietly, 'as are all the others that I know of in the vineyards there. But Andalusia's problems are what they've always been—an ineffectual monarch and corrupt government, an all-powerful Church, and absentee landlords milking huge, ill-run estates. Those are the things that have to change...will be changed *violently* before very long, if they aren't corrected in any other way.'

Phoebe suddenly remembered something else. 'My great-grandfather came here a hundred years ago. Even then in his journal he seemed to be anticipating that just such violence would eventually be required.' She shivered despite the golden warmth of the day, and then for the first time smiled naturally at her companion. 'I'm so glad you found Lucía and Manolo for my father; he'll be relieved to be in touch with them again.'

She was attractive when she smiled, he realized, and her husky voice was unexpectedly charming; but he found her a disconcerting mixture of engaging child and opinionated young woman of a privileged class. Thank God his promise to Henry Maynard could be considered fulfilled as soon as he deposited her back at the hotel. Thereafter, with his Spanish search complete, he would hand Archibald back his client and think no more of the Maynard family. But he took away with him to Jerez a vivid memory of the drawings in Phoebe Maynard's sketchbook that refused to be put aside.

Henry paid his visit to the couple who had been

76

his servants, drank the unexpectedly good sherry that Manolo offered him, and understood that even if they'd known hardship in the past, there was no need to worry about them now.

'It is all thanks to Asunción,' Lucía said proudly.

He asked about her, of course, in rusty Spanish...tried to sound unconcerned as he suggested that their daughter probably now lived at the other end of Spain.

'No...no—she's been here since her marriage,' Manolo explained instead. 'That's why *we* came to Seville.' He smiled at his wife, unaware that she hadn't yet made up her mind how much to say. But when their guest finally stood up to go it was she who pressed a printed card into his hand.

He walked away in the direction of the hotel...stopped...read the card with difficulty, because his hand trembled too much to hold it steady:

Señora Asunción Rodriguez Vargas
Barrio Santa Cruz, no 6
Sevilla

She was a five minute walk away—too near, because he arrived with not enough time to discipline himself into calmness again. Her house in what had been the old Jewish quarter of the city was noticeably grand—perhaps he should have expected that, knowing her changed standing in the world. A manservant left him waiting in a charming courtyard, but he was beyond appreciating the laughing bronze boy astride a dolphin in the middle of the pool. His hands were clammy and his heart thudded like a young man's, terrified at making his first call on a woman.

Then, just as he decided how wildly insane he'd been to come at all, Asunción stepped into the sunshine from the dimness of the house. He knew her age precisely—thirty-four; fifteen years younger than himself. But her hair was still dark as a blackbird's wing, and her beautiful mouth was smiling.

'My dear, I shouldn't have come,' he stammered, '...no permission to call...no arrangement. Forgive me, Asunción.'

She held out her hand, and unthinkingly he bowed over it and kissed it—any gentleman greeting any Spanish lady. But he didn't release it as the gentleman was required to do.

'I had to see you again...just to make sure that you were all right,' he said unevenly. 'I couldn't do it before, but I came as soon as I could.'

She stared at him, easily recognizing in this middle-aged but still handsome Englishman the lover who had transformed her life. The remembered wonder of that time had been not only an introduction to love more passionate and tender than most women knew in a lifetime; but the fact that nursemaid and grand English gentleman had come together for a little while as perfect equals.

'My husband, Carlos, died two years ago,' she answered gravely. 'I still miss him, you

78

understand, but otherwise I'm the most fortunate of women.'

'I lost all trace of Lucía and Manolo for years...managed to track them down only recently, after my wife died. Lucía gave me your address...' Henry's expression suddenly relaxed into a charming smile. 'I think she wasn't sure whether to or not; then decided that I might be trusted with it!'

Asunción nodded, accepting what he said but not commenting on it. 'Your daughters, Lydia and Phoebe—you see, I still remember their names—are they also here?'

'Only Phoebe—Lydia is married with children of her own. I didn't bring Phoebe to see you because I couldn't have said what I've waited fifteen years to say. I was the cause of Manolo sending you away from Santolina. You went in disgrace, and I was left in absolute despair. I've never forgiven myself.'

Asunición's lovely smile reappeared. 'It was at Ronda that Carlos found me—I should thank you, not forgive you.' She registered a fleeting look of disappointment in her visitor's eyes; they were still so memorably blue and honest that she knew he didn't want to be reminded of her late husband.

'I refused to go in shame,' she confessed gently. 'How could I when Don Enrique had loved me!'

She saw now a different expression on his face. The years were rolling away—he was a young man again, and she was a girl, bewitching and heavenly-kind. He held out his hands, but even before he dared touch her, the faintest little movement of her head told him that he never would touch her again. The past was dead, and he was a fool. He let his hands fall to his sides. The meeting was over and he must bow himself out of her house—Rodriguez's house—with as much grace as he could muster.

'It's...it's time to say goodbye, I think,' he managed, more or less calmly.

'Not quite,' said Asunción. My two younger children, Luis and Marilar, are out, but Juan is here. I think you should meet him before you leave.'

5

Lydia, pouring tea on the Rectory lawn, gave a little sigh of relief.

'It's nice to have you home—we missed you.'

'So your daughter was kind enough to say, but her pleasure at seeing us back seemed to be mixed with strong resentment that we'd gone away at all!'

'Helena's yardstick,' Lydia agreed ruefully, 'it's only what affects *her* that counts.' She surveyed her sister and made a discovery. 'Father was right—the change has done you good. I can't quite put my finger on it, but Spain's had an effect on you.'

' "How much a dunce that has been sent to

roam, Excels a dunce that has been kept at home",' Phoebe suggested helpfully. Then she grew serious again. 'I doubt if anyone comes back from Spain quite the same as when they went. But unforgettable as it was, I'm very glad to be back at Hindleford.'

'Poppies in the corn, village cricket on the green, and the Church fête looming—in fact, rural England in July! Is *that* what you're glad to come back to?'

Phoebe heard the note of desperation in her sister's voice but stared at the sky above their heads. Even on a perfect day like this, it was a softer, hazier blue than Andalusia knew. 'I happen to like rural England,' she said after a while. 'Spain was altogether too much for me—always *sol* or *sombra*, like the seats in the bullring; never any gentle English in-betweens!'

'Is even England gentle any more? Last year's strike by the police would have been unthinkable before the war, and the world is changing whether we like it or not. Mrs Briggs's daughter isn't coming back to domestic service in the village because she can earn more money in the Birmingham telephone exchange. And old Will Tomkins's son won't stay to be sexton when his father dies; that isn't what he thinks he and his friends fought for in Flanders.'

'All right, England's changing...probably *needed* to change for people like Elsie Briggs and Charlie Tomkins. But I think Father's right—we're not what revolutionaries are made of. Changes can come gradually here, because we'd rather allow for the other man's point of view than kill him.

I'm not at all sure that's how things work in Spain.'

'What about Father...was it all too much for him as well?' Lydia asked.

'No, I was wrong about him and Spain—he never hated it at all; in fact he'd been longing to go back. His lawyer, Hugo Taverner, had managed to trace Lucía and Manolo Vargas so he was able to see them. He didn't say much afterwards, but it must have been a great relief to find that they were in good health and, thanks to Asunción marrying very well, comfortably settled.' Phoebe frowned over the memory of her own lunch-time encounter with Hugo Taverner, but decided that there was nothing in it to interest Lydia.

'Enough of Spain—tell me about the Fan-shawes instead,' she suggested. 'Are *you* behaving as Dr Martin says you ought?'

'I'm swelling visibly, as you can see, and counting the months until November...how I loathe being pregnant! But at least Francis has abandoned the name of Hermia for Rosalind, which I reckon to be a slight improvement.' She watched her husband cross the lawn towards them, and poured more tea as he sat down beside his sister-in-law. 'I thought you were taking the twins for a walk,' she reminded him. 'Have you mislaid them somewhere?'

Francis smiled at his wife, wondering whether he would ever look at her without his heart beating a little faster. 'We only got as far as the churchyard because Will was digging a new grave and the job seems to fascinate them. They were down in the hole when I left, looking for worms, and listening to one of Will's stories. He'll bring them back when he's had his little breather.' The Vicar sipped his tea and thought of something else. 'I'm sure Richard will enjoy having the Harkness boys here, but Helena may be a different matter.'

Phoebe looked from one to the other of them. 'The...the *Harkness* boys, did you say?'

'I hadn't got round to the family news,' Lydia explained. 'Imagine it after all these years—Cecily Harkness wrote last week asking if they could come and stay during the school holidays while George makes another trip to Oxford. She suggested that it was time the children met, but I can't help thinking *she* wants to inspect Hindleford—for some reason that entirely escapes me.'

Phoebe shook her head. 'I think you're wrong, Lyddy. George said she'd hate it here, because she's too bright and clever for our little backwater; it *must* be the children she's thinking of.'

Lydia thought better of what she might have said next and asked instead for their prayers for fine weather. 'Then at least we can send them all out of doors.'

It brought the conversation to an end, but Phoebe continued to think about it as she walked home. It was odd not to have mentioned Father's intimidating lawyer, met in Seville, whose voice had been so unexpectedly angry for the wrongs done to Andalusia. But she had matters nearer home to worry about. Harkness reminders were the last things Lydia needed in her present, keyed-up state, and it seemed perverse and dangerous of fate to spread the members of that family in front of her so that she *couldn't* forget them, even if she would. Then there was Charles's brother, George. Phoebe decided that the only solution open to herself was not to think of him at all. She'd briefly met a charming man who had seemed to step easily into the world she inhabited herself. This time he would be half of a couple called 'George and Cecily'—the father of three sons who no doubt needed all the attention that his wife could spare. She might not even see him alone, however much she would have liked to explain that the water lily bowl was always the last thing she saw every night before she fell asleep.

Before the Burslem visitors arrived Henry Maynard had a funeral to attend. The University Church of St Mary's in the High in Oxford was crowded for the occasion with dons and neighbouring gentry, whose affairs old Archibald Taverner had handled with firmness and discretion for nearly sixty years, but would handle no longer. Afterwards, as they all sipped sherry in the library of Brasenose College, Henry smiled at the man beside him.

' "A devilish fine turn out", can't you just hear your father saying? It's a pity *he* couldn't hear what his friends were saying this morning.'

'It's a drawback of funeral orations,' Young Archie agreed sadly. 'The person who would appreciate them most is always missing. My father would have enjoyed the anthems, too. Give him the sound of boys' voices soaring up in English church music and a glass of fine port and he was that rare creature—a perfectly contented man.'

Henry stared across the room at another Taverner who surely hadn't found contentment yet. Hugo's dark head showed above most of the people around him, and he looked both tired and withdrawn.

'I like your nephew, Archie. If you need to be spared taking on all your father's clients, push me in his direction. He accomplished my Spanish task very well, and even obliged me to the extent of looking after my daughter there as well.'

'*Most* unusual! Hugo isn't much of a lady's man these days. In fact even some of our elderly gentlemen find him a little too abrasive for their taste. They stop short of saying it, but have a suspicion he'll turn out to be a socialist!'

Henry smiled, knowing some of the gentlemen himself. 'Fifty-eight Labour members in the House now, and the Party officially in opposition ...I'm afraid socialists are almost respectable!'

He said goodbye to his friend and threaded a path through the crowd to where Hugo Taverner was standing. Phoebe had been so brief in mentioning her luncheon with him that it was clear *he* hadn't suited, any more than Paris had, and Henry could see why. There was something intimidating about this large and taciturn man, and his wartime mutilation only increased the strong impression he gave of being different from other people. Abrasive was perhaps too harsh a word for him but he would certainly prefer to alienate people rather than have them splash pity over him. It was an understandable attitude, Henry thought, but it probably sent away those who might have been his friends.

'Your uncle and I have just agreed that Old Archibald would have enjoyed this morning's eulogies,' he said with a pleasant smile. 'But how we shall all miss him.'

Hugo nodded, knowing that he had yet to make up his mind about this man who apparently found it so easy to be charming. Lack of effort seemed to equal lack of merit to someone like himself who found charm very hard work indeed.

'It was good of you to mention us to Sir Joshua Harkness,' Hugo said briefly.

'Well, I thought that to find the Spanish-speaking lawyer he needed in Staffordshire might present a difficulty! I hope all the red tape has been tied neatly.'

'It will be, as soon as documents have been signed. I offered to go to Burslem with them but George Harkness insisted that he had other business in Oxford as well.'

'I know—some huge college order for porcelain. The result is that his family are due to descend on us *en masse*. Spare time to call on me at Hindleford yourself as soon as things settle down again—there's another matter I should like to discuss with you. *Adiós*, Hugo!'

After two postponements the Harkness cavalcade

reached Hindleford on as beautiful an August afternoon as even Lydia could have prayed for. The Rectory lawns were shaven, the larders full, and the house smelled of beeswax polish and flowers. She found herself disinclined for this visit but nevertheless she was outside on the gravel sweep as soon as Francis appeared. Behind him, borrowed from her father, Jim Wilkins drove the trap, and behind *him* Andy Briggs brought up the rear with a gig that seemed appallingly full of luggage. But while Francis was handing down Cecily Harkness, Lydia thankfully counted two nursemaids as well as three children. They hadn't come for weeks after all, and she could manage to smile a welcome on her guests.

'My dear Cecily...I'm full of admiration. Francis and I are almost ashamed to travel with our children; unlike you, *we* arrive bedraggled and distraught and all out of temper with one another!' It wasn't entirely true, but it had the merit of making Mrs Harkness smile complacently.

'With the arrangements left to George, I'm sure it's how *we* should arrive. I don't interfere with his precious pots, but everything else I make sure *I* see to.' Cecily's large eyes, rather too pale in colour but beautifully fringed by dark lashes, subjected Lydia to a frank stare. 'I hope we aren't going to be too much for you. I hated guests when I was expecting, but perhaps a vicar's wife has to get used to visitors at inconvenient times.'

She turned to assemble her straggling family,

sent instructions flying like hail about their heads, and then peace was restored. Later that evening, wishing that Cecily Harkness could be disliked without reservation, Lydia was forced to admit to Francis that George and his children didn't *look* in the least unhappy or downtrodden.

'On the contrary, my dear,' he said mildly. 'They're a family for any woman to be proud of, and since George's sweetness of character quite balances Cecily's more...ah...astringent qualities, the combination works admirably!'

Lydia could see for herself that it was true, but she stared mournfully at her husband. 'Do you suppose people regard you and me like that—bearable if we're lumped together, otherwise not? If so, I can't say I care for the idea.'

Francis crossed the room to bend down and kiss her cheek. 'My dear girl, you would if you were me,' he said simply, and made her smile.

Beyond asking Jim Wilkins if the visitors next door had arrived safely, Phoebe refused to be concerned about them. They were Lydia's guests; she would bring them over when she was ready to. Meanwhile an unfinished task of her own was all the excuse she needed to hide herself in the studio. The job was done and she was washing out brushes when one of the visitors walked in. She scarcely recognized him for a moment in a light tweed suit and soft-collared shirt, but his warm glance was the same, and so was his lovely, gentle smile.

'Your father thought you wouldn't mind if I came and said hello.'

She gestured rather wildly to the picture propped up on the drawing board. 'I *was* b-busy, but it's d-done now.'

He recognized it at once, but stood looking at it for so long that she could get used to seeing him, and even speak naturally again.

'It's for an old friend of mine here—she used to be the village schoolmistress, and played the organ beautifully for us on Sundays, but she's too frail to come now. Francis always takes Communion to her, but she wanted a painting of the church. I hope she'll think this will do.'

He'd forgotten the husky sweetness of her voice—like a choirboy with a cold, only that didn't nearly convey its attractiveness. She was dressed in paint-stained overalls that his elegant wife would despise as being not nearly smart enough—it was a word George hated, but Cecily set such store by smartness that he'd never had the heart to tell her so. Still, paint-splashed and shabby, he liked the look of Phoebe Maynard very much. He liked her painting of the church too.

'Your friend is fortunate,' he said definitely. 'It will do very well.'

They smiled at one another then. Friendship, found in the spring greenness of the very churchyard she had painted, had had to be abandoned; but it was only waiting to be picked up again, and came to them as naturally as breathing. They seemed to be able to manage without words, but George remembered that conversation was customary.

'We've both been to Spain. I only had the chance to look at Seville, but there were more beautiful human beings, more proud horses and more sheer gaiety than I may ever be lucky enough to watch again; and, oh, the sparkle in the air, Phoebe—golden by day, silver by night! Were you knocked sideways by it, the same as me?'

She smiled, but shook her head. 'The Feria was over by the time we got there,' she remembered slowly, 'and *you'd* better see Granada before you give your heart to Seville. I couldn't stop to draw half I wanted to, but I copied quite a lot of things in case they might make patterns for you to use, but then I didn't send them in case they wouldn't do!'

'You weren't sure about the painting, either,' he pointed out gently. 'It mustn't become a habit to doubt yourself. I never do when I *know* it's something I know about!'

She could be confident in his company...could be happy without effort too, just because he was there. 'The water lily bowl is my greatest treasure,' she confessed suddenly. 'I like to imagine it being made.' Her hands drew its shape in the air, but he moved towards her and took hold of them, almost roughly.

'No, not like that—look, your left hand goes outside the clay, holding it in position; the right hand is inside the thing you're making, always exerting pressure in the opposite direction. It's...it's quite simple, really.'

90

She heard what he said clearly enough, even remembered it afterwards, but all that mattered now was his hands holding hers in a grip that hurt, the warmth of his body against her, and the closeness that brought his mouth to brush her cheek. A tranced stillness kept them standing there, world and time forgotten, until Cecily's sharp voice spoke from the doorway, driving them apart.

'So *this* is where you've got to, George. Do you remember, by any chance, that you were going to show me the sights of Hindleford, such as they are?' She transferred her attention to his companion, noting without pity the effort Phoebe was making to recover herself. Cecily had met such girls before—dowdy, but dangerous because they admired so openly, and it was well known that men were fools who could never resist the lure of flattery.

'You're Lydia's younger sister, I suppose, though not at all like her to look at, I must say.'

'Yes, I'm Phoebe.'—'I'm *myself*—not a poor, dull version of my sister who must always be apologized for.' The words rang in her brain, shocking her with the fear that she'd shouted them aloud. But she couldn't have done—Cecily was smiling now, confident that she was in control and the opposition negligible.

'We haven't met before. I should have remembered if so, because I never forget a face. It's just as well,' Mrs Harkness explained sweetly. 'George can't ever think who people are—they're his bosom friends one minute, and the next he's forgotten meeting them entirely. Quite embarrassing it is at times, especially with ladies, who always expect to be remembered!'

Phoebe wanted to hear him say it wasn't true but, although he refused to diminish what had happened by explaining that merely a little pottery lesson had been in progress, he seemed to be agreeing with his wife as usual.

'I hope I don't embarrass you too often, my dear, or give too much offence to slighted friends. Now, shall we leave Phoebe in peace and take our little walk?'

She was thankful he didn't suggest that she should go with them. When the door closed behind them she had to sit down because her legs were trembling violently. Too much seemed to have happened very suddenly—huge chunks of experience unknown before...excitement dancing in her blood, physical longings that she didn't recognize, and sheer, shameful hatred of another human being. They were emotions enough to nearly freight down her little boat, and she dimly saw the danger she was in of being shipwrecked.

But during the next difficult days help came from an unexpected quarter. Instead of hating Cecily's children, she discovered that her greatest comfort came from watching them with the twins. Charming, solemn Edward, aged nearly nine, had had the sense to see that he must rule or be ruled by Helena. He firmly declined a command to push her round the garden on her tricycle in the blazing heat, and made a suggestion of his own instead. Her grandfather's village was out of bounds to them—a fact she had sadly had to admit to—but there was no reason why they shouldn't construct one of their own in the garden outside.

A site was chosen under the cedar tree, and the rest of the work-force—James, Young Josh, and Richard—sworn in, to gather the stones, twigs, leaves and moss that would be needed. Phoebe was allowed to offer a little artistic advice, in return for the pleasure of watching them at work. It suited her better than pretending that she felt at ease in Cecily's company, while George was absorbed in the affairs that had brought him to Oxford. She could almost persuade herself that those few electric moments in the studio had been the fevered longing of a dream, so aloof from her did he now seem. Then, one morning when she went outside he was there as well, squatting under the cedar tree, to have the layout of the village explained to him. His smile was a caress, and she couldn't think of an excuse to leave again, even when Edward was summoned by Helena; Young Josh was raiding a tombstone in the churchyard for its shining green pebbles, apparently, and needed discouraging.

'Shouldn't we go and help?' Phoebe suggested after a moment or two when the silence between them seemed to become threatening.

George shook his head. 'I don't think so. Edward's the Gaffer...we must leave him in charge until he asks for reinforcements. He seems fairly able to keep the other three in order—quite a strong character is Ned.'

She smiled at the sight of the small figure of her niece plodding along purposefully beside Edward. 'I can believe it. Helena is usually the one issuing all the orders—this total subjugation is unheard of.'

George's long fingers adjusted the wavering outline of a barn picked out in pebbles on the grass in front of him.

'Young Josh is the attraction at home, especially with his grandfather, and Cecily favours James. Edward's blossoming *here* because he's very happy...just like his father.'

'They're...they're sons to be proud of,' Phoebe muttered with difficulty. She had stayed long enough...could now get up and walk away if only George weren't looking at her as if trying to imprint on his memory an image that would never fade.

'You asked me once if I would like a different sort of life,' he said quietly. 'The truth is that I can see it very clearly here. It's as out of reach as the man in the moon, my dearest Phoebe, but I wanted you to know how...how very desirable it looks.'

She blinked away the tears that pricked her eyelids and tried to smile, but her little boat was sinking now—weighed down by more pain than she could bear. Then two arms wound themselves round her neck, and Helena's rosebud mouth planted a damp kiss on her cheek by way of consolation.

'Iss'orl *right*, Aunty Phee, no need to cry...us made Josh put all the stones *back*,' she said virtuously.

Phoebe hugged her niece's small, warm body in the sudden anguish of knowing that this might be as near as she would get to filling the emptiness at the centre of her heart. Her sister's children might have to be comfort enough, together with the knowledge clung to through lonely nights that George Harkness would have shared his life with her if he could.

The visitors stayed one more week at the Rectory. By then the neighbouring gentry had been inspected and pronounced upon—dowdy provincials, one and all, in Cecily's view. Oxford was a shabby, disappointing sort of place, not worth half the fuss that was made about it; and she'd been able to point out to Lydia several ways in which the parish at home was well ahead of Hindleford. Her desire to be helpful was genuine, and she took her place at Henry Maynard's dinner party on their last night confident of having done her best for her relatives.

She reckoned that the same couldn't be said of her husband. The sooner he was back in the life that suited him at Burslem, the better. No lasting harm had been done, of course, but even temporarily she couldn't allow any part of his attention to wander from Harkness, herself, and the boys; he belonged to them completely. It was an added irritation that the threat should have come from someone as insignificant as Phoebe Maynard, who now looked pale but calm at the foot of her father's table. Seated next to her but one, Cecily would have left her alone but for the fact that George, further along on the opposite side, was silly enough to glance too often in her direction.

'You'll be glad to see the back of us, Phoebe; other people's children soon wear out their welcome and become a nuisance,' Cecily said brightly. 'In any case they've kept you from those little bits of painting that seem to fill up your time.'

A taunt from someone who knew nothing about art didn't worry Phoebe, but the rest was easy, too. 'The children would never be unwelcome here,' she said simply. 'Helena for one will roar the house down when she has to say goodbye to Edward.'

'I dare say, but she'll learn soon enough that she can't keep what doesn't belong to her. It's something we *all* have to learn.' Cecily's smile left no doubt of the direction of her message, and it seemed to another guest at the table that only a huge effort of self-control kept Phoebe Maynard sitting there, white-faced but composed. Hugo suddenly found himself obliged to intervene.

'You'll be visiting Spain next, Mrs Harkness, now that Sir Joshua owns the pottery there,' he suggested.

'I *very* much doubt it. It wouldn't be *my* idea to bother with a place so primitive and dirty and violent. If we need to learn anything from the Spaniards, I shall be very much surprised.'

Phoebe watched a little smile touch Hugo Taverner's mouth and, amid her own distress, had the strange certainty that he was deliberately drawing Cecily's fire away from her. It was even more strange to feel so sure that she could trust him.

'No need to learn from Spaniards at all,' he was agreeing affably; 'by all means let us ignore the fact their potteries were turning out works of art several centuries before the English even got going in Staffordshire!'

Cecily measured him under dark lashes and decided that it would be prudent to concede the point without ill humour. 'All right...they make what suits *them*, I'm sure. But if Phoebe's scratchy little copies of their squirts and squiggles are anything to go by, their patterns won't suit *us*. George is too soft to say so, but fortunately my father-in-law won't be.'

Hugo looked from George Harkness's rigid face to Phoebe's pale one, and thought he understood at last. 'Then we shall have to rely on Sir Joshua,' he said ambiguously, and turned to talk to Lydia on his other side.

The following morning the procession re-formed for the return journey to Oxford station. Phoebe hugged the children goodbye, promised that she and Helena would inspect the village under the cedar tree every day, and prayed that she might never have to see Cecily's smiling face again. She supposed George clasped *her* hand and kissed *her* cheek, as he had done Lydia's, but she couldn't ever be sure afterwards. All her concentration was pinned to a moment when he would no longer be there. Then, with shouts and jingling of harness and clattering of hooves, they were moving off. There was only silence left in the stableyard, and the terrible emptiness that filled her heart.

A week later the long spell of fine weather broke in a great end-of-summer storm. For a night and a morning thunder rolled round the valley, and the heavens flung down torrents of rain. At lunch time the next day when the assault finally seemed to be over, Phoebe squelched across the sodden lawn to the cedar tree. The children's village lay strewn over the grass, its carefully arranged patterns just disordered heaps of pebbles now, and twigs and leaves floating on rivulets of water. She stood staring at it for a long time, too sad at heart even to weep, and then turned and went back towards the house.

6

Francis proved to be right in anticipating a second daughter. His Rosalind was born on one of November's dreariest days, but joy transfigured him as he walked through the village afterwards. Everyone who met him thought they must be mistaken about the weather; there was no winter murk after all and the sun was shining from a cloudless sky.

His wife, lying in bed in the Rectory, was aware only of the exhaustion that followed long labour, and of the midwife kindly making allowances on that account for her patient's sad lack of joy. Lydia promised herself she would pray when she felt less tired...ask God in his mercy to let her love this child as she loved Helena and Richard. But if Rosalind belonged especially to Francis at least it made things fair at last: he had a child who was unquestionably his, and now she need have no more children.

Phoebe arrived quickly to admire, but got waylaid by a disgruntled niece.

'*She's* a girl as well,' said this maiden disgustedly, 'an' she's orl red and cross-looking, besides.'

'Well, give her time,' Phoebe advised. 'We had to wait for *you* to improve as well.'

Helena shook her bright head, certain for once that her usually reliable aunt needn't be taken seriously. 'I'm the prettiest thing in natchur—old Mr Hobbs says so every time he comes to tea.'

It was broadly true, Phoebe reflected. Even just released from the womb, Helena had been different from most other babies, and she would probably never be anything but beautiful. It would be Lydia's thankless task to try persuading her that beauty, besides being a gift she'd done nothing to deserve, carried certain penalties.

'I promise you'll get used to your sister in time,' Phoebe said now, 'and be very glad that she's another girl.' It was cowardly not to point out as well that Richard would enjoy having another sister, but sharing him with the newcomer was something else the enchanting, headstrong child would have to learn. Just at this moment Phoebe was more painfully aware on her own account of all that there was to learn. Each day got through with apparent cheerfulness was a small victory unnoticed, she prayed, by anyone else. Each night was a different matter; in dreams Cecily Harkness didn't exist, and she could run towards George as if he were a lover waiting for her. But she always woke to find herself alone again, with tears drying on her cheeks.

One morning just before Christmas she finally remembered to ask who was to be Rosalind's godfather at the forthcoming baptism, and was unpleasantly surprised to be told 'Hugo Taverner'.

'Whatever for?' she asked too sharply. 'We don't know him—he's just Father's lawyer now that old Mr Taverner is dead.' Her pale face was suddenly flushed with colour, and Lydia was made aware that her usually reasonable sister had found someone to be unreasonable about at last.

'Perhaps you haven't taken the trouble to notice that he now comes to Hindleford as an invited friend,' she answered with a trace of severity in her voice. 'He and Father have discovered that they enjoy each other's company.' She saw that her sister looked unconvinced, and tried again. 'Francis approves of my choice. I expected Hugo to thank me for the invitation and refuse, but he seemed rather pleased to be asked.'

'Because it meant that Rosalind would be brought up with the help of *one* godparent, at least, who would keep her feet on solid, egalitarian ground—no High Church, High Tory, High any other nonsense for Mr Taverner,' Phoebe said tartly.

'That *was* more or less what he said,' Lydia admitted, staring curiously at her sister, 'but unlike you, he said it with a smile. You ignore the poor man completely when he's here—how does it come about that you're so well acquainted with what he's likely to think?'

'I'm not, but I forgot to mention that he turned up in Spain while Father and I were there,' Phoebe mumbled. 'We didn't exactly take to each other, but no doubt we shall be able to manage a gracious nod across the font at Rosalind's christening.'

'Generous of you!' Then the dryness in Lydia's voice gave way to sudden concern. 'Are you all right, Phee...not unhappy or bothered about anything?'

Phoebe shook her head, even managed a bright smile. 'Not bothered at all, thank you; only trying to make up my mind whether to enrol at art classes in Oxford after Christmas or teach myself how to handle clay. One of us ought to learn what our forbears seem to have been born knowing, don't you think?'

Lydia had no view on the matter. Like her mother before her, she felt no pride in the fact that the Harknesses were part of Staffordshire history; but she couldn't entirely disown Eliza's family, even if she'd wanted to—Charles Harkness had seen to that.

'Dear Cecily sent modified congratulations on the birth of Rosalind,' she reported with a wry smile '—daughters not ranking as high as the sons *she* is able to produce without the slightest difficulty! Whatever Francis may say, she's a cow of a woman who doesn't deserve George Harkness.'

'Well, perhaps,' Phoebe agreed with difficulty, 'even if it isn't the sort of thing a vicar's wife is supposed to say!' She found relief in talking about the people who inhabited her private thoughts, but it was dangerous as well. If she wasn't very careful and resolute, her fragile wrapping of self-control would be in tatters, leaving her naked to the world. 'I'm not on correspondence terms with Cecily, thank goodness, but dear Edward has got into the habit of writing to me—largely so that I can pass on messages to Helena about important things, like his tadpoles, and his first attempts to become a potter.'

For the twins that Christmas was memorable for a perfectly-timed fall of snow. For Phoebe it brought the strange moment afterwards when she stood making her god-parent's vows beside the tall, unyielding form of Hugo Taverner. After the service they hurried from the coldness of the church to the warmth of the Rectory fireside.

'Your father hasn't joined us, I see,' Hugo said, going straight to the point as usual without the social formalities that most people found necessary.

'He was feeling a little tired.' Phoebe intended to be equally brief, but Hugo's frowning expression demanded an explanation which she gave reluctantly.

'There's always a lot that he's expected to do in the neighbourhood at Christmas time. He insisted on doing it, but it seemed more of an effort than usual this year.' Having no more to say, she would have turned to walk away then, but her arm was suddenly clamped in Hugo's right hand.

'*You* might have tried insisting that he *didn't* do it, but I suppose you were too wrapped up in yourself to care.'

The brutality as well as the unfairness of the attack drove the blood from her face, but she was roused to such pure anger for a moment that she almost lost sight of what they were quarrelling about.

'Perhaps you enjoy issuing instructions, Mr Taverner. I don't make a habit of *insisting* that my father does anything at all. It isn't the way we live together.' She stared pointedly at his hand, still gripping her arm, but he wasn't ready to release her.

'Then use whatever methods your tender little way of life does permit, but persuade him somehow to consult a doctor.'

The flash of anger died, leaving her cold and afraid.

'I don't know why you say that. My father hasn't complained of feeling ill, and he hates to have people fuss about him.'

'And no doubt he hates to admit that he's losing weight and tiring too easily for a man of his age.'

She closed her eyes for a moment against the lawyer's accusing stare, but saw clearly imprinted on her memory the different image of her father casually explaining that he'd given up his after-dinner cigar because he no longer enjoyed it. If Hugo Taverner was right she might have to thank him for noticing what both she and Lydia had failed to see, but she couldn't bring herself now to be contrite to this man who judged without mercy. His hand let go of her but her flesh retained the memory of his clasp. Her mind retained something else—the recollection of him crossing swords with Cecily at her father's dinner-table. He had been kind then, and perhaps was trying to be helpful now.

'I'm sure my father will agree to see Dr Martin if I ask him to.' She fought with herself and produced one more stiff sentence that he could only just hear. 'Thank you for...for being such a good friend to him.'

'I hope friends are forgiven when they seem interfering! *Vaya con Dios*, Miss Maynard.' The lovely Spanish valediction took her by surprise, and so did the fleeting smile that touched his mouth with gentleness. Even if she couldn't understand or like him, that brief softening reminded her that it was still the season of the year when they must offer one another goodwill. She would have said her thanks again as if she meant them this time but it was too late; he was already turning away, and Helena was tugging at her skirt, demanding attention.

For as long as the arctic weather gave Henry Maynard a reasonable excuse to stay working quietly in his studio, Phoebe left him in peace. He was happy there, and surely safe from harm. Alerted now to anxiety, she tried to resist the temptation to be always watching him. But she was often aware that, whatever model of barn or cottage was growing under his fingers, his thoughts were not of Hindleford. When he sometimes caught her looking at him, he would smile, and then the two of them would go on working contentedly together. In a strange sort of way she *was* content, even though the joy her heart had craved was always going to be denied her. She had been made to glimpse herself through Hugo Taverner's eyes, and seen a selfish, dejected creature she was ashamed to recognize.

Her first tentative suggestion to her father that their old friend Dr Martin might be glad of a chance to call met with an astonished stare.

'My dear girl, you make it sound as if he needs a guinea from me to save his children from starving! I imagine the truth is that he's run off his feet with winter ailments.'

Phoebe abandoned tact for honesty. 'I'm worried about *you,* not Dr Martin. Would you let him examine you...just to please me?' She thought he was going to refuse again, and was just deciding that she would risk his displeasure and ask the doctor to call anyway, when her father suddenly changed his mind.

'He'll only diagnose indigestion and other

such-like indignities, but let him come if it will make you happier.'

It *was* what Henry could usually persuade himself his trouble was likely to be, but there were sudden moments of acute pain that suggested something more serious and reminded him sharply of his own mortality. Then, the concern for Phoebe that always hung on the margin of his mind suddenly swamped him with anxiety. As the village people said, the time would come sooner or later for his thread to be broken, and then she would be very much alone. Lydia and Francis, thank God, were next door, but there was scarcely anyone left on his side who could be a companion to her. The Maynard blood had grown thin over many generations; an only child himself whose parents had died young, he'd inherited Hindleford from his father's bachelor elder brother. The widow of a cousin who had lived in London was the only family connection he cared about.

'You haven't got nearly enough relatives or friends,' he said now, with a little frown of worry; 'I should have been less selfish...done something about that.'

Affection for him lit her thin face to beauty. 'I have all the friends I need...in fact, I have *everything* I need,' she said firmly.

'Your mother's people, Phoebe—you could make an effort to see more of *them.*'

'I dare say I could,' she agreed, smiling at him. 'I could also encourage my suitors in the village—dear old Colonel Wyndham or Lady Monkton's unpleasant son! The truth is I'd much rather stay here.' Her father's face still looked anxious and she forced herself to talk about the Harknesses instead. 'Lydia hears from Burslem, and I'm sure it isn't the moment for a visit *there*. Jane has given up the Fabians—as being not advanced enough!—and flaunts the fact that she's become a founding member of the Communist Party instead. Sir Joshua thunders that his daughter is bringing discredit on them in Staffordshire, and Cecily's father tells him that they'll be the laughing-stock of Birmingham, which is thought to be much worse!'

Henry Maynard suddenly grinned, having had the experience denied to Phoebe of meeting both Joshua and George's pushing father-in-law. 'As you say, *not* the time for a visit, my dear.'

Dr Martin came soon, and suggested so casually a check-up with a 'very good man' at the Radcliffe Infirmary that she was relieved rather than alarmed. Her father had to confess afterwards that a little more than indigestion had been diagnosed, but he talked much about the idle life he intended to lead from now on and scarcely at all about the heart condition the very good man had warned him of. Phoebe pretended not to notice this omission, knowing that it was all she could do for a man whose lifelong habit had been to keep grief or pain to himself. She still avoided Hugo Taverner on his regular visits to the house, but no longer resented him—he gave her father a different sort of companionship from her own, and it was something to be grateful for now. Occasional snatches of their conversation reached her, and the two men rarely seemed to agree about post-war social unrest, or the pros and cons of tariff protection; but they argued without heat, and listened with enjoyment to each other's point of view.

Phoebe imagined that her absence wasn't noticed on these occasions, but one mild spring evening as she and her father walked slowly about the garden he suddenly spoke of Hugo.

'I'm sorry you still don't like him, my dear. He's not the easiest man to get to know, I grant you, but in all the months he's been coming here I've found nothing in him that I should wish to change—not even his convictions that I don't happen to share. I reckon he's entitled to those.'

She answered only after a long pause. 'That says a good deal for Mr Taverner,' she said eventually. 'All the same I think we've agreed, he and I, *not* to warm to each other.'

Henry nodded and left the subject of Hugo Taverner there...he had something else that needed talking about at last.

'Memory is a damnably persistent thing, Phoebe. Even now, given all the years we've been back in England, I can still remember every detail of that house and garden at Santolina. I loved Spain as much as your mother came to hate it.'

She glanced at him, doubtful of whether she did right or wrong to speak of the memories in her own mind.

'I remember the flowers, and the brightness, and the maid singing—Asunción, you once told

108

me her name was, only it seemed to make you angry to think of her.'

Henry Maynard stopped suddenly, as if held motionless by some remembrance of his own. 'I didn't tell you at the time, but after I'd called on Lucía and Manolo last spring, I went to see Asunción as well.'

'What...what happened to her?' Phoebe asked in a low voice, not sure that he was even aware of speaking his thoughts out loud.

'She was sent away, up to Ronda where her uncle kept a lodging-house. It was much patronized by our officers at the time, who used to ride over from the garrison on Gibraltar to see the famous gorge. But a Spanish gentleman, not young but well-to-do, went with some English friends one day and was entranced enough by Asunción to marry her. It was a very unequal match by the world's standards, but apparently a happy one. She is a widow now, with...with three children. Her husband became a wealthy man—that's why she was able to let her parents give up being servants to other people.'

Phoebe remembered something Lydia had said, long ago it seemed now, about Asunción Vargas...'not as lovely as her name, by any means'. In the same moment her father spoke again.

'Your mother took a dislike to her, of course, but I'd like *you* to know the truth. Of course I had no right to fall in love with her, but she was simply the kindest, most beautiful creature I had ever known—I think she still is.'

Phoebe saw the past fall into place at last.

109

Not even her father had really been to blame. The Fates who governed men's lives had sent the Maynards to Spain, and Asunción to work for them there.

'If she loved you as well, I hope you were happy together,' she said after a long pause, '...oh, I do hope that.'

Henry surveyed his younger daughter, with a half-rueful, half-loving smile. 'You were supposed to be shocked...disapproving at the least! Yes, my dearest, we *were* happy—even Asunción remembered that, after a contented marriage of her own. I'm glad to think she said so when I saw her again.'

'You...you mentioned that she's a widow now,' Phoebe hinted diffidently; then stopped because her father was shaking his head.

'I'm afraid she intends to remain one, sweetheart; but it doesn't matter now, and still I'm happy.'

She remembered that gratefully a few days later. Going into the studio one morning she found her father already there, but he was slumped over the unfinished model on his work-table of Colonel Wyndham's great Tudor barn. He was still alive then, but died on the way to the Infirmary, holding his daughter's hand.

The church was crowded for the funeral service; all Hindleford was there, come to remember a courteous, gently-spoken man who had always done good to them by stealth, preferring it that way. Old friends and acquaintances arrived from all over the county, even brother-officers of long

110

ago who had known Henry before he sold out of the Army to settle down to country life and marry Eliza Harkness. Standing beside Lydia and Francis, Phoebe greeted them and thanked them in her husky voice, but it all seemed quite unreal until she suddenly saw George Harkness standing there. Sir Joshua had come too, but she didn't notice *him*, being only aware of the comfort of having George smile at her.

Hugo Taverner watched her, wondering whether she even realized yet that when all these well-meaning visitors went away she would be left alone. He knew she had not long passed her twentieth birthday, although she seemed older today. The black clothes that flattered Lydia's golden beauty made Phoebe look sallow and plain.

He knew the contents of Henry Maynard's will, and regretted that it would soon be his job to make them known—it was a great pity that Old Archibald wasn't still alive; they could have done with *him* today. Then he told himself he'd been a fool to break his firm rule of never making a friend of any client—the result was that he felt far too responsible for Henry's younger daughter.

He still thought she was managing the dreadful occasion rather well when Sir Joshua's heavy-handed attempts to pump him drove him into the quietness of the library for a moment. It had always been Henry's favourite room, and still seemed to hold the essence of the man who'd become his friend. The shock was all the greater, therefore, to find it already being used by a couple who stood in one of the window embrasures. It was Phoebe there, locked in the arms of her Harkness cousin.

Hugo tried to remember that sympathy and comfort were acceptable and right, and certain to be offered on a day like this. But the entrancement in their faces would have given them away if nothing else did. He recognized that what Phoebe was being offered and accepting had nothing to do with a relative's conventional concern over a bereavement. With the sick taste of bitterness in his throat, he remembered trying to shield her in this house from the malice of George's sharp-tongued wife; he even remembered thinking that Harkness could be trusted to deal carefully with a young girl's temporary infatuation for a man years older than herself. He told himself now that he had no bloody right to be a lawyer at all if he could misread human nature to this extent.

Seconds crawled by while none of them found anything to say. George's arms let go of her but even now, Hugo noticed, she didn't move away. Her face was very pale, having been flushed a moment ago, but it made him more angry still that she should now look not plain at all, but rather beautiful. He spoke only to George because he couldn't trust himself to speak to Phoebe.

'Your father is waiting to leave, I believe. Perhaps you should at least tell him that you're otherwise engaged.' Then he turned and left the house without waiting to say goodbye to Lydia.

The silence that he left behind in the library seemed to Phoebe to last a very long time but, for fear of saying the wrong thing, she said nothing at all.

'My fault, sweetheart,' George muttered finally. 'You've been very brave, but you looked so sad that it seemed the most natural thing in the world to...to...'

'To comfort me,' she finished for him unsteadily. He must know at once that she recognized those moments in his arms for what they were; she expected nothing more, because there was nothing else that he could offer. She tried to smile, but grieved as she looked at him for the change in his face since last summer's visit. He looked older than his thirty years...more careworn now. Had he been lonely, too? His hand touched her cheek in a little gesture of tenderness, then hid in the pocket of his coat, in case it should be tempted to repeat itself.

'We can pretend that it was for comfort's sake, but I'm afraid Hugo Taverner knew better,' he said at last. 'I held you because it's what I've dreamed of doing for months past—that's the truth of it, my dear one, and I can't pretend about it any longer.'

It was almost more happiness than she could bear coming on top of the day's grief for her father. Still with nothing to say, she simply stared at him, colour staining her pale cheeks again and her eyes luminous as amber.

He took hold of her hands then, because touching her again was necessary after all.

'Phoebe love, I had no right to say what I've

just said, and if your father were still alive I wouldn't be saying this now. I can't change anything for a long while yet—the boys are too young to be left to Cecily and, for all that she seems very confident, she couldn't manage on her own.'

'I don't expect you to change anything...don't want you to,' Phoebe said hoarsely, '...at least, not till you're sure you could, without hurting them too much.'

He let out his breath in a long sigh, because in her own way she'd told him what he needed to know. They stared at one another, conscious of a kind of joy; it scarcely mattered that he must go away and she be left without him—they understood one another.

'There'll be no dishonour, sweetheart, if you *should* get tired of waiting,' George murmured.

She smiled because it seemed such an extraordinary idea, and he leaned forward and kissed her mouth again because she looked so beautiful.

Hugo was obliged to return with the will the following day, but at least a subdued Mrs Jim thought it proper to conduct him to the dining-room, not the library. Lydia and Francis were already there, talking to a pleasant-faced woman whom he knew by name—Anne Maynard, the widow of Henry's only cousin, who now eked out life on the small pension he had left her. Phoebe only walked in as they seated themselves round the table; deliberately, Hugo thought, she had timed her arrival so as not to have to meet him alone.

While he set out papers in front of him she was free to glance at his withdrawn face. It registered nothing as far as she could see, not even sadness for his dead friend. She was to understand that he came now as an impersonal stranger, merely to see to her father's last wishes. His intrusion into the library the day before was something he preferred to ignore.

The list of bequests was dealt with matter-of-factly, although Hugo managed to smile when he announced Henry's gift to Anne Maynard. But, watching the lawyer's face with interest, it seemed to Francis that Hugo was steeling himself to read out the provisions for disposing of the main part of the estate. The Rectory had been in Henry's personal gift, and he had given it outright to Francis and Lydia. The Manor itself was to remain Phoebe's home for as long as she wished to stay there, and it would be maintained by the income from the estate. If she married but continued to live there, the inheritance would eventually be shared between the children of Henry Maynard's offspring. If she left Hindleford, the manor house would be sold and the proceeds split equally between the present heirs—that was to say between Lydia, Phoebe and...Henry's son, Juan Rodriguez. Hugo heard the stifled gasps around the table, but went steadily on...'who had been given his mother's married name when Asunción Vargas became the wife of Carlos Rodriguez.'

115

Hugo looked from one shaken face to the other, waiting for someone to put their feelings into words.

'His *son*,' Lydia whispered at last. 'So Mama was right all the time...Asunción trapped him into...into...'

Phoebe suddenly interrupted her fiercely. 'No, that's *not* how it was.'

'Of course it was—how can *you* know...you were only a small child.' Lydia confronted her sister across the table, white-faced and trembling, but Francis held up his hand, refusing to allow them to descend to quarrelling.

'I take it that there's no...no doubt about the parentage of the boy?'

'Not the slightest,' Hugo confirmed briefly. 'Apart from anything else, I've *seen* Juan Rodriguez and he looks remarkably like his father.' A faint, ironic smile touched the lawyer's mouth as he addressed himself to Lydia. 'Don't imagine that he is any more anxious to be recognized than you are to recognize him; he insists on thinking of himself as the son of a Spaniard he loved and respected very much.'

'Juan Rodriguez would have loved his *true* father if he'd had the chance to know him,' Phoebe shouted, all her hostility now directed at the man who sat at the head of the table. He watched them with distaste, she thought—or the impersonal curiosity of a scientist waiting for mice to perform for him in a laboratory. She hated him for his cold and analytical approach to life, and forgot the moment at a lunch table in Seville when, anything but cold, his voice had suddenly been rough with feeling for the downtrodden people of Spain.

'Suppose you let me tell you the facts as I received them from your father,' he suggested unemotionally. 'Asunción was sent away from Santolina as soon as her parents realized that she was pregnant. Henry suspected the reason, but Lucía and Manolo denied it; there was less disgrace if it was simply never admitted to. Your mother insisted on returning to England, and for as long as she was alive your father had no knowledge of what had happened to the Vargas family. When she died he felt free to ask me to trace them, and I finally found them in Seville.

'We now know that Asunción's child was born at Ronda, and that soon afterwards she met and married Carlos Rodriguez. He was forty-one then, twenty years older than she—a prosperous man who went on to become a wealthy one.

'When your father went to see Lucía last spring she gave him her daughter's address, probably for the same reason that Asunción must have decided to introduce Henry to Juan—it was a terrible thing to deny a man all knowledge of his only son. The boy didn't know the truth then; when he was told afterwards he refused to acknowledge his real father. He's at present fifteen—English-looking in some ways, but wholly Spanish in temper, and determined to have nothing to do with his father's relatives. That fact explains the final clause in the will that I haven't yet read out to you. Your half-brother has been given fifteen years in which to change his mind. By 1935 he will be thirty. If he is of the same mind then as he is now, Hindleford and the residue of the estate are shared only between Lydia and Phoebe. For what it's worth, my impression of him is that he will *never* change his mind.'

Lydia let out a deep breath, and smiled for the first time. 'Well, that's all right then; the whole sordid story can die with poor Papa, and no-one else need ever know about it.'

Anne Maynard murmured something that seemed to agree, and Francis Fanshawe nodded without saying anything at all. Hugo refused Lydia's courteous suggestion of sherry, and they were all drifting towards the door when Phoebe found words to hurl at her sister.

'It isn't "all right", because you understand *nothing*. I hope Juan never does come here, because I should have to hate him for rejecting a man who had already lost his only other son.' Her voice broke under its weight of sadness, and tears sparkled on her lashes. 'Asunción was beautiful and good...and my father loved her greatly. I won't believe that there was anything sordid about their story.'

It was Francis who broke the silence. 'Then don't believe it, my dear,' he said gently, 'but try as well not to hate Juan Rodriguez.'

She stared at him for a moment and then walked away across the hall to the open front door. Hugo watched her go, and wondered whether the time would ever come when he felt certain, one way or the other, of the truth about Phoebe Maynard.

118

7

Lydia had often wondered in the past whether she would be *bored* to death with the repetitious duties of vicarage life, or stifled by her husband's high opinion of her. Now that there was a change she found it unexpectedly irritating and hurtful. Francis didn't blame her openly for the rift between sisters who had always agreed before, but in the matter of their half-brother in Spain she knew that he shared Phoebe's opinion, not hers.

It was the unfairness of it that she found hard to bear. Phoebe might go on blinding herself to the fact that their father had been a less than honourable man, but Francis had no right to. A clergyman was required above all to uphold the sanctity of marriage, not condone licentiousness that left respectable families encumbered with illegitimate children and much unhappiness besides. She had only to think of her father's bastard son and her mother's permanent state of misery to be convinced all over again that it wasn't for *her* to admit that she was in the wrong.

Phoebe read the danger signals and stayed tactfully out of range until it was finally necessary to confess to Lydia that her plan for the future had finally been decided upon; she intended to invite their father's cousin, Anne Maynard, to come and live with her at Hindleford.

'It's a good idea, don't you think?' she suggested hopefully, in spite of her sister's unpromising expression. 'Anne's bound to be more comfortable here, and there's room to spare for the two of us.'

'Why ask me?' Lydia queried, with a sudden flush of anger in her cheeks despite the fact that she could see it was a very good idea indeed. 'You are free to do whatever you like; my views needn't weigh with you at all.'

Phoebe knew that she was required to apologize for more than her decision about Anne if peace was to be restored, but she no longer felt inclined to trail obediently behind her sister. Loving George and losing her father had made an adult woman of her. 'I thought it was time I stopped relying on you and Francis,' she said quietly. 'If I don't think for myself occasionally *you'll* go on feeling responsible for me.'

'No doubt your next decision will be to write to Juan Rodriguez and assure him that if he's prepared to think well of Father after all, we shall welcome him to Hindleford.' Phoebe's tell-tale blush made Lydia add bitterly, 'Yes, I thought so! Well, I have no intention of inviting him to the Rectory—it would be an insult to Mama's memory.'

'I had no intention of writing to him,' Phoebe said in her own defence, even though it now occurred to her that it might be the very thing she *ought* to do next. 'I only thought of writing to Asunción—where would be the harm in that?'

120

Lydia stared at her in horror, struggling to find words strong enough. 'You're mad, Phee. Can't you see that our only sane course is to have nothing to do with these people? Thanks to a will Hugo should never have allowed Father to make, we must wait fifteen years as it is to be sure we are rid of them. But *don't*, I implore you, do anything to encourage the connection.'

'They are part of our lives already, whether we do anything or not,' Phoebe said gravely. 'We have a brother with whom we may have to share Hindleford, whether we like it or not.'

'Then we must pray *hard* that Hugo is right and Juan Rodriguez goes on refusing to admit that he's a Maynard.'

Phoebe didn't reply, but her expression said clearly that in this matter she had no intention of praying at all. It came as no surprise to Lydia—for a gentle-seeming girl Phoebe had always been amazingly intractable; even in childhood, with her colours nailed to the mast, she had been immovable. It had been inconvenient at times, but Lydia had always felt then, and did now, a faint stir of pride in such stubbornness. She suddenly kissed her sister's cheek, and it was a little gesture of reconciliation. Even so, her husband's attitude still rankled—he should have sided with *her*, not Phoebe.

Still feeling irritated with Francis, she walked across the Rectory lawn towards the house. The twins were there, throwing a large yellow ball at each other, and afternoon sunlight held them in brilliant illumination. Lydia caught her breath and suddenly stood still. The light that shone on Helena's bright curls showed her Richard's head as well with the same perfect clarity—fairish too, but turning much more red than fair...his father's hair; nothing to do with Charles Harkness, after all. While she stood there, Richard threw the ball back at his sister, watched her drop it, and suddenly rocked with laughter—hands on hips, head thrown back; it was not only Francis's very attitude, but his same infectious chuckle.

At last she waved to the children but walked on, no longer merely irritated, but filled with sick anger for the years of unnecessary anguish.

Francis was in his study, composing a sermon on spiritual pride, but his wife's face when she walked in told him that a subject he found fascinating would have to be put aside.

'Phoebe is becoming *very* difficult since Father's death,' she said without preamble. 'No discussion with us—she's simply decided to invite Anne Maynard to come and live at Hindleford.'

His temptation was very strong to point out that Lydia had scarcely encouraged her sister to confide in them recently, but he said instead, 'Perhaps discussion wasn't necessary—it's such an excellent idea from every point of view.'

'You think all Phoebe's ideas are excellent nowadays,' she snapped. 'That has been made abundantly clear.'

Francis gave a little inward sigh. Every nerve end shrank from an open quarrel with his wife, and he was well aware that something more deep-seated than her present disagreement with Phoebe was fuelling anger now. It was the only grief of his life that she didn't love him as he loved her. He was too humble a man not to find this reasonable, but his sadness lay in the knowledge that he might never be able to make her happy.

'My dear, you've been a wonderful elder sister but it's time to let Phoebe stand on her own feet,' he said gently. 'She must take charge of her life even if it means that you won't like some of the things that she decides to do, such as inviting Anne here.'

'Of *course* I like it.' She almost shouted the words, and her resentment was entirely against *him* now, for misunderstanding what it was she had objected to. 'But it's only the beginning; taking charge of her own life is even going to include being hail-fellow-well-met with the Rodriguez family. I shall have to rely on Hugo Taverner to discourage her from that.'

'Because you can't rely on me?'

The quiet question halted her in mid flight. With a single sentence he had chosen to go straight to the failure at the heart of their own lives.

'It's true, isn't it? I've been a great disappointment to you,' he said bluntly. 'I only ever wanted two things in life—to be a good priest, and to make you happy; but sometimes I think I've failed in both.'

Every Sunday she listened with pleasure as he repeated the lovely cadences of the King James

123

Bible, but now his deep voice was rough with sadness. The despair in his face warned her that they had reached a point of crisis—they could go on together better than before, or worse, but they couldn't go on in the same way. She saw him put his hands in the pockets of his cassock to hide their trembling, and knew that, because he was a man who lived with humility, he would accept without complaint whatever she said. She almost had to shout the truth to him.

'You're the *best* of priests. Everyone else knows that even if you don't.'

'But I haven't been able to make you happy.' He stated it as a fact, and she understood why. She hadn't admitted it to herself before, but it was clear now. It had been easier to punish him than deal with her own sense of guilt, and to blame him because a terrible war had denied her the life she should have shared with someone else. Refusing to see the evidence that the twins were his was part of the same shabby pretence. Suddenly she was caught in a bright beam of truth that revealed the dark corners of her soul.

At last she lifted her head and stared at him, but her gentle husband had become a stranger now—erect and unyielding. She had lived by his side night and day for the past five years...believed herself to be his strength; but she saw what the truth was now—he would manage without her if he had to, much better than she could manage without him.

'If I haven't been happy it's been my fault, not yours,' she said slowly. 'I've been like a child—determined that because what it had set its heart on had been refused, nothing else would do.'

The sternness left his face, and suddenly only love remained. 'My dear, you were worth much more than I could offer—a different life altogether.'

'I was vain enough to think so,' she confessed, 'but I'm beginning to understand that what I was offered instead should have been enough for any woman. Will you give me time to go on learning, or have I spoiled things too much?'

He stared at her for a long time until at last a smile transfigured his face. 'My dearest, I love you—how could anything be spoiled?' Then he held out his arms and she went into them, to be held against his heart.

Matters of legal business forced Phoebe to see more than she wanted to of Hugo Taverner because her father had left the administration of the Hindleford estate in the lawyer's hands. He was always polite and businesslike, never referring to the scene he'd interrupted in the library on the day of her father's funeral. She would have preferred him to; it would have been a relief to quarrel, but even when she announced that Anne Maynard had accepted her invitation to live at Hindleford, he disappointed her by taking the news calmly.

'Good—it's out of the question for you to stay here alone. But it must be made clear to Mrs Maynard before she gives up her present home that she can't count on being here permanently—otherwise she is being brought here merely to suit *your* convenience.'

Phoebe had honestly tried, remembering her father's high opinion of Hugo Taverner, to think more kindly of him. It was no good—she would always dislike him quite as much as he despised her.

'If Anne is happy to stay, this *will* be her permanent home,' she said distinctly. She saw his dark eyebrows rise, and knew what the gesture meant: it was as far as he would allow himself to go in reminding her of George Harkness. Her next words were flung at him like a challenge. 'I have no intention of leaving Hindleford. There have been Maynards here for generations, and I shall continue to do as best I can whatever my father did for the people here.'

He was still not inclined to believe her. Practising law didn't lessen a tendency to distrust human nature, and he felt sure that as soon as George Harkness decided to abandon his family and Burslem for an illicit life with her somewhere else, she would forget the good name of Maynard in Hindleford. But he admitted to himself that Phoebe Maynard's direct gaze would have confused anyone who knew less about her than he did. She had lost weight recently, he noted, and her soft brown hair was drawn back from a face that now looked very thin. Temple, cheek, and jawbones were too prominent, and the sudden sparkle of amusement that had been her principal charm in the past seemed to have been lost with the death of her father. Almost against his will, he felt sorry for her; and most certainly he would have been glad to lay his good right hand on George Harkness.

It was Phoebe who broke the silence that had fallen between them. 'I want to write to Asunción Rodriguez,' she said abruptly, 'but I need *you* to give me her address. Lydia strongly disapproves, so I'm afraid you will have to displease her or me.'

He was made aware that his displeasure wouldn't trouble her at all, except in so far as it might deprive her of the information she wanted. More so than Lydia Fanshawe, she was truly her father's daughter, and it was something to remember in his dealings with her.

Because he hesitated she asked another question. 'Do you wish to know first what I might say to her?'

'No, because if I had the slightest fear of it being something unkind, I should refuse to help you.'

The blunt answer pleased her, and she allowed him in her mind the saving grace of being anything but stupid. As her father had said, it meant that however inconvenient his convictions might be, they would always be worth listening to.

For a moment she was tempted to confide in him, because she thought he missed her father, too; he might understand how daunting it was to try to take Henry Maynard's place at Hindleford. But she knew his sympathy

127

would stop short of condoning what she felt about George Harkness. She had no right to the happiness of being loved—that was what Hugo Taverner would say. All the same, she wavered on the edge of begging him to listen, but he was intent on putting papers into his briefcase, awkwardly with one hand, and failed to recognize the sudden moment of entreaty in her face.

The next time Hugo came to the house she was no longer alone. Anne Maynard had arrived, and he greeted her so pleasantly that she congratulated Phoebe afterwards on having a lawyer who was not only efficient but charmingly kind. Her own experience of Hugo's profession since being left a widow had been entirely different.

'Efficient I'll allow,' Phoebe conceded, 'but I'd say he has the charm of a fighting bull, waiting to charge and impale the *torero.*'

'Then let his tormentors be warned! My sympathies are always with the bull.'

So, in general, were Phoebe's, and she put aside the discussion of Hugo Taverner aware that she hadn't chosen her simile very well. Instead, she reverted to the subject of Anne herself.

'I expect it's too soon to ask if you'll be happy here, but can you at least be sure of not regretting that you've left London?'

The earnest question made Anne Maynard smile. 'Regret? My dear, shall I tell you about life in rented rooms in Addison Grove, West Kensington? A railed-off patch of tired grass and two sad laburnum trees comprised the grove! Then there was my landlady, with eyes as black and hard as the jet brooches she always wore, waiting to complain if I played the piano louder than a whisper! I'm ashamed to say I began to hate her, when I suppose I should have felt sorry for her.'

Anne looked round the white-panelled walls and flowered chintzes of what Phoebe had designated *her* sitting-room, and tried not to weep for joy. It now contained the piano which, with no flint-eyed landlady to object, she could play soft or loud as she felt inclined. Next door, her bedroom windows overlooked a sweep of lawn and an amelanchier tree just coming into snowy blossom. She lay awake in the dawning for the pleasure of listening to birdsong instead of traffic, and hoped it wasn't selfish to pray that she might always be allowed to stay at Hindleford.

She smiled tremulously at the slender, brown-haired girl in front of her, determined that if the moment came to leave again, she would go cheerfully.

'I can't tell you how happy I am to be here, but it must only be for as long as I can be useful—I insist on that being understood between us, Phoebe.'

Her hostess, following a train of thought of her own, scarcely heard. 'I can't think why you weren't allowed to escape that landlady much sooner—you should have been here long before this.'

'I think there *was* a reason; your father thought

us stupidly improvident and extravagant. I expect we were, but Malcolm couldn't live life in any other way. Perhaps he always knew there'd be no sad old age for him!' She smiled and Phoebe saw restored in her the youthful charm that had captured Malcolm Maynard. 'I don't regret anything but losing him, my dear, nothing else—not even Addison Grove!'

As the summer days lengthened, their liking for each other grew. Anne Maynard saw with contentment that she was needed, and Phoebe watched her fit naturally into village life as if she had always belonged there. Francis being without a regular organist, Anne offered to try to play the instrument in church. He overheard her practising one afternoon, stayed to listen in the farthest pew, and walked up the aisle at the end of the rehearsal announcing that she was unanimously elected to the post. He liked this kind, cultivated relative-by-marriage very much and, more clearly than she realized, understood the pricelessness of the gift Phoebe had given her. A lonely, childless woman was no longer condemned to living entirely for herself; at Hindleford she was not only part of their family, but part of the village as well, with all the pleasures and duties that belonging entailed.

When she had happily gathered up her music and gone away, Francis remained in the familiar peacefulness of the church, content to be there alone. Then the door latch gave its customary squeak as he got up from his knees, and Phoebe walked in with her arms full of golden and flame-coloured lilies. She misread his glance at them and looked doubtful.

'A bit too gloriously pagan, do you think? I'm afraid Lady Monkton's bound to say so.'

'She may think whatever she likes, but let the rest of us enjoy a feast of beauty.' He smiled lovingly at his sister-in-law, noticing more about her than she would have wished. The hours she spent working in the gardens had dusted her hair with sunlight and warmed the colour of her skin, but it was only a surface glow.

'You should always wear a sprinkling of golden lily-pollen on your nose; it suits you,' he said solemnly.

She grinned to please him, but he had the impression that her thoughts weren't on the flowers at all. He would have liked to ask what troubled her nowadays, but the wearing of a cassock didn't entitle him to walk uninvited into the hearts and minds of the people he ministered to; he was certain that something had to be left to individual privacy and dignity.

'I was saying my prayers when you came in,' he explained simply '—thanking God for this peaceful corner of England, and wishing that everyone else could know such blessings.'

'Only *they* don't,' Phoebe pointed out with a rare touch of asperity. 'I doubt if embittered miners and striking dockers think they have much to thank heaven for. *They* must reckon that they're very far from living in the land

131

fit for heroes that Mr Lloyd George promised them.'

'Politicians can never resist making promises,' Francis pointed out sadly. 'They seem to think that we expect it of them. But even the Prime Minister can't single-handedly right the wrongs of the world—the tragedies of the war will be with us for years, and the difficulties of peacetime are only just beginning I'm afraid.'

Phoebe nodded, then abruptly abandoned the world's difficulties.

'Lydia says you're to be spared another visit from Burslem. Poor Edward, unable to come to see his friend Helena again because George can't spare the time to bring him.' She might have added in her sadness that nor could he find time to write letters himself, but it wouldn't have been fair—*she* had been the one to insist that they must manage without a shameful, clandestine correspondence. Only she hadn't understood then how desperately she would come to need *some* contact with him.

'The Harkness company is having the same problems as everyone else,' she was dimly aware of Francis saying. 'A short-lived post-war boom, followed by a relentless drop in world trade, from which all manufacturers are suffering. Added to that, Sir Joshua is old and ailing...I don't wonder George can't find the time to visit us.'

Phoebe turned her head away to answer. 'No...I don't wonder at it, either.' When she looked at him again the pollen-dust now made a damp golden smear across her face, but she was making a pretence of smiling.

'It seemed better not to enquire in front of Lydia,' he said diffidently, 'but I've wanted very much to know whether your letter to Señora Rodriguez received any reply.'

'I didn't write it in the end,' Phoebe met the Vicar's glance with her usual directness. 'The truth is that I probably would have done if Hugo Taverner had made me obstinate about it, but he was clever enough to hand over Asunción's address without any fuss at all.' She frowned at the next thought that occurred to her. 'He didn't even mention it again, being also clever enough to know that when it actually came to writing, I'd be unable to find anything to say that didn't seem impertinent. It's hard, isn't it, to like people who are so invariably right as Hugo Taverner!'

Instead of smiling, Francis shook his head. 'Not invariably right, I'm afraid. His choice of a future wife wasn't very good.'

Phoebe looked surprised. 'Is *that* why he never mentions the poor thing?'

'They didn't marry in the end,' explained the Vicar. 'Your father told me the story. When Hugo was invalided out of the Army his fiancée was kind enough to say that she would still be his wife provided she was never required to look at what remained of his left arm. Not unnaturally he released her from their engagement, and quite soon afterwards she married someone else.'

Phoebe found nothing to say: what *was* there

to say about the havoc that the war had caused, or its permanent damage to men's lives? Then she heard Francis revert to the subject of Asunción Rodriguez.

'I think it *was* better not to write to Spain, my dear. The legal position has been clearly explained, and unless Juan ever decides to come to England we must assume that he and his mother prefer the connection to have died with Henry.'

He looked at his sister-in-law's pensive face and thought how pleasant it would have been to stay and watch her deal with the lilies; some other well-meaning ladies contrived to produce effects that the flowers themselves must weep over, but Phoebe handled them with love.

'I must go,' he said regretfully. 'There's bound to be something I'm a little late for already. Still, it's a pity young Edward's not coming—while he was here last summer he had a *most* beneficial effect on Helena!'

He lifted his hand in a little farewell salute and walked away out of the church. Yes, it was a pity, Phoebe explained to the recumbent effigy of a long-dead Maynard ancestor...much, much more of a pity than he realized. His stone face smiled up at her, serenely insisting that it didn't matter—really, nothing mattered when, as the Arab saying had it, life was so much shorter than death.

'You're *wrong*,' she told him wearily. 'It matters dreadfully when you're afraid of never being allowed to live at all.'

8

In the world outside the river valley there were signs and portents during the passing year that were significant for the future. But Hindleford, with its own affairs to consider, scarcely noticed that the guardians of world peace were assembling in Geneva for the first time; scarcely guessed that another innovation—the invention of broadcasting—would last longer and affect its life much more. Hindleford's daily round was still regulated by the seasons. At the tag end of the summer that meant Harvest Festival, then autumn ploughing, interrupted by the annual celebration of the Feast of All Saints, that brought them the Bishop of Oxford in a flurry of purple. The village let others worry about the rumblings of a threatened national strike among the coal-miners, and prophecies of doom that England's traditional markets overseas were being stolen by the wicked Americans and Japanese.

Phoebe worried about these prophecies for George Harkness, and read *The Times* diligently, explaining to Anne Maynard that she was bound to feel a family interest in the problems facing her Burslem relatives. She didn't confess to something else—that nowadays time travelled for her at an entirely different speed from that of anyone else she knew. When people complained that this or that occasion passed too quickly she always agreed, fearing that their measurement of time was more accurate than hers.

Almost a year after the death of her father she reached her twenty-first birthday—on St Valentine's Day, 1921. Mrs Jim and her husband told her, as they did every year, that it was the day when the thrushes mated for the coming season. Lydia told her, in the course of bringing early-morning birthday good wishes, that Dr Martin had confirmed that she was pregnant again.

'A sort of extra birthday present,' she suggested when her sister didn't immediately reply '—unless you've gone off nieces and nephews by now.'

Struggling with what she recognized as bitter, unadulterated envy, Phoebe made haste to deny it. 'Certainly not—it's the first duty of an aunt to be constant in her affections!' She stared at Lydia's face for a moment, noticing a difference in it. 'Am I right in thinking that you feel happy about *this* baby?'

Lydia nodded, smiling faintly. Her conversation with Francis wasn't for sharing, even with Phoebe, but she made a different confession instead. 'I'm not in quite such a muddle as I was—and about time too, you'd be forgiven for thinking!'

'I might, if I weren't aware of muddles of my own,' Phoebe agreed ruefully. She tried to look cheerful, not knowing that her eyes were shadowed with sadness. 'I'm getting left behind—you had the twins by the time you were my age. I can't even claim the model village as *my* achievement—it's really Father's work. Now that it's finished I shall make the County Museum a gift of it in his name.'

Lydia hesitated on the verge of asking how matters stood between her sister and their Harkness cousin; there was *something* between them, she felt sure, but even now she couldn't bring herself to pry uninvited into Phoebe's innermost state of heart.

'There's no need to belittle your achievements,' she pointed out instead, 'you make these gardens beautiful at each season of the year, and you're indispensable to Hindleford—at everybody's beck and call for miles around.'

'Oh, I'm in great demand,' Phoebe agreed solemnly.

She turned her attention to unwrapping the present Lydia had brought, and was exclaiming with pleasure over a topaz pendant on an antique gold chain when the twins burst into the room shepherded by Anne Maynard. They had come with presents of their own, but the real purpose of the visit, Phoebe suspected, was to enquire whether her birthday made any difference to a tobogganing rendezvous already fixed upon. Had she suddenly become too old, Richard asked anxiously, knowing that some ladies of their acquaintance would certainly object to toiling uphill with the toboggan after every airborne descent. She felt able to deny it and to prove it spent an exhausting morning with them on the snowy slopes of Goose Hill.

But dressing for dinner at the Rectory that

evening, she stared at her reflection in the bedroom mirror, examining it with much more than usual care. No, she wasn't too old yet—for toboggan rides and birthday parties and the bright courage of youth, but slowly as the days dragged by, time *was* wasting. Like the Lady of Shalott who also looked too long in her glass, she might at last grow 'half-sick of shadows'. A sudden wave of loneliness gathered and broke over her head, drowning courage in its icy waters. For a panic-stricken moment she felt entirely alone—bereft now even of her few memories. She couldn't remember how a man's hands had once felt against her skin, couldn't recall the image of his face.

Her only aid and comfort was still the water-lily bowl. She picked it up and its message was so clear that panic slunk away. George didn't know it was her birthday, so how could she expect to hear from him? The little bowl reminded her that she was loved; she needed nothing else.

A clock chimed outside in the passage, reminding her that she had been getting ready for Lydia's dinner-party. She stared at herself once more, surprised to find that the storm of emotion of a moment ago had left no visible trace; then she turned out her lamp, and went downstairs.

Anne was not yet waiting for her in the drawing-room, but someone else was there, and her little exclamation of surprise made him turn round from staring into the fire. He was a tall and unfamiliar figure in evening dress—impressive after his own craggy fashion, she supposed, but producing in her always the feeling that they were antagonists in some way. It was the one point on which she and Anne had had to disagree—Hugo Taverner found favour with Anne Maynard.

'Nellie told me to wait in here,' he said after a little pause. 'Congratulations, Phoebe! At last you can be rid of some of the tiresome advice that lawyers can never resist inflicting on clients who haven't come of age.'

'I hadn't thought of that,' she said gravely. 'Does it mean that I can do exactly what I like from now on with no let or hindrance from Messrs Taverner & Taverner?'

'Well, not quite. What you decide to do with your inheritance is still dependent on Juan Rodriguez. I'm afraid you won't be entirely free of me until that is finally settled.'

'Then I don't seem to have gained very much.' She misread the flicker of emotion that changed his expression for a moment and felt obliged to apologize. 'I'm sorry—that was an ungracious thing to say. I don't think birthdays agree with me.'

'My feelings weren't hurt, if that's what you're afraid of.'

'Of course not—are they ever?' The sharp question slipped out and she remembered five seconds too late what Francis had told her about the fiancée who'd preferred to marry an unmutilated man.

Hugo watched with interest the colour that suddenly stained her cheekbones.

139

'I see you know my sad little story. Don't think you have to apologize again—it all happened a long time ago.'

Genuine remorse gave way at once to the hostility he always managed to arouse. Even now they didn't meet on equal terms; she was still to be put in her place as the tiresome charge he'd been saddled with, even if she *was* indisputably twenty-one.

'Birthdays are supposed to agree with you for a few more years yet. Why don't they?' he asked suddenly.

It was an unfair question when he thought he knew the answer, but he was curious to know what she would say. She hesitated over a reply and he looked at her while he waited for it. He didn't know whether her dress was fashionable or not but, disliking stiff, shiny materials, he approved of its softly floating chiffon, and the old-rose colour suited her. She had grace and a gentle dignity of her own, and Hugo valued both qualities in a post-war world that seemed hell-bent on more strident attractions.

At last Phoebe smiled faintly. 'I expect I'm suffering from keeping my end up with the twins this morning. Francis and Lydia very sensibly declined their invitation to go to Goose Hill.'

She had evaded his question and knew that he knew it, but she was saved from being told so by Anne hurrying into the room, flustered and apologetic.

'Am I very late? My fine feathers were discovered at the last moment to be a trifle moth-eaten—so some running repairs were necessary.'

Hugo answered her, thereby explaining to Phoebe for the first time why he was there at all. 'Lydia sent me much too early to escort you both to the Rectory.' He smiled at Anne and his usually impassive face was full of warmth and humour. 'There's nothing wrong with the feathers now that I can see—in fact the effect is charming!' He remembered to give a little bow, too, in Phoebe's direction but she couldn't help but see it as an afterthought. A shared love of music had made Anne and Hugo friends, and it was shaming to begrudge Anne Maynard companionship other than her own, but she couldn't help feeling lonely all over again.

'Shall we go?' she suggested abruptly. 'Lydia will think the escort has lost his way.'

Hugo followed them out into the hall, certain now of the cause of her distress. She was foolish and tiresome and worse than unkind to hope that Harkness would abandon his family for her benefit, but it was difficult not to feel sorry for her—impossible not to fear that, in one way or another, she was doomed to be unhappy.

When they arrived there were guests already gathered in the Rectory drawing-room. Phoebe could see through the open doorway several old friends—the Bellinghams, and Colonel Wyndham and his forceful spinster sister, and a charming historian friend of the Vicar's much given to forgetting dinner invitations while he refought the Second Punic War. Lydia, who usually loved entertaining, came into the hall looking distracted for once.

She greeted her sister with relief, and drew her aside.

'Well done!' Phoebe whispered. 'How did you manage to get Humphrey here?'

'Sent Francis to fetch him, although now I'm not sure it was such a good idea. It turns out that we've got a rather different sort of historian about to come downstairs.'

She grimaced at the ceiling, but rushed on *sotto voce*. 'You'll never guess who turned up an hour ago—George's sister Jane, and a strange bearded creature called Ernest Larkin who claims that he's a disciple of Marx, or some such thing. They're still up there changing into less outlandish clothes than the ones they arrived in because I said it was the *least* they could do in Oxfordshire on your birthday.'

Phoebe's startled expression gave way to a grin, but it wasn't the moment to ask whether it was Oxford or her birthday that Lydia considered required dressing up for. 'They couldn't have known it was my birthday—so why on earth are they here?'

'They're on their way to Staffordshire, but want Francis to marry them first by special licence. Jane's all for free love, apparently, but her friend insists on a wedding before he confronts old Joshua, and I can't say I blame him. Francis is dying to get into an argument with him about his strange creed, but it will give Colonel Wyndham apoplexy if they do. Damn them for turning up this evening—I had the dinner-table beautifully arranged.'

'Well, I'll have the bearded creature,' Phoebe

142

suggested nobly, 'and Anne can keep the Colonel happy.'

'What about Jane?'

'Why not let her partner Hugo? That should make for an interesting conversation!'

Lydia nodded and disappeared to rearrange her dinner-table. Phoebe walked into the drawing-room, smiling at a shower of good wishes from the other guests. Suddenly the evening she had been dreading an hour ago looked enjoyable after all.

Before it was over she had to admit that her little spurt of malice received its due reward. Hugo, seated next to wild-eyed, intense Jane Harkness, even appeared to be enjoying his dinner companion. Phoebe looked in their direction as often as she dared, trying to see in Jane some faint likeness to her brother. If it could have been found she would have forgiven Jane any mad philosophy that she felt drawn to; but all she and George seemed to have in common was the capacity to buttonhole the attention of whoever they talked to. Phoebe saw it with a shaft of pain, remembering the brief times when George had seemed absorbed in *her,* just as Jane was now absorbed with Hugo. At the end of the long meal he still remained beside her but, very tired of Ernest Larkin, Phoebe thankfully handed over to Humphrey Caldicott the defence of capitalist society, the Monarchy, and the Empire. She took refuge with her neighbours, and talked with them of local affairs until Lydia opened the piano lid and invited Anne Maynard to perform.

143

Unexpectedly, Anne chose to play the beautiful, fiery music of Spain—de Falla, Granados, and Albéniz. Phoebe gave herself up to the torrent of sound, half-astonished that it should be her placid companion of every day re-creating such passionate beauty, and half-lost in the pictures of Spain that it evoked so vividly in her mind.

At the end of the interlude Anne explained to them that she owed the discovery of the music she'd just played to Hugo Taverner. Then to Phoebe's further astonishment, as she played the opening bars of the accompaniment to something totally different—Schubert's lovely 'Im Frühling'—Hugo got up and sauntered over to the piano.

His voice was deep and darkly beautiful, and he sang without the slightest trace of self-consciousness...perhaps, Phoebe thought, scarcely aware that they were even there. She regretted not being able to understand the German he sang, but it mattered very little. Words and music and voice and piano made a collaboration of such pure beauty that when the recital came to an end she was on the verge of tears. She could only explain to Lydia that it was because she missed having their father at *such* a birthday celebration.

Lydia agreed but, as usual, turned her attention to more practical matters. 'Phee dear, I'd meant Hugo to stay here, of course, but with Jane and Ernest Larkin turning up we're suddenly short of bedrooms. Can *you* have him for the night?'

If the alternative was to face Ernest at

144

the breakfast-table tomorrow bent on another pitched battle in class warfare, Phoebe thought she could certainly agree to having Hugo Taverner; but when they walked home across the moonlit, frost-bound gardens she wondered why she should feel so strongly that she had been manipulated into taking *this* unexpected guest. As soon as they got inside the house Anne basely abandoned her, as it seemed to Phoebe, by bidding them good night. She was left to cope with him alone and felt inadequate for the task.

'I'm not sure how you...how you have things arranged at home,' she began awkwardly... 'I mean...'

'You mean, can I manage to get myself to bed with one hand? Easily, with long practice, but thank you all the same.'

She accepted thankfully what he said but thought of something else. 'Do all men require a night-cap? My father always did.'

Hugo, who disliked spirits late at night, assured her that a glass of whisky would be welcome. She had no choice but to lead him into the drawing-room and wave to the decanters set out on a Pembroke table, while she busied herself with reviving the dying embers of the fire. It seemed typically perverse of him that, having ignored her for most of the evening, he should now be reluctant to go to bed. But at least it provided the opportunity for something she was obliged to say herself.

'The music was very beautiful...Anne's playing, of course, but your songs as well.' She stopped herself in time from adding uselessly that she hadn't known he could sing; the truth was that she knew almost nothing about him, except that they didn't like one another.

'But for the war I should have thrown up the law and become a church organist,' Hugo said surprisingly. 'Old Archibald understood but my father, who was a professional soldier, didn't. In the end, of course, the problem settled itself and I made do with singing, but Anne is a fine accompanist.' He took a sip of whisky, and stared at Phoebe's downbent head as she sat on a low stool by the fire. 'I understand your father's village is finished...what will you occupy yourself with instead?'

He thought a tinge of colour suddenly stained her thin cheeks, but it might have been the glow from the fire. 'I expect you think it ought to be harmless "good works", but I'm going to become a potter...learn how to handle clay.' She lifted her chin in a little gesture that said he would probably misunderstand, but it didn't worry her if he did. 'My mother was a Harkness...I'm bound to be interested in how china and porcelain are made.'

'And are you also bound to feel interested in whatever George Harkness does?'

It was the first direct reference he'd made to the scene he'd interrupted almost a year ago. She wasn't prepared for it, but there was relief in having it out in the open at last.

'I'm *very* interested,' she said quietly, 'but I think you knew that already. We have to be patient, George and I, because for the moment he must stay where he is needed most; but young Josh is nearly six, and as soon as the children are old enough to manage without him he'll come here and share Hindleford with me. By then I hope we shall have deserved happiness together.'

Hugo put down his glass, feeling suddenly sick. She was foolish beyond permission, and trusting to the point of madness, but entirely lovely as well in the simple perfection of her belief that one ordinary mortal man called George Harkness wasn't ordinary at all.

'I know what you're thinking,' she went on '...I've no right to encourage George to be unfair to Cecily. But we try not to behave badly. I haven't seen him since the day of Father's funeral, and we don't even correspond.'

He could feel her loneliness in his own heart, and it suddenly made him angry.

'You *don't* know what I'm thinking,' he shouted. 'You don't have the faintest, bloody idea. Stop telling me what *hasn't* happened, for God's sake, and I'll tell you what *has* happened.'

Having got so far, he stopped suddenly, unable to go on, but Phoebe forced herself to put into words the fear that made her voice shake. 'Did Jane say that...that something was wrong? Tell me, please.'

'She wrote to tell her sister-in-law that she intended coming here to get married. Cecily replied with the news that *she* is expecting another child...apparently she and George fancy the idea of a daughter this time.'

147

Hugo picked up his glass and took a gulp of whisky that seared his throat; then he made himself look at Phoebe. It was absurd to imagine that she had shrunk since a moment ago, but she reminded him of a wild animal that had been wounded and retreated into itself to survive disaster. For a long time she said nothing at all, and Hugo almost gave in to the temptation to hold her, as he would have held a stricken child. But his ex-fiancée had taught him a necessary lesson: the touch of a man with a stump for an arm was probably repellent to any woman.

'My dear...I'm very sorry,' he said at last in a voice she didn't recognize.

Phoebe lifted her head to look at him. 'Is that why you stayed so close to Jane all the evening...so that she couldn't blurt out the news to me? The poor girl must have thought she was making another convert to the Communist Party.' She stood up, staring at him with eyes that seemed fever-bright in the whiteness of her face. 'I shall have more time than I thought to catch up with George. There's no rush about the pottery class after all. Perhaps I can persuade Anne to come to Spain with me and took at the lovely things the Moors managed to make. In any case I owe it to Father to give Spain a second try...it was the country he loved best next to England.' She was unable to stop talking, and unaware of the tears that had begun to brim over her eyelids and trickle down her face.

Hugo's right hand suddenly cut off the flow of chatter by gripping her shoulder and shaking her hard. 'Listen to me, Phoebe. Go to Spain if you like...do anything else that occurs to you...but in the name of all the saints in heaven *forget* about George Harkness. He is tied—he is bloody well *chained*—to Cecily and the Harkness Pottery, now and always.'

She wrenched herself away from him with a travesty of a smile twisting her mouth and stepped back to put a safe little distance between them. 'I think my birthday has lasted long enough; in fact it seems to have been interminable. Your room, when you feel like going to bed, is on the right at the top of the stairs, and a bathroom is opposite it. Good night, Mr Taverner.'

It was the last he saw of her, because only Anne Maynard shared breakfast with him the following morning, explaining that Phoebe was nursing a headache in her bedroom. For the next three or four days she went mechanically about her duties in the village, and spent more time than usual on her knees in the winter quietness of Francis's church without knowing exactly what it was she prayed for. She saw Jane and Ernest married by special licence, and felt relieved when they left. Then George's letter arrived...the only one she had ever received from him...and she knew before she opened it that Jane and Cecily hadn't lied. When she read it, it was clear he hadn't known that his wife had already passed on her news...imagined that *he* was the one to be telling her that their lovely dream would never materialize after all. Joshua was failing, and the Harkness Pottery would need all his care and attention if it was to survive the next difficult years. The work-people there depended on him but, more than that, it was impossible to desert a good wife who had wanted a daughter so much that she had pleaded for another pregnancy.

The letter was like George himself—kind and loving. Phoebe saw with aching clarity that it was his special charm, to make people love him; and his special danger to them, because not even he could make them all happy at the same time. Unhappiness was dreadful, but bearable if he wasn't obliged to see it at first hand.

She read the letter again, and afterwards slowly tore it into small pieces and watched them consumed in the flames on the hearth. Then she went downstairs, and suggested calmly to Anne that they might find the spring warmer in Andalusia than Hindleford.

9

The suggestion, born of a moment of desperation, became the thing they were bound to do, but with retreat cut off, Phoebe found herself equally desperate to be gone. In saner moments she could remember that no-one but Hugo Taverner had known of the future she'd expected to share with George; then imagination pictured again the whole of Hindleford discussing her pathetic little dream. So, to Spain they would go, and she insisted to everyone who spoke of their journey that they were going as serious students. To prove it she set herself and Anne a course of daily reading. Ford's monumental *Handbook,* Lady Holland's *Spanish Journal* and Whishaw's *Arabic Spain* were especially in evidence if she suspected that Hugo Taverner was likely to call.

He came more often than she thought necessary—apparently to see his friend, Anne Maynard, or his god-daughter at the Rectory next door. When possible, she avoided him, and was able to believe she carried out quite well the village duties that had belonged to her father. The truth would have astonished and displeased her—that Hugo used whatever excuse he could find to keep a watchful eye on her little household and on her responsibilities in Hindleford.

Their business meetings were always brief, and their conversation on the night of her birthday was never referred to. But when he spoke one morning of a new tenant needed for a Maynard cottage, she was obliged to admit that she would soon be unable to deal with that or anything else from the depths of rural Spain. His raised eyebrow was irritating when she was certain he already knew that they were going away, but she was uncomfortably aware of being in the wrong.

'I'm sorry...I expect I should have mentioned it before...Anne and I leave soon for Spain,' she explained briefly.

'It will be the best time of all to see the wild

flowers of Andalusia,' Hugo agreed. 'I assume that *is* where you're going?'

She was obliged to adopt a lofty tone. 'Moorish Spain—that's what I *particularly* want Anne to see: Toledo, Córdoba...Granada most of all, of course.'

'Seville too, perhaps?' he suggested helpfully.

Phoebe hesitated for a moment before deciding that there was no way of dealing with a bull except to grab it by the horns. 'Certainly Seville—we plan to go up the Guadalquivir by steamer from Sanlúcar.' Hugo was now frowning, a fact that enabled her to smile at him. 'To go to Andalusia a *second* time and miss the Holy Week processions would be not so much a misfortune as sheer carelessness, don't you think?'

The neatness of the quotation pleased *her*, but it seemed that her lawyer didn't care for apt little allusions to Oscar Wilde. His frown deepened and he sounded stern. 'To go to Seville with the intention of spying on the Rodriguez family would be both foolish and unfair. If that's your real motive I'd rather you said so.'

Colour stained her cheeks, but she didn't look away from him. 'I'd rather *you* admitted that Anne has already told you exactly what our plans are.'

'And now you're evading the issue by dragging in a red herring—it's a typical woman's trick.'

Phoebe made a huge effort to hold on to the remnants of self-control. 'I'm not sure yet *what* I shall do, because Lydia still wants us to pretend that someone of the same flesh and blood as ourselves doesn't exist there. But if I decide to call on Asunción Rodriguez and my father's son, it will *not* be because I'm prompted by vulgar, spiteful curiosity.'

She half-expected a shouted command not to go there at all, and was bracing herself to shout back, when she discovered a change in the forbidding frown in front of her. Hugo was far from smiling, but for once his expression was rueful, hinting at the possibility that he might have been wrong.

'You must behave as you think right, but I retract that unpleasant word "spying". Please remember that Lydia is justified to *this* extent, though; whatever you decide to do about Juan may have an effect on your life that can't be cancelled afterwards. I speak as your friend, Phoebe, as well as your lawyer.'

She only nodded by way of an answer, and after a moment's hesitation he finally left the room.

The library windows overlooked the drive, and from where she stood she could watch him climb into the waiting trap and be driven back to Oxford. The little more she knew about him now had come from Anne. John Smithers, the taciturn servant outside, had been his batman in France—wounded in the same night attack that had cost Hugo his left arm. She thought master and man well matched—two self-sufficient males who had remade their shattered lives in a way that firmly excluded women.

He said he had spoken as a friend, but she didn't regard him in such terms. Friends trusted

153

one another, and although she trusted him as a lawyer, as man and woman they were adversaries still, each determined never to give way to a change of heart.

Much hindered by a despondent Helena, who had insisted on watching her aunt pack in order to sigh and mutter 'goin' away *again*' at frequent intervals, Phoebe hadn't got very far when Lydia also appeared and despatched her reluctant daughter back to the Rectory.

'Lyddy dear, is something wrong?... You look very shaken,' Phoebe said quickly when they were alone.

'Francis has just had some dreadful news from India. Do you remember his sister Louise? She and her husband, Lionel Carteret, came here to say goodbye before they went out to Bombay.'

Phoebe nodded, calling to mind after a gap of eight or nine years a tall, willowy woman with the same shy smile and freckled skin as her brother. Louise had confounded her conventional relatives by marrying an Anglo-Indian doctor, and turning her back on England.

'Yes, of course I remember Louise,' Phoebe agreed.

'Well, there's been some dreadful epidemic raging—cholera, I think. Whoever else Lionel has managed to save, he hasn't been able to save his own wife; Louise died the week before his letter was written. It makes heart-breaking reading...he obviously adored her and doesn't seem to know how he's ever going to manage on his own.'

154

'There was a child—a daughter,' Phoebe remembered. 'At least the poor man still has her.'

'No, he doesn't. There was a chance to send her away out of that damnable place and he took it. Holly is on her way here, where he thinks she will be safe. She's on board ship *now*, with an Indian nurse, in the care of an English family coming home. Francis must go down and meet them at Tilbury in a month's time.' Lydia stared tragically at her sister. 'I think it was the cruellest thing Lionel could have done to a seven-year-old child who has just lost her mother, but I suppose he was slightly mad at the time with grief and overwork.'

'Anne and I will still be in Spain,' Phoebe murmured. 'Would you rather we didn't go?'

Lydia shook her head. 'Of course you must go, but I'll need your help with Holly when you get back.'

Phoebe stared round the disordered room. The sea of tissue paper and piles of neatly-folded clothes waiting to be packed reminded her of a journey planned as an escape from her own despair, but it seemed almost unimportant now. Her mind was filled with different pictures: of a small, solitary child torn from everything in life that had been familiar and dear, and a woman's grave that might have seemed less lonely under an English sky.

'Perhaps you didn't guess that I've been slightly mad myself,' she confessed suddenly. 'It actually seemed possible—even something I'd have a right to if I waited long enough—that

George should abandon everything he had known in order to come here. I was running away to Spain from the knowledge that he could *never* have done so, however much I longed for him to be happy at Hindleford.' Phoebe stared at her sister with huge, shamed eyes. 'Hugo knew, and despised me...or pitied me for being such a fool. I don't know which is worse.'

'I hope he's blaming George Harkness—I certainly am,' Lydia said bluntly. 'In fact, I'm ready to hate the whole Harkness tribe if it'll make you feel any better. You wouldn't have fallen in love with a married man without the strongest encouragement; that I'm sure of.'

'I hope you *won't* hate him,' Phoebe insisted with gentle firmness. 'He wanted to make me happy, but in the end he couldn't make Cecily *un*happy. I should have known that about him if I hadn't been so flown with the idea that I was loved.' She saw Lydia about to protest and shook her head. 'It's over now and we won't talk about it any more. Does Helena know about her cousin coming to live with you?'

'Not yet, but they'll either be bosom friends or enemies sworn—there are no half-measures about my daughter.'

'If enemies, what then?'

Lydia answered with a serenity Phoebe hadn't seen in her before. 'Then I shall have to rely on Francis. He makes an art of seeming ineffectual, but I know the truth about us now. I'm all surface force and competence. He's our deep, quiet source of strength.'

'The perfect combination?'

'I rather think it is,' Lydia agreed slowly. Then she kissed her sister in a rare gesture of affection and went away, but Phoebe made slow progress with her packing. Amid all the tangle of sadness in her mind, a thread of unexpected joy shone brightly. At least Lydia was nearer happiness than Phoebe had ever known her. It was *something* to remember with gratitude.

A March gale tried the travellers severely, reminding Phoebe of Nathaniel's similar experience of the Bay of Biscay. Cadiz when they reached it looked all the more pearly-white and inviting for being solidly anchored to its long tongue of land, but there was no time to linger there if they were to be in Seville for Easter. They steamed, calmly now, up the green waters of the Río Guadalquivir to a city getting ready for the great, high moment of the year. Less prepared than her companion for its beauty, Anne gazed in such wonderment that Phoebe had to put her own grief aside, remembering that it was the very lesson Spain always taught—*sol y sombra;* life might inflict pain carelessly, but to those who would accept it, it offered joy that was just as undeserved.

By Palm Sunday excitement was at fever pitch, and as part of a huge crowd they stationed themselves where they could see the first of dozens of processions wend their way from each parish church to the Cathedral. Every procession was escorted by soldiers and the Guardia Civil, perhaps to underline the age-old trinity of Spanish authority: Monarchy,

Church, and State. Then came the weirdly-gowned and hooded members of every *cofradía* or brotherhood concerned, escorting their own particular float. Each one depicted some lifelike, climactic scene in the life of Christ, or carried a much-loved statue of the Virgin Mary—elaborately dressed, richly jewelled, painted face even shining with glass tears. Beneath each float's trappings of brocade and velvet a score of men sweated for twelve hours to carry their heavy loads about the city. Behind them came the barefooted penitents, staggering under the weight of wooden crosses and dragging the chains that were fastened around their ankles.

Phoebe found it a bemusing combination of sacred and profane. The porters occasionally emerged from beneath their fearsome burden to exchange repartee with friends in the crowd or refresh themselves with cigarettes and casual swigs of wine; and it was undeniable that the Virgin Mary looked sometimes more like a painted trollop than the Queen of Heaven. But then a penitent's exhausted, pain-racked face would insist that he *was* in body, mind, and spirit carrying the cross of Christ, and the noisy, irreverential jollity of the crowd would suddenly be silenced by the unearthly song of a *saeta,* launched 'like an arrow thrown skywards to pierce the side of God'. Phoebe listened, on the verge of tears, and imagined that she heard her father's voice saying, 'It's Spain, my dear...don't expect the mixture to be like anything else on earth'.

On the morning before they were due to

158

leave she excused herself from joining Anne on a final walk through the gypsy neighbourhood of Triana. Her own destination was on the other side of the river among the narrow lanes and tiny squares of Santa Cruz. She found the house she was looking for, and another combination of extremes—dazzlingly white walls and the blackness of wrought iron grilles at every window. The effect was secretive and forbidding until a servant ushered her into a charming inner courtyard, bright with flowers and greenery. Rudimentary Spanish had sufficed so far; now, feeling sick with the nervous fear that she would have done better not to come at all, she was suddenly aware that a real conversation with Asunción Rodriguez would probably be impossible. Hugo Taverner had been right as usual.

'Miss Maynard...Phoebe?' a clear voice enquired behind her.

She spun round to see a woman who was not quite a stranger even after so many years. Her figure was no longer that of the eighteen-year-old nymph who had enchanted Henry Maynard, but her hair was still black and lustrous, and her face was beautiful. Phoebe looked for a smile that she might recognize to ease the difficult moment, but Señora Rodriguez remained grave, waiting for *her* to speak. The silence in the courtyard was unnerving, and Phoebe finally spoke the only words that came into her mind.

'You used to sing me Spanish songs—to match the nightingale.'

'And *you* tried to catch tiny lizards, and laughed out loud when the sunlight made a rainbow in the fountain!'

They stared at one another—elegant Spanish matron who had once been a nursemaid, and slender English girl in a simple jacket and skirt of grey worsted who had been the nursemaid's charge.

'My Spanish is very bad,' Phoebe said next. 'I was suddenly afraid of not being able to talk to you.'

'Carlos, my husband, made us all learn English, but now it is less good, because my children prefer to speak their own language.'

'I was also afraid that you would answer my note by saying that you didn't wish to see me,' Phoebe confessed, glad to make a clean breast of her anxieties.

'It's what Juan wanted me to say,' Asunción agreed calmly, 'but I was...curious!' After a further inspection she made up her mind. 'You do not resemble your father.'

'No—Lydia did. Don't you remember? She was the pretty one.'

Señora Rodriguez nodded, as if she recollected that about the children they had been. The same gesture served to bring the servant back with a tray of coffee, and Phoebe was led to a group of comfortable chairs at one end of the patio. The pouring of the coffee gave her time to reflect how seriously she had underestimated the difficulty of conversing with someone who, in the course of nearly twenty years, had become virtually a different woman. Asunción had been the wife,

160

then widow, of a rich and cultured man; who but an idiot would have supposed that anything of the laughing, singing maid-servant could have remained?

'Why *did* you come?' the señora enquired, then suddenly smiled '—perhaps you were curious too?'

The smile made communication possible after all. Phoebe's strained expression relaxed, and she answered with her usual directness. 'Our lawyer, Hugo Taverner, accused me of that. Perhaps it's partly true, but I thought it was time for you to know something my father once said. For as long as my mother was alive he never talked of Spain, but afterwards I was privileged to know what it had meant to him...what *you* had meant to him. You were the kindest, most loving, and surely the most beautiful, person he had ever known.'

There was so long a silence that Phoebe was afraid of having made a grave mistake. Then Asunción spoke at last, slowly, as if what she said had never meant to be shared.

'I wanted to die when my parents sent me away from Santolina. At eighteen I cared very little for the mortal sin I was committing; all I could see was the joy your father and I shared.' She turned away from that glimpse at the distant past to smile at Phoebe—a smile acknowledging that they were both women together, and therefore both acquainted with the happiness as well as the pain of being alive.

'I expected you to resent my son, Juan...and me also, perhaps.'

Instead of bothering to answer, Phoebe merely shook her head, and Asunción spoke again. 'I was wrong...you *are* very like your father, I think.'

The more difficult topic of Henry Maynard's will remained to be tackled, and Phoebe was still wondering how to go about it when a young man's voice spoke to someone inside the house; then the owner of it suddenly appeared in front of them.

'He looks very like his father,' Hugo had said, and Phoebe could see why. Juan, at sixteen, was already taller than most Spaniards, and his thick mop of hair, although dark, missed by far the night-blackness of Asunción's. He had inherited her eyes and olive skin, but the long, straight nose and mouth had come from Henry Maynard.

She introduced him with a deliberate formality that Phoebe thought was meant to remind him of the courtesy due to a guest. But he scarcely touched the guest's hand, and his manner was hostile. She told herself that the situation would have taxed someone much older than Juan, and that he *had* made it clear that he intended to go on considering himself Carlos Rodriguez's son. Still, there was her father's grief to remember, when a boy who didn't understand had rejected him out of hand.

'You know my father is dead, Juan?' she asked slowly.

'Yes—the lawyer told me...' He might have added 'I'm very glad', if it had been necessary to speak the actual words.

'I'm sure the lawyer also made clear to you the terms of my father's will.' She still spoke slowly, even though it wasn't his command of English that was any bar to understanding.

'Everything is clear, but Señor Maynard's will is nothing to me. I told my mother and the lawyer so. There was no need for *you* to come here as well.'

She felt his antagonism like a blow across the face but shook her head quickly when she saw Asunción about to intervene. The issue was between the two of them—strangers who happened by an accident of blood to be half-brother and sister as well.

'You may change your mind...perhaps decide one day that you *would* like to see your father's home in a different country...'

It was as far as she was allowed to get before his voice, breaking with rage, flung back at her what she was saying.

'He was *not* my father...this Englishman. He betrayed my mother and then left her alone. I told *him* when he came here that my name is Rodriguez. I am glad he is dead.'

'Juan, *tesoro*...' Asunción's shocked murmur scarcely reached the white-faced girl and boy who confronted one another.

'You understand *nothing*,' Phoebe cried, unaware that it was exactly what she had accused Lydia of a long time ago. 'My father didn't know about you...wasn't allowed to know. His first son died in England as a tiny child—given the chance, he would have loved you with all his heart. He never stopped loving your mother.'

163

It was an appeal passionate enough to have reached the heart of almost anyone else—but not this intractable mixture in front of her of English obstinacy and Spanish pride.

'I burned the lawyer's letter. You, Señorita, may burn your father's will. I, Juan Rodriguez, am not interested in England.'

'Then my father would have pitied you for a fool,' Phoebe said distinctly.

She saw the flash in his eyes, and braced herself for an explosion but Asunción's hand, lifted in a silent appeal, seemed to steady him. He managed a creditable, ironic bow instead and walked away into the house.

Phoebe was the first to break the silence he left behind. 'I'm sorry...I didn't manage that very well.'

'On the contrary,' Asunción said unexpectedly. 'My son *heard* what you were saying. I assure you it was more than he intended.'

Phoebe hoped without much confidence that it might be true. 'I *can't* burn my father's will,' she pointed out. 'Juan still has fourteen years in which to change his mind. But if he ever *does* decide to come to Hindleford, he must come as a friend. Perhaps he will understand that for himself later on.'

Asunción stared sadly at her visitor's pale face. 'I am sorry, Phoebe...it has been painful for you, this meeting. But will you try to understand that the only father Juan knew was my good, kind husband, who treated him exactly as if he had been a true son. It is a matter of *pundonor,* we say in Spanish, for him to revere the memory of Carlos, and to teach his younger brother and sister to do the same.'

Phoebe nodded, accepting without question this time what was clearly true; then she stood up to go. 'My cousin and I leave Seville in the morning, and perhaps I shall never see Juan again or you. Shall we agree to remember only the singing and the laughter and the rainbows in the fountain?'

'I think we shall agree to remember your father as well,' Asunción added gently. She leaned forward to kiss Phoebe on both cheeks. 'I am very glad you came, after all.'

Of the walk back to the hotel Phoebe recollected nothing. Her mind was filled with images of past and present that swung about like the shifting pictures in a kaleidoscope, but the one that remained uppermost and would stay with her longest was the stormy face of a boy who had reminded her of Henry Maynard.

She found Anne already back at the hotel, and confessed that she had been to call on Señora Rodriguez.

'Was she as you remembered her?' Anne asked gently.

'Yes, and no; but I think we parted friends.' She couldn't, after all, bring herself to refer to her brief meeting with Juan...the boy who might have smiled at her with his father's smile if only he hadn't seen her as an enemy. With a huge effort she put aside the memory of the morning.

'Enough of Seville—it's time to think about Granada. As a serious student of Moorish

Spain, dear Anne, you must promise me to be properly stunned by the Alhambra, and knocked speechless by the gardens of the Generalife!'

Anne agreed to do her best, and pretended not to notice that her companion's hazel eyes were bright with tears.

10

'I don't *like* it here...I want to go home.' The words varied sometimes, but never the intensity; then defiance would suddenly crumble into a plea to break the listener's heart. 'Why doesn't *M-Mama* come b-back?'

In the month that her husband's niece had been at the Rectory Lydia had heard it many times, but she was no nearer discovering how to deal with it, nor how to persuade a small, inimical child that the world she'd been abandoned to wasn't entirely hostile. Francis kept murmuring that time was needed...time, and the patience of a saint, Lydia corrected him in her mind. Her first reaction had been the right one; Lionel Carteret should never have sent Holly away.

Even the *ayah*, who had come from Bombay speaking no word of English, pined so visibly that the warning Francis received at Tilbury from Lionel's friend was soon seen to be true. 'She'll only turn her face to the wall and die,' he'd predicted cheerfully. 'Far better to ship *her* home if you don't mind my saying so.' There had been nothing for it but to agree, and arrange a passage back to India. Lydia saw her go with relief; life was difficult enough without a woman in the household who couldn't be communicated with and was therefore totally beyond the reach of comfort.

Holly made no fuss when her last link with India was driven, sobbing noisily, to the railway station. But her shuttered little face spoke the anguish that she wouldn't put into words. Another child might have responded to the new affections being offered to her; not *this* child, Francis slowly realized. With a strength of will far beyond her years, Holly Carteret was simply bent on surviving alone until the adults who ruled her life allowed her to go back where she belonged. Until then she would ignore Rosalind, now a flaxen-haired toddler beginning to take an intelligent interest in the world, spurn Richard's shy attempts at making friends, and fight with Helena on every possible occasion. If the cause of the battle was clearly Holly's fault and Lydia remonstrated with her, she would reply in an unintelligible stream of Hindi—the language she insisted on using for any deeply-felt occasion. Well-meant demonstrations of sympathy or affection were simply endured until she was released again, and Lydia's unconfessed nightmare became that Lionel Carteret might eventually forget that he had shipped his daughter back to England.

She managed not to say so, but when Hugo called one day he observed her drawn face, and heard her sigh of relief as she sat down.

'You're looking very tired; more ructions with Holly, I suppose,' he pointed out with his usual bluntness.

Lydia nodded wearily. 'Francis has had to attend the induction of a neighbouring priest, and she's always at her most difficult when he isn't here. I shall finish up believing what *she* clearly does—that we're to blame for her being here.' She heard the tremor in her voice and tried to smile. 'I dare say I'm as much irritated as anything else. It's downright humiliating not to be able to come to terms with a seven-year-old child!'

Hugo thought that she *would* see it in that way. He knew her well enough now to understand how much she expected of herself; failure with Holly would be her personal failure. 'What does Francis say—that she'll accept you all in the end?'

'Yes—what else *can* he say? But I don't think she will. There's something implacably alien about her. When I look at my own children, or the children in the village, I can usually guess what they're thinking. But Holly's eyes tell me nothing—it's like staring into bright, black glass!'

'She's bound to seem alien,' he said calmly; 'so would you if you'd been born into that teeming continent she's come from. Think of it—heat and squalor, burning skies and vivid, brown-skinned people; that's all you know of the world. Then you're given *us* instead, and the quiet green heart of England—the Gorbals

168

in Glasgow would probably have seemed less strange!'

'Well, yes, you're right,' Lydia conceded, and amusement glimmered in her tired face for a moment. 'I'm afraid it irritates my sister that you very often are! However much Holly exasperates me, I do remember her grief, but it's difficult to deal with when it takes the form of rage at being here. There's something else to remember as well...India is in her veins. Lionel's father was a District Commissioner out there who committed the social sin of *marrying* an Indian girl. His granddaughter may be three-quarters English, but that last fraction of Punjabi blood is still there...you can even see it in her looks.'

'All right, she's exotic by our standards,' Hugo agreed, 'but it needn't prevent her settling down here if she has to.' A rare and charming smile suddenly changed his face. 'The advice of a childless bachelor noted for his unfeeling heart is probably the last thing you need, but will you let me suggest something? Don't try too hard with Holly. It's not a bad rule where small, wild animals are concerned—to let *them* come towards you.'

She nodded, no longer taken unawares by his kindness or his perception. 'I think it's the advice Phoebe would give me, too, if she were here. She doesn't believe in hedging people in any more than you do.'

'When do the travellers return?' Hugo enquired casually.

'In a week's time.' Lydia hesitated, then went

on. 'Phoebe's last letter, by the way, mentioned that she was going to call on Asunción. I should have expected that she would; *nothing* deflects my sister when her mind is made up, and she's convinced that we're bound to love Father's bastard son. I just hope he refuses to be loved.' Then Lydia smiled suddenly. 'But for all that she infuriates me at times, I shall be *very* glad to see her back.'

'So shall I,' said Hugo calmly. He saw the astonishment in Lydia's face and felt obliged to explain. 'I miss Anne's music, and I prefer *Phoebe* to be where I can keep my eye on her.'

'Don't tell *her* that—she likes to imagine that she does rather well by Hindleford without Father.'

'So she does, but he was my friend, and I can't help feeling responsible for her.'

Lydia stared at his reticent face, thinking how little they knew of him compared with what he knew of them. 'I've never asked, but...no family of your own, Hugo?'

'Not much, apart from Uncle Archibald's tribe in Oxford. My mother was a lovely person—a musician as talented as Anne, but she died much too young when I was still at school. My father eventually retired from the Army to the Suffolk coast. He's content there on his own, watching birds and painting them rather badly. We meet occasionally, as polite strangers who wish each other well.'

The bald account explained quite a lot about Hugo Taverner. It hadn't included a reference to the girl who'd changed her mind about wanting to marry him, but Lydia hadn't expected that it would. Instead she reverted to her sister again.

'You know so much about our muddled affairs that I dare say you were perfectly well aware of what was happening between Phoebe and George Harkness. It was bound to be hopeless from the very beginning because Cecily—much as I dislike her—didn't deserve to be abandoned. Since George knew that better than anyone, it was downright wicked to have encouraged Phoebe to fall in love with him. With another child coming, he'll never leave Burslem now. She accepts that, but I doubt if it will stop her loving him—he's still the blasted "parfit, gentle knight" of her imagination. I could *kill* him for wasting all her goodness and funny, sweet ways.'

'Not entirely wasted,' Hugo suggested. 'Everyone who knows her enjoys the experience—even I do!'

Lydia was not to be comforted. 'Treasured sister, favourite aunt, friend of everyone hereabouts. What damned good is *that*, Hugo, when she deserves a lover and a husband of her own?'

'Put in those terms it isn't any good at all,' he agreed quietly, 'but I think you're right—an idealized vision of George Harkness is in her heart. She won't relinquish that for some other *real* man.'

It was depressing to have him agree with her so readily, and only after she'd waved Hugo goodbye did she realize how profoundly regretful he'd sounded.

Anne found the long journey home tiring, and was glad to be instructed to stay in bed and rest; but a perfect dawn in late May lured Phoebe out to rediscover her private kingdom. Spain was grandly, astonishingly beautiful, and on a second visit she had understood it much better than before, but *this* green, river-bounded world was home.

She wandered through the meadows, still dew-wet, where buttercups and marsh marigolds waited for the sun to open them, but the faint, unmistakable smell of river water drew her to watch families of swans float by. The moorhens were busy about their nests, and little water rats scurried in and out of holes in the river bank, intent on the morning task of finding breakfast. At last, reluctantly, she reclimbed the stile into the grounds of the Manor. It was still too early for Jim Wilkins to be at work, but a flash of colour caught her eye among the bronze-green willow fronds on the boundary of Maynard land...perhaps an eager fisherman already out considering the water, or a tramp who'd found a quiet riverside spot in which to spend the night. She almost left him in peace, then decided that he might be glad of bread and a mug of the strong tea that Mrs Jim offered her husband at intervals throughout the day.

But it was no tramp she found among the streamers of mist that clung like cobwebs to the margin of the river. A child stood watching her, uncertain whether to stay or flee. Moisture beaded her fringe of straight black hair, and her dark eyes were fixed warily on the stranger's face. She was very thin and long-legged, and clearly meditating escape if she could only be sure of the direction in which escape lay. She looked much too self-contained to be merely seven years old, but Phoebe had no doubt of her identity. At that age local children, being familiar with the river, came to no harm, but Holly Carteret was still new to Hindleford, and Lydia would be horrified to discover that her niece wasn't safe in bed at the Rectory.

'If you're thinking of making a race of it, I can still run quite as fast as you,' Phoebe pointed out gently. She smiled in the hope of winning some response but the child's face remained taut and hostile, concentration entirely fixed on some inner purpose of her own.

'If you're Holly Carteret, I'm your Aunt Lydia's sister,' Phoebe explained, 'and I live in the house next door. I know the morning is lovely, but it's very early to be out by yourself. Shall we walk home together?' The word 'home' was a mistake, but she realized it a moment too late.

'This *isn't* my home,' Holly shouted. 'I don't like it here and I'm not staying...I'm going home to Papa.' She picked up the little drawstring bag at her feet, that presumably contained all she needed for the journey, and edged carefully round the unknown obstacle in her path. But unfortunately the obstacle moved, too.

'Then I'll come with you,' said Phoebe cheerfully, 'only I'm afraid you're going the

173

wrong way. For India, we have to travel down the river.'

'I don't *want* you...I can go by myself. And *that* isn't a river,' Holly said with deadly scorn, 'it's just...just rain puddles.'

Phoebe could see the truth of it; to someone who'd clapped eyes on sacred Mother Ganges a Thames backwater must seem very small beer indeed. But she was also beginning to understand the despairing tone of Lydia's letters to Spain.

'I'm sorry you don't want me, because I quite refuse to be left behind,' she said firmly. 'Shall we make a start?'

Holly's considering glance took time to recognize a stubbornness that matched her own. But the effort to wake so early was being wasted and her aunt's household would soon be rousing. She gave a little shrug that accepted the inevitable, and they began to trudge in silence through the meadows and out on to the road that led to distant London. Once, Holly gave a little sigh and changed the drawstring bag, already growing heavy, to her other hand, but she went steadily on. Phoebe glanced down at her companion's set face, wondering how far in the direction of India they would have to walk until this fierce little creature gave in and behaved like any other child who was tired, hungry, and deeply unhappy.

They were in sight of Clifton Hampden before a solution presented itself. Phoebe stumbled realistically, gave a bitten-off groan of pain,

174

but limped on without speaking. Holly stared out of the corners of her eyes, looked away again, then turned a moment later for another glance at the companion who now hobbled by her side. Phoebe struggled on until a convenient gate in the hedge gave her an excuse to stop, sigh with relief, and lean against it.

She smiled faintly at the child who was watching her. 'I'm sorry, Holly...I should have liked to come with you, but I can't walk any further. Now you will have to go by yourself after all.'

Holly looked at the ground, making up her mind, and Phoebe prayed earnestly to God, the Father, not to forsake her at a moment when His help was needed so badly. If this ruse failed, she would be worse off than before, unless her ankle could suddenly be found to have mended itself. The issue hung in the balance for a moment, then in despair she watched Holly begin to march doggedly on. It took another fifty paces for her to accept the fact that a hurt companion, however much unwanted, couldn't be abandoned by the roadside. Her expression was still hostile as she turned round, but at least she was coming back. Phoebe said, as matter-of-factly as she could, that she would ask the first farm cart that came along for a ride back to Hindleford. Clifton Hampden church clock chimed seven; a morning stillness lay over the countryside. Holly squatted on the grass verge, bag clutched to her thin chest and a look of brooding sadness on her young-old face. Fearful of doing or saying the wrong thing, Phoebe finally broke the silence.

'Holly dear, it's a *very* long way to India, and I can't help thinking that you ought to wait until you're older and stronger than you are now...grown up, in fact. Will you agree to come back with me to Hindleford if I *promise* to tell you when the right time comes?'

The child's dark eyes examined the face of a fellow-traveller who, in the course of their silent walk, had somehow already grown familiar. She didn't resemble Aunt Lydia or Helena at all, and therefore didn't seem to insist that it was wrong not to have their white skin and golden hair. She didn't pat or kiss or exclaim, either, as seemed to be the habit of all Aunt Lydia's friends. Holly found herself not minding this quiet lady whose name she didn't know, but who no longer felt a stranger. From Phoebe her gaze wandered to the road in front of them. In the distance it disappeared round a bend, and the fact that she couldn't see it any longer suddenly distressed her. Dimly she understood that what she couldn't see she might not be able to manage on her own. The known boundaries of the Rectory garden, the churchyard, and the village, almost seemed desirable, because it might be very lonely out here, away from them on her own. A hard dry sob suddenly racked her whole body, suggesting defeat, as well as grief, and Phoebe held out her arms, but let them fall again. The time *might* come when Holly asked for comfort, but it wasn't yet

176

and must be waited for.

'I don't like Helena...nor Aunt Lydia much,' the child muttered, 'and Hindleford's all wet and green, but I'll come back for a little while.'

'All right, I understand. My name is Phoebe, by the way. Shall we play "noughts and crosses" while we're waiting?'

They were still drawing squares in the damp earth with pieces of twig when the rattle of a wagon sounded on the road. It was being driven by someone she knew—Will Cooper, the tenant of the Maynard Home Farm—on his way back to Hindleford.

Phoebe explained again a story that seemed to get more deceitful with each telling, but she told herself that it was justified. Will hoisted her without fuss on top of the bales of straw in the back of the cart, and then invited Holly to a share of the driving seat. With only a little hesitation she climbed up beside him, and Will's mare clip-clopped them sedately home. It seemed to Phoebe that she'd left the house hours ago, but they restored Holly to the Rectory so little late for breakfast that no-one had even realized she wasn't there.

In order to lend colour to her story of a sprained ankle, Phoebe wore a bandage for a day or two. She had told Lydia the truth about the escapade, but it was Francis who was given the task of talking to Holly. He explained the situation with a firmness that left no room for doubt; for the time being she had to consider them her parents, and herself their daughter, as much as Helena or Rosalind.

She weighed the proposal carefully before answering. 'Just until I'm old enough to go home?'

'Until then. What do you say, my dear...shall we slap hands on a bargain?'

The expression was new to Holly and not fully understood, but she memorized it afterwards, because the solemn ritual that seemed to go with it of shaking hands pleased her—at this rate she'd be grown up in no time. But there was something else to make clear.

'My friend Phoebe promised to tell me the right time for going...she lives next door.'

'I know she does, and you may trust what she says.'

Holly thought so too, and all in all she was reasonably content with the outcome of her morning walk. She now knew that escape was easier than she'd thought from the chattering cousins who seemed childish to her, and from the clucking ladies who kept calling at the Rectory. She had only to walk out of the garden to find the little rain-puddle river that in truth she rather liked, and the old grey church her uncle visited every day. She liked that too; its peacefulness was something she approved of, and the green and gold and crimson light that came slanting through its dimness, making patterns on the stone floor. Beyond the churchyard was where Phoebe lived. Holly was certain of the promise that had been made, but it would do no harm to call there occasionally...just to make sure.

11

On her first visit to the Manor Holly got no further than the kitchen garden, where Jim Wilkins was planting out young leeks. She stopped to watch, and didn't mind the friendly grin he gave her when he stood up to straighten his back.

'Want to lend a hand, missie?' he suggested. 'One seedling in each hole, and a drink of water to make it feel at home, like.' Then, without waiting to see if she stayed or went, he bent down again to the neat rows of holes he was making. After a moment's hesitation she took a tiny plant from the pile in the trug and followed his instructions...then another, and another. By the time the bed was complete with a slender green shoot waving from each deep hole, her sandals were very wet and her hands were muddy, but she felt content and smiled at her new friend.

'I'll come again tomorrow...will there be something else to do?'

'There's always summat that needs doin' in a garden,' he agreed. He watched her walk away and then went indoors to ask his wife whether the Reverend next door would mind his niece getting herself good and dirty in the garden. Mrs Jim thought not, but reckoned the child would soon lose interest anyway. He only smiled and drank the tea she put in front of him; for once his usually all-knowing wife was wrong, but better not tell her so, he thought.

Holly's visit was reported to Phoebe, but she only half-considered it as she walked through the churchyard with an armful of white peonies. The chancel flowers needed changing, but she knew with the other half of her mind that she was going in the hope of finding Hugo Taverner. He and his uncle closed their Oxford offices at noon on Saturdays, and he had fallen into the routine of a long tramp from his own cottage to listen to Anne practising the music for the following morning's service. Afterwards, more often than not, he went off alone again, but sometimes when the twins lay in wait they successfully lured him back to the Rectory for nursery tea. It still surprised Phoebe that they sought his company so eagerly, and she'd seen them tug at the empty sleeve of his jacket without the smallest hesitation to attract attention when they needed to. He hadn't called at the Manor since she and Anne returned from Spain. It wasn't that she'd missed him—she was quite certain of that; she merely required to see him on a matter of business.

The peonies were arranged and lit the altar with their pure, perfect beauty, but there was no sign of Hugo. Presumably he'd been told that Anne was away from the village for a few days and had cancelled his usual visit. The sharpness of her disappointment came as a surprise, reminding her that it was stupid to have got into the habit of relying on him.

As usual with things to think about, she went to her favourite seat on Ebenezer Bates's moss-covered tombstone. After more than a hundred years it now leaned at a very comfortable angle, and from where she sat she could enjoy the stone figures in the niches of the church tower—no satanically grinning gargoyles these, but surely the cheerful faces of medieval Hindleford citizens. It was in this very place that she had fallen in love with George Harkness. More than anything for herself she'd wanted *him* to be happy, and *there* had been her mistake; calmly now, she could see how useless it would ever be to think that she could know best what someone else might need for happiness.

'Welcome home, my dear Phoebe,' Hugo's voice said suddenly beside her. 'No bandage, I see—the ankle must have mended.'

It was enough to make her heart stand still, repeating so exactly the moment when George had appeared long ago.

'There was never anything wrong with my ankle, though I shan't forgive you if you tell Holly so.' She sounded cross, to conceal the fact that she was caught off balance and very short of breath.

'*Not* in merry pin today, I fear!...I can always go away if you were hoping for your own company.'

He made the suggestion lightly, but it reminded her that he was a man who valued privacy himself. She looked at him then, and in the shaft of sunlight that found a gap in the trees and fell on his dark head, saw him clearly for the first time. His hair was sprinkled now with silver; she didn't know his age—had always thought of him as a contemporary of Anne Maynard's, and therefore at least a generation older than herself. His face was unrevealing, not telling her whether he was happy or not, but the lines etched in it from nostrils to mouth spoke their own message of self-discipline that had had to be fought for. 'No man is an island', John Donne had once said, but *this* man was surely more 'entire of himself' than any other she had known, and for some reason she didn't understand the knowledge was hugely saddening.

'As it happens, I was hoping to see you,' she said finally, after a pause that seemed long because her thoughts had travelled far in a short space of time. 'If you'd care to walk back to the house, I could offer you some tea.'

The prim suggestion made him smile, but he propped himself against a neighbouring tombstone and shook his head. 'I'd rather stay here and contemplate the picture you present: the personification of youthfulness in a delicate white dress, sitting on what remains of old Ebenezer—one of those philosophical "problem" canvases that Victorian academicians used to delight in!'

She eyed him doubtfully, aware of a mood in him that was unfamiliar to her. Had she realized that he found it unfamiliar in himself she might have been still more disconcerted.

'You were hoping to see me,' he reminded her helpfully when she hesitated over what to say next. 'That *is* what you said, but perhaps you've thought better of it by now.'

She could easily have agreed, except that it was downright absurd to imagine there was anything to fear from her father's detached, sardonic friend, even in the loneliness of the churchyard. She took a deep breath and plunged into the matter in hand.

'Did...did Lydia mention that I was going to c...call on Asunción?'

Hugo didn't reply for a moment; when he did his voice was entirely businesslike again. 'Yes, she mentioned it. Shall I guess that you came away disappointed because Juan Rodriguez *didn't* fall into your arms, swearing brotherly love?'

'You make me sound very stupid,' Phoebe said, stung to fierceness. 'I didn't expect him to do that, but I thought we *might* have begun to become friends.'

Hugo suddenly stepped away from his leaning-post and stood looking down at her—no unfamiliar gleam in his face now; the frown that replaced it was all too recognizable, and so was the biting anger in his voice.

'No wonder Lydia says you're as stubborn as a mule. For God's sake try to learn once and for all that certain things aren't going to alter because you want them to. Juan isn't going to change his mind and accept his parentage or you; George Harkness isn't ever going to be anything but an imaginary lover who inhabits your dreams at night. He never was! Wake *up*, Phoebe...look at reality for a change.'

'Stop shouting at me and telling me what to

do,' she cried, flushed now where she'd been pale a moment before. 'I'll think what I like, dream what I like, and go to perdition in my *own* way if I have to, not yours.'

She had sprung to her feet without realizing it, and stood confronting him. A strangely-glimmering, regretful smile touched his mouth as he looked at her, then faded again.

'Yes, sweetheart, I'm terribly afraid that you will.'

She heard what he said, but there was no time to take it in before his hand gripped her shoulder and pulled her towards him. She felt his mouth suddenly hard and urgent against her own, and she was encompassed in a wave of delight, fierce and unknown till now. Then all too quickly the moment was gone; she was bereft, and alone again. Hugo's tall figure was striding along the path...had already disappeared among the trees.

Nothing had changed—the churchyard was still peaceful and beautiful, she could hear the usual summer-afternoon noises of the village, smell the scent of honeysuckle carried by the breeze; but she felt more lonely than she had ever been in her life before. At last she wiped a trembling hand across her mouth, and forced her legs to move and carry her towards home.

Afterwards, when she'd succeeded in re-membering why she had wanted to see Hugo, she'd managed to write a letter instead, asking for Juan to be reminded that her father's will must remain in force for the years he had specified. The note was couched in terms of awe-inspiring formality, and she was pleased with it until Hugo's reply arrived. His letter used as many long and legal words as he had been able to think of, but she couldn't rid herself of the suspicion that he'd been smiling when he dictated it. Having entirely lost her own sense of humour for the moment, and with 'stubborn as a mule' still rankling, she concluded the whole matter by frostily requesting Lydia not to discuss her with their lawyer in future. But by the time they next met she was herself again, only taking her sister to task more typically for neglecting to rest enough during her third pregnancy.

'I hardly like to ask, but are things any better with Holly?' she also enquired.

'If armed neutrality is better than open warfare, I suppose they are,' Lydia agreed. 'She and Helena have to share the same nursery, and Miss Carlton's schoolroom at Wittenham Hall with the Bingham children; otherwise *they* now ignore one another. She mostly ignores *us*, too—no-one could accuse her of being a talkative child.'

Phoebe agreed, remembering her own brief meetings with Louise Carteret's self-sufficient daughter. 'She prefers her own company unless someone else strikes her as a kindred spirit—Jim Wilkins, for example; she follows *him* about the garden like a shadow.'

'Well, no-one could object to Jim, but Francis found her halfway to Little Wittenham the other day, hobnobbing with old Jervis, the road mender—she said she was helping him, if you please! Short of locking her in, it seems impossible to be sure of finding her where we expect her to be.'

'Do you ever hear from India?'

'One letter in the months Holly has been here, and even that scarcely referred to her. If you ask me Lionel has forgotten that he *has* a daughter.' Lydia frowned at her ankles that were beginning to swell—a deplorable result of pregnancy. Then she suddenly smiled instead. 'We've had *one* charming letter this week—from Edward Harkness. He remembered to hope that we were keeping well, but then came the nub of the matter. At nearly eleven he is now considered old enough to travel on the railway by himself; he thought we'd like to know in case we should find it convenient to invite him to Hindleford this holiday!'

Phoebe thought it sounded exactly like George's eldest son—thoughtful, solemn, and irresistible. 'So, is he to come?'

'Of course—directed by Helena, Francis has written to tell him so. We shall just have to pray that he takes no notice of Holly while he's here; otherwise the fat *will* be in the fire. My darling daughter remembers him as her exclusive property.'

'Well, a house full of children is the last thing *you'll* be needing—send them over for Anne and me to deal with.' Phoebe said it more confidently than she felt, foreseeing the sort of uproar that would ensue if Edward discovered this time that he preferred a companion nearer his own age.

Alone after the conversation with Lydia,

there was something else to think about. When Edward's visit the previous year had been cancelled because his father was too busy to bring him, she'd been almost felled by disappointment. Now, although she thought of George with no less affection, the excitement leaping in her blood, and the pain of missing him, were gone. He'd become inseparable in her mind from Cecily. It had been merely an illusion, beautiful but unreal, to believe that Phoebe Maynard mattered more to him than anyone else in the world.

Seeing the truth clearly now, Hugo Taverner's demand for her to face reality seemed all the more unfair and infuriating. But it was a mistake to think of him at all. At times she could persuade herself that she'd forgotten those few moments in the churchyard. Then, without warning, she'd be transfixed again by the memory of being held against him; she even found herself wiping away the touch of his mouth, as though her lips insisted on remembering it. She tried never to be where he was likely to appear, and explained briefly to her family that she left his company to those who enjoyed it. But with the model village presented to the County Museum, she was desperately aware of needing something to do. She was on the point of enrolling in an Oxford art class when their friend Humphrey Caldicott introduced her to someone even more eccentric than himself.

Humphrey merely explained that Brian Starkie had returned from the war in need of healing.

Phoebe paid her first visit to him expecting to meet a nerve-shattered recluse. Mr Starkie turned out to be a blue-eyed, red-bearded giant, with bare feet thrust into disciple sandals. She liked the proud motto he'd inscribed above his door—'Noble as the king, but not as rich'—and liked still more what he was producing in the pottery behind the cottage he rented from Humphrey at Brightwell. His motto he might owe to the Aragonese, but the inspiration for the lovely things she could see came from a more southerly part of Spain.

'Not much like the stuff your relatives turn out in their Burslem factory,' Brian Starkie said...derisively, she thought.

But it was true. The only decoration on the stoneware bowl she was holding was a delicate swirl of colour—as airy as the arabesques of Moorish calligraphy. On other pieces, glazed a tender green or blue, there was merely the hinted outline of a pomegranate or passion flower.

'They're nothing like,' she was bound to agree reluctantly, 'but that doesn't mean George Harkness wouldn't appreciate them—he *would*.'

Brian Starkie's smile was hidden in his beard, but he answered with unusual meekness. 'Sorry—no offence intended to the great name of Harkness!'

His visitor accepted the apology with a duchess's gracious nod, 'None taken,' and then spoiled the effect by smiling at him. 'I can scarcely quarrel with you, Mr Starkie, when I've come to ask a favour! I can draw a little,

188

but I want to learn how to throw pots—would you teach me?'

He was sure he was about to say that he had better things to do with his time than waste it on a lady of the manor who fancied she could dabble a little in watercolours. What he heard himself say was, 'You can come twice a week until you or I get tired of the arrangement.'

Her luminous smile shone again, making him glad he hadn't said no, and when she went away without overwhelming him with thanks he knew he hadn't made a mistake about Phoebe Maynard.

She described her visit to Lydia, who expressed grave doubts about the Brightwell potter. 'Mark my words, Phee—a contempt for socks *always* goes with a contempt for morals—to men like Brian Starkie the "simple life" means no responsibilities at all and free love on request in the middle of the afternoon!'

Phoebe tried hard not to smile, failed, and burst into helpless laughter. 'Lyddy dear, perhaps—but not with me! I'm not the sort of woman to appeal to Mr Starkie. He has an eye for the beautiful.'

Nevertheless, by the end of her second lesson their friendship had progressed by leaps and bounds, and she was becoming less convinced that her teacher saw her only as a student potter. Her strongest impression, though, was of his innate goodness—there was nothing to fear from continuing to visit him.

Driving out of Hindleford on the morning of her third visit, she overtook the solitary figure

of a child trudging aimlessly along the road.
It spoke so vividly of boredom and loneliness
now that the long summer break from lessons
had begun that Phoebe instinctively reined in
the mare.

'I'm on my way to Brightwell. There's room
for us both, if you'd like to come too.'

Holly had no idea where she would like to
go—could dredge up no other name on the spur
of the moment from the sad, empty blank in her
mind. Aware that the trap still waited, she finally
nodded and climbed in, and Phoebe suggested
to Dulcinea that they could now start moving
again. Suggestion was one thing, acceptance
another. By the time she had cajoled, begged,
and finally shouted at the mare, Holly's stony
face had come to life, and she even listened to
Phoebe's explanation of why they were going to
Brightwell. She enjoyed being perched up on
the box seat, with the sun warm on her face
and a little breeze ruffling her hair. It was also
a comfort, although she didn't say so, not to
feel alone for once. With Helena and Richard
she always *was* conscious of being outside the
magic circle of their twinship, and Rosalind was
far too young to be a friend.

The cottage they eventually stopped outside
pleased her as well, although she announced in
tones that forcibly reminded Phoebe of Lydia
that it would be all the better for a little
tidying-up.

'Well, don't tell Mr Starkie so,' she suggested.
'He likes it the way it is.'

He also looked a little put out at the sight of

the second visitor, but with Phoebe's pleading eye upon him he managed to smile at Holly and greet her cheerfully. She stared around her at the racks of drying pieces waiting to be fired, sniffed at the characteristic pottery smell of wet clay and enamel paints, and watched without saying a word as a soggy, grey handful of material thrown down on the wheel grew under the potter's hands into a little vase that he said could be hers after it had been in the kiln, then glazed, and fired again.

When the lesson ended they drove home in silence until the grey tower of Hindleford Church came in sight.

'Can I go with you again...*please?*' For once Holly's face was unguarded. Longing had wiped away its usual withdrawn sullenness, and her voice cracked with the fear that she was going to be refused. Phoebe nodded after a moment or two, trusting in Brian Starkie's good nature; he was too kind a man to turn away an unhappy child, however much he would have preferred to do without a chaperon.

By the time Edward Harkness arrived at the Rectory, to be appropriated immediately by Helena, it was an established routine that Phoebe and Holly should visit Brightwell together. Allowed to 'wedge' the wet clay at last for throwing on the wheel—rather as a baker kneaded dough—Holly was an absorbed, contented child. She watched and listened with fascinated concentration, and understood what she was told to do with the minimum of explanation.

191

One morning when she was sent to the cottage to draw shapes of jugs that wouldn't topple over, Phoebe tried to thank Brian for his kindness. 'She's transformed here, but a different child at home as well, because there is *this* to look forward to. I wish I knew how to sound adequately grateful.'

It was some time since he'd thought of Phoebe as being inadequate in *any* situation. Her thin face was attractively browned by summer sunshine, but his glance lingered on its expressive eyes and vulnerable mouth. She'd been far wrong in imagining that his taste ran to obviously beautiful women; on the contrary, everything about *this* woman pleased him.

'You *sound* grateful enough,' he said brusquely, 'but I wonder what would happen if I asked you to prove it?' His eyes held hers, and their message was so clear that her cheeks were suddenly tinged with colour. The moment Lydia had predicted was upon her after all, but she couldn't help feeling a little glow of satisfaction as well as embarrassment; surely it was *something* to have appealed to such a connoisseur? Then, as usual she grabbed the nettle with both hands, not knowing what else to do with it.

'Is it to be a...a condition of continuing to help Holly?'

She thought the question fair and scarcely expected the flash of anger in his blue eyes.

'I've a damned good mind to say yes, except that sharing my bed with a sacrificial maiden offering herself on the altar of family duty

192

would kill even *my* lust stone dead. Dear Phoebe, I should like to make love to you now and forever, but it takes two for true delight—a man and a woman entirely intent on giving and receiving pleasure. Now, having made that simple fact clear, shall I ask the question again?'

Despite the flush in her cheeks she faced him with the directness he was coming to recognize as the essence of her personality. In fact so candidly did she seem to be considering him that lust as well as anger threatened to melt into inconvenient amusement.

'I'm afraid it wouldn't work then,' she answered with genuine regret. 'The duty I *could* manage in a cause as good as Holly, but not the delight.' He made a stifled sound that she feared might mean offence taken, or too much hurt inflicted. 'It's not at all *your* fault,' she explained earnestly. 'I'm sure any woman in her right mind would...would *leap* at the chance; it's just that I...' Another snort silenced her and gave him away as he lost the struggle not to shout with laughter.

'Phoebe...heart of my delight, s-say not another w-word!' he gasped at last. 'You shall continue to bring that p-pot-mad child here until I can no longer b-bear the pangs of unrequited passion!'

He mopped his streaming eyes, and seeing that she still looked anxious, smiled at her with so much warmth that for a moment she wondered whether she'd been mistaken. But

193

delight didn't come with merely wishing—she knew *that,* even if she was ignorant of much else of the mysteries that lay between men and women. Doubtful of apologizing again when it seemed to cause him so much mirth, she kissed his cheek instead by way of ending the conversation.

But driving home, *she* was the pensive one while Holly rattled on about their next visit. Whatever Lydia pretended, Brian Starkie was an attractive as well as an experienced man, and Phoebe felt a twinge of aching regret for herself as well as him. Her only experience of love seemed now to have been as unsubstantial as a dream. Love's true reality was a man who would smile at her, touch her, claim her because he had a right to do so. All she'd known was a promise that didn't materialize; all she was left with was the prospect of the years ahead lived only through what she knew of other people. It suddenly didn't seem enough—she passionately envied women like Lydia and Asunción who, for all their moments of despair, knew joy at first hand as well. She tried to imagine herself explaining to Brian that she'd changed her mind; after all, delight *might* come if she applied herself to it, heart and soul. But the more she thought about it, the more unlikely it became—because try as she would to see herself finding passionate fulfilment with Brian, there hovered inexplicably in her mind instead the dark, sardonic face of Hugo Taverner, still telling her to face reality.

12

The man himself materialized unexpectedly soon afterwards. After weeks of miserable summer weather the sky had cleared at last and Phoebe crossed the garden to the Rectory one late-August afternoon in blazing sunshine. Francis and Anne were in Oxford, he officiating and she the organist at the wedding of an old friend's daughter. Lydia, therefore, was likely to be alone and glad of company. Nothing of the kind, Phoebe discovered a moment later, because sitting on the lawn beside her long chair was Hugo—who should have been still safely away in Spain.

The two of them looked at ease together, and Phoebe was sharply aware of several things at once...of *not* being at ease, and of having only herself to blame for the fact; of the pleasantness of Hugo's brown face when he was smiling, and of the completeness of his intimacy nowadays with the Fanshawe family—*she* was the one on the outside of that friendship. Spain had suited him—she'd never seen him looking so relaxed and content; or was it some gift Lydia possessed for charming him into gentleness? She felt suddenly sick with the strength and unexpectedness of her own jealousy, and it required a huge effort to walk towards them, smiling as if nothing troubled her.

'All well, Lyddy?'

'Yes, if that allows for my present resemblance to a landed whale! Wouldn't you think the Lord God Almighty could have made procreation a little less unsightly?' Lydia was aware of scarcely needing an answer. With the child due to be born in less than two months' time, her body was heavy and cumbersome, but she still looked, and knew that she looked, radiantly beautiful. *This* coming child was anything but regretted, and she didn't mind who knew it.

'I thought *you* were going to Spain,' Phoebe said next, looking directly at Hugo for the first time.

'I went...I'm back, and—thank you for asking—I enjoyed the visit very much!' The solemn mouth and eyes gleaming with amusement were a combination she was becoming familiar with, but she was no nearer knowing how to deal with it.

'By the way,' Hugo went on, 'I called on Asunción Rodriguez in Seville—I thought you would like me to.' He sounded so smugly virtuous that she should have been amused but, unlike Lydia, she wasn't in the habit of laughing with him.

'I expect you went to please yourself, and she merely told you how much worse I'd made things with Juan by going there myself in the spring,' Phoebe said tartly.

The gleam of mockery in his face disappeared, and instead she saw there only understanding. 'That *wasn't* what she told me. Knowing her son better than you could do, she wisely left

196

the subject alone. It took several days for *him* to mention it, and even then he didn't refer to your father, but at least he admitted that he'd been wrong to distress you.' Hugo registered Phoebe's disappointed expression. 'If it sounds too little of a climbdown, I promise you it isn't. The phrase "I am wrong" doesn't exist in the Spanish language, but even if it did no right-thinking male would dream of using it. Juan is more English than he realizes!'

Hugo was smiling at her now, with such true...such warm...kindness that where she had been deeply, illogically unhappy only a few moments ago, she was now deeply, illogically content.

'It's a beautiful day,' she announced, as if she'd only just made the discovery, and blushed at the look of enquiry in Lydia's face. 'It's also wonderfully peaceful—have you anchored the children somewhere in the middle of the river?'

'Rosalind's asleep indoors, and Holly is engaged on the weekly task of composing a letter to her father—refusing to be deterred by the fact that she almost never gets a reply. The twins and Edward are in the churchyard, "helping" Will Tomkins dig a new grave. Helena will have shed tears as usual for the dear departed—poor old Mrs James in this case—and then taken charge of the operation, because she always knows better than anyone else!' Lydia looked at the fob watch pinned to her dress. 'Teatime...they'll be back any minute. At least Richard and Edward refuse to let Helena make them late for meals.'

197

But it was Holly who appeared, clutching the little bowl that was the first piece she had been allowed to throw on Brian Starkie's wheel and shape more or less unaided. It had been hidden in her bedroom until now—all the more precious, just as a backward child is precious, for being slightly less than perfect. But an almost wordless friendship had been struck up with Hugo Taverner, and she wanted *him* to see what she had done.

He put it on the wide wooden arm of Lydia's chair to examine it with proper care just as the other three children came running through the shrubbery that hid the Rectory garden from the churchyard. With a little more warning Holly would have retrieved her bowl, but it was too late; Helena saw it at once, leaning slightly askew because the potter wasn't yet entirely mistress of her craft.

'It's all funny-looking and ugly,' said Miss Fanshawe, made blunt by jealousy. '*Silly* old bowl!'

Edward Harkness observed the stricken look on Holly's face, and stepped into the breach with the quick sweetness of spirit that Phoebe recognized as having been inherited directly from his father. 'It's not ugly at all...it's lovely,' he assured its creator, and he spoke with the authority of generations of Harkness potters behind him. Left there, the situation might still have been saved, but Edward was prompted to make matters clear to his dear Helena. '*You* couldn't make anything at all—you're all fingers and thumbs!'

It was perfectly true; Helena's only physical flaw was what Andy Briggs was known to describe as Missie's cag-handedness. She didn't mind in the least when Andy said it, but Edward was a different matter...Edward, *her* friend, her *best* friend...it wasn't to be borne that he should side with Holly, especially when her cousin was standing there, listening to it happening. She pounced on the bowl, flung it as far as she could, and watched it shatter on the stone flags of the path.

There was a moment of silence and of complete stillness, while Hugo, Lydia, and Phoebe all struggled to find something to say. Then, with a choking sob, Holly was off, running like a deer, long thin legs flying over the grass towards the river. Edward almost went to collect the fragments of the bowl, then set out after Holly instead. Helena burst into hysterical tears, and made for her mother's lap; Richard flung himself at Hugo, both children aware of needing security in a world that suddenly seemed awry. It took Hugo a moment or two to struggle to his feet, hand the small boy over to Phoebe, and start running himself. He kept to the path, assuming that it would lead him to the Rectory's little landing stage; it did, but he didn't know about the short cut the children always used.

He reached the water's edge in time to see Edward twenty yards away take a flying leap and land on the old raft Holly had already pushed clear of the bank. He was still tugging off shoes and socks when Phoebe flung herself round the last bend in the path.

'There's a punt at *our* landing stage,' she gasped '—shall we run for it?'

'Too far away; besides, I couldn't control it well enough—but I *can* still swim.'

'The raft's rotten and Holly *can't* swim,' she cried desperately.

'All right, but they're still just afloat at the moment. *You're* to stay here—there'll be enough of us in this bloody river as it is.' Then, in a raking dive, he was in the water, striking out for the raft, already a good fifty yards ahead of him. At the end of a much wetter summer than usual the water level was high and the current running swiftly. There hadn't been time to warn him how perilous the backwater was—clogged near the banks with the submerged roots of trees and rushes, exceptionally deep in midstream because of old gravel-pit workings. Further down, it churned into what was now the main river below the Clifton lock. Remembering that, she began to run along the path, as if the terrors in her head could reach the man driving himself through the water. Insanely, she heard herself repeating out loud Lionel Carteret's plea to Lydia...'Keep Holly for me—she'll be safe in England'—oh, dear God—*safe!*

The ancient raft did its best, lowering the children almost gently into the water as the rotting planks finally disintegrated. Nearly level with them now on the bank, Phoebe saw Edward clinging to the almost submerged timbers, but Hugo's dark head was beside him, and Holly's arms were round his neck.

Phoebe was scarcely aware of praying; but kept afterwards a recollection of such huge promises made that, if not broken, they would surely guarantee her a place in heaven.

It was perhaps five minutes later by her watch but seemed as long as eternity, when she reached down and pulled Holly out of Hugo's clasp on to the bank. Edward was still a little way behind but, remembering a boy's proper pride, Hugo allowed him to finish the swim unaided. When he'd finally been heaved on to dry land, Hugo hauled himself out of the water. Phoebe's sheet-white face tried to smile at him, and failed. She wanted to throw herself against his dripping body and weep instead.

'Now, shall we all go home?' he suggested, a trifle out of breath.

She stared at him, unable to answer, then at last nodded and took Holly's wet hand.

At the Rectory Lydia and Mrs Briggs attended to the children, while Phoebe was instructed to take Hugo to the Vicar's dressing room and find him dry clothes. There she saw what he'd managed to conceal so far—a long gash in the sleeve of his sodden shirt, through which blood still oozed, mingled with river water.

'A scratch,' Hugo explained, 'I didn't notice a nail sticking out of a drifting bit of raft. It's nothing to fuss about.'

'Of course not; and it doesn't matter a bit that the nail was certain to be rusty,' Phoebe agreed. She could hear a cold, unfriendly voice that surely didn't belong to her? She wanted to thank this man, not treat him like an enemy.

'Well, rusty or not, there's no need for you to play Florence Nightingale. I'll get Mrs Briggs to bind it up for me.' Then he politely held the door open, waiting for her to leave, apparently unaware that water still ran down his brown face out of wet hair and blood dripped down his empty sleeve. Phoebe stared at him, almost overset by too many emotions; but she fastened on sheer rage as the one she could deal with best. Good, kind Mrs Briggs might be allowed to help him, but *she* was to be lumped with the feeble, cruel fool who had deserted him when he came back from the war.

'Mrs Briggs is busy,' she shouted at him. '*I'll* play Florence Nightingale if I want to.' It sounded deplorably childish, and his expression told her so, but she was goaded into rushing on, tact forgotten now. 'Don't be so ridiculously proud of being different. There were *dozens* of men with amputated limbs at the Radcliffe Infirmary. I should know—I was a nursing auxiliary there.' It sounded grand and it was partly true, even if a volunteer of seventeen towards the end of the war had done nothing more harrowing than wash dishes and sweep floors. His impassive face revealed nothing at all, but she waited to be told that she could go and not come back. Instead, when he spoke again she was taken entirely by surprise.

'Have it your own way then. I shall be dry and decent in ten minutes or so.'

She was back within the allotted time, resolved despite inner quaking to remain calmly professional or die in the attempt.

One sleeve of his borrowed shirt was rolled high, enabling her to see at once why he could still swim so strongly—his left arm was intact to halfway between elbow and wrist. The stump was ugly, and for a moment undeniably shocking, but she scarcely hesitated—concentration now fixed on the long jagged gash above it that needed attention. He seemed disinclined to talk while she worked, but touching his skin seemed so intimate a thing to do that she was nervously obliged to chatter.

'Holly and Edward are being bathed and put to bed, worn out with excitement. Helena is genuinely full of remorse, and hunting through her treasures to find a peace offering. Contrition won't last, but for the moment she's as biddable as a lamb.'

Hugo's attention appeared to be elsewhere. 'You must have made rather a good child nurse!' he remarked at last. 'Gentle hands, and some light conversation to take the patient's mind off the agony being inflicted on him!'

'Agony...?' she looked up in dismay from the job of applying iodine, and saw that he was smiling. His expression confused her and she tried to remember that he too might be a little overwrought from the events of the afternoon. 'I was only allowed to do the most humdrum duties at the Infirmary,' she confessed, 'but you've probably guessed that already.'

He nodded, content to watch her absorbed face, aware that it wasn't his exertions in the river that had made the afternoon momentous.

'What happened today was my fault,' Phoebe

said suddenly. 'Helena asked several times to be taken to the pottery and I refused.'

'Why—because, compared with Holly, she has more than a child needs already?'

'Partly that but also, I suppose, because there's a limit to even Brian Starkie's good nature.' Phoebe blushed, remembering her last conversation with him. 'Lydia pretends to disapprove—Arcadian whimsy she calls the way he lives, but I don't really see why a man should trim his beard or wear socks if he doesn't want to.'

Hugo's nod seemed to agree. 'And by the same token a man should always do what he *does* want to do...I expect you'd think that only fair, Miss Nightingale?'

'W-well yes—within reason, that is,' she stammered, fearing where this discussion might lead them. 'B-Brian's very impressed with Holly, by the way...thinks she has the makings of a natural potter...' But the rest of what Brian thought was lost, because Hugo's fingers were gently laid against her mouth, stemming the flow.

'Light of my life...I'm glad Helena's so full of remorse. I'm delighted that Holly is talented, that Edward is brave, and Richard's the nice, bright child he is. I'm devoted to my god-daughter and even to her parents as well—but right now I'd much rather know why the mention of Brian Starkie should make you blush.'

She scarcely heard the question, having taken in very little of that speech except its beautiful opening phrase. He hadn't meant it, of course—it was the kind of thing a wily lawyer might say in order to be disconcerting. She looked for mockery in his face and thought she saw it in the teasing mask he wore.

'Brian's kind enough to be a little in love with me,' she suddenly shouted. 'Why shouldn't he be, even if I *can't* hold a candle to Lydia. You can go on admiring *her.'* It wasn't the effect she hoped for because her voice shook, and she was making a hopeless mess of trying to roll up the bandage she was holding.

'I do like and admire Lydia, and of course Brian Starkie has had the sense to fall in love with you,' Hugo agreed, 'but I was asking about *you.* Can you only see merit in potters, who are bound to have two good hands?'

With an effort she was unable to appreciate, he asked the question lightly, giving her the chance to retreat to safer ground. But it hung in the air between them, waiting to be answered.

'I once imagined myself to be in love with George Harkness,' Phoebe muttered. 'I'm very fond of Brian Starkie—that's all I have to say about potters.' She sounded regretful, but very firm, and didn't see the smile that touched Hugo's mouth.

'What about lawyers who can't even tie their shoelaces unaided—what is there to say about them?'

'Only that they shouldn't be so damnably proud and difficult,' she cried, '...nor so stupid as not to know that a wife, if they had one, would be proud to tie their shoelaces.' The truth, torn out of her heart, lay waiting to be slain, but when the silence had lasted so long that she had to look at him, she saw only yearning tenderness in his face.

'My dearest...are you sure? You don't have to feel grateful to this extent for me fishing Holly out of the river. I'm still no ideal lover...just the awkward, ugly customer you've been so careful to avoid!'

The pot of gold at the end of the rainbow was within her grasp now, dazzling and beautiful, and she began to smile. 'I'm very tired of dream lovers... Oh, Hugo!'

Gashed, mutilated arm and sound one were hard about her now, and his mouth insisted that the reality of love was what they were going to share. When he finally lifted his head to smile at her she saw him transformed into the young, ardent man that war and self-concealment had almost destroyed.

'I've known for ages what I wanted most in the world,' he murmured, 'but the more clearly I knew it, the further you seemed to slip away from me.'

Phoebe wound her arms more closely round him to deny the smallest intention of slipping away in the future. 'I've been in a fearful muddle...until this afternoon; then it was all perfectly clear,' she said with immense contentment.

'Does that mean I have to leap into the river whenever...'

She reached up to kiss him into quietness, and then explained. 'Do you remember what you

206

said on the riverbank?...“shall we go home?”.
We've both been lost for ages, but now that's
where we're going, Hugo, my love—just home.'

She was still wrapped in his arms when the
door opened and Lydia walked in.

'Let me guess—the nurse is consoling her
patient,' she observed dryly. She was aware of
a sharp and shameful twinge of jealousy because
she counted Hugo *her* friend; knew in the same
moment that she was behaving like her daughter
and felt deeply mortified.

'Appearances to the contrary, the wounded
one's been wonderfully looked after,' Hugo
said, 'and, dear Lydia, you may wish nurse
and patient joy!'

She smiled at them then, jealousy swamped
by sheer affection.

It was Hugo who settled the matter of where
they were to live by deciding that he would be
the one to move.

'You're saying that to please me, but there's
no need,' Phoebe insisted. 'Why can't I be like
Ruth, "lodging where thou lodgest"?'

'Because, dear heart, this house needs to be
inhabited and loved, at least until Juan's right to
a share of it finally expires. In any case, there's
John Smithers to be considered.'

She was tricked by his solemn afterthought
into staring at him in astonishment.

'The poor fellow *needs* to be uprooted—he's
getting very set in his ways!' Then, having
kissed Phoebe's quivering mouth, he spoke
more seriously. 'I couldn't possibly turn him

away—we've been through too much together. But if you agreed, we could make comfortable quarters for him in the coach house here—he'd like that.'

'Oh, of *course* I agree,' she said quickly, 'but there's someone else to be thought of, too. Anne is determined to leave...says she never intended to stay so long in any case; but I simply won't allow her to go back to the world of dreary rented rooms and dreadful landladies. Will you help me persuade her that this is still her home?'

Hugo took so long to reply that she grew anxious. 'My dear, of course I will,' he said finally, 'if *you'll* consider another suggestion first? Willow Cottage is for sale—I saw it as we drove past. I thought we might sell my house at Iffley and buy the cottage for her. She would still be part of the family and the village, but a woman with a home of her own at last. Don't you think she might prefer that?'

'Of course...oh, Hugo, of *course* she would, but how do we get her to accept such a gift? She's fearsomely independent, and determined not to be what she calls "a burden".'

'Simple—I shall threaten to back out of marrying you; no ceremony unless she agrees, and that's scarcely to be thought of when the entire village is already blowing the dust off its wedding finery!'

'*Always* marry a lawyer,' Phoebe advised herself, torn between laughter and tears. 'He has the answer to every problem, and if you happen to love him very much as well, life is perfect indeed.'

Hugo smugly agreed, then spoiled the effect by asking with sudden, touching gravity what he'd done to deserve such happiness.

'Endured much *un*happiness, my dearest dear,' she answered '...been brave and resolute and kind, and altogether...' but it was as far as she was allowed to get before he cut short the discussion of his virtues by kissing her instead.

The wedding was considerately delayed until after Kate Fanshawe, Lydia's fourth child, had made her entrance into the world. At much the same time the news reached Hindleford that Cecily Harkness had also safely given birth to a girl. Phoebe had no doubt that, dearly as he loved his sons, George would treasure a daughter, but it required an effort of memory now to recall a time when she'd felt sick with envy of Cecily for that unborn child.

She didn't expect Burslem guests at her wedding, but George arrived, apologizing for Cecily's absence. The baby, to be christened Joanna, was too tiny yet to be left, and in any case Sir Joshua depended on Cecily very much nowadays.

'The poor girl wanted to come, but somehow she seems to be indispensable to us all up there,' George explained with a mixture of regret and pride.

Phoebe was able to answer sincerely. 'I'm not at all surprised—she's what they describe as "deedy" in these parts, and it's a term of the highest praise.'

He smiled, remembering more vividly than he'd bargained for other occasions when it had been easy to smile at Phoebe Maynard.

'You look very happy...beautiful, in fact,' he said gently. 'I'm glad, even if I do feel rather elderly by comparison. It won't be long before I'm decked out in Joshua's gold watch-chain!...do you remember how we laughed about that a long time ago?'

Phoebe nodded, but he could see no trace of regret in her face. 'I remember everything,' she said simply. 'When I'm a very old lady and sit down to write my memoirs I shall recall with pleasure my dear friend, George Harkness.'

His charming, wistful smile, passed on to Edward, accepted that she had tactfully closed the subject of things past. In future when they met they would talk only of the family, the children, the pottery perhaps.

Phoebe's wedding-day seemed a good enough excuse for a village holiday. All of Hindleford intended to cram itself into the church to hear the Vicar marry her to 'the Captain', as they'd been taught to call him by John Smithers. George's sister, Jane, arrived from London wearing shorter skirts than any so far seen in a conservative country neighbourhood; Brian Starkie arrived wearing socks, to Lydia's great relief; and Helena—highly pleased with herself in Kate Greenaway bonnet and frilled muslin—set off for the chancel steps without waiting for Holly, her fellow-bridesmaid, or the bride. Restored to her proper place by Lydia, the ceremony went joyously without a hitch, and Anne and her assistant small boy on the bellows galvanized the old organ into a triumphant rendering of the 'Wedding March' from *Lohengrin*. Phoebe and her husband walked smilingly down the aisle until she heard Hugo's sharp intake of breath at the sight of an elderly man standing stiffly upright in the back row.

'Something's wrong?' she whispered anxiously.

'No, dear heart...only something very unexpected. I made sure my father wouldn't trouble himself to come, but he's here after all.'

Phoebe smiled at him from under the brim of her beautiful flower-petal-strewn hat.

'It makes the day *entirely* perfect,' she said without any doubt.

'Yes...I rather think it does,' Hugo agreed, and kissed her hand that he held, thereby causing Mrs Jim to burst into tears.

'The dear souls looked so pretty,' she explained afterwards to her husband, 'there was nought else to do but have a little weep.'

PART TWO
1932

13

At the age of seven Holly had thoroughly approved of an arrangement that brought Hugo Taverner to live next door, and she never saw reason to change her opinion as the years of growing up went slowly by. The Rectory was where she lived, but home was with Phoebe and Hugo. She had no secrets from *them* except one, but that was too precious and too painful to be shared with anyone. On the eve of her eighteenth birthday she was seriously taking stock of her future, unaware that it was also being discussed elsewhere.

Pressed to admit that Holly needed thinking about, her aunt sounded irritable. 'I *know*, but I can't think what's to become of her. She can't help looking plain beside Helena, but she could do *something* to make people like her. That's too much trouble, apparently.'

'It's not effort she begrudges,' Phoebe pointed out, 'only time wasted on people who can't teach her anything. I'm afraid poor Miss Carlton comes into that category.' She stared at her sister with a little frown of worry between her eyes. 'I promised years ago to tell her the right time for going back to India. Perhaps the time is coming.'

'Oh, for heaven's sake, Phee—what would she go back *to*—a father who never gives her a thought, except to pay money into an Oxford bank account?' Lydia inspected a smear of dust on the table-top beside her. She would have preferred to talk about the folly of village girls who dreamed of factory jobs in Oxford instead of domestic service, but Phoebe would certainly drag her back to the subject nearer home.

'Helena scarcely listens, either, to a word Miss Carlton says,' she confessed, 'but in her case it doesn't seem to matter. Young men will be beating a path to our door before she's much older, but they aren't going to do that for Holly. She wouldn't notice them if they did—all she thinks about is your potter-friend at Brightwell.' Lydia always qualified Brian Starkie in this way, as if it reduced the level of a friendship she had never quite approved of.

Phoebe thought of several things she might have said by way of retaliation but abandoned them. Lydia dreamed of a grand marriage for a daughter as beautiful as Helena; she wouldn't admit that a childhood attachment to Ned Harkness had never wavered, any more than she could be brought to see her niece's unconventional attractiveness.

'Brian isn't odd at all,' Phoebe said firmly instead, 'and he's been a true friend to Holly. What's more, he thinks she has quite exceptional talent, so you shouldn't regret the pottery either.'

'Talent or not, she'll need a suitable husband when the time comes, like any other girl. But you'll climb on your high horse again if I insist

216

that hobnobbing with Brian Starkie isn't going to help her find one.'

They were no nearer a solution to the problem, but Lydia suddenly abandoned it to speak in a different tone of voice. 'Dearest...no better news from Dr Martin?'

Phoebe shook her head and tried to smile, unaware of the shadow in her eyes. 'Two miscarriages are to be the extent of my motherhood—I'm even forbidden to try for another pregnancy. Nature lacks common sense...some poor overworked woman in a city slum can scarcely *stop* producing babies, while I...' her voice trembled on the edge of tears, but she swallowed them and tried to sound cheerful. 'Don't pity me—I'm the most blessed of women, and Hugo insists that there are already more children growing up around us than we know what to do with, yours and George's!' Then she touched her sister's hand and Lydia knew that the subject was closed. 'We haven't seen the Rural Dean for days—too busy with Parish affairs?' Phoebe asked instead.

'Busy, but entirely happy until this morning. Then a summons arrived from the Bishop which seems to indicate that the mantle of the retiring Archdeacon is about to be offered to him.'

'Well, you wouldn't mind, and you'd make a lovely Archdeacon's lady—another Mrs Grantley!'

'I shan't get the chance, because Francis will refuse. He'll thank His Grace very sweetly, and then explain that God intended him to be a parish priest, not a housekeeper for the Church.'

She said it so serenely, and smiled so beautifully as she got up to go, that Phoebe had difficulty in recalling a time when Lydia herself had been desperate to escape from Hindleford. She was a contented woman now, who had come slowly and with difficulty to that condition.

Phoebe reckoned it a very saving grace in a decade that, outside their own quiet lives, had been stormy. The pre-war Edwardian years seemed now to have belonged to a different, sunlit world. A Labour government for the first time in history hadn't, after all, spelled the end of England, but nor had it cured social unrest and the relentless slump in trade. Desperate misery had finally brought about a General Strike, and shock waves still battered the entire financial world after America's Wall Street crash. They had lived through interesting times but, as Hugo pointed out, the Chinese wished *that* on their enemies as a curse.

Phoebe abandoned the depressing train of thought with a sigh, reflecting that her conversation with Lydia had done nothing to solve the problem that confronted *them*. But a day or two afterwards Holly herself raised it in the forthright way Phoebe realized they might have expected. The shared weeding of a rose-bed was in progress when Holly suddenly laid down her fork and stared at her friend instead.

'Aunt Phee...they don't know at home yet, but I'm not going to do any more lessons with Miss Carlton after the summer holiday. She must have a terrible time, poor woman, trying to keep one step ahead of us; but I don't even *want* to know about artesian wells or the poetry of Alfred, Lord Tennyson.'

Phoebe raised an eyebrow. *'None* of it?' She was tempted for a moment to offer a choice morsel calculated to change *anybody's* mind—perhaps 'now sleeps the crimson petal, now the white'—but Holly's set expression reminded her that a more serious discussion was in front of them.

'Well what *do* you want to know about...India? We talked of that a long time ago, if you remember. Do you want to shake the dust of England off your feet?'

The mobile, olive-skinned face next to her changed again and, watching it, Phoebe marvelled that Lydia should be so blinded by her own daughter's golden beauty. Holly might not be able to compete with Helena, but she didn't need to. Glossy, short, black hair framed a face that was fascinating to watch, and her eyes set wide apart under perfectly-shaped brows, were beautiful. At the moment they were full of sadness.

'I've grown used to England...like it here,' she answered slowly. 'Even if I didn't, there'd be no point in going back to India. My father doesn't want me there.' She saw Phoebe about to deny it, and shook her head. 'It's true...I know, because I wrote and asked him.'

'Dearest, you...you misunderstood,' Phoebe struggled to suggest. 'Your father was...was afraid *you* might find it hard to settle down after ten years in England.'

Holly stared at her with huge, dark eyes that

219

refused not to see the truth, however much it might hurt. 'I burned his letter...but I made sure of understanding it first.'

Phoebe wondered if she were swelling visibly with rage. Her only relief would have been to lay rough hands on Lionel Carteret, and pummel his self-righteous, unfeeling breast until he confessed that love, like charity, was intended to begin at home. No doubt it was praise-worthy to shoulder the white man's burden—but at the cost of rejecting his own child?

'Not India, then,' she agreed, when she could trust herself to speak calmly. 'I talked you out of it once before and I'm bound to say I should *still* hate to see you go...and so would Hugo. We can't help feeling that you belong with us.'

Her companion suddenly smiled, sidetracked into thinking how typical it was that Phoebe should say 'belong with', not 'to'; she made no claims, and exercised no rights, but simply offered love to other people.

'One day I should like a pottery of my own,' Holly now confessed, 'but I'm not ready for that yet. Brian says that I can be promoted to the job of paid assistant, but I just like helping, and learning from him all the time.'

Phoebe looked thoughtful, wondering how to deal with a subject that, however delicate, seemed to need touching on. She was suddenly forestalled, and now Holly's face glimmered with amusement.

'It's quite all right, Aunt Phee—Brian and I are the best of friends, but he doesn't at *all* want to seduce me. He was kind enough to explain, in case I should be feeling slighted! Apparently another lady took his fancy long ago.' Deep in thought, she failed to observe the sudden colour in Phoebe's cheeks, and went on mapping out her own future.

'I'm going to use the money my father sends, and enrol at the Ruskin School of Art in Oxford. I'm bound to end up a potter, but it won't do any harm to get a general grounding first.'

Phoebe hastily confirmed that it was sensible and right, and the very thing she'd regretted never doing herself.

'After that I'd like to go to Spain,' Holly finished up. 'I want to see where Brian's inspiration comes from for the loveliest things he makes.'

'You could visit the Harkness Pottery in Seville,' Phoebe suggested, 'but there's always Burslem itself until you're old enough to be independent. I'm sure Ned could arrange it with his father for you to work there.' She saw the change in Holly's expression, but it came and went so fleetingly that she thought she must be wrong—surely it was no sudden shaft of pain that had made a young girl look old beyond her years.

'I don't know that I should care for Burslem, Aunt Phee...but I'm certain of something else. Helena wouldn't allow it, in any case!' Then she kissed her friend and went away, leaving Phoebe to work out the significance of that remark.

But the conversation was still in Holly's mind as she rowed herself upriver one May morning.

As usual at a weekend, Ned was at the Rectory, having cycled over from St John's in Oxford. He was in his third year there—a brilliant classics scholar, according to her uncle, who lamented privately the waste of seeing him eventually follow Sir George as the head of Harkness. Holly avoided him when she could; it was a painful temptation to watch for his shy, sweet smile, but Helena always made sure of intercepting it. She'd had to share Richard with young Josh once they were at Rugby together, but she was never going to share Ned with anyone.

It was a relief to be away from them, on her own. A breeze blew coolly off the water but the day was fine, and she soon found something to sketch—the contorted but lovely shape of a willow tree leaning out of the bank in front of her. Then the picture was disturbed by the sight of a man walking towards her along the path. He was a stranger, at least—no-one from Hindleford who would feel entitled to stop and ask why she wanted to draw a vexatious old willow tree that, as everybody knew, always grew much too fast where it wasn't needed at all.

Nevertheless the newcomer *did* stop, ten yards away, and she was obliged to pay attention to him. She saw a dark-haired man above average height, perhaps ten years older than herself. He was dressed not quite in the style of the men she knew round about, and yet there was something in the cast of his face that looked vaguely familiar.

'Good morning...I am looking for Hindleford Manor—can you tell me if *this* is how I find my way to it?' A faint stress on the word seemed to suggest that, if so, he wasn't very impressed with it. And a faint carefulness in the way he spoke gave her a clue as to who he might be—one of Hugo's Spanish relatives, speaking very well a language that wasn't properly his own. She thought him stiff and arrogant...poor Aunt Phee, to be saddled with such a visitor.

'Perhaps you've come across the meadows from Appleford,' she suggested crisply. 'If so, you missed the lane leading to the main road. Why not walk all the way back to it and try again if you'd prefer a grander approach to the Manor.'

He wasn't attuned to English voices, nor to English irony, but the coolness in her manner was obvious and provoking. An answering smile touched his face but didn't warm it.

'I make it a rule never to travel back the way I have come—it seems not sufficiently adventurous, don't you agree?'

He had the clear advantage of being older and more experienced, and she remembered Hugo's advice: 'never fight when you're out-gunned, Holly love'. Disengagement being advisable, she picked up her sketchbook and stepped out of the boat. He could see now that, though tall and slender, she was still only a schoolgirl. Her pleated skirt revealed long, beautiful legs, and her hair and eyes were dark enough to belong to a Spanish girl.

'I'm going past the Manor myself,' she said briefly. 'I'll show you the stile that leads into the grounds.' He made a polite bow, and fell into step beside her.

'I suppose Mrs Taverner is expecting you,' she suggested as they walked along.

'You suppose wrong, I'm afraid. I was promised a welcome many years ago, but she may have forgotten that by now.'

Unable to identify a man she didn't know existed, Holly pointed to a path beyond a wooden stile, winding among banks of honeysuckle and wild tree-lupins. 'There you are—keep following that. It will bring you to the orchards and a kitchen-garden, and finally the house. There will probably be large dogs roaming about, but perhaps you'll find *them* adventurous, too!'

She smiled as if the idea pleased her, but he merely bowed again and climbed the stile—agilely enough, although he wasn't a countryman, she decided. At the Rectory she mentioned that a foreign-seeming visitor had arrived next door, but her aunt was too immersed in parish duties to do more than mutter, 'Oh, really? One of Hugo's friends, I expect.'

Juan Rodriguez followed the instructions he'd been given, met neither slavering dogs nor Holly's friend, the custodian of the kitchen-garden, and arrived unscathed at the far end of the Manor lawn. He believed, perhaps rightly, that Seville was the loveliest city on earth, and had come to Hindleford convinced that nothing in *this* alien place could give him pleasure. Nevertheless, he was obliged to stop and stare—there were flowers everywhere, and blossoming trees that dropped their petals like snowflakes on the brilliant grass, and an ancient house of rose-red bricks perfectly worked on by time and weather.

The woman who walked towards him had been cutting tulips; there was a rainbow-coloured sheaf of them in the trug she carried. Visitors didn't normally arrive from such a direction and she glanced at him uncertainly.

'Excuse me...I took the wrong route, and then was directed through the gardens.'

She still hesitated for a moment, but across the years chimed the echo of this same resonant quality in his voice; there was something familiar in the cast of his face too, insisting that she wasn't mistaken. Greatly though he'd changed, she could see that this self-assured and watchful man was exactly what the fierce schoolboy she had met so long ago would have grown into.

'It *is* Juan Rodriguez, isn't it?' she asked, holding out her hand. 'I'm Phoebe Taverner now, no longer Maynard, but you may have known that already from your mother.'

He could see in *her* the added poise that had come with the years of marriage; otherwise she seemed the girl who had outfaced him in his mother's courtyard. She hadn't been able to hide distress or anger at that other meeting, but he thought she wouldn't reveal herself now; she was on home ground, and entirely mistress of the situation.

He bowed over her hand but released it immediately. 'I should have asked if I might call,' he said with cool formality. 'But I...I

225

wasn't certain that there would be time.'

'And even if there were, you hadn't *quite* made up your mind, perhaps, whether you intended to come or not!'

Hugo would have sympathized with a man who'd had no time to grow used to his wife's disconcerting directness. But Juan only hesitated for a moment.

'That is also true,' he finally agreed.

She commended him in her mind for being honest, but felt chilled by his manner. If he'd come as friend, the fact wasn't obvious, and it was a relief to see Hugo walking towards them.

'Here is my husband,' she said thankfully. 'I believe you've met him in Seville.'

Juan nodded, remembering clearly the tall, quietly-spoken man who had called on them. The 'very large dogs' rushed towards him too, but so obviously with the intention of *kissing* a visitor to death that it was clear the dark-eyed girl in the boat had been enjoying herself at his expense. It was a useful reminder that he was among people whose ways and humour were different from those of Spain.

They walked towards the house almost in silence, even Phoebe's normal habit of putting guests at their ease deserting her. She was weighing the pros and cons of sending for Lydia to meet the visitor, while Hugo reflected inevitably on the matter of Henry Maynard's will—still with three years to run. Juan was simply regretting having come at all, but his face was expressionless, offering them no clue.

Inside the house Hugo poured into delicate glasses the golden *manzanilla* that his mother's family produced in Jerez. 'One link, at least, between this country and Spain,' he suggested with a pleasant smile. 'The English have always been loyal consumers of Spanish sherry!'

'No doubt they enjoy what they largely own,' Juan pointed out. 'The sherry trade is almost as much theirs as ours.'

It was scarcely a promising start. Listening to it, Phoebe could take no pleasure in the unexpected visit. Instead she was reminded of another meeting, and a boy who'd shouted that he was glad his father was dead.

'You didn't come to discuss our ability to recognize a good thing when we see it,' she said suddenly. 'Why *have* you come?'

He realized that it was the very tactic she had used outside, and found himself wondering whether it was Henry Maynard who had passed on to her this habit of going straight to the heart of things. In the days that he'd been in England, even with many other things to occupy his mind, he'd been irritated to find that he couldn't stop thinking about the man who had been his father. Now, in this book-lined room that was both elegant and shabby at the same time, surely echoes of the past were all about him...here, no doubt, the Englishman had read, written letters, perhaps remembered the life he'd abandoned in Spain, and the girl whose child he'd fathered.

Juan shook off the vision of a man he'd taught himself to hate, and answered at last

227

the question he'd been asked.

'I finally decided that it was time to visit England—you suggested a long time ago, if you remember, that I should find it interesting. My friends are still in London, but I wanted to see Oxford. I didn't intend to come *here*, but as I walked about the streets my mother's voice kept saying in my ear, *"por cortesía,* Juan, you *must* go to Hindleford"!' He smiled faintly at them, looking his true age for a moment. 'I am not always in the habit of listening to what my mother says, but this time I did.'

Phoebe smiled too, ready to lay wariness aside. 'Perhaps she would also say that you should agree to stay for a little while, now that you're here—will you?'

Hugo watched them both and knew even before Juan answered that his wife was going to be disappointed.

'Thank you, but I must go back to London this evening—we catch the boat-train to Dover tomorrow morning.'

'Well...well, there's time for you to meet Lydia, at least, and to lunch with us, and...and look around...' Phoebe's husky voice faltered and stopped because Juan was shaking his head.

'There is no reason to look around...and no need, I think, to meet anyone else.'

'Because you are still determined to refuse Henry Maynard's gift?' Hugo asked quietly, to save his wife the task.

Juan found it easier to speak to him. 'It is what I have come to tell you...for the last time.'

Even to his own ears it sounded graceless and abrupt, and he held out long, brown hands in a sudden gesture that asked them to understand.

'Señor Maynard intended to be generous...I see that more clearly than I did. But I am Juan Rodriguez, *not* Maynard, and nothing can change that now. My life is in Spain, my true brother and sister are Luis and Marilar...*they* and my mother are my family.'

The words themselves were blunt, but it seemed to Hugo that Juan spoke them to make matters clear now, not to inflict unnecessary pain. Phoebe said nothing for a moment or two, then went to stand beside her husband; because things that were difficult became easier when she was near him. It was very strange to feel so great a sense of loss now that her father's son was actually there. Perhaps there would be nothing they could ever agree about, but even so she might have learned to love him.

'I won't urge you any more to accept what you don't want—us, or any share of Hindleford,' she said quietly. 'But perhaps you'll agree not to lose touch with us completely? There might be something we could do in the future to help Asunción's family.'

Hugo found himself holding his breath, willing Henry's son not to hurt Phoebe by rejecting her a second time. But there was a change in Juan's expression, and suddenly a rueful smile curved his wide, straight mouth.

'Thank you, but you might come to regret your offer. Marilar is fifteen...very pretty and very good—even if we don't expect her present

229

ambition to outdo Teresa of Avila in saintliness to last!'

'But Luis is a different matter?' Hugo suggested calmly.

'He's seven years older than his sister, and supposed to be studying at Seville University, but I'm afraid Law makes very little appeal. He's been introduced by his grandfather to men who believe they are the only saviours of Spain. Their new religion is called Anarchism, and their god is a Russian—Mikhail Bakunin. Knowing nothing of Spanish problems, you won't be able to understand what dangerous but exciting companions they make for a boy of twenty-two.'

'It sounds as if you don't share their religion,' Hugo commented.

'Luis would tell you that my political convictions are so far to the right of *his* extreme Left ones that we are in danger of meeting round the other side! The truth is that I believe the old ways work best in Spain. We need reforms of every kind, but Luis's friends would sweep away everything that has made Spain uniquely different from the rest of Europe.'

'So, having got rid of General Primo's military régime, and sent the King into voluntary exile, you pin all your hopes of peace and progress on the new Republican government.'

'What else can we do?' Juan stared consideringly at Hugo. 'I'm sorry—I was wrong; you clearly *do* know something about my poor country. In that case you will understand that we are intolerant people...difficult if not impossible to govern. But we are also tired of being intimidated—by the Army, the Church, or the Guardia Civil. What is left but a republic?'

Hugo nodded, and Phoebe could see how deeply he was interested in the discussion. But Lydia's voice sounded unexpectedly in the hall, and although Phoebe could now have wished her not there, it was out of the question to let her go away in ignorance of Juan's presence.

She was brought into the room and Juan remembered what Asunción had told him—there'd been two small English children at the house at Santolina. Here was the elder of them, approaching forty but still beautiful in the fair, blue-eyed English way. She was a pleasure to look at, but he could feel at once that she had no welcome for him. *This* sister wasn't going to urge him to share an inheritance with them. The atmosphere that had warmed almost into friendliness grew strained again when Lydia enquired after his mother. Although she managed not to refer to Asunción, the nursemaid, her very carefulness made it unnecessary.

Phoebe struggled to remind herself that Lydia hadn't seen Asunción Rodriguez. No-one who knew her as she now was could think of her in the terms that Lydia still did. It was a relief when Mrs Jim came to announce that lunch was ready. With Hugo exerting himself to entertain, and Lydia doing her best to be amiable, the conversation went easily enough,

231

but Phoebe was sadly aware of failure. Juan would leave soon, thanking them politely, and almost certainly making up his mind never to visit them again. Watching his intelligent face, and the rare smile that reminded her so poignantly of Henry Maynard, she regretted most intensely that her father had never known his son.

When luncheon was over he rose to go, and there was nothing she could do but summon John Smithers to drive him back to Appleford.

Out in the drive Juan kissed Phoebe's hand, but didn't immediately release it. 'My mother was right,' he said unexpectedly, 'and I am glad I came.'

'You'll remember what you agreed, won't you?' she reminded him earnestly.

He nodded, turned to say goodbye to the others, and then was driven away.

'*What* was agreed?' Lydia asked, as they watched the car turn out on to the road.

Knowing that his wife was close to tears, Hugo put his arm round her shoulders and answered for her.

'Juan is going to let us know if we can ever be of help,' he said blandly, 'but once and for all he rejects any share of Hindleford. We can tear up your father's will as far as he's concerned.'

Lydia scarcely attended to Hugo's first sentence, being too attracted by the rest of what he'd said. The wife of a Rural Dean wasn't supposed to worship Mammon as well as God, but God must remember that she had four children to launch in the world. How could she not be thankful that their inheritance wouldn't have to be shared with the brood that a Catholic Spaniard would surely father? But there was another blessing just as important: the story of her father's bastard son need never now become the gossip of the neighbourhood. Once and for all, as Hugo had said, they could finally forget about their Spanish connections.

14

They had owed Juan's visit to Asunción, and it seemed natural to Phoebe, therefore, to write and thank her for it. *Some* contact had been made; she wouldn't lose it again if she could help it. But the habit caught from Hugo of studying the news of events in Spain gave her very little comfort. The new Republican government, *The Times* said magisterially, was doing its best; but, in trying to haul the country into the modern age, it was bound to outrage everyone who had traditionally ruled Spain—the Church, the Army, and the land-owning grandees.

'Am I right in thinking that in that poor, wretched peninsula *everybody* distrusts or hates everybody else?' she asked Hugo despondently one day.

'More or less, sweetheart,' he was obliged to agree. 'The only comfort I can offer you is that it's nothing new. What would look like the end of all things anywhere else manages in Spain to be what they've survived for the past hundred years—in fact ever since they threw out the French, with a little help from Wellington's troops. Governments come and go in Madrid, but the people themselves *don't* change, thank God.' He smiled, knowing why she still looked unconvinced. 'You think I'm biased—ready to grant them all the virtues they undoubtedly possess and a good few more besides!'

'Not that...you can grant them anything you like; but an accumulation of misery and misgovernment *does* change people. The downtrodden Russians eventually overthrew the Tsars, and even millions of feckless Italians are allowing Mussolini to transform them into drilled and disciplined *fascisti*...so where is your theory now?'

'Intact,' said Hugo calmly. 'For one thing, the examples you mention may not last—almost certainly won't, in my opinion; for another, the Spaniards are a different kettle of fish from the Slavs, and the Italians.'

'Juan spoke of a new religion.'

'I know, and a lot of hot-headed young men like Luis are bound to be its disciples; but they'll grow up in time and become quite staid and reliable citizens like the rest of us!'

She thought he spoke confidently for her benefit, and agreed to accept comfort where she could—there were enough other problems that seemed intractable. As the year wore on the world's money markets remained in turmoil; the slump persisted, and the dole queues grew longer. Another Labour government fell, and England came off the Gold Standard for the second time. Hugo frowned over the newspapers and Phoebe imagined that it was these domestic problems that troubled him. He didn't confess to finding developments abroad even more ominous—Germany's total economic collapse, for instance, and on the other side of the world land-hungry Japan's invasion of Manchuria.

In the autumn of the year, just as Ned Harkness started his final year at St John's, with an honours degree well in sight, Holly became a student at the Ruskin School of Art. She emerged from her first bewildering day there to find him waiting outside. He'd taken to wearing spectacles now that made him look older than twenty-one, but his mop of auburn hair was untidy as usual, and his smile lit the misty evening. Her heart turned over with the pleasure of seeing him, but she forced herself to sound indifferent, almost sharp.

'You're supposed to be poring over some musty tome of Ovid or Euripides, not lolling about out here.'

'My musty tomes can wait—I thought you might be feeling a bit adrift today. Are you going back with Uncle Hu? If so, I'll walk with you to the Turl.'

She could scarcely speak for the pleasure of knowing that he'd thought about her...no wonder she loved him so dearly.

'No, he's out of Oxford this afternoon,' she managed to say. 'I'm catching a train to Appleford, but you don't have to shepherd me

235

to the station—I know the way.'

Ned merely took her hand to guide her across the road, as if she were a child who needed looking after, and she was smiling when he glanced at her again.

'That's better—you were sounding cross before!' His shy grin came again, but Helena was nowhere in sight and it was entirely for *her* this time.

'Aunt Lydia would say I was being my usual ungracious self! The truth is I've hated feeling "new" all day and not knowing what I was supposed to do.'

'Very unsettling,' he agreed, 'but you'll soon get over it and be happy there.'

'Yes, I expect so...Ned, thank you for coming. I should have said that before.'

He simply waved the idea aside and walked beside her, thinking that it wouldn't be long before she had no need of a companion known since childhood. She was a vivid, attractive figure—scarlet beret, matching her jacket, pulled down over dark hair. He realized that the lovely pastel colours Helena always wore wouldn't have suited her at all. Holly Carteret was herself, different from any other girl he knew; he suddenly found himself hoping she'd stay that way.

'One more year here, Ned,' she said suddenly, 'then what? How does a classics degree fit in with being Sir Edward Harkness eventually—businessman and inheritor of a large chunk of the Potteries?'

'It doesn't fit in at all...wasn't meant to,' he

answered simply. 'My time here is a generous gift from Father—something I shall always be grateful for.'

The note of yearning in his voice made her realize how deeply he might have wished his life to be ordered differently, but she sensed correctly that it was something he would prefer her not to say. 'Afterwards it's Burslem, and the Harkness empire?'

'Of course; that's always been understood—by James as well when he gets through Cambridge. I'm not so sure about young Josh! But I shall have had all this...' his hand gestured at the city around them, '*and* Ovid and Euripides too!'

Holly touched his hand in a little gesture of comfort intended to be momentary, but Ned's fingers closed round hers again and they walked on together hand in hand—Ned unusually thoughtful, and Holly wondering whether she was dreaming this journey home.

There was nothing prearranged about their shared walks after that, she always took the train, and whenever he could Ned would be waiting at the school entrance. The days slipped by towards Christmas like coloured beads on a string, each one that she saw him glowing more richly than the rest. At weekends he cycled over to the Rectory as usual, to laugh and dance with Helena, and then Holly took refuge with her friends next door. She seemed now to live intimately with joy and pain because, like the inheritance that bound Ned to Staffordshire, she knew that his belonging to Helena was something else that had always been understood.

At the end of term there was the carol service to attend as usual with her uncle in Christ Church Cathedral. It had been an annual treat since they were children, but this time she sat more than ever entranced by the candle-lit beauty of the ceremony. The soaring trebles of the choristers, and her uncle's deep voice affirming in the lesson he read that 'the glory of the Lord shone all around' seemed almost more loveliness than she could bear. She was on the verge of tears when Ned smiled at her, and happiness opened like a flower in her heart. He went home, of course, afterwards for Christmas, but it didn't matter; there was the new year, the new term in Oxford, to look forward to.

Her contentment lasted until a cold, grey day in January. The sullen-looking sky promised snow, or the worse misery of sleety winter rain, but Aunt Lydia had reminded them of a task that had to be performed. It was almost Twelfth Night, and the tall fir tree in the Church remained to be dismantled of its decorations. Holly trudged through the garden with the twins, aware that Helena was even more bored and rebellious than usual.

'I am sick to death of being the Vicar's dutiful daughter,' she complained bitterly as they let themselves into the cold church. 'I loathe and abominate the smell of candle grease, dusty hassocks, and dry rot!'

'Quite so, but you aren't the only one to suffer,' Richard pointed out, 'so stop grizzling, for pity's sake, and hold the ladder steady—it's me that has to risk life and limb to rescue Ma's precious angel.' He grinned down at her through the fragrant branches of the tree but she refused to smile.

'Bilious!...too much Christmas plenty, I expect,' he added consideringly as he descended again. 'Never mind, dear heart...now be a good girl and help Holly or we shall be here all night.'

Helena flicked a cold glance at her cousin, methodically winding long strips of tinsel into a ball, but still stood hunched inside the old cloak borrowed from her father. She occasionally chose to wear it, liking the contrast of its soft, dark cloth with her flawless skin and golden hair. Her brother thought she was being tiresome, but forgave her because she looked forlorn.

'You're missing Ned,' he said more gently. 'He'll be here soon...you know he always comes well before the start of term.'

'Tell that to Holly...I'm sure *she's* missing him as well!' Sparkling malice suddenly brought Helena's face to life as she stared at her cousin. 'No-one to smile at sweetly in church...no-one to keep her company on lonely walks!'

Holly had imagined a moment before that the icy coldness of the church was penetrating her very bones; now she was suddenly feverish with heat and rage and hatred of Helena, but she did her best to speak without shouting.

'Ned sometimes shares a walk with me in Oxford—is that what you're talking about?'

'Of course—but why do you think he comes? I *asked* him to take pity on my poor little cousin because she's such a duffer at getting on with

239

people! Kind, darling Ned didn't mind...well, not at first...but it wasn't meant to grow into a habit.'

Holly stared at her tormentor—known and lived with intimately since childhood; but become now a white-faced, smiling stranger wrapped in the darkness of the old cloak. They confronted one another, unaware of Richard. He watched the confrontation, desperately conscious of needing someone else—anyone would do—to walk in and interrupt a scene he didn't know how to deal with.

'You're lying,' Holly said at last, in a voice that scarcely trembled. 'Ned might have come out of kindness, but it was his own kindness, nothing to do with you. I suppose some village gossip has seen us at the station and mentioned that he sees me to the train occasionally. What if he does?...you don't own him, Helena.'

Her cousin's smile insisted that she did and her blue eyes, bright as jewels in the pallor of her face, held some final, killing knowledge that she was about to use.

'Ned can't help feeling sorry for you—all that grand fuss made about going to learn to become an "artist", and it turns out that you hate the silly classes after all!' She kissed a hand at her brother, announced that she was now going home, and swept out of the church, leaving utter silence behind.

'Not...not quite her usual merry self,' Richard said miserably at last. 'She's always cantankerous when she's bored, and *not* at her best without Ned. Now, shall we finish this damned tree?'

Holly nodded, unable to trust her voice. She would go on winding tinsel as if life depended on it, sweep up pine needles, do anything not to have to stop and realize that Helena hadn't lied after all. No-one else on earth, not even Aunt Phee, had been told that she wasn't going to stay much longer at the Ruskin School of Art—only Ned Harkness knew, and *he* must have told Helena.

She spent the remainder of the holiday working with Brian Starkie at Brightwell. It wasn't unusual and caused no comment at the Rectory, and if Brian wondered what made his assistant more withdrawn than usual, he knew her well enough not to ask. When Holly Carteret felt like talking, she would talk; otherwise not.

But when the school term began again, she was waiting in Hugo's outer office for him to come out of his own room and leave for home.

'Train not good enough for you now?' he enquired when she appeared for the third evening running.

She answered his question with a hesitant one of her own. 'Is it a nuisance if I come here? It's...it's just that I want to avoid someone.'

He suspected a troublesome fellow-student and smiled.

'I didn't suppose it was *my* elderly company that was suddenly irresistible!' She made an effort to grin, but his impression that she was discouraged and unhappy remained. 'Anything else I can do, apart from escort you home?'

She shook her head and tried to sound unconcerned. 'Nothing else, but thank you all the same.'

He reminded himself to consult his wife—the only person in whom she might confide—and ushered her out the door.

Then a day came when John Smithers drove him over to Blenheim, to advise the Duke's agent on some point of tenancy law; for Holly it would have to be the train back to Appleford. She spent the lesson hours in needless agitation because no tall, untidy young man waited for her at the entrance. Of course, he'd given up coming...no, not even that; Helena had cancelled her previous instructions.

She was trapped on the pavement at Carfax by a river of bicycles flowing past when Ned caught up with her.

'Never wear a scarlet beret if you want to be invisible,' he advised, a trifle out of breath. He scarcely heard her little gasp, smiled as she turned her head, and it was the warm, sweet smile he'd offered her at the Christmas carol service. To escape from it she would have blundered into the path of yet another cyclist if he hadn't hauled her back again. He didn't let go of her, and they were suddenly isolated there, unconscious of the home-going crowds that parted, swirled around them, and then came together again.

'I thought you hadn't come back this term until I asked at the School. Why haven't you been coming out at the usual time?'

She managed a little shrug, and called on

the memory of Helena smiling at her in an icy church. 'I prefer to wait for Uncle Hu when he's in Oxford—a comfortable ride home, and no boring trudge to the station.' Boring?...those lovely shared walks when they'd 'tired the sun with talking and sent him down the sky'? The gods above should strike her down for the hugeness of the lie, but Ned was staring at her, more puzzled than hurt.

'What's wrong, Holly?'

The simple question went like an arrow through her defences, allowing the rest of the world to penetrate as well. This frozen moment of time would have to stay in her memory now, linked to a raw January evening and the sound of Great Tom in St Aldate's chiming the hour, followed by half a dozen other church or college clocks apologetically trying to catch up with it.

She thought it would have helped to feel angry, so that she could shout the truth at him; but the greatest part of the truth was that she herself had been such a fool.

'Nothing's wrong,' she said finally, 'except that I shall miss my train if I stand here much longer.'

He turned as if to cross the road with her, but she spoke again in a cold, flat voice that even to her ears sounded dreadfully final. 'Don't come with me—I prefer to go alone.'

His hands suddenly clamped themselves on her shoulders in a grip that bit through the stuff of her coat. She was a prisoner, helpless to avoid his mouth that fastened on hers in the only kiss he had ever offered her—hard

243

and hurtful and without tenderness, because he himself had just been hurt. When he lifted his head she saw instead of dear, gentle Ned a stranger she scarcely recognized.

'There won't be any need to hide in Turl Street in future. You can go home any damned way you like.' He stared a moment longer at her trembling mouth, then turned and shouldered his way through the crowd, leaving her with despair for company.

She stayed where she was, trying to remember what it was she had to do next, until an elderly woman stopped beside her, curious to know why she waited to cross an empty road. Then she began to walk again in the direction of the railway station.

Easter was approaching when an unexpected visitor arrived at Hindleford, to be shown into Phoebe's drawing-room.

Brian Starkie grinned as a startled housemaid closed the door behind him. 'It's the quietest outfit I possess—I searched the wardrobe for it!'

'Perhaps, but Nellie isn't accustomed to gentlemen paying morning calls in a waistcoat made of furnishing brocade. Of course, if you came more often she'd get used to it.'

Her smile hadn't changed nor lost its power to tug at his heart, but he bowed grandly over her hand, trying not to hate Hugo Taverner. 'Furnishing brocade be damned, Phoebe love—this was woven for me specially, I'll have you know. And I might just as well reproach you for never coming to see me.'

'I know, and I'm sorry, Brian; but at least Holly is always going back and forth between us with the latest news.

'She's my reason for coming now,' he said baldly. 'I had to tell her that I plan to go away for a month or two...it's years since I've been back to Spain, and suddenly the urge is on me to see Andalusia in the spring again.'

'Did she by any chance ask to go with you?' Phoebe enquired.

'No, but I know she's praying that I'll invite her. It's my own fault for running on so about the marvellous pots and tiles they still turn out there.' He eyed Phoebe guilelessly for a moment. 'You're supposed to wring your hands with horror at the mere idea of a wicked old rake like me running off with your ewe lamb. And even if *you* don't, Francis Fanshawe and his wife will certainly do so and forbid her to come.'

'I doubt if it would stop her,' Phoebe said slowly. 'She's a very redoubtable girl.'

'I know,' he agreed, serious again. 'That's why I'm here. If you tell me it's the wrong move, I shall simply say that I'm going alone. If not, *you'll* have to persuade your sister and brother-in-law that she won't come to any harm with me. I'm assuming, of course, that that is what you think.' He smiled through his beard but she wasn't misled; he waited quite anxiously to know what she would say.

'She will come to no harm at all,' she answered gently; 'you'll look after her as Hugo and I would.'

Her reward was a kiss on her cheek—light as the touch of a butterfly's wing, but still it made her blush.

'Holly needs to get away,' Brian pointed out next. 'I expect *you've* noticed that.'

Phoebe nodded, relieved that they were impersonal again. 'The art course hasn't worked out; she doesn't complain about it, but endless life classes are time wasted to a girl who was meant to be a potter. Something *else* is wrong, but she keeps *that* to herself as well. A trip to Spain would be a godsend, I think.' Then a little frown of worry shadowed her eyes. 'There's a problem, though. My brother-in-law may not know a great deal about present-day Spain, but Hugo certainly does.'

'Then he knows that foreigners who don't meddle in local politics have nothing to fear,' Brian said calmly.

She nodded, and smiled at him. 'It's wonderfully kind of you, but you always *have* been kind...since that very first morning I turned up at the pottery with my prickly little waif.'

'And *you* have always been very grateful!' He mimicked her without malice, and then leaned down to kiss the tip of her nose this time. She forgave him the liberty and assured him that his waistcoat would probably become all the rage.

'Happiness is like a perfume about you,' he said abruptly. 'I always *wanted* you to be happy, even when you had the deplorably bad taste to prefer Hugo Taverner to me.'

She touched his hand in a little gesture of

affection, and then reverted to the safer subject of what had brought him there.

'Let me tackle Lydia before you say anything to Holly about Spain.'

He nodded and got up to go. 'By the way, you can also tell your sister that Holly has the makings of someone quite unique at her craft. I'm a pretty good potter myself, but the day isn't far off when she'll leave me behind for good.' He smiled as if the idea actually pleased him, then said goodbye and went away.

Phoebe reported most of the conversation to Hugo that evening and was happy to find that he endorsed Brian's view. It was true that Barcelona had the reputation still of being a violent city, but that was because the Catalans still yearned for independence from Madrid; Seville was much less unsettled and he could see no reason not to let Holly go. Phoebe's satisfied expression made him smile.

'My opinion should have been the least of your worries,' he pointed out. 'How are you going to convince Francis and Lydia that Brian Starkie is a suitable travelling companion for a nineteen-year-old girl? You could, of course, tell them the truth—that he would do much more for love of *you* than just take the greatest care of Holly!'

She stared at him, too taken aback to have the presence of mind to pretend that what he'd just said wasn't true.

'He came to our wedding,' Hugo explained. 'I can still remember the look on his face. I felt very sorry for *him,* as well as insufferably pleased with myself!'

Phoebe was bound to smile at such a speech but she answered seriously. 'I know he rather enjoys the Bohemian label that people have tied on him, but he's a very kind man, Hugo, and he's sure that Holly will become a *brilliant* potter—so she's wasting her time at Oxford.'

'I agree entirely, my love, so between us we must make sure she has this Spanish visit. I shall bully Lydia and leave *you* to cajole Francis—that should do the trick.'

She kissed him gratefully and said, not for the first time, that she was *very* glad she'd had the good sense to marry him.

It proved less difficult than Phoebe had anticipated, perhaps because Lydia recognized that Rectory life would be smoother without her niece. There was no denying that *she* and Helena had firmly refused to become friends, but that wasn't all. The twins agreed about most things but not about Holly, and although Rosalind was content to be Helena's acolyte, red-headed, fiercely independent Kate fought impartially with both of them whenever the subject of their cousin arose.

'You're pigs,' was her forthright, twelve-year-old epithet for a pair of elder sisters who excluded her as well as Holly from their confidence. 'Holly's cleverer than you—that's why you don't like her.'

Helena took refuge in sarcasm, 'Is it clever to splosh about in buckets of wet clay? I hope

248

I shall find something more exciting to do with my life than that.'

'*Edward* likes Holly's sploshing...I've heard him say so.'

It was a well-aimed thrust, and Kate observed with pleasure the angry flush in Helena's face. 'When another wretched lump of earthenware is brought for him to admire, he's too kind to say anything else, you stupid child.'

Kate knew she was safe in ignoring this last insult. She had overheard her father once explaining to a parishioner that his youngest daughter was showing signs of exceptional intelligence. At the time she'd been displeased, wishing to be distinguished for valour instead, and had staked her claim to it by climbing on to the back of Will Cooper's largest Shire horse; but she was beginning to see that intelligence might be more useful in later life.

'Well, Uncle Hu's in the drawing-room talking to Mama about Holly's "lumps of earthenware"...I went in to ask her something and got told to go away.'

'Good,' said Rosalind virtuously. 'You listen to other people's conversations far too much.'

Kate forsook battle on the lofty plane of intelligence and made an evil face at her instead. Their mother came into the room and caught them eyeing each other like fencers seeking their opponents' weak spot, and knew that Holly was almost certainly their bone of contention. As usual, Hugo was right—one troublesome female the less in her household would at least be a help.

Once it was agreed that Holly should be allowed to go to Spain, Phoebe busied herself with the writing of several letters, and finally managed to wring from Lydia permission to explain to Holly their connection with a family she was likely to meet.

The brief story of Henry Maynard's love-affair was accepted so calmly that Phoebe resolved to convince Lydia that her own children might as well be told about it too. They had grown up in a different world, and Victorian discretion in such things now struck them merely as Victorian hypocrisy. Holly was much *more* disconcerted to discover that her aunt's half-brother was the arrogant stranger she'd encountered by the river all those months ago, and disliked on sight.

'I know you had different mothers, but he might have managed to be a *little* bit like you,' she complained. 'I don't *have* to meet him again, do I, or his family at all?'

'Yes, I'm afraid you do,' Phoebe said with unaccustomed firmness, 'because I've already told Señora Rodriguez that you will call on her.'

Holly smiled involuntarily, aware that when her dear Aunt Phee spoke thus she was not to be trifled with. But she made one last bid for her usual lonely independence. 'I'm not going to investigate Spain or the Spaniards. My only reason for being there will be to learn all I can, and to...escape from Oxford.'

Phoebe glanced at her companion's face and saw the sadness that said she was already no stranger to grief, nor to the necessity to manage

250

without her heart's desire. Holly stared at her long, thin fingers, paint-stained as usual, then looked up to find Phoebe still watching her.

'I'm really running away from *here*,' she confessed jerkily. 'Ned doesn't really see anyone but Helena...never has since we were children.'

'It's time you had a break from Hindleford,' Phoebe agreed after a moment or two of not knowing what else to say. She could give no comfort by denying what Holly had said, and only berated herself privately for not understanding sooner what the real problem was.

'It's been mostly my fault, not Helena's,' Holly insisted. 'Years ago I think she even felt sorry for me, because I wasn't growing up a raving beauty like the rest of the Fanshawe family. But by then I'd got so proud of being different, and difficult, that I even managed to ignore what Aunt Lydia has never once pointed out—I should have been deeply *grateful* to my mother's relatives, instead of a constant thorn in their flesh.' She looked round the sunlit garden just breaking into leaf and blossom, and her voice trembled on the edge of tears. 'I'm sure Spain will be exciting, but it can't be more beautiful than this. I want to go, but oh, how I shall miss *you* and Hindleford, Aunt Phee.'

'We shall be here for you to come back to,' Phoebe promised gently. She hesitated for a moment, then spoke again. 'It won't be any comfort, because other people's experience never is, but years ago I did exactly what you're doing—went to Spain imagining that my heart had been given for ever to a man who belonged to someone else. I believed it so stubbornly that I didn't see for a long time the true joy that was waiting for me with Hugo.'

Holly didn't answer, and Phoebe understood why. For all her prickliness, her heart was very kind...*too* kind to say that it *was* no help at all, because her own love was more steadfast and would never change.

15

Holly and Brian set out a fortnight later—Lydia finding it necessary to explain to the neighbourhood that her niece was being escorted by Mr Starkie on a journey to visit family connections in Spain. Holly left what had been her home for more than ten years with an unsettling mixture of emotions. For all that time she'd been an incubus foisted on her uncle's family—they'd had no choice but to feel responsible for her. Now, allowing a little for her travelling companion, she was on her own, grown up more or less, independent more or less.

Resolution wavered when the moment came to say goodbye...funny, fierce Kate, prim Rosalind, Richard, and even Helena, had been part of the only real life she could remember...the years in India were now only a distant dream. She had grown to love her gentle uncle, and how was she to say goodbye to friends as dear as Phoebe and Hugo? Only the memory of Ned saved her from weeping. He would soon be at the Rectory for the Easter vacation, but this time she wouldn't be there to watch him smile and dance to Helena's piping.

She and Brian travelled easily together, observing with relish whatever went on around them, and happy to share anything that struck them as beautiful or strange. At the end of a leisurely southward journey Seville awaited them, smoke-blue with jacaranda blossom—a May-time vision that Holly never forgot. She also remembered afterwards her companion's first little sigh of contentment; memory hadn't lied...the combination of green river, golden stone, brilliant blossom and blue Spanish sky was just as intoxicatingly beautiful as he'd remembered.

His only lament was that in dawdling too long among the Moorish enchantments of Granada they had missed the Feria.

'Perhaps we did worse,' Holly suggested. 'We missed the Holy Week processions as well, and Aunt Phee says that once seen, they're never forgotten.'

'How right, how true,' Brian Starkie agreed feelingly. 'I *have* seen them, my child, and once is enough by my reckoning...hundreds of grown men in ridiculous fancy-dress, and thousands of otherwise perfectly sensible citizens in the grip of religious hysteria—*not* my idea of a spectacle to watch at all.'

'You're very severe...*and* serious,' said Holly,

surprised by this last discovery.

He nodded, but recollected that it was a subject on which he and a priest's niece might not think as one.

'Mother Church doesn't need *us* to argue about her,' he suggested hastily. 'Our happy task is to savour what remains of a civilization that the *Reyes Católicos* did their infernal best to abolish, root and branch. I rejoice to say they failed. Five hundred years after the *reconquista* Southern Spain is *still* utterly different from the rest of Europe, praise be to God and Allah.' He bowed to the deities concerned, then led Holly to the Alcázar for a lecture on the significance of the colours used by the original tile-makers—white, he said, denoted the Umayyads who had founded the Caliphate; blue kept demons at bay; red was for royalty; and green was the very colour of the Prophet himself. He touched a plain green tile almost reverently. 'Look at that, Holly love; you'll see ones just like it in any present-day pottery. Remember when you do that they've been made here for a thousand years.'

She nodded, fully understanding at last his pride in a craft whose traditions had survived the turbulence of centuries. Then, as casually as possible, she broached an important matter of her own.

'I thought I'd call on the Harkness Pottery tomorrow, while you visit your own friends. Sir George was kind enough to give me a letter of introduction, and apparently the manager speaks English, so I'm sure I can manage on my own.'

He was a little surprised by this show of independence, but agreed all the same. 'All right—if it turns out to be more interesting than I expect, we can both go again. Isn't it also about time you called on your Rodriguez friends? They'll think it odd that you're wandering about Seville on your own, but the Spanish proprieties might be even more upset if you strolled in with me on your arm.'

'They *aren't* my friends,' she said categorically, 'and I don't much care *what* they think. If it wasn't for a promise to Aunt Phee, I wouldn't go at all. I bumped into Juan Rodriguez once at home, when he was visiting Hindleford—more grand than a grandee! I could easily imagine *him* keeping his hat on in front of the King.'

She grinned suddenly, remembering the savage dogs that he'd been told to look out for in the Manor garden. Knowing now what his unexpected connection was with Phoebe and Aunt Lydia, she felt curious to meet the woman who had bewitched Henry Maynard; but much more important would be her visit to the Harkness pottery.

At dinner the following evening Brian found her strangely untalkative on the subject. Yes, she'd been to the pottery; no, she didn't think he would enjoy it—the young man deputed to show her round had seemed apologetic, not proud, that their methods and designs had never changed. Spain was very backward, he'd said...*she* must have noticed that, coming from England.

'Bloody idiot,' Brian exploded. 'Tell George Harkness to fire him when we get home.'

Holly smiled fleetingly, then grew serious again. 'I don't seem very good at saying "thank you",' she muttered, apparently at random. 'Helena does it beautifully—give her a sixpenny bangle from Woolworth's and you'd think she'd been made a present of the Crown Jewels. Give *me* an unforgettable journey through Spain and I'm completely tongue-tied.'

Brian watched her, aware of a tension in her slender body that seemed altogether too excessive for the apology she was bent on making. He had found her constant company nothing but a joy, much to his own surprise, because appearances to the contrary, he knew himself to be a difficult man to please. His taste approved the way Holly looked, and the way she behaved; in fact he liked her very much, and knew he would have done so even without her extraordinary gift for handling and painting clay.

He answered her more seriously than usual—not as adult to child, or teacher to highly promising student, but as man to woman. 'I think you've just expressed gratitude so nicely that I'm bound to return the compliment. I can't call to mind *any* previous travelling companion who has failed to try my patience at least once! But there are still pleasures in store, as well as the journey home. We needn't start thanking each other yet.'

Her huge dark eyes were fixed on him with an expression he couldn't read—pity, sadness, regret? He hadn't made up his mind when she answered him.

'There isn't any journey home for me. I'm staying here.'

Coming from anyone else of her age, the firm statement would have made him smile. Coming from *this* girl, he was more inclined to pray for help to any divinity that would listen to him. He knew her very well by now. She wasn't in the habit of saying anything she didn't mean, and his imagination baulked at explaining to Lydia Fanshawe, much less Phoebe, that the maiden entrusted to his care had been left loose and unguarded in the depths of lawless Spain. He tried a little bluster in the forlorn hope that *that* would work.

'Don't be daft, my idiot child—home is where we both have to go. There are commissions waiting for me at Brightwell, and *you've* got to make up your mind what you're going to do—throw in your lot with me, or find someone else you'd rather work with.'

Holly shook her head, and he knew his situation was desperate. 'I've already found a job—I'm going to work for Harkness here...only decorating to begin with, but I expect they'll let me throw the clay when they're sure I know what I'm doing.'

'I should bloody well think so...remember who taught you!' he bellowed, distracted for a moment from the real argument. Then, looking at her, he made a discovery that irritated him still more—he would miss her very much indeed if he was forced to leave her behind.

'I'm sorry,' she said contritely, 'I should have told you what I intended to do. It wasn't a spur-of-the-moment whim yesterday. I knew when I left Hindleford that I was going to try to stay in Spain.'

The deceptiveness, the sheer damned dishonesty of Woman! He was about to embark on a tirade, delivered *fortissimo*, when the haunted expression on her face halted him. 'Do you hate your family as much as that?' he enquired almost gently instead.

'I don't hate them at all,' she confessed, 'but it's time to make my own way, and this seems a good place to start. I shall write and explain to Aunt Lydia, and to Phoebe...they *won't* blame you, I promise...I'm too well known for being difficult and unmanageable!'

'Who cares about blame?' he shouted. 'Down here you'll be a thousand miles from home, and you're scarcely more than a child yet. Why couldn't Burslem have been a good place to start?'

Her mouth twisted in a little grimace he didn't understand. 'No, that wouldn't have done at all.'

Almost defeated, he fired the only shot remaining in his locker.

'I'll be fairer with you than you have been with me, Holly. We'll *both* go and see Señora Rodriguez. If she agrees that it's feasible for you to work here and find somewhere suitable to live without coming to harm, then I'll go back without you; if not, I'll put you on the train home, even if I have to do it by brute force.'

258

She hesitated for a long time before accepting. Without knowing Asunción Rodriguez at all, it was a risky bargain to make, but ever since arriving in Spain the certainty had grown that she was where she was *meant* to be. She must put her trust in fate, and rely on it to help her now.

She knew what to expect the following morning—Phoebe had described the house in the *barrio* of Santa Cruz behind the great looming bulk of the Cathedral. Even so, the contrast was startling—secretive-looking outside, with shuttered windows and heavily barred door; within, feminine, fragile beauty—because they were shown into a courtyard filled with flowers, light, and the sound of falling water. She hoped it might be an omen, much-needed now that she was feeling so nervous. However clearly *she* could see what fate intended, there was no reason why the unknown Señora Rodriguez should.

For a visit that Brian had made crucial, it began badly; the tall figure coming towards them was immediately recognizable. He hadn't been friendly at their first encounter, and looked even less so now. Her impression was of a most un-Moorish reserve...no faint, inherited vestige here the traditional desert welcome that travellers to bedouin tents enthused about. He was half-English by blood, but Phoebe had explained that by choice he was wholly Spanish. There was a flicker of unwelcome recognition in his face, and she found herself regretting her behaviour on the river bank at home, especially when he refused to refer to it. 'Good morning, Miss Carteret...I am Juan Rodriguez. My mother hoped to have returned by the time you arrived, but she has obviously been delayed a little. She will be sorry to keep you waiting.' His glance moved from Holly to the man beside her. By Brightwell standards Brian had dressed formally for the occasion, but she could see that a cream linen suit, flowing floral tie, and wide-brimmed panama hat scarcely fitted Juan Rodriguez's idea of a reliable Englishman. Then there was the wild, red beard speckled with silver, and blue eyes bright with curiosity.

Convinced already that it had been a mistake to come, Holly made an effort to sound cool and dignified.

'This is my friend and teacher, Mr Brian Starkie, Señor...we are travelling together, inspecting ceramics mostly.'

Juan bowed, certain of having identified the slender young woman in front of him, even though she looked entirely grown up now. Her clothes were sophisticated—a jade-green jacket and skirt that matched the soft beret that clung to her dark hair; but her voice hadn't changed. He remembered also the little charge of hostility that had run between them once before like an electric current.

'For ceramics you should be in Valencia,' he suggested briefly. 'There are two excellent museums there.'

'But no working pottery that belongs to my Aunt Phoebe's family,' Holly said firmly. 'I'm still a student, but Mr Starkie is a famous potter in England.'

'I believe Señora Taverner mentioned that in her letter to my mother.' As clearly as if he'd put it into words Holly heard the depth of his disapproval. To this extent, at least, he was entirely his mother's son. A young woman was meant to be secluded from the world, handed, when the time came, from a father's to a husband's care without any unsettling whiff of freedom in between. She did *not*, in the view of this poker-faced Spaniard, wander about Europe with a man old enough to be her father who contrived nevertheless to look anything but fatherly. Holly told herself that Juan's view needn't concern her, but it was beginning to seem more and more unlikely that Asunción Rodriguez would do anything but agree with him. She would certainly have been reared from the cradle upwards to believe that however much women might propose, men ultimately disposed of them.

It was time to accept defeat and go away, but as she opened her mouth to say that they would leave, a servant appeared with a tray of glasses and a decanter of sherry, misted and ice cold.

'Served in the Spanish way, I'm afraid. Perhaps you don't care for that,' Juan commented as he poured the wine.

'Instead of our dreadful habit of leaving it opened in a warm room for days or weeks?' Brian took a sip, then smiled beatifically. 'Señor, give me the Spanish way every time!'

It couldn't be said that their host smiled in return but his expression relaxed a little. Holly thought he might even be going to exert himself

261

to the extent of keeping the conversation going, but it proved not to be necessary. The sound of a woman's voice talking to someone inside the house was followed by footsteps on the tiled floor of the patio. Holly saw Juan's face change and guessed that the newcomer must be his mother.

Asunción was still and always would be beautiful. That also Phoebe had explained, but Holly wasn't at all surprised to see Brian Starkie make the obligatory gesture of getting to his feet seem more like an act of homage. Here was metal worthy of his steel, said the gleam in his eyes as he was introduced, and kissed her hand with a grace to rival any Spaniard. Holly watched the little scene and, because it pleased her, smiled. Juan observed the change and found it disconcerting. An offhand, precociously adult young woman shouldn't suddenly become a girl not much older than his sister, with merriment putting warmth and mischief in her face. For a moment he regretted having no excuse to stay for the rest of the interview, but she had come to see his mother and he could only bow over her hand again and walk away.

'Forgive me—I meant to be here sooner, but my mother always finds little reasons to keep me with her longer than I intend,' Asunción explained. She smiled at them both, and invited Brian with a graceful gesture to pour more sherry. 'You are having a successful visit, I hope. Phoebe's letter spoke of your interest in ceramics. I call her that because I can only think of her as the small child who clapped and laughed when I sang to her...*so* long ago, it seems!'

Holly thought of the story she had been told. It no longer seemed strange that a conventionally brought up Englishman should have been captivated by the girl Asunción had been; nor that Phoebe had stubbornly refused to remember her with anything but love.

Suddenly it was Brian who took charge of the conversation. 'Señora, may I explain why *I'm* here? Our visit—entirely successful and enjoyable, I may say—is almost over, and we are expected back in Hindleford next week. But Holly has decided that she would like to stay in Spain...in fact to work here in the pottery that belongs to her aunt's cousins. They will be fortunate to employ her, but the arrangement may not be feasible in other ways. When we left England she was entrusted to my care. She has agreed—reluctantly—to accept the ruling of a Spanish lady—yourself, I'm afraid it has to be: if you say that it is unthinkable for a young English girl to live and work here on her own, then she must return to England with me.'

Asunción looked from his face, grave now, and troubled, to the girl who sat watching them. She remembered what Phoebe's letter had said about Holly's arrival in England, and the difficult years of childhood and adolescence. She could see why this girl looked older than her years and bravely self-controlled, even though her fingers were gripped together tightly in her lap.

'It would be most unusual,' she answered

slowly after a long pause, '...so unusual that I suppose I should say that it *is* out of the question.'

'The *job's* not out of the question—it's all arranged,' Holly said, struggling not to weep, 'and I thought perhaps I could lodge in a convent...I'm not a Catholic, of course, but would they mind that? You see, I want...I want very badly to stay, Señora.'

It was impossible *not* to see; her voice shook, and her eyes were huge with the fear that she was going to be rejected.

'My dear child...your aunt and uncle would certainly expect me not to encourage you...is that not so, Mr Starkie?'

'Well, yes it is,' he agreed. 'On the other hand, they know as well as I do that Holly doesn't need encouragement to go her own way. She's accustomed to taking decisions for herself...Francis and Lydia have had plenty of time to grow used to that.'

The scene was becoming unbearable. They should never have come, Holly realized, and the sooner they went away the better. She stood up and managed to smile at Asunción.

'Señora, I think we had no right to trouble you, and it was equally unfair of me to come to Spain without telling my kind friend here what I wanted to do. I see that I shall have to go back...at least for the time being.'

Brian heaved an inward sigh of relief, felt absurdly proud of his pupil's dignity in defeat as if it was something *he* could take credit for, and then heard Asunción say, 'Perhaps Mr Starkie

264

could face your aunt and uncle if they knew you were going to stay here with me?' She smiled at the expression on Holly's face—dawning hope mixed with the fear that she had misunderstood. 'You will be busy, of course, at the pottery, but perhaps at weekends you and my daughter, Marilar, could be company for each other. She misses Luis...he is twenty-three now, and not as inclined as he once was to spend time with a much younger sister.'

Holly was certain now that she hadn't misunderstood. In a gesture that took Brian Starkie wholly by surprise because it was so foreign to her usual reserved behaviour, she walked across to Asunción and bent down to kiss her cheek. There seemed no question about it now—Holly was staying here and he was going home alone to face the combined wrath of her family.

Asunción remained outside in the sunlit patio after her visitors had gone. The scent of carnations already in bloom was all about her in the perfect combination of morning freshness and the day's increasing heat, but for once she was scarcely aware of these things.

'Lost in memories, Madre?' asked Juan's voice beside her. 'Perhaps I should leave you with them.'

She opened her eyes and smiled at him. 'No, don't go...I want to talk to you.'

'About your English visitors?' he suggested when she seemed to hesitate. 'You're horrified, I expect, that Miss Carteret's family should have allowed her to travel with only a middle-aged man for company.'

'I'm a little surprised,' Asunción agreed slowly. 'It isn't our way of doing things. But I had something else to say to you. I've invited Phoebe's protégée to stay here for a while...a few months, perhaps.' She watched her son's face and knew that he wouldn't have shared the impulse that had prompted her invitation. 'You disapprove, I see!'

He disapproved so strongly that for once he was tempted to be rough with a woman he loved deeply. 'This is your house...you must do as you please,' he managed to concede at last. 'But if you imagine that Miss Carteret will make a suitable companion for Marilar, I'm sure you're mistaken.'

She was shaken, having grown accustomed to relying on his judgement, but tried to sound firm. '*Tesoro,* this is unreasonable...how can you know? In any case, Phoebe loves this girl...why should we not grow to like her, too?'

Juan's expression didn't relent. 'If I remember it correctly, Phoebe's letter mentioned that Holly Carteret has *never* fitted into her aunt's family—for the good reason, I suspect, that she is both independent and wilful.'

'Not, of course, what we encourage Marilar to be,' Asunción agreed with a faint smile. She made a little gesture with her hands, pushing aside doubt. 'We must wait and see, of course, but the truth is that I *wanted* to help her, Juan. She hopes to stay and work at the Harkness Pottery, but that is out of the question unless she has somewhere safe and respectable to live. Perhaps she will be happier here than with her aunt's family, and therefore not wilful at all.'

Juan bent down suddenly and kissed her cheek. 'Very well, *cara*—she is bound to come if you feel sorry for her! You shall continue to pity her, and I shall hope that homesickness soon drives her back to England.'

It was the end of the conversation and he didn't refer to it again. But while Marilar excitedly chattered about the *inglesa's* arrival, and even Luis deigned to speculate about her, Juan thought he understood the real reason for his mother's impulsive invitation. If only distantly by marriage, Holly Carteret was connected to Henry Maynard and his daughters. It made her in Asunción's eyes someone who had to be helped...even loved, if possible.

16

Luis Rodriguez saw Holly for the first time in the lobby of the hotel. He'd come because Asunción had insisted on this courtesy to their English guest, but it was an irritating waste of time to someone deeply involved in more important matters. Anticipating a girl like Marilar scarcely out of the schoolroom, he was afraid the hotel clerk had made a mistake—*this* slender, elegant creature, dressed in a turquoise-coloured jacket and skirt, whose dark head rose several inches above the Spanish women around her? But she turned when he spoke her name, and then he saw that her eyes were brilliant with unshed tears.

'I am Luis Rodriguez, Señorita,' he explained gravely, '...here to escort you to my mother's house.'

A moment earlier she'd been engulfed in loneliness, a stranger in an alien land, but now she could almost smile at him. 'I've just been saying goodbye to a dear friend, and trying to remember that I'm still here because I very much wanted to stay in Spain!'

Luis bowed over her hand, grace personified, and then summoned a hotel minion to deal with Holly's luggage. The gesture was imperious, and she couldn't help wondering whether a convinced anarchist shouldn't be ready to manhandle suitcases himself. She would ask him the question one day, but for the moment she was grateful for his kindness in being there at all. It had been a dreadful moment when she'd watched Brian Starkie being driven away. She blinked her eyes free of tears and looked at Juan's brother—half-brother, she corrected herself, and saw that the difference in parentage was very noticeable. Beside Juan he would look fine-boned, almost delicate, as if some distant Moorish ancestry had contributed a strain more exotic than Henry Maynard had bequeathed to *his* son. Holly had no idea whether she would like him or not, but loneliness retreated when he smiled at her, and it was comforting to realize that he approved of her.

Ten minutes later they were at his mother's

house, but it wasn't Asunción who waited in the courtyard to welcome her. A plump, raven-haired girl stood there, ready to explain in slow, careful English that she was deputizing for her mother, who was visiting a sick relative.

'Shall I show you round first?' she enquired, anxious to perform her duties in the right order.

Holly smilingly agreed, curious to see more than the charming courtyard. The house was typical of its kind, she discovered later—shuttered and tile-floored against the heat, sparsely furnished with heavy, dark pieces that were intricately carved. Against the whitewashed walls the effect might have been stark, except for the glow of porcelain and glass, and the sumptuous colours of the hangings Asunción had chosen. As well as an inner staircase, a flight of stone steps led from a corner of the courtyard to an arcaded verandah exactly like the one on the ground floor. Long glass doors opened from all the first-floor rooms on to this airy corridor. It was a beautiful house, and Holly said so when they were back in the bedroom that was to be hers.

Marilar seemed to take no pleasure from the compliment. 'Beautiful, yes...but unfair also, Luis says. Many people here are poor, you understand...and hungry. Luis says *we* have too much, they not enough.'

'And Juan...what does *he* say?' Holly asked curiously.

'He and Luis, they...' the English word failed

269

Marilar, and she locked her fingers together in an expressive gesture.

'They argue—disagree? Brothers often do, I'm told.'

'Yes, but here it is important, what they argue about. Juan says Luis's friends care nothing for Spain...only for destroying...' again Marilar's speaking hands completed her meaning.

'They destroy everything—what is good as well as bad?'

She nodded, pleased with her new friend who understood things so well. Then, in another swift gesture, she grasped Holly's hands and examined them. They were long and thin-fingered, but otherwise no different from her own.

'Mama says you are going to work as...as an *alfarera*. Is that not very strange? Juan thinks it is.'

Holly felt a twinge of pleasure at the news, but answered calmly. 'Women can be anything they choose in England—doctors, lawyers, go into parliament even. My choice is to work as a potter...I've been learning since I was a small girl.'

Marilar missed the letter of some of that speech, but she grasped its spirit, and dimly understood that through their ancient, iron-barred door had come with the *inglesa* some new way of looking at life, which Juan might also think very strange. She smiled her mother's entrancing smile, and said shyly, 'I'm very glad you're here. I love the convent nuns dearly, but I'm sure I'm too old for lessons, and I

270

miss Luis. He used to talk to me, but he's too busy now.'

Holly had a sudden glimpse of a life more protected than her own had been, and rigidly controlled by what Spanish *costumbre* would permit. She felt sorry for a girl who simply waited to be married off to the first man her autocratic elder brother thought suitable.

'Will you talk to me instead?' she suggested gently. 'I need you to teach me Spanish.'

Again, blowing faint but exciting against her cheek, Marilar felt the little breath of change. No-one else had thought that she could teach them anything.

Their first lesson was already under way when Asunción returned. Luis had gone out, Marilar explained, for once without regret. It hadn't mattered, though; she and the señorita had found much to talk about. Asunción smiled a welcome at their guest. Juan was rarely wrong, but he wasn't infallible, and it began to seem that Phoebe's protégée might be one of his mistakes.

Holly was relieved to discover he'd gone away—to Madrid, Luis explained later, to help defend the ringleader of a right-wing revolt against the Republic.

'They'll be imprisoned, of course,' he said coolly, 'but without expert help they'd be executed instead. They are my brother's friends...he's bound to defend them.'

'You sound as if you don't approve,' Holly suggested.

'How could I, even though I know them, too?

They call themselves Catholic Monarchists; I and my friends call them fascists...traitors in effect.'

She raised her eyes to heaven, bemused by anarchist logic. '*They* are against the government in Madrid, and so are you. How *can* they be your enemies?'

He smiled pityingly, forgiving her because she was English, and a girl, and altogether worth forgiving. '*Cara,* this is *Spain.* Here, we believe in the truth—*our* truth, of course—with passion. We scorn *your* ridiculous habit of seeing everybody else's point of view.'

She thought he sounded condescending and silly, and normally would have told him so. But there *was* something valiant about him as well, and Brian had pointed out another truth in his ridiculously impartial English way. Luis's anarchist friends might be destructive, but there was a great deal of social evil to destroy. Luis himself might sound stupidly bigoted, but he was scarcely older than Richard Fanshawe and his friends, and *they* didn't concern themselves with slum waifs or farm labourers who were unemployed.

'I shan't be able to understand what's being said at the moment,' Holly confessed regretfully. 'When I *can,* will you take me to one of your meetings?'

Luis's smile was a flash of white teeth in an olive-skinned face. What she suggested was out of the question, of course, remembering some of his companions, but he was touched and happy to be asked.

'*Querida*, I think not, even though half the things Juan says of Anarchists simply aren't true. *Some* are violent, naturally, but how else are we to achieve the society we dream of? We use the methods forced on us by the Army and the Guardia Civil.'

He stared at Holly with eyes grown suddenly sombre. 'My grandfather, Manolo Vargas, understands—it was he who introduced me to the brotherhood. But my father's relatives are rich bourgeois—living in Cadiz, thank God, not here. Juan agrees with *them*. My mother tries not to choose between us, but one day she will have to, I think.'

Holly shivered at the note of foreboding in his voice. There was nothing extravagant or vainglorious about him now, only a sober conviction she found frightening that a day of reckoning was bound to come. He saw her distress, and suddenly touched her cheek in a little gesture of tenderness.

'You've been here only a few days and seem to belong already. I'm glad you came, little *inglesa!*'

She saw with surprise that he meant it, and remembered that Marilar had said the same thing. It was more than her Fanshawe cousins had ever done, but she couldn't blame them; she hadn't *wanted* to feel welcome there, and the childish habit of staying aloof had been something she'd become branded with. She couldn't blame Ned, either, for loving Helena instead of her. It was easier to understand now, among these fatalistically-inclined Spaniards, that life arranged itself in certain predestined ways. Human beings could do nothing but accept them, with courage if possible.

The days also arranged themselves in a pattern that she began to enjoy—a long morning's work at the pottery, followed by the leisurely Spanish luncheon eaten out of doors in the courtyard. The late-afternoon heat required a siesta, and then it was time for the evening *paseo* before dinner. To Holly's fascinated eyes it seemed that almost everyone gravitated to the cooling streets, as naturally as tides responded to the moon, *'para tomar el fresco'*.

When she said this about Seville one day Asunción corrected her. 'Almost everyone in *Spain*, cara. There is no village so small that it doesn't have a *paseo* of its own. We live in troubled times but still cling to the old ways when we can.'

'So does the pottery,' Holly said contentedly. 'I could have worked for Harkness in England, but the joy of being here is that nothing has changed—no machines, no mass production, no two pieces exactly alike because they're still crafted by hand. It's hard to explain how satisfying it is to a potter like me to stack a brick kiln for a firing, knowing that it was built when the Moors were here.'

'You explain it very well,' Asunción remarked with a smile. 'I hope your family understands as clearly as I do.'

'Aunt Phee certainly does, and Uncle Francis is putty in her hands, so *that's* all right.' Holly grinned with pleasure at the idea, then grew

274

serious again. 'What isn't all right is my staying here, Señora. I should like to remain in Seville for perhaps as long as a year, but I can't be that much of a nuisance to *you*. Someone at the pottery must have a mother or a grandmother with a room to spare, and I can easily afford to pay the rent such a landlady would charge.'

'She might offer the room because she is poor, but you would be displacing several of her children,' Asunción suggested. 'My dear, such people still scrape a living here...I should know—I was born among them, shared their hardship.'

She made the admission without self-pity, simply stating a fact; she was not only beautiful and kind, Holly realized, but remarkable in other ways. It was no wonder at all that Henry Maynard had loved her.

'That hardship is what Luis and his friends want to change,' Holly said impulsively.

'I know, but they refuse to believe that others might want to change it too—by different methods.' Asunción sounded sad, but made the graceful gesture with her hands that Marilar was learning to copy. 'We were talking of you, not Spain. While you live *here* your family need feel no anxiety about you, and nor need I. But I ask you to stay for my daughter's benefit as well, Holly. She was very lonely and bored before you came; now you are like the sister she has never had.'

Perhaps it was a peculiarly Spanish grace, Holly thought, to offer a gift as if it were being made the other way round. She accepted it with her transforming smile, but registered a proviso. 'I'll stay until you get tired of me...just until then!'

A week after that conversation Holly returned from an expedition with Marilar to find a change in the atmosphere of the house.

'Juan's home,' Marilar said instantly. 'I can always tell. It's less peaceful, of course, because Luis can't help arguing with him, but I still *like* him to be here.'

Being unable to agree, Holly said nothing at all. She knew by now that Carlos Rodriguez had died when Marilar was still a baby. Juan's autocratic ways, second-nature to any Spanish male, had been made worse by the loss of a father. As a youth he had had to take charge; now it was probably an ingrained habit to tell other people what to do.

She stayed in her room until it was almost time to go down to dinner, then went to see the little fountain that she never tired of watching in the centre of the courtyard. The sound it made would be one of the memories she would take away from Spain; another would be the scent of carnations and geraniums lingering on warm air.

'*Buenas noches, Señorita,*' Juan's voice said behind her. 'Marilar tells me that your Spanish has made great strides.'

She turned to look at him, and saw that he looked tired and sad. He was twenty-eight, but could have passed for a man ten years older. Spain seemed to hasten maturity on its young

276

men, in a way that her own country didn't.

'Did the trial in Madrid not go well?' The impulsive question was out before she remembered that they were still strangers; he only didn't seem so because Marilar often talked about him. Now she remembered that he probably didn't even want her in his mother's house. His sudden frown confirmed it, prompting her afterthought. 'Not my affair, you're thinking...or something you don't want to talk about to a foreigner.'

His eyes inspected her, noting that Spanish air and sunlight suited her. The cotton dress she wore was simple, but its coral colour was lovely against her sun-tanned skin.

'You don't know *what* I'm thinking,' he pointed out. 'But since you ask about the trial, it went badly enough—my friends are now in prison, for trying to correct some of the wrongs that bedevil this country.'

'All right—it went badly enough, but at least they are still alive,' Holly insisted, surprised by her own desire to lift some of the strain from his face.

'Very true—let us be grateful for small mercies...isn't that a saying in your country?' He didn't expect a reply, and spoke again in a voice he tried to make less bitter. 'My mother tells me that you enjoy being here. Enjoy it while you still can, Miss Carteret. The time is coming when we can no longer pretend to be a civilized race; the veneer is dangerously thin already.'

As usual, she was stubborn when she knew she should have held her tongue. 'Aunt Phee's husband, Hugo Taverner, says that nothing is ever quite as bad here as it seems. Crises come and go, but the Spanish people survive them because *they* remain unchanged.'

'That's to say they all remain convinced that *their* vision of the future is the only one that's true. Your countrymen would probably argue about it; mine are more inclined to kill each other.'

Again his pessimism irritated her. 'Luis claims that as a virtue in them—*anything* is preferable to our cold-blooded indifference, he says.' She thought it sounded even sillier now than when Luis had suggested it, and regretted the fatal impulse to argue that Juan Rodriguez aroused in her.

'My brother says a lot of foolish things—he needs no encouragement from you.' The cold, flat statement was justified, but no more welcome for being so. If it was the way he spoke to Luis himself she could see no hope at all of their ever understanding one another. She was hesitating on the verge of saying so and getting another snub for her pains when Juan spoke again.

'Marilar tells me that the two of you went walking through the gypsy quarter by yourselves this afternoon.'

'I suppose *she* needs no encouragement from me either,' Holly said sweetly. 'In no time at all she will become *much* too independent and unmanageable, following my dreadful English example!'

She waited to be told that such rash

expeditions wouldn't be tolerated in future...saw, with complete astonishment, that Juan had begun to smile instead. 'I was only going to say that she enjoyed it,' he observed mildly. 'In fact she seems happier altogether than I have ever known her...thanks to you, according to my mother. Now, shall we go inside, Miss Carteret?'

Unable to find any other answer, she nodded and walked docilely with him into the house. Marilar had been right about one thing: it couldn't be called peaceful at all when her elder brother was inside its walls.

Her letters to Phoebe, and less frequent ones to the Rectory, described a summer like no other she had known. For Hugo's benefit she reported faithfully the Government's futile efforts to rule a bitterly divided country; for Phoebe's, she wrote of Asunción's unfailing kindness. The occupants of Hindleford Manor also heard much about the pottery, and her friend, Marilar, but she kept to herself a conviction that was beginning to occupy her mind. It seemed very strange that Luis should have decided to fall in love with her, but she recognized the signs—she'd seen them often enough at home in young men entranced by Helena. It made the summer memorable in yet another way, but she trod carefully between encouraging and snubbing Luis, mindful that she was a foreign guest whose novelty value would soon fade.

To Asunción, torn between the clashing political creeds of her sons, the long, hot days seemed full of brooding danger. Another *pronunciamiento* designed to change the government of Spain had failed as usual; this time the general involved had fled to Portugal but been captured on the wrong side of the frontier.

'What will happen to General Sanjurjo?' Asunción asked sadly at dinner one evening.

'Don't worry, Madre—no summary trial and firing-squad for the "Lord of the Rif"!' Luis said with bitter irony. 'It's only anarchists without friends or influence who get *that* treatment.'

'Your friends are treated as common criminals because it's precisely what many of them are,' Juan pointed out coldly. 'Sanjurjo has been a great soldier—served Spain faithfully in Morocco. He thought he was *still* serving her by trying to dislodge a government that is incapable of running this country.'

Luis looked from his mother's anguished face to Holly, now watching him with compassionate pleading in her eyes. He knew what she was asking and, for once, instead of shouting at his brother, got up and flung out of the room. Holly smiled reassuringly at Marilar's pale face, and suggested a promenade together.

'Thank God for our guest,' Asunción said when they had gone. 'It's becoming hopeless, isn't it? Spain itself is becoming hopeless, but there are times when I could *kill* my father for introducing Luis to those people.'

'My dear, if not him it would have been someone else,' Juan pointed out in the gentle voice he always used towards her. 'No-one as intelligent as Luis could have grown up here

280

in the last twenty years without aching to change what he sees all around him. But he won't understand that his friends' vision of Spain—no priests, no politicians, no-one in authority at all—is simply a dream. To try to make it come true they're ready to riot and burn and murder.'

Asunción sat without speaking for a while. At last she raised troubled eyes to Juan's face. 'Should we send Holly home...has it come to that?' His expression defeated her; she had to wait for him to answer.

'Not yet, at least. After a failed coup things have a habit of quietening down. In any case you'd have to think of some other reason for sending her away—she's English, don't forget...convinced that she's bound to ignore mere local disturbances!'

Asunción almost pointed out what she could see from his suddenly rueful expression he'd already remembered for himself. Instead, she said quietly, 'I'm sorry you haven't changed your opinion of Holly. I like her very much, Marilar adores her, and for the first time in his life Luis is tempted to forget about politics. It was *her* influence, not mine, that kept him from quarrelling with you just now.'

'I know...' Juan agreed after a moment or two. 'I apologize for a jibe against the English, Madre.'

He hadn't apologized about Holly, but she saw him glance at a pottery bowl on the table, filled with fruit. A skein of geese in flight circled the rim of the bowl, pure white against a background of deep cobalt blue. It was simple but spectacularly beautiful, and he knew that Asunción cherished it for its own sake and because Holly had made it for her.

'She was supposed to have come here to learn,' he said slowly. 'I doubt if there's anything our craftsmen can teach her.'

'No, but Spain has other lessons to offer. My impression is that she's learning quite a lot about herself; she's not the girl who arrived here in the spring.'

'You understand her because you've grown fond of her,' he said almost accusingly.

'Yes, I have, and I think Phoebe expected that I would.' A glimmer of amusement touched Asunción's face. 'But *you* are free to go on disliking her, *tesoro*, if you want to!'

Juan gave a little bow that not only thanked his mother for the concession, but seemed to indicate that it was exactly what he *would* do.

After the burning heat of summer came a gentler warmth that reminded Holly of autumn at home. She remembered with a pang of homesickness a green valley turning to gold, hedgerows hung with sparkling spiders' webs, and the smell of chrysanthemums and bonfires.

'You're looking sad, *querida*,' Luis murmured, when she sat for a long time one morning with a letter from Hindleford in her hands. 'You need diverting! I know...we'll go to Ronda. It's just the day for seeing the Sierra and the gorge.'

'It's also a day when you're supposed to be getting ready to go back to the university,' she reminded him with a smile.

'There's always mañana in Spain, little protestant! Today I declare a holiday.'

His sudden gaiety was infectious, and she was obliged to agree, even when Asunción insisted that Marilar must remain at home to nurse a slight fever. The three of them usually made expeditions together because Holly refused to leave Marilar behind, but she couldn't help acknowledging to herself that a day spent alone with Luis was certain to be more exciting.

The journey itself was staggering enough not to have been missed—along a road that climbed and curved so never-endingly that it seemed impossible to imagine there could be a town at the end of it, hanging in space.

'*Not* sorry you came after all?' Luis asked, when a brief flat stretch of road allowed him to glance at her. She shook her head and smiled at him so beautifully that for once he thought he knew what it felt like to be completely happy. 'There's a railway as well as this road from the coast up to Ronda,' he explained. 'The brain-child of one of *your* energetic countrymen, needless to say! No-one else would have been mad enough to believe it could be done, much less risked his own fortune doing it.'

'Hurrah for the English,' Holly agreed. 'We have our uses if you *do* think we make rotten revolutionaries.'

He had to return his gaze to the road, but the image of her smiling mouth remained with him. In all the weeks she'd been in Seville he'd never kissed it, but he'd promised himself he was going to do that very soon now.

'Being English, you probably share Juan's view,' he pointed out next. 'Anarchists are a disorganized assortment of wild-eyed visionaries and even wilder criminals, held together by a common hatred of everyone who has misruled this country for centuries. The hatred is true, Holly, but we do *know* what we want in place of what we have to destroy—a just society, governing itself, and caring equally for *all* its members—no corrupt State, no oppressive Army, no cynical, greedy Church.'

'It sounds like heaven on earth,' Holly agreed gently, and then said nothing more because ahead of them was the place they'd come to see—clustered fantastically at each end of the bridge that leapt across its famous gorge.

Their inspection of the town was made and they were sitting over coffee at the end of lunch when Luis suddenly began to speak of personal things. 'This is a special place, you know—my parents met here. Carlos Rodriguez saw a young woman working in her uncle's lodging-house and fell instantly in love with her.'

'Who wouldn't have done?' said Holly. 'She must have been entirely beautiful—still *is*, for that matter. Aunt Phee told me so before I came to Spain.'

'I'm afraid you've missed the point of the story, *querida.*'

'No, I haven't. You were tactfully explaining that Asunción's parents were servants, and your father's family thought he'd done something unforgivable in marrying her. Well, my father's

284

father married an Indian girl, and that was thought to be even *more* unfortunate by the people *he* lived among.'

Luis's hand touched her cheek in a little gesture of tenderness. 'So *that* explains the lovely difference. Before you arrived I expected a girl with a pallid complexion that would turn bright red under our Spanish sun, wispy yellow hair, and an air of despising everyone who wasn't English! Instead of that, I got *you*...who might have been born here.'

His voice trembled a little, and the expression in his eyes warned her that he had no intention of wasting Marilar's absence from the outing. Not sure how she would answer him, she tried to postpone the moment that was coming inevitably. 'A girl born in Spain wouldn't be allowed to spend a day alone with you, even in *this* year of grace, and I'm bound to say you're judging the English rather harshly. Come to Hindleford and meet my cousin Helena...I swear that you, like everyone else, will be bowled over by her entirely anglo-saxon beauty!'

'I shouldn't even notice her,' Luis said simply. 'I only look at you.' His hand covered hers, lying on the table. 'Darling Holly, I can't promise to give up fighting for Spain—that's part of me now, and anyway you understand how important it is. But I'll do anything else *you* want if only you'll marry me one day. I'll go back to university, and work hard, and *try* not to get into trouble! I'll love you more than any woman has ever been loved before.'

The words poured out in a breathless torrent

of Spanish that by now she could understand. She was shaken by their sincerity, and deeply troubled by the knowledge that she felt bound to disappoint him.

'You don't answer me...*say* something...say *yes*, Holly,' he almost shouted.

'I can't answer without hurting you,' she said slowly, 'and I doubt if I can make you understand. I grew up awkwardly, you see—lonely even among a flock of cousins, resentful because life seemed to have been unkind to me. Among my cousins I picked out one of them to love, *knowing* that he was already Helena's property. Perhaps, I even chose *him* so that I would have one more thing to feel resentful about.' She frowned over that idea, fearing that it might be true, then stared at Luis with huge, troubled eyes. 'I came to Spain believing that I should always love Ned Harkness. I think I still do, but I should have to see him again to know for certain.'

Luis took the news more calmly than she'd expected, except that they *were* sitting in a public restaurant. 'Now, I know at least that I must make you forget this Englishman, who must be stupid enough to *deserve* forgetting!'

She was reminded of what Phoebe had said about being stubbornly determined to stay blind to happiness, and said less firmly than she'd meant to that Ned was anything but stupid.

Luis smiled, with so much tenderness that she couldn't help but smile back. 'All right, *tesoro*, not stupid if you prefer; but he is far away and we are here. Almost I feel sorry for him.'

286

'Generous,' Holly conceded, and discovered that Luis had taken advantage of the moment to lean forward and kiss her mouth. What began gently became fierce when he felt her lips quiver beneath his; but the rest of the world was still about them, and the waiter was standing there, mournfully offering their bill. They walked away from the restaurant having little to say, then or on the long drive back to Seville. But Luis occasionally turned his head to smile at her, and Holly was aware that she might look back on Ronda as Asunción did—as one of those special places where life had taken a turn that was always to remain significant.

17

The new university term began and Luis returned to his law studies with a diligence that surprised his brother, though not Asunción. She also realized how much she'd come to rely on Holly, and checked Juan sharply one day when he complained that, far from discouraging Luis's wild ideas, she seemed to be doing the reverse.

'Because they're going to visit my father, you mean?' Asunción asked. 'Of *course* Luis would take her. He wants Holly to know that he's *proud* of a man who used to be a servant. I find nothing to regret in that.'

'And nor do I, as you perfectly well know.

But she will be charmed by your father, as everybody who meets him *is*. He will talk about the evils of the past, and explain that everything must be swept away before the millennium can arrive. He's a natural orator—persuasive and dangerous.'

'And Holly comes from a country where tradition counts for much, and *no-one* is inclined to sweep things away,' Asunción insisted calmly. 'She'll make sure she informs him of the fact!' She saw Juan's face relax into a reluctant grin, and added gently, 'Don't worry about her, my dear. Luis is very much in love with her, but she'll do him nothing but good.'

'And what about her?' he asked after a moment. 'Is she in love with him?'

'I can't be sure yet. All I do know is that they've become true friends. She arrived here unhappy about another young man, but I doubt if she ever thinks of him now.'

Holly would have had to confess that Asunción's guess was correct. Even when she tried she could scarcely reconstruct the image of Ned's face in her mind's eye. The pottery at Brightwell, Hindleford itself, were equally remote. Reality now was the life she led in Seville and when little sparks of excitement fizzed in her blood like champagne they were caused by Luis's smile and the touch of *his* hand on her. One day she would have to decide whether she was going to marry him and stay for good, but there was no frantic rush to make up her mind. For the moment Luis was content just to have her close at hand. She could go on walking to the pottery each morning and lose herself in the sheer pleasure of working there. All its straggling yards and workshops were known to her now, as was the pattern of its daily rituals repeated without change because no change was necessary. She knew the men who arrived at five o'clock every day to stoke up the wood fires beneath the kilns, and those who judged when the clay-slip in the settling ponds was clean enough to be wedged and thrown; she worked with men and women who shaped and painted clay with a skill passed on to them by their ancestors.

So ordered was this daily routine that she could write calmly to Phoebe about the general situation around them. Yes, there was unrest, bitterness, and the ever-present threat of violence...she was bound to be aware of that; but in the end Spain survived, as Hugo insisted it always would. Her letters, Phoebe once observed plaintively, never mentioned Juan...did *he* not live in Asunción's house as well? He did, but Holly merely reported that he was very often away. She thought Phoebe would be distressed to know that *he* was the only one who made her feel unwelcome.

But one afternoon, when she thought him still in Madrid, and she was tending Asunción's plants in the courtyard, she suddenly discovered that he was watching her.

'*Are* you talking to those flowers, or do I only imagine it?' he asked, giving away the fact that he was there.

'Aunt Phee taught me to,' she answered,

turning round to look at him. 'Plants don't respond nearly so well if they're not loved.' Rather than stand facing him, she went back to the task in hand—potting-up carnation slips for a new season's flowering—but she was very aware of him still there, and wished that he would go away. He was altogether larger, more solid, than his brother, and the truth was that she'd have been intimidated by his air of authority if she hadn't simply made up her mind not to be.

'Do you anticipate being still here to see the fruits of your labours next spring?'

The question was politely asked, but it stung her into bluntness. 'Why do you ask...because you think I've been here too long already?'

It was the direct approach favoured by Phoebe Taverner, he remembered—perhaps she'd passed on *this* habit too. He stared at Holly and, because she'd raised her head to challenge him, saw her profile delicately outlined against a background of shadowy foliage. She was a slender, graceful figure, standing there, and the long legs that he'd noticed at their first meeting were still beautiful.

'What I think doesn't matter,' he said slowly—'you are my mother's guest. But one thing *does* concern me...my brother's peace of mind. Don't play with Luis. If you intend *not* to marry him in the end, it would be kinder to leave very soon.'

'I don't know yet *what* I intend, but Luis and I understand one another,' she muttered, with heightened colour in her face.

Juan came towards her, close enough to have touched her without moving, and she was acutely aware of things she hadn't noticed before—the fine texture of his brown skin stretched tautly over the bones of his face, the mouth that was beautifully carved, and stern at the same time.

'Our customs are not the same as yours. Here, if a young man is allowed to offer a girl a passionate embrace he's entitled to feel certain that it's his future wife he is embracing.'

She was caught off balance, and humiliated to think that he had observed the only time when Luis had trapped her alone and kissed her very thoroughly. But Juan's disapproval was entirely for her, she realized; *she* was the one to have been tried, and found guilty.

'Luis was trying to make me forget someone in England,' she explained as coolly as she could manage. 'Perhaps you have the same saying as we do—"all's fair in love and war"!'

Juan's gaze was unnerving, and she was conscious of wishing that she were more able to deal with him, more experienced altogether.

'All is *not* fair to my brother,' he said at last, 'there are heartbreaks enough ahead of him without grief over *you* as well.'

Holly heard caution whisper that it was time to end the conversation by walking away, because if she argued with this man she was certain to lose. But her stubbornness refused to concede him the last word. '*Not* heartbreaks, necessarily,' she insisted. 'Why should *your* friends be the ones to win, and his to lose?'

Juan's frown pulled dark brows together above a formidable nose, but he didn't shout at her, as she thought he might have done.

'For God's sake don't encourage him. He's fed enough intoxicating madness by his grandfather. There's no chance that his friends can win, and probably no chance that my friends, as you call them, can win either. We shall *all* be losers...Spain as well.'

She was silenced, not only by his argument even though it seemed unanswerable, but the sheer weight of sadness in his voice. Whatever else she didn't know about this reserved and complex man, she now knew that he loved Luis and the country that had become his, despite an English father.

'I don't encourage Luis...in *any* way,' she said quietly, 'and I hope I shall never hurt him.'

There was nothing more to say, and she picked up another carnation stem with hands that trembled slightly. After a moment or two she knew that Juan had gone away—not because she'd heard him go, but just because the courtyard seemed empty now.

It was a relief to be told by Marilar the following day that he'd gone away again—to visit Germany with his friend, José Antonio Primo de Rivera.

'They were law students together, but afterwards José Antonio became a member of the Cortes,' Marilar explained earnestly. 'Luis calls him a fascist, an enemy...but, Holly, he is so beautiful, so charming, that I don't care whether

292

he is a fascist or not.' Then she blushed to have given herself away.

Holly only smiled, and nodded wisely. 'Quite right, *tesoro,*' she said—using, as she often did, Asunción's way of addressing her daughter. 'Never let politics stand in the way of common sense—only misguided males do that!'

Marilar's solemn expression melted into a grin, but it faded again and an almost tragic look replaced it as she thought of something else.

'We ought soon to start making the Christmas crib, but Luis pretends now that such things are childish superstitions. I *hate* him when he talks like that.'

Her eyes filled with sudden tears, and Holly's heart ached for a grief that she knew was real. One girl's bewilderment might be of small account measured against the conflicts of belief that were tearing Spain apart, but it didn't seem unimportant to Marilar that her own brother was now required to deny the truth and beauty of the Nativity itself.

'*Cara,* he's learned a different religion for the time being,' Holly suggested gently. 'It may not last, but in any case it doesn't stop *us* making the crib.'

She repeated this part of the conversation to Luis as they took their places one evening in the usual pre-dinner procession along the avenue bordering the river. 'You needn't pretend to believe what you can't...but don't say anything to hurt her, please.'

He stood still, and turned her to face him, holding both her hands. His eyes examined her face, still tanned from the summer sun, framed by its wings of glossy dark hair. 'You're kind as well as beautiful,' he said unsteadily. 'I love you more than life itself, and I think I shall go to England and kill your stupid lover there.'

The smile that he always waited for lifted the corners of her mouth. 'Dear Luis, there's really no need! He never was my lover, and my heart is proving as fickle as Aunt Phee *said* it would...I can scarcely remember what Ned looks like now!'

She was enclosed for a moment in a hard, breathless hug, and then released so that they could walk on again. Luis smiled brilliantly at everyone they met, whether he knew them or not, and she realized that she couldn't say truthfully to Juan now that she had given his brother no encouragement. She was glad he was away in Germany, and there was no need to face him; but even so it was quite unnecessary for Marilar to wish, as she often did, that her elder brother would come home again, because Asunción's house still seemed full of his compelling personality.

The clay figures had taken a long time to make at the pottery—Holy Family, Wise Men, shepherds, and an attendant menagerie of animals for the stable; but they were finished at last and brought home carefully to the house. She was inspecting them in her room one morning when the Señora knocked and was invited to come in.

'A surprise for Marilar's crib,' Holly explained. 'I wanted them to look primitive and unglazed,

294

but now I'm thinking *she* might have preferred them shiny.'

Asunción gently touched an irresistible long-eared donkey, moved almost to tears by the beauty of the little, painted figures. 'My dear, how could she *not* love them? She'll understand that she's being given something very precious, and she will cherish them for *her* children.'

Reassured, Holly smiled at her visitor, and Asunción remembered the envelope she'd come to deliver. 'Early Christmas greetings from England, perhaps!'

Holly withdrew the telegram and read Phoebe's message. She stood still, staring at the piece of paper in her hand, and finally managed to force words through the sudden dryness in her mouth.

'Not greetings...my dear friend, Brian Starkie, has been badly hurt in an accident...he came with m...me to see you once.' She raised stricken eyes to look at Asunción. 'I shall have to go home...I can't *not* go.'

'Of course,' Asunción agreed quietly. 'Perhaps you should tell Luis yourself, but I will break the news to Marilar...oh, my dear, what a sadness for us, and how much worse for you.' She kissed Holly's pale face, and tried to smile at her. 'But when poor Mr Starkie is recovered, you will return to us, of course.'

That same evening Holly waited at Seville station for the train to arrive from Cadiz. Luis was with her, tense, and tragic-eyed. 'I should be coming with you.' He'd said it over and over again '...it's not a journey for you to make alone.'

She explained once more that she could perfectly well manage on her own, but knew that what she said scarcely penetrated the pall of misery that wrapped him round.

'You won't come back, *querida*...once you're in England they'll keep you there...you'll forget about Spain.'

She shook her head, trying not to weep. 'I've *promised* you, and Marilar. I'm leaving most of my heart here...how could I *not* come back?'

He held her and kissed her for the last time and their tears were salt on her mouth. Then, the clamour all around them rose to a new pitch as the train hissed and snorted its way into the station. A moment later, still within touching, speaking distance, they were already in different worlds—he left standing there desolate, she seeming to be torn from everything that had become familiar and dear. She had the dreadful sensation of belonging nowhere...her life in Seville suddenly as much of a dream as England had become; the only reality was this lonely journey through the darkness. She could no longer see Luis as the train gathered speed, plunging towards the first range of mountains that separated them from the rest of Europe.

Daylight revealed a snow-covered landscape swept by bitter winds. The frontier brought a change of trains, and the sound of French vowels instead of rasping Spanish consonants, but she didn't notice these things; as the long hours passed her tired brain was haunted instead by the image of Luis's tragic face, and her memories of Brian Starkie—now dying in a hospital in Oxford.

Phoebe, writing letters, saw her crossing the lawn from the direction of the river path. She walked as a sleepwalker might, unaware of anything except the compulsion to keep moving. Her clothes were the ones she'd set out in with Brian, and for a moment the illusion was complete that time had stood still; she hadn't been away at all. Then, as Phoebe threw down her pen and ran out into the wintry cold of the garden, the deception was shattered. She hadn't seen this white-faced girl for almost a year, and much had happened to her since then.

'Dearest...why didn't you let us know? Hugo and John would have met you.'

'There wasn't time. I left the same night after your telegram arrived and went straight to the Infirmary this afternoon...but even so I was too late. I did *want* to see him again, Aunt Phee...just to say thank you.'

Phoebe held out her arms and Holly went blindly into them, tears trickling down her cold face.

'Sweetheart, he wouldn't have wanted thanks...he was so *very* proud of you,' Phoebe murmured. 'His legacy to the future, he always called you. We've seen him often during the past few months...I think he missed not having you at Brightwell.' She talked almost at random, Holly lifted her head and smeared her wet cheeks.

'Tell me how it happened. They were very

297

kind at the hospital, but I couldn't talk to strangers.'

'The details don't matter very much,' Phoebe said slowly, 'but there was an accident. A motor car frightened a horse and made it bolt. A child was in the way and would have been killed, but Brian managed to save it at the cost of being trampled on himself. There was never any real hope, but he lived longer than we expected.'

'Where...where did it happen?'

'On the Clifton Hampden road—where you and I took our first walk together, on the way to India.' She saw Holly close her eyes against the scene that imagination painted, and registered again the pallor and exhaustion in her face.

'Dearest, you look as if you haven't slept or eaten for days, and you're half-frozen besides.'

'I can't remember anything about eating,' Holly muttered, '...yes, I can—a roll and a cup of coffee before the boat docked, early this morning.' She stared at Phoebe, and a smile trembled on her pale mouth. 'You don't look any different. I'm glad about that—even if everyone else changes, *you* have to stay the same.'

Phoebe promised to do her best and then tearfully suggested that the garden with an east wind blowing was no place to continue the conversation. 'You need food, a hot bath and a long sleep, my love. After that Hugo will be home and we can properly inspect one another.'

In fact, Holly didn't wake until the following morning, and went downstairs to find breakfast in progress.

The firelit room known since childhood, Phoebe's welcoming smile, and Hugo getting up to hug her...it was so familiar that perhaps she'd never been away at all...had simply dreamed the long, hot, leisurely days in Spain, lived in the heart of a different family.

'I don't know where to begin talking,' she muttered unsteadily. 'Yes, I do—I'll start with a confession. Spain's harsh light has shown me things I didn't see before. Jim Wilkins would say I had the wrong sow by the ear! Instead of being eternally grateful for what I was offered, I got stuck in the habit of feeling sorry for myself. I don't know how you and Aunt Lydia's family put up with me at all.'

She smiled tremulously at them across the table, and Hugo observed the changes in her with more immediate certainty than Phoebe had done. The structure of her face was clearly defined now, temple and cheekbones more prominent under the creamy skin; but some experience of the heart had added softness to her mouth as well, and knowledge to her huge dark eyes. The aloof and independent-minded adolescent had become a woman...Spain had worked its usual alterations.

She got up to kiss Mrs Jim, who appeared in the room with more coffee, and when they were alone again, looked directly at Phoebe.

'Aunt Phee, is it all right if I stay here with you? I'll go to the Rectory after breakfast, of course, but *you* were Brian's friend too...it seems right to be here, somehow, just until I go back to Spain after the funeral.'

She saw Phoebe's change of expression, and got up at once to go and put warm arms around her. It wasn't a gesture she would have made unthinkingly a year ago, Hugo realized.

'Don't be hurt if I go back,' she pleaded. 'It isn't that I don't love being here with you and Uncle Hu...it's just that I feel more *needed* there.'

Phoebe smiled at her, smoothing away the little frown of anxiety between Holly's dark brows. 'Dearest, there's no need to explain—Asunción's letters make it perfectly clear that *none* of them can do without you!'

'Well, *Juan* can...he thinks I shouldn't be there at all. But he's away so often that it isn't too much of a problem.'

She went back to her own seat at the table, in time to hear Hugo say quietly, 'I'm afraid there is *another* problem, though.' His face looked so preoccupied and grave that both she and Phoebe waited for him to go on, but he addressed himself to Holly.

'Before you decide about hurrying back to Spain, you must know what I already know. Brian began by renting his Brightwell set-up from Humphrey Caldicott, but he bought it all some years ago. A young couple have been living with him at the cottage for the past month or two, and I've asked them to stay on until things are settled. But in Brian's will everything he owned—the pottery, cottage, land—goes to *you*. He imagined that you might be ready to come home by now...it gave him joy when he was dying to think that he could help you get started on your own.'

Hugo's deep voice stopped, and silence flowed back into the room again. In its quietness Phoebe heard the echo of something Brian had once said... 'I always wanted you to be happy'. Outraged but not embittered by a dreadful war, he had seen life afterwards in terms of making other people happy.

'What...what about the couple?' Holly asked after a long pause, and this time it was Phoebe who answered.

'They're a brother and his older sister, called Annie and Arnold Blake. Brian heard them in the covered market in Oxford—Annie singing, Arnold playing the mouth-organ. They were there whenever he went, valiant but heart-breaking. In the end he offered them the job of looking after the cottage and the garden for him. But the boy is frail, and so Brian began teaching him to be a potter instead...he said Arnold showed almost as much promise as *you* had done at that age.' She looked at Holly who sat motionless, long fingers laced round her coffee-cup, dark hair falling forwards over thin cheeks, concealing her expression.

'My dear, I think you'll have to go to Brightwell, and *then* decide,' she said gently.

Holly looked up at last, and tried to smile at them. 'Yes...yes, I shall. But first I'm going to make my peace with Aunt Lydia.'

'She's not quite twenty,' Phoebe murmured as Holly walked out of the room. 'It's not fair to put this responsibility on her shoulders.'

'It wouldn't be fair, or feasible, for most

girls of her age. But she isn't *like* most other girls, sweetheart.' Then Hugo did what Holly had done and walked round the table to kiss his wife. 'All the same, I should like to know what's been happening to her in Spain.'

18

Holly spent most of that first day walking alone, scarcely aware of the winter landscape or the damp, mist-laden air that covered her head in a veil of moisture. But during the evening, shared with Phoebe while Hugo attended some all-male dinner in Oxford, she talked about her life in Seville—the contented hours of working at the pottery, the joy of living in the house at Santa Cruz, and the mixture of delight and despair that was present-day Spain. She spoke much of Marilar, more than she realized about Luis, and not at all about Juan, except to say that being left in charge of Carlos Rodriguez's family had not improved a disposition that inclined to the autocratic. Phoebe suggested that it *might* also include, hidden as yet, some of the warmth that had belonged to her father, but Holly looked very unconvinced.

The following morning she borrowed Jim Wilkins's bicycle and rode over to Brightwell, having after some thought refused Hugo's offer to go with her.

Brian's garden, even in its dormant winter

state, looked more attractively cared for than she'd seen it before—grass neatly cut, flowerbeds dug and weeded. The brass knocker on the door gleamed like gold, and every small window-pane shone with polishing. She was tempted to see if the pottery seemed more familiar in its working clutter and untidiness, but something insisted that this must be a formal visit, with the new owner treading very carefully. Her knock on the door was answered immediately, and a tall, thin girl stood there, reddish hair wound in a thick plait round her head, freckled white skin, and a slightly bent nose that might have been broken when she was a child. No smile was offered, and no welcome either.

'My name's Carteret,' Holly explained tentatively but got no further before she was gestured inside.

'I know...Mr Taverner said you'd be coming.' She led the way to the kitchen, indicated a chair for her visitor, but didn't sit down herself. Holly was aware again of some domestic love or skill at work, because a once cheerless room had been made homely and attractive; the kitchen welcomed, even if the girl didn't.

'It looks nicer than it used to,' she said impulsively.

A quiver of something that might have been pain touched Annie Blake's pale face, then it was expressionless again. 'Brian was s'posed to use the parlour, but more often than not he'd come in here with us. I expect you'll be wanting me and Arnold to leave now. We...we didn't reckon to stay, anyway...it just...just suited quite well to be here for a bit.' Her voice stopped suddenly, for the very good reason, Holly thought, that she couldn't trust it any longer. She could look at her visitor and not blush for the lie she'd just managed to get out, but the thin hands hanging at her sides were trembling. Holly glanced away, pretending not to have noticed. The visit was going to be even worse than she'd anticipated, and she found that she was struggling with a mixture of anger with Brian and compassion for Annie Blake that would certainly be rejected.

'I wish *you'd* sit down,' she said bluntly, 'because there's a lot to talk about. Perhaps your brother should be here, too?' She thought the girl was going to refuse both suggestions, but after a moment or two Annie pulled out a chair, then hid her shaking hands in her lap.

'Arnold's better left in the pottery...he understands now that Brian isn't coming back, but it's been a shock...just when he was beginning to feel safe and happy here.' Annie's flat voice cracked, and Holly glimpsed in her suddenly anguished face more pain than *she* had ever known existed.

'Tell me about Arnold,' she suggested gently. 'I gather he has the makings of a good potter.'

'Yes...not as good as *you*, Brian said, but better than most he'd come across.' She reported it with a touch of pride that seemed to make it easier to go on talking. 'We came here to look after the house and garden. Brian thought it might be too much for us because it was all in such a mess, but after an Oxford lodging-house *this* looked like the kingdom of heaven. Arnold isn't like me—he was always delicate and nervous as a small boy; that's why I had to take care of him after our mother died. Brian could see that he wasn't up to heavy labour outside, and put him to work in the pottery instead—it was a kind of miracle while it lasted...like showing a dying duck a pond of cool, clear water!' Afraid of having given away too much, she suddenly stopped talking, then stared at Holly with eyes that saw the truth steadily. 'Brian's kindness died with him—I realize that. We can find someone else to work for...there's no call for *you* to take us on.'

Holly supposed that she was about to agree, and a moment later heard herself launch confidently on the only lie she had ever told.

'You're free to go wherever you like, of course, but in Brian's will he *hoped* you'd want to stay here and help me keep the pottery going.'

Annie examined her visitor's face, trying to believe what she had heard, while unaccustomed tears brimmed over her eyelids and slid down her pale, freckled cheeks. 'Arnold has...has a lot to learn still,' she whispered.

'I know...but I think it's time I met him, don't you?'

The congregation crowding the church for Brian Starkie's funeral would have pleased him, Phoebe thought—surrounding gentry, who until he died heroically, hadn't quite approved of him, far outnumbered by all the villagers who had.

There were also people like Sir George Harkness and his eldest son come to pay tribute to a man who'd been one of the supreme craftsmen of his generation. Flanked by Edward Harkness and Richard Fanshawe, Holly got through the ceremony by remembering all that she'd known of Brian alive—the flamboyant, generous man who had been endlessly kind. Only afterwards did it seem strange that it was Richard's hand she'd gripped at the cruel moment of committal. The tall young man on her other side had become a stranger who, she dimly sensed, disapproved of her a little for flouting good Methodist and Burslem conventions with her Spanish adventure. Mostly because of *him*—she'd grown up jealous of Helena, and at odds with nearly everyone else as well. It was almost unbelievable now, because when he left her to talk to Anne Maynard, she didn't mind at all.

Afterwards, helping Phoebe to dispense sandwiches and sherry, she moved about the crowded room apparently engaged in greeting acquaintances she hadn't seen for months. But all the time she was trying to decide whether it was an illusion that she alone had changed. Uncle Francis might be fractionally more vague, and Aunt Lydia—by compensation—marginally more brisk; but Richard was exactly as memory pictured him, and Rosalind remained her sister's faithful but less vivid echo. Hindleford *was* just the same, smugly insulated from the world outside, and filled with kind but self-satisfied people who knew nothing of Spanish hardship, or the agony of divided creeds, or the bright flame of passion. She wanted to see Marilar's face when Asunción gave her the crib figures...wanted to tell Luis that she'd seen Ned Harkness and knew the truth about herself at last. She'd had to leave without saying goodbye to Juan Rodriguez and even that seemed to leave unfinished something that had been important too.

In the warmth of the room she felt the sudden damp prickle of faintness on her skin, and bolted past Mrs Jim and Nellie in the kitchen to let herself out into the garden's raw December air. Then someone came to stand beside her and put an arm about her shoulders.

'I watched you turning a little green in there,' Hugo said quietly. 'You want very much *not* to stay, don't you? My dear, something else can be arranged. Brian would have hated to think he'd burdened you with something that stood in the way of your happiness.'

Holly turned to look at him and he saw the sadness in her face. 'I've been wrong in the past about happiness; maybe I'm wrong again to think it's waiting for me only in Spain. I *promised* to go back, Uncle Hu, but first I have to finish what Brian started here. After *that* I'll go, and I hope it can be before something very bad happens. When that does, I want to be there to share it with Asunción and her family.'

Hugo smiled at her with huge affection. 'I should, of course, insist that you stay here, but since it wouldn't do a particle of good I shall simply say that we must make the most of having you till then.'

She kissed his cheek gratefully, and then they went back indoors.

Nothing was allowed to vary the time-honoured rituals of the season...the carol singing, the mince pies, the Vicar's usual Christmas sermon, all had to confirm that whatever happened in the world outside the valley, Hindleford remained the same. Even the unpredictable quality of the school Nativity play was part of the familiar pattern. Would the Three Kings arrive late and breathless after a tussle outside, or Will Cooper's donkey disgrace himself *again* on the stage? There was one novelty this year—for the first time in history the King broadcast a Christmas message to his people, and those who could hear it reckoned it added something to the day. Those who couldn't didn't worry—it was still Christmas, and a good day's holiday.

For Phoebe and Hugo another of the day's customs was dinner at the Rectory. Holly went with them aware that more than a nod across the pews in church would be required for Helena. She'd been away staying with her Harkness relatives, and they hadn't spoken to each other since that malice-laden confrontation in the church a year ago. It had been the spur that had sent her galloping off to Spain; *now*, she had cause to be grateful to Helena, but that might be hard to admit to a girl she'd always been most bitterly at odds with.

Finally face to face with her cousin in the Rectory drawing-room, she felt absurdly at a loss and could only say the first obvious thing that came into her head.

'How was Burslem?'

'Less exciting than Seville, I expect...in fact, not exciting at all if I'm strictly truthful. It was a dreadful temptation to run amok in the Harkness Museum and start throwing plates about; but I closed my eyes and thought of England, as the saying goes, and fortunately the madness passed!'

Holly smiled at this confusion, feeling suddenly at ease with her cousin. 'I can see the problem, with the ghost of old Sir Joshua daring you not to worship at the family shrine.'

Helena changed tack suddenly. 'When you walked in just now I thought you looked as if you'd rather be somewhere else...back where you've come from?'

'I miss my friends there,' Holly admitted after a moment, 'but I didn't mean to make it so obvious; nor will I bore you by running on about people you don't know.'

'It's ridiculous *not* to know them when we're so connected. Imagine Mama and Aunt Phee hugging Grandfather's secret all those years—as if anybody cares about such goings-on nowadays.' She fell silent for a moment, her lovely face shadowed by some different train of thought that she found depressing. 'I envied you going off to Spain. Sometimes I think I'll die of boredom here if I don't rush out in search of an adventure of my own. The trouble is I'm not clever like you...I can't think of anything to do.'

She smiled as she spoke but there was

309

suddenly a glimpse of a different Helena Fanshawe from the beautiful, confident creature who'd always seemed to dance her way through life.

'I thought it was only me envying *you,*' Holly said honestly. 'Why hadn't God given *me* golden hair, and a twin brother, and parents to love?'

'There was Edward, too, wasn't there?' Helena asked the question in a casual tone of voice, but Holly had the impression that it wasn't casual at all.

'Yes, there was Edward,' she agreed after a little pause. 'I envied you *him* most of all.'

'I know. I lied to you about Ned, by the way. He gave away the fact that he was meeting you in Oxford, and enjoying himself too much...I knew it was serious because he didn't *mean* to tell me. That's why I pretended *I'd* asked him to take pity on you. I've always known I'd have to tell you the truth one day, but I can't think why I've chosen this festive moment to unburden myself.' Her face was serious and sad, and for the first time Holly was aware of feeling sorry for her.

'I wanted to kill you at the time,' she admitted, 'but since I couldn't do that I ran away to Spain instead—where Aunt Phee says everyone with a broken heart should go! It never fails to cure, apparently.' She smiled at herself, and then grew serious again. 'If you're going to marry Ned one day, as I assume you are, won't *that* be your great adventure?'

'I suppose so.' Helena considered what she'd

just said and made a little grimace of self-disgust. 'Sorry if that sounded grudging. With Mama out of earshot, my forthright sister Kate would call me a spoiled, ungrateful cow! I do love Edward...always have done...but what goes with him strikes terror in my heart—factory chimneys, outings for the workers, and acres of china I might find myself wanting to smash!'

Holly tried not to grin, because the matter was clearly grave. 'Burslem wouldn't seem nearly so bad if you knew what goes on there. You could start finding out by coming to Brightwell occasionally.'

It was a challenge that, much to her surprise, Helena finally accepted after a moment's thought. 'All right, I will; but I'd better warn you I'm still cag-handed...although it's thought to be my *only* flaw!' She grinned, herself again now, and Holly smiled back, thinking how strange it would be if she finally learned to like Helena Fanshawe.

It couldn't be said that Helena was a born thrower of clay, but as winter gave way to the spring of a new year she often cycled over to the pottery. Instead of regretting an invitation given on the spur of the moment, Holly came to enjoy her visits and congratulated her on managing to get Arnold Blake to talk.

'Most people do *without* needing encouragement,' Helena pointed out.

'Not when they've been regularly beaten throughout childhood by a drunken father. He did it once too often and Annie walked out with Arnold—*walked* out; they hadn't any other means of getting away. I haven't heard all their story yet—Annie only releases a little bit at a time because she's so ashamed of it. But I know now why they see Brightwell as little short of paradise.'

Helena stared at her cousin's face wishing that she was better at reading its swift changes of expression. She knew that Holly would be uncommunicative if asked directly about Spain, but perhaps a sideways approach would yield results.

'Uncle Hu says that you're turning out things here that are different from any other pottery.'

'Different from any *English* pottery, perhaps, but Brian Starkie would have recognized their inspiration.' She examined her fingers, paint-stained as usual, and rubbed at a blob of colour absent-mindedly. 'I thought I'd find it heart-breaking, working here without him, but in a strange sort of way he seems to be here all the time. I could swear he's behind me, watching, and that he'll suddenly say as he used to do, "Well done, Holly love, that isn't bad at all"!' She smiled but her face looked so sad that Helena risked another question.

'*Are* you going to stay? Mama thinks this is a strange life you lead, but Father says we all find different roads towards contentment. Is this *your* road?'

'I don't know, but it happens to be the road I'm on, and by the time I've made a potter out of Arnold it may be too late to change my mind.'

312

'We could ask Edward's father to find Arnold a job—*then* you'd be free.'

'So I would,' she agreed, and abruptly ended the conversation by telling Helena it was time she got her white hands dirty.

But as the months passed, Holly's fear grew of being too late for something that had been precious. Her letters to Spain were answered, but with a lack of warmth and interest that seemed deliberately intended to hurt. As plainly as if he'd actually written the words, Luis made his own disappointment and anger clear. He hadn't understood why she felt obliged to stay in England, and believed instead that she had learned once more to prefer it to the dangerous excitements Spain offered. The truth was the very opposite; every day she became a little more certain that she belonged with Luis in Seville. But every day she wrestled with the longing to turn her back on the Blakes, and lost. They couldn't be left yet. But then, for two weeks running no letter arrived from Spain at all. When it finally did it was a note so brief that she put it aside without comment.

'Not bad news, I hope,' Phoebe ventured.

'No news at all, except that Luis is too busy to send any. His law studies are getting forgotten again; political meetings seem to take up all his time.' Her withdrawn expression didn't encourage questions but Phoebe decided for once to persevere.

'Dearest, Brian thought he was *helping* by leaving you the pottery; it wasn't meant to be a millstone round your neck. If it's costing you greater happiness you must leave it and go back to Luis. Hugo will find someone to help Annie and Arnold.'

Holly didn't answer for a long time, because she had to be sure of knowing what she meant to say.

'It's a temptation, because Luis is so unhappy and angry with me. I *promised*, you see, and now he thinks I'm breaking the promise. But there'll be plenty of time for us, if he'll only be patient; for the moment he's got studies to finish, and I've got work to do here.' Her strained face finally managed a smile. 'So the answer to your kind suggestion is that I'm not going back yet...Spain has to wait a little longer.'

'You haven't abandoned it altogether,' Phoebe pointed out. 'George Harkness came back here very excited after his visit to Brightwell, murmuring about ancient traditions. I didn't need telling, of course, but he was *very* definite—your work is becoming sought after by collectors.'

She sounded so gratified by the thought that Holly smiled again, wholeheartedly this time.

'I was mixed up about the pottery at first,' she admitted '—very proud, but resentful in a way as well. I might *not* have kept it on without Annie Blake to shame me into it. Now, whatever happens between me and Luis, I shan't ever regret giving Arnold *his* one, precious chance.'

Phoebe nodded, aware that she was meant to be reassured; but George had been right—all Holly's memories of the place she'd had to put aside were being poured into what her hands

314

created so unfalteringly. The very colours of Andalusia were in the glazes she was constantly experimenting with—umber, terracotta, brilliant blue, and a silver-green and grey that spoke of olive trees ruffled by the wind. What she made was unique and beautiful, and more and more lovers of ceramics were coming to understand the fact.

'We could invite Luis here—Marilar as well,' Phoebe suggested, before the subject of Spain was finally closed between them.

Holly firmly shook her head. 'He wouldn't come. This country is full of the sort of bourgeois people he most despises. Luis has no high opinion of England.'

'Nor had Juan years ago, but I think he's much more tolerant now.'

Holly stared at her, astonished by an idea so contrary to the truth. But being too kind to destroy what it gave Phoebe such pleasure to believe, she merely kissed her instead and said that it was time to be pedalling over to Brightwell.

19

The year spun its coloured threads slowly— different by far from what memory kept reminding her she'd known at this or that same time last year. Loving messages still arrived from Asunción and Marilar, but Luis's occasional scrawls were now merely to confirm that heart and mind were caught up in the vortex of Spanish politics. Holly thought of Richard Fanshawe and his friends—much the same age as Luis but debating merely cricket scores or how most enjoyably to spend the long vacation. She enjoyed their company now, but knew that a serious Spanish anarchist would have found it frivolous. Her heart ached for Luis, but away from him the violence *his* companions engaged in seemed not only dangerous but futile. When she mentioned her change of view to Hugo one day he answered more seriously than she expected.

'Even for *our* young men life may get real and earnest soon enough; let them loaf away the summer days until it does, say I!'

'Because the madness that is destroying Spain will spread?' she asked gravely.

'Not quite the same disease, perhaps, but I'm afraid it's in the air.' Then because he saw anxiety in her face, he shook his head. 'Take no notice, Holly love, I'm just an elderly gent staring into his rather cloudy crystal ball! All shall be well, and all manner of things shall be well, so long as we keep our heads and don't give in to the barbarians.'

She recognized that this comfort was for her; for himself he didn't believe in it. It was necessary to smile because he wanted her to, but her thoughts returned immediately to Luis. She wanted for *him* the carefree pleasures her cousins knew...wanted for herself the happiness of being loved, and *not* to be a thousand miles away from him. She couldn't regret seeing

316

Annie Blake feel safe enough to laugh again, and a frail and frightened boy discover the talent that would make him confident. But she might regret it bitterly one day if Luis's Spanish pride refused to wait for her. And as clear as *his* changing image in her mind—now melancholy, now gay, or tender—was the unyielding face of Juan Rodriguez. She could imagine him eager to point out to his brother the drawbacks of a foreign wife too stubborn to relinquish English ways and learn how Spanish women behaved.

The summer was dying in a blaze of September glory when the twins celebrated their nineteenth birthday.

At a great party in a marquee on the lawn, Francis announced the engagement of his eldest daughter to Ned Harkness, and Lydia finally abandoned her dream of a more illustrious son-in-law. Richard hoped, *sotto voce,* that Ned would be more successful at keeping Helena in order than he'd been himself; Kate, rather flown with the pleasure of wearing her first long dress, doubted this in language learned from Colonel Wyndham's groom; and Rosalind didn't listen, wondering instead with the agonizing intensity of fifteen years whether *any* of Richard's friends would ask her to dance with them.

It was Helena's face that stayed in Holly's mind long after the party was over. Out in the water meadows with Hugo's setters the next morning, she saw again in her mind's eye the picture of her cousin dancing in Ned's arms—beautiful as always, but content at last as well. It made her own prospect of happiness seem painfully remote, but she went home telling herself that she mustn't once again fall into the trap of envying Helena—she'd spent too many years doing that already.

She walked into the house and found only Nellie, hovering anxiously in the hall. The Captain and Mrs Taverner were out, and there was an unexpected visitor waiting in the library. She went in, anticipating a neighbour or an Oxford friend. But the tall figure standing by the fireplace had come from much further away than that.

'Did...did we expect you?' she enquired stupidly. With heart beating less frantically and legs feeling more firm, she might have been in a condition to notice that Juan Rodriguez also looked off balance for the first time in her acquaintance with him.

'I thought you lived at the Rectory,' he said almost accusingly, and then answered her question. 'No, I'm not expected...it's a habit of mine to call here without warning.'

It was the only reference he'd ever made to their first meeting on the river-bank, and the memory of it suddenly released her from the shock of seeing him again.

'I've lived here since I came back from Spain. There's...there's nothing wrong at Santa Cruz? That isn't why you're here?'

'Nothing is wrong my mother and Marilar send their fondest love.'

'They write, and so does Luis when he remembers, but I'm bound to say your family

318

make rotten correspondents.'

'They're Spanish, and would therefore rather talk than write! Apart from that, my mother made Luis and Marilar promise not to urge you to return to Spain—she thinks, quite rightly, that the times we live in are too unsettled and dangerous.'

It was an explanation so obvious and consoling that it had never occurred to her. A smile of luminous beauty lit her face and she offered it to Juan as a reward. 'I was beginning to think they'd forgotten me,' she said simply. 'Nine months is a long time to leave a promise hanging in the air.'

Juan suddenly left his place by the hearth to come and stand in front of her, as he'd done once before. She was obliged to take the hand he held out—it was hard and warm against hers, and strangely familiar.

'We forgot the formalities, Señorita...my fault, but you took me by surprise—I was expecting Phoebe to walk in.' He didn't release her hand immediately as formality certainly required, and the smile that lifted the corners of his mouth was gentle and sweet.

'You...you should have arrived yesterday, in time for the twins' birthday dance,' Holly found herself stammering nervously. Then she wished she hadn't mentioned the evening before. To remember Helena held close in Ned's arms was to remember all over again what she lacked herself away from Luis. She longed to beg the man who stood in front of her to confirm that Luis still missed and needed her. But Juan Rodriguez would probably despise such weakness. She was saved a moment later by Phoebe hurrying into the room, followed by Hugo.

'My dear Juan...if only we'd known; there was no real need to go out this morning. But Nellie says you have a bag in the hall, so there can be *no* reason not to stay the night at least.' She smiled with the warmth he remembered...a woman who probably won in the end against any rebuff through sheer goodness of heart and spirit.

'I meant to find a room in Oxford,' he admitted, 'but I think I should like very much to stay here with you.'

Hugo smiled at the happiness in her face as she left the room to give some instructions. When she returned he was pouring Madeira wine, and Holly had established herself on a window-seat, seeming to say that he was their guest, not hers.

'Now we can talk,' Phoebe said with great contentment. 'Dear Juan, I think *you* should begin.'

It was his turn to smile, thinking it absurd that she should still look and sound so like the girl who had outfaced him in his mother's courtyard all those years ago. He knew her age—the same as the century's—but it was hard to believe that she approached her middle-thirties now. Holly sat turned away from them, he noticed, thin hands locked round her knees as she stared out of the window. The pose, withdrawn but graceful, was typical of her—he'd never seen her make an ungraceful movement.

'I came to London with an old friend,' he said, suddenly remembering that he was supposed to talk. 'We studied law together, but afterwards he went into the Cortes, representing Cadiz. During the past year he's founded a new political party—it's called the Falange in Spanish.'

'So your friend is José Antonio Primo de Rivera, and he came to London to meet Sir Oswald Mosley. It was reported in our press,' Hugo commented.

Juan watched him across the width of the hearth. 'Am I right in thinking that you disapprove?'

Hugo held up his hand in a little gesture of apology. 'Forgive me...I know nothing of your friend except what distant connections tell me. He's the charming, talented son of a man who did more than anyone else this century to rescue Spain from chaos, and then was deserted by the very people who had brought him to power.'

'Knowing that, and obviously aware of our present turmoil, why do you object to General Primo's son?'

The two women in the room didn't interrupt; the duel was between two intelligent, strong-minded men who both loved Spain.

'I object because, like the man he came to London to see, your friend is a fascist. You'll tell me that Benito Mussolini has been the saviour of Italy, that Adolf Hitler intends to rescue Germany from defeat and degradation. Unarguably you'll insist that successive régimes

321

and governments in Spain have gone from bad to worse. The fact remains that I distrust all fascists, and abominate the methods they use.'

'Then you must hate as well the methods José Antonio's opponents use—incessant strikes, sabotage, arson, and assassination, to name those that come immediately to mind.'

There was silence in the room. It still looked familiar and comfortable and safe, but Phoebe shivered suddenly, touched by the shadow of fear and the distant memory of Nathaniel Harkness's journal, prophesying a disaster that had yet to arrive. As if aware of her distress, Juan smiled at her reassuringly.

'I'm sorry, Phoebe. I came about a personal problem, not to argue politics with Hugo.' He glanced again at Holly, but she still seemed entirely absorbed in the view outside.

'You know a lot about my brother already,' he went on, 'but perhaps you aren't aware that his friends become *more* lawless, *more* violent, all the time because the Government itself swings back more and more to the right. Anarchist leaders are being caught and imprisoned, sometimes executed. Luis has received his own baptism of fire—a severe beating by the Guardia Civil. The situation is almost certain to get worse, and I need to be sure I can get him out of the country when it does.' Juan looked across at Phoebe, then at Hugo. 'Could he come here, or is it too much to ask? He wants to learn Russian, which I'm sure he could do at Oxford, but he would badly need friends as well.'

He was answered almost before he'd finished

322

speaking. 'My dear Juan, of *course* he will come here,' said Phoebe, 'and between them Hugo and Francis can certainly find him a Russian tutor.'

'Between us I'm sure we can,' her husband obligingly agreed, 'but will a fiery young revolutionary allow himself to be shipped off to sleepy Oxford?'

Once again Juan stared at Holly and this time her eyes were lifted to his in a grave enquiry that made him answer with the sort of deliberate emphasis that made his meaning clear.

'I think Luis will allow himself to be shipped *here.*'

Holly spoke for the first time, hoarsely repeating what Phoebe had said to Juan. 'Of *course* he must come—it's madness for him to stay in Spain now.'

Juan nodded, aware of her anxiety and of some emotion of his own. It felt so shamefully like envy of his brother that he gave a careless shrug as well, to prove that he didn't mind whether she was concerned for Luis or not. Phoebe broke the awkward silence by suggesting that they should walk over to the Rectory, where Fanshawes and Harknesses were still gathered in force after the previous day's party. Holly was glad of the excuse to move. She found Juan's presence altogether too disturbing until the explanation occurred to her as she walked along behind the rest of them—he reminded her too much of Spain. Next door Helena obligingly confirmed the theory.

'So gorgeously intense looking,' she murmured wistfully, as her father led the visitor away to admire a garden view of the church. 'Who'd want to be a pallid Anglo-Saxon if they could have *that* colouring and fire?'

'Spanish eyes and hair I grant you,' Phoebe conceded, overhearing. 'Otherwise he grows more and more like your grandfather. He even walks in the same way—Spaniards don't as a rule, they flourish an imaginary cape and sword!'

'I'm sorry to have to agree,' Lydia said rather shortly. 'This time Juan almost looks as if he belongs here.'

Theory sadly shaken, Holly wandered away from a discussion she preferred to avoid. If she couldn't think of Juan Rodriguez as reminding her of Luis, she preferred not to think of him at all. Jim Wilkins was in the Manor kitchen-garden, and she stopped to pass the time of day and accept the offer of a taste of his late strawberries; then she climbed the stile on to the river path where she and a hostile Spanish visitor had parted company long ago. A moment later she found him there again, and realized she should have expected him. As at other points in her life, what was happening now was pre-ordained and inevitable.

'Your uncle found another visitor already waiting for him in the church,' Juan explained, 'so I left them together.'

'He'd forgotten, I expect. He does sometimes, if a glorious new way of looking at one of the Gospel stories suddenly occurs to him.'

'A perfect priest,' her companion agreed gravely.

She looked at his unrevealing face—so maddeningly *English* in its reticence that Helena was wrong, and Aunt Phee right after all. But because she suspected him of laughing she blew on a poor little flame of anger. 'I suppose we all strike you as trivial, or ridiculous...you despise young men who have nothing better to do than bang tennis balls about, and absent-minded priests who actually believe in the mystery of Christ's life, and all this gentle English greenness everywhere, instead of harsh sierras and blood-soaked bullrings.'

She stopped for lack of breath, and so long a silence followed that she had to turn and look at him. When she did so a little electric charge started pulsing round her body, strangely causing weakness and excitement at the same time. It would have helped to believe him similarly affected, but she knew him to be hard, and impenetrably resistant to the clamour of the senses. *That,* some foolish, still-functioning remnant of her brain insisted, seemed *very* sad...sad not to know how sweet was tenderness, how rapturous the give and take of love.

'I must have said something to offend you,' he observed mildly at last.

It was, she had to admit, a sublimely English comment on *her* splendid Spanish outburst. Suddenly all the anxieties of the past months were transmuted into a heaven-sent, releasing gust of laughter. Juan stared at her, mouth twitching, until he was obliged to join in. At last he wiped his eyes and spoke unsteadily.

'I also said something to amuse you. I don't know what it was but it never does to analyse a joke.'

Holly mopped her own wet cheeks, agreed, and suddenly grew serious again. 'Is it very bad in Spain now, and do you really think Luis will agree to leave?'

'He'll understand that he must if he wants any future anarchist leaders left alive. That and his need to see *you* will bring him to England. He's been missing you very much.'

Relief shone in her face, but 'What about Spain?' she asked again.

Juan turned to look at her, and his expression wasn't reticent now. 'Spain is riding the whirlwind, I'm afraid. A good and patriotic king thought he must choose exile to save his country from a civil war, but he might as well have stayed...the war is coming anyhow one of these days.'

She closed her eyes against the picture of Juan and Luis caught up in a struggle that compelled them to try to kill each other. 'Tell Asunción that when Luis comes we'll do our best to keep him,' she whispered.

She suddenly felt Juan's hands gripping her shoulders through the thin material of her dress. She opened her eyes and saw that he was trying to smile.

'My mother would thank you with a kiss if she were here...perhaps I should offer it instead!'

But it wasn't anything like the kiss Asunción

would have given her. Torn between fierce anger, and terror for the response his mouth aroused in her, she could only ride out the storm until he released her. When he raised his head at last she struggled to find the breath her body needed. His eyes registered the turmoil she was in, but he turned the moment aside with something approaching a careless smile.

'As a thank you, it got a little out of hand, I'm afraid! Never mind, Señorita. I dare say my brother can spare me one small kiss. I hope he comes here as fervently as I hope *you* never come back to Spain.' Then he turned away from her and went striding along the path.

She sat at the same dinner-table with him that evening, stood with the others to wave him away the following morning, but they had nothing more to say to each other.

It was spring by the time Luis finally arrived. He'd held out as long as honour demanded, sharing his friends' risks and dangers. But their numbers were shrinking and someone had to survive to lead a persecuted band when the moment of final revolution came—the *successful* moment next time, not an ill-planned uprising like the last one that had left the miners of the north fighting a brave but hopeless battle entirely alone. He wouldn't have chosen England as a temporary refuge—it was a soft and decadent country now, by all accounts, full of the sort of people he most despised. But Holly was there, and for her he could suffer smug, capitalist fools with the *cortesía* that Asunción had begged him to remember was obligatory in a guest.

He stayed in London only long enough to change stations—glimpsed in a taxi-ride from Victoria to Paddington a fraction of the size and clamour of the metropolis, and saw its springtime greenness with astonishment. But it was Oxford that concerned him, where Holly had promised to be waiting. In spite of himself he was curious about Juan's English connections. His mother had spoken warmly of the woman in whose home he was going to stay, and he remembered Holly insisting once that he would find her Fanshawe cousin beautiful.

In the event it was Helena who went with her brother to meet their aunt's Spanish guest.

'Funny business,' Richard said as they waited on the platform for the train from London to arrive. 'I can only remember Grandfather Maynard as a quiet gentleman in his workroom, politely requesting *you* for the umpteenth time not to meddle with the models he was making.'

Helena nodded. 'I know...hard to think of him as a rumbustious young man in Spain, seducing gorgeous servant girls.'

'There was only one seduction,' her brother pointed out fairly, 'and for God's sake don't chatter about servant girls in front of Luis—she's his mother, remember.'

'According to Aunt Phee, who's much more forthcoming than Mama, she was perfectly beautiful.' Reminded of her own reputation, Helena peered anxiously in the mirror of her powder-compact—but there was nothing

328

to worry about; all was perfect there as usual.

Richard was frank, also as usual. 'He's Holly's friend, not yours, and I'm not having you play fast and loose with a dashing Spaniard while Edward's toiling in New York on behalf of Harkness.'

'He should have taken me with him—I asked him to.'

It was still a sore subject with Helena, who rightly blamed Lady Harkness for the fact that her offer to accompany him to America had been turned down. She would have gone on grumbling about it now, but the arrival of the train was signalled and a moment later it steamed into the station.

No prizes, Richard decided, for spotting untidy dons and their ladies returning from vacation visits to outlandish places, hung about with even stranger trophies. But coming towards them was someone as easily identifiable. With olive skin and his hair so dark and smooth that it shone like black lacquer, Luis Rodriguez couldn't be missed. A raincoat was draped about his shoulders like a cloak, and if the effect was studied, it was also very graceful. Richard strolled towards him, tall and broad and incapable of any effect at all save that of being stubbornly himself. Even Helena, not given to scrutinizing sharply anything outside herself, was struck by the contrast between the two young men and thought she preferred her brother.

'Holly's cousins—well, two of them,' he explained pleasantly, holding out his hand.

'I'm Richard Fanshawe, and this is my sister, Helena. Holly wanted to be here, but she's been laid low for a few days with a dose of 'flu.'

Almost in a trance of disappointment Luis scarcely registered the bright-haired, smiling girl over whose hand he seemed to be bowing correctly—she was not Holly...she did not concern him. Helena made no claim to intellect, but lifelong practice had honed her skill in estimating the effect she had on men, and the fact had to be faced that she was making no effect at all on Luis Rodriguez. She enquired almost nervously about his journey—yes, it *had* seemed rather long and, no, it hadn't rained quite the *entire* way from Dover. Seeing his sister for once in difficulties, Richard signalled hastily for a porter and led the way outside.

He drove them back along the Broad, pointing out the Bodleian and the Sheldonian Theatre, crossed Magdalen Bridge, waving a hand in the direction of Oxford's ancient botanic gardens, but still no flicker of interest disturbed the tragic expression of his passenger. Richard gave an inward sigh of relief—thank God he was Aunt Phee's guest, and Trinity term would start in another week or two. They delivered him to the Manor and then turned into their own drive.

'Not exactly a friendly sort of chap, would you say?' he suggested as they got out of the car.

'No, but he bows very beautifully,' Helena said with a faint smile. 'I think we should look upon him as a challenge!'

At that moment he was greeting Phoebe next door with a grave speech of thanks whose *cortesía*

330

scarcely concealed the fact that he was wishing he hadn't come at all. Then Holly came down the stairs, wrapped in a silk dressing-gown, and Luis threw formality to the winds to enfold her in his arms. Watching them, Phoebe thought she understood why Juan had been so sure his brother would consent to come to England.

'*Querida*...dearest love...I meant to go on being very angry with you for not coming back to Spain; but now that I see you I can't be angry at all.' His smile, like his bow, was beautiful—a flash of very white teeth in a brown face; he resembled Asunción, Phoebe decided, but she could see no likeness to his half-brother at all. Luis would be entirely Spanish—passionate or melancholy or entrancingly gay, as the spirit took him.

'I *wanted* so much to come back,' Holly was explaining with a little colour in her pale cheeks now. 'You'll understand better why I couldn't when I take you to the pottery. I also meant to be at the station just now, but Aunt Phee forbade even that! Still, at least it means that you've already met Richard and Helena.'

He agreed, but seemed so unaware of the fact that Phoebe reported to Hugo when he came home that Luis Rodriguez seemed to be made of different metal from other young men.

'It's just as well, of course,' she said thoughtfully. 'We can very well do without the complication of having him fall hopelessly in love with Helena...although I'm bound to say that at the moment he seems *much* more inclined to be in love with Holly. He's a very serious young man, but I suppose that comes of being an anarchist. He'll go back to Spain thinking us very flippant and trivial.'

Hugo suggested with a grin that they could leave time to work its usual adjustments, but for the first week Luis remained an unenthusiastic guest, coming to life only when Holly was there to make him smile, and talk about Seville. But gradually he began to show a glimmer or two of interest in the strange race he found himself among. His host insisted to Anne Maynard that the credit went to Phoebe, who was well known to be irresistible. His wife thanked him for the compliment but explained that it was actually the change in the weather that had been providential. Dreary rain had suddenly gone, leaving them a succession of perfect spring days. Tennis, croquet parties, and even punting on the river were suddenly possible again, and Luis showed signs of learning to enjoy himself.

'Learning?' Anne asked in surprise. 'You mean that he's having to be taught these simple country pleasures?'

'Yes, but the children are *devoting* themselves to the task of making him fit for Oxford life! He certainly wasn't when he arrived—apart from being with Holly, all he wanted to do was to argue with Hugo and make him admit that *his* friends are the only saviours of Spain.' She smiled lovingly at her husband. 'For a man who isn't *naturally* tactful, my dear Hugo did very well!'

Anne smiled, but returned to the beginning

of Phoebe's speech. 'If you ask me, Helena is devoting herself to subjugating a new slave—any resistance and slaughter will be the more merciless in the end!'

Phoebe looked anxious for a moment, aware that Anne's opinions were never based on malice, only on interested observation.

'Holly won't neglect the pottery, so it's true that during the day Luis is often next door,' she admitted at last, and I suppose Helena can't help expecting him to fall in love with her, because young men always *do*. She hasn't met someone like Luis before, with his heart and mind only fixed on serious things such as plotting the next revolution. Poor boy, he's suddenly in the peaceful heart of England where we haven't had a revolution for three hundred years and don't, in any case, feel they're anything to boast about. He tries to despise us, but it's a struggle when he discovers that he enjoys whacking a croquet ball quite as much as the rest of us!'

Anne smiled, but noticed how skilfully her dear Phoebe had switched the topic of conversation. They had been talking about Helena, not Luis, and a girl engaged to a far-distant fiancé was better off *not* spending most of every day in close proximity to a young man exotically and dangerously different from Richard's usual circle of friends. It was Anne's considered view that they'd been safer with the uncommunicative stranger who had first arrived than the charming guest Luis had now become.

'Term starts soon,' Phoebe said suddenly. 'In

fact Josh Harkness arrives tomorrow to spend the last few days of the Easter vac at the Rectory. Luis will have to start *his* studies at the same time, so all their frolicking will soon be over.' She sounded thankful, and Anne was left with the impression that perhaps after all Phoebe herself had found something disquieting in the situation.

If Holly shared their anxiety, she was careful not to show it. She went every day to Brightwell, sadly aware that her obstinacy about working there irritated Luis. Equally his refusal to show the slightest interest in the pottery irritated *her;* but far outweighing irritation was pity for his exile, and her longing for him to be happy in England.

One fine Sunday morning, instead of setting off with the others for her uncle's church, she agreed when Luis demanded a walk by themselves for once. Hand in hand but saying little, they climbed the long slope upward to the Wittenham Clumps. A little wind blew up there, bringing them the Sunday sound of church bells ringing. The landscape was a spread quilt of vivid green, latticed with the darker green threads of hedgerows, and overhead a lark sang as it flew towards heaven. Holly was content to sit and stare at England, wondering what her companion made of it, or even if he saw it at all.

'I know it's not the Ronda mountains, or the Guadalquivir, but doesn't it strike you as worth loving in its own quiet way?' she asked after a little while.

'I came determined *not* to think so,' Luis admitted. 'I was going to find Juan's English connections, apart from *you*, not worth bothering with either. Stupid...childish of course that was.' He caught her hand and kissed it by way of apology. 'But nothing else is changed, Holly...I still want to go back to my *compañeros* as soon as I can, and take you with me, for good this time.' Her averted face didn't help him guess what she would say. It was familiar again now, but she wasn't quite the same girl who had left Seville and the fact both frightened and excited him.

'The Englishman you were once in love with isn't here,' he said suddenly. 'I should know if he were.'

Holly turned her head to look at him, with a rueful smile lifting the corners of her mouth. 'You might *not* know, because it no longer matters to me whether he's here or not, except that he remains a friend. At the moment he's in New York, but in any case I'm truly glad to say he's going to marry Helena in the summer.'

Luis leaned towards her gripping her hands. 'Why didn't you say that the moment I arrived? Oh, *Dios*, now I feel better...now I think you *will* leave England behind. Dearest, let's forget my prosy old Russian professor, and the fools at home who think they can prevent the coming of a new dawn...we'll go back now...tomorrow!'

Love and all the careless optimism of youth glowed in his face; he was her senior by four years but she felt old by comparison. It was hard to speak the truth without hurting him, but he guessed what she would say from the shadow in her eyes.

'It's still that damnable *cerámica* that your friend had no right to burden you with. *Querida*, give it away...we'll burn it down if you like—*anything* to make you stop thinking about it. You shouldn't have to spend the days with your beautiful hands covered in disgusting, slimy clay.'

She shook her head, trying not to smile because he sounded tragically intense again, and it wasn't the Andalusian way to treat serious matters lightly.

'Dear Luis, I'm not free to leave yet and nor, for Asunción's peace of mind, are you. Apart from that, I *like* clay, and you must allow for the fact that I shall go on being a potter *wherever* I am. If that idea is more than a true-born Spanish male can bear, you had better say so now!'

His hands suddenly pushed her back until she was lying on the grass, pinned there by the weight of his body.

'Juan warned me that English women were different—brought up to be independent...not content to be loved and looked after, and to bear their husband's children.' He looked unhappy for a moment, then gloom was wiped away by a transforming smile.

'It's all the fault of English *men*, of course, who don't know how to love their wives. Spaniards know, my dear one, and I promise

336

that I shall make you happy.'

She was bound to believe him...and to rely on what she was sure was true. In Spain there would be no tug-of-war between them; loving would be easy and natural again, and there would be nothing to fear. Gripped by the sudden longing to be reassured, her hands pulled his head down towards her so that she could whisper against his mouth, 'Make me happy *now*, please.'

They were alone on a hill above the rest of the world, and Luis's smile was full of tenderness and triumph as his lips touched hers...gently at first, then more and more insistently. The frustrations of months past melted in a shared feverish desire that could suddenly bring them to fulfilment. She was almost certain of it when Luis suddenly dragged his mouth away from hers and lifted himself away, to look at her.

'*Tesoro*, I was nearly mad just then,' he said unsteadily. 'Forgive me. *Our* complete act of love must be beautiful and unhurried and private, not *this* ugly taking here, like a beast in the field.' His hand gently smoothed her disordered hair, but bereft of the comfort of his body against her own, she felt cold and lonely, and the racing excitement of a moment ago was drowned in a wave of self-disgust.

'We were *both* a little mad,' she said truthfully, but he still looked so remorseful that she tried to smile at him. 'It was my fault, dear Luis, and no harm has been done, unless some village gossip has seen the Reverend's niece "behaving very unseemly"!'

He pulled her to her feet and stood with her face cupped in his hands. 'It *will* all be perfect when the time comes...this I promise you.'

She must believe it now because she was committed, to him and to Spain. Luis was smiling at her, tender and confident, and she would refuse to listen to an echo in her brain of Juan's voice saying that he hoped she'd never go back to Seville.

'Have you remembered something about an anarchist's creed, sweetheart? *We* see no need for a venal and ignorant priest to bless our relationships, but what would your uncle, who is neither venal nor ignorant, think of that?'

'He'd be horrified,' Holly admitted, 'and so might I, as a matter of fact—not being a fully-fledged revolutionary myself.'

Luis kissed the hand he still held as they turned to descend the hill. 'Then in that case a wedding you shall have!'

They walked home after that sedately enough to mingle with the congregation leaving Hindleford Church. But Phoebe, observing them more carefully than most, was aware of a change. There was a new contentment about Luis, and about Holly the quietness that came from a decision taken. She could guess what it was, and accepted sadly that she had only herself to blame—she had wanted so much to keep Asunción and Juan in their lives. It was too late now to regret that the cost was going to be losing Holly to Luis Rodriguez.

20

On a late April day that might have strayed out of mid-summer by mistake a croquet party was assembled on the Manor lawn. Phoebe had declined to join in, but promised to watch from the terrace for any vestige of foul play. Richard partnered his youngest sister, Josh Harkness played with Rosalind, and Luis and Helena made up the remaining pair. Phoebe was bound to admit to herself that she couldn't blame Helena for Holly's absence at Brightwell, where an exhibition piece demanded urgent attention; but she strongly suspected her niece of arranging the couples to suit herself. They made a strikingly contrasted and attractive pair, she and Luis, but Phoebe wondered whether it was necessary for Helena to adjust his grip on the mallet so frequently, or encourage him so often with her captivating smile.

'I've been sent over from next door—Aunt Lydia said you were all out here,' a quiet voice suddenly murmured beside her.

She turned to find Edward Harkness standing there, offering her his charming, shy grin.

'Dear Ned...what a *lovely* surprise—I'm sure Helena said it would be another fortnight.'

'It should have been, but suddenly I found I could get away earlier, and I was sick of New

339

York. I didn't cable...thought I'd let it be a surprise for Helena.'

Phoebe smiled at him affectionately; she loved all George's children, but knew in her secret heart that if she had a favourite it was Ned. 'Shall we interrupt the game, or wait for them to spot you?'

'Let's wait—it looks too serious to interrupt, and I'm happy just to sit and watch.' He waved a hand round the scene in front of them, 'I used to dream of this in New York.' Then he shaded his eyes against the sun. 'I suppose that's your Spanish guest playing with Helena? One of her letters mentioned meeting him at the station—*very* stiff, I gathered; but he seems at home enough now.'

Phoebe's glance followed his to the picture Helena made on the lawn—thin blue jersey and skirt blown against her body by the breeze, outlining the lovely curves of breast and thigh. Sunlight gleamed on her cap of bright hair, and anyone who watched was bound to see the smile she offered her partner when his ball went through the hoop.

'Yes, that's Luis,' Phoebe agreed, feeling the need to make some explanation. 'He wasn't at all happy when he first came...we've had to rely on everyone to be very kind to him.'

'Why need he be here at all?' Ned asked bluntly.

'Because his political beliefs don't find favour with the present authorities. He risks being imprisoned, or beaten senseless by the Civil Guard. Shocking, is it not?'

'Well, we might think so; but remember how *his* friends behave too, Aunt Phee.'

She stared at him, aware that the past few months on his own in America had made a change—there was a new self-reliance about him now...more *gravitas* altogether, she could hear Francis saying. 'You seem to know quite a bit about Spain,' she commented with a faint air of surprise. Then he smiled and she recognized him again.

'We own a pottery there...we *need* to know what's going on.'

There was no time to say that he sounded like old Joshua, because the players on the lawn were suddenly appealing for Phoebe's verdict on a disputed stroke. Looking towards the terrace, they saw two figures where there should only have been one, and Richard and Josh called out noisy greetings. But Helena, who should have moved first, seemed rooted to the spot. Her paralysis was so complete that Phoebe thought she might even have ceased to breathe. Then just as the delay became intolerable she threw down her mallet and began to run—stiffly, as a mechanical toy might move again because it had suddenly been rewound.

'Ned...darling Ned...how dare you sit there so quietly, watching this stupid game. It's *lovely* to see you, but I don't in the least understand how you come to be here.' She leapt the terrace steps and flung herself into his arms in an embrace that Ned would once have found embarrassingly public. This time, it seemed to Phoebe, he didn't mind—the

341

whole world, including Luis Rodriguez, could know that they were overjoyed to be together again.

'I came as soon as I could,' he said simply. 'I read your letters a dozen times, but you still seemed dreadfully far away.'

'That's because I'm such a rotten letter-writer...Richard says I'm scarcely educated at all, in spite of poor Miss Carlton's most patient efforts.'

'No need to listen to brothers...I never take any notice of mine,' Ned advised. He smiled broadly as Josh and Richard now climbed the steps towards them, and then was introduced to Luis. Seeing that no-one now seemed inclined to finish the game, Phoebe went into the house to ask Nellie to bring out beer and lemonade. She was surprised to find how strongly she wished Hugo were at home; somehow in his company even the most ill-assorted guests were lulled into angelic harmony. But she was being ridiculous—merely a harmless group of cousins and friends sat talking outside when she went back to them.

'Another Easter vac over,' Richard lamented sadly. 'The petty tyrannies of term-time again for us, and a worse fate still for poor old Ned—he'll soon be hidden in Burslem chimney-smoke again.'

'Not for long,' Ned admitted after a slight hesitation, '...Father wants to pack me off to Seville next, as part of my Harkness education.' He looked at Helena and saw an expression on her face that he could easily recognize. 'It will

342

only be for a few weeks, sweetheart, while you're getting ready for the wedding.'

'If you're going away *again,* I'm going with you this time,' she said categorically. 'I don't care *what* your dear mother says.'

Phoebe knew that there were ways of leading Ned Harkness, and there were ways of driving him that simply wouldn't work. It was hard to believe that Helena hadn't discovered them by now, but harder still to believe that after a separation of several months she was deliberately picking a quarrel with him.

'I shall *hate* going off again without you,' he said quietly, 'and it has nothing to do with my mother. I should be mad to think of taking you anywhere near Spain, even if your father were to permit you to come with me. Law and order, if they ever existed there, have completely broken down.'

It was true, of course—Luis's very presence confirmed it; but Phoebe couldn't help thinking that Ned had deliberately and untypically chosen to abandon tact. At the same time she registered the effect on Luis, and knew that they were back where his visit had begun. He was remembering that he'd come ready to despise these smug Anglo-Saxons with their eternal compromises and their lack of passion. But it was to Luis that Helena suddenly appealed—eyes darkly blue and pleading in the whiteness of her face.

'Tell Ned that there's no reason why I shouldn't go to Spain. Foreigners don't get involved, but even if they did, I shouldn't mind—I'm sick to death of safe, *boring*, little Hindleford.'

Phoebe saw Richard frown, and thought he shared her anxiety for the position Luis had been forced into. But then it seemed from her guest's charming bow towards Helena that he didn't mind in the least having to choose whether to side with her or Ned.

'You're right—foreigners are outside our struggles; we fight only each other for the future of Spain. Visitors who cannot even understand our problems have no part in the battle.'

Helena thanked him with her most ravishing smile before turning back to Ned. 'There you are, you see—I *can* go with you, and I *won't* be left behind.'

She seemed blind to the sudden grimness in Ned's face, and to the fact that the confrontation had changed. It was between him and Luis now, and the girl who had begun it was put aside by both of them.

'We can *understand* your problems,' Ned said almost insolently. 'It's the way you go about solving them that defeats any rational human being.'

Phoebe thought she heard Richard pray under his breath—'Oh! God Almighty'; Luis flashed a smile at Ned, but it was bright and dangerous as naked steel.

'Our way is too violent for a good English bourgeois, of course! But Spaniards are not ashamed to love their friends, and hate their enemies; and they hold their country to be

344

worth dying for if need be.'

'So do we, if nearly a million men—my father's brother among them—are anything to go by.'

Luis was silenced for a moment by a reply that was unanswerable. He stared from Ned's rigid face to Richard and young Josh, and saw in all of them the same mixture of embarrassment and dogged certainty that their point of view was right. Had Juan not said something about this, too? It was the very certainty that always made them hard to beat.

'Forgive me...I meant no offence,' he said stiffly, 'even though you speak without knowing the truth about Spain. Our poor people there have been ground into the dust for generations by the cynical conspiracy of politicians, priests, and generals. For them the only hope now is the violence you condemn. They wouldn't understand your Oxford undergraduates who voted last year *not* to fight for King and country.'

Phoebe stared round the ring of faces—the young men aware in spite of themselves of listening to the pure intensity of feeling that fuelled revolutions and bred martyrs for a cause; Helena and her sisters listened too, but almost certainly *saw* only Luis's ardent face and tense, lithe body. Then it was Richard's turn to enter the conversation.

'That Union vote *sounds* bad, I grant you, Luis, but there's a thing you have to remember about the English—they very often say what they don't mean.' A gentle smile made his

345

face pleasant. 'Very confusing it must be for other people until they get the hang of it!'

Then, in some way having taken charge, he thanked his aunt for putting up with them and announced that he was ready to escort his sisters and cousins back to the Rectory. When they had gone, Luis offered Phoebe a rueful apology.

'A very serious lack of *cortesía*, my mother would say—forgive me, Señora Phoebe, for behaving so badly.'

She smiled at him with her usual kindness and said, 'I'm not sure how *else* you could have behaved,' but it was a relief when he suggested borrowing a bicycle so that he could ride over to Brightwell and escort Holly home. The past hour had been a strain, and she was still left with troubling images in her mind—Helena dazzlingly gay with her partner on the lawn, but desperate and defiant with a fiancé who himself had changed; and Luis being made to look at Spain's bleeding wounds with different eyes, afraid of seeing them as self-inflicted after all.

The following morning Edward let himself quietly out of the Rectory before even Francis Fanshawe was likely to be stirring. He knew the Vicar's habits by now and, much as he cherished his prospective father-in-law, wanted to avoid an invitation to walk or pray with him this morning.

The fine weather held, although an early mist veiled the furthest reaches of the garden. In the stillness about him the world seemed to be holding its breath; there was no sound at all until a blackbird near at hand but invisible began its morning song. It was a far cry from New York, or even from his own home, and tomorrow he must leave again.

At the river he turned upstream, and then hesitated, almost deciding to turn back. But a twig snapped beneath his feet, giving him away, and Holly's young spaniel began to bark, sure of having met a friend. She stood waiting for him to come up with her, and held out her hand.

'Aunt Phee *said* you were back early...welcome home, Ned.'

'Two of us out before the rest of the world is awake,' he said with a smile. 'Couldn't you sleep either?'

'Oh, I like this beginning part of the day, but I usually have it to myself.'

She said it without resentment, but equally without any suggestion that she would mind if he walked away. Pique was ridiculous when he'd come out to be alone, but he watched the mist beading her dark hair and suddenly remembered a time when she *had* been content to walk with him, not wanting the world to herself. He hadn't seen her for a long time, not since she'd gone to Spain. The spare grace he remembered was more noticeable now, needing no frills or finery to make its effect. As a child she'd probably hated being different from the fair Fanshawe girls; if she bothered to think about it at all, the contrast between them might seem an advantage now. She walked beside him companionably enough, but he was certain that her thoughts were not on him; he found himself wanting her to be aware, at least, that he was there.

'Did Aunt Phee also tell you that I upset her Spanish friend yesterday, and embarrassed everyone else?'

The direct approach made her turn to look at him, and for the first time she saw the tiredness, discouragement almost, in his face.

'Luis is *my* friend, too,' she said gently. 'In fact one of these days he's going to be kind enough to marry me!' She grinned at the expression on Ned's face and felt obliged to explain. 'Anarchists don't marry, as a rule, being very against a Church that they reckon has despoiled the Spanish people for centuries.' She was aware still of something that seemed like shock in the tall figure walking beside her, and tried again. 'I expect Luis was partly to blame yesterday. He longs to be back in Spain, so it would have been hard to hear that you were going when he couldn't. Apart from that, it must be maddening to hear *us* running on about his poor country's ills as if we had no injustice or misery *here*.'

Beside the path a fallen tree made a convenient seat, and they made for it, both aware that they were glad not to be alone after all. Holly began to disentangle a burr from the spaniel's silky coat, while Ned seemed content to sit and watch mist rising like smoke from the surface of the water.

'Do you remember the day Hugo fished us both out of the river?' he asked suddenly.

She nodded, looking down the vista of years to a moment that had set much else about her life in motion. 'I thought of *you* as my hero that day, and for years afterwards too! No wonder it took me such a long time to become friends with Helena...but we've finally managed it, I'm glad to say.'

Ned thought of a moment on a busy Oxford pavement when he'd kissed her mouth for the first and only time, and then shouldered his way manfully—or perhaps ridiculously—through the crowd. There seemed to be nothing to be said about that, given that she was going to marry Luis Rodriguez and he was engaged to Helena; but it was an effort, all the same, to put the memory aside and talk about present pains.

'If you've become friends perhaps you can tell me why Helena's unhappy,' he suggested, with his eyes on the river again. 'Yesterday's quarrel was apparently about not taking her to Spain. You know more about the wretched place than I do—was I wrong to refuse?'

'Probably not,' Holly answered slowly, 'except that she *is* very bored—craves adventure, and sees more chance of it in Seville than Hindleford.'

Ned remembered Helena's face as she looked at Luis and recognized his brave glamour, but it seemed impossible to say to the girl Luis was going to marry that his own fiancée saw adventure in terms of people, not of places.

Instead, he muttered something that was almost as painful.

'I expect the truth is that we've known each other too long. There's nothing very exciting about marrying your childhood friend and sweetheart, and God knows there's no great adventure in being taken to live in the Potteries. Helena scarcely even understands what we do there.'

Holly scrambled thankfully on to firmer ground. 'That's not true, Ned—she's been coming to Brightwell for months past.' She saw the trouble in his face, and wanted to make him smile instead. 'Helena knows *more* about ceramics than Luis does, if that's any consolation; I can't get *him* to take the slightest interest in clay at all!'

'It sounds as if you should be marrying *me,*' Ned pointed out, but he smiled as he said it and she was almost certain that he'd meant it as a joke. All the same, she hurried on, in case a silence should become embarrassing.

'I know that giving advice is the quickest way to lose a friend but it seems to me, dear Ned, that you should make your visit to Spain as short as possible. Come back as soon as you can and marry Helena—she's like Aunt Lydia...happiness depends on being busy and indispensable! And *stop* being apologetic about Burslem. The Harknesses are part of Potteries history, for heaven's sake.'

There *was* a little silence now; then Ned said solemnly, 'I hear ye, missus!...and speaking of Aunt Lydia, unpunctuality at meals is still a

350

cardinal sin, so I'd better be getting back. You coming too, Holly?'

'Not yet—Jasper here hasn't found nearly enough ducks to chase, or rabbit holes to get stuck in.'

Ned got up to go, but stood looking down at her, reluctant to walk away. As usual, she sat with long, slender hands linked round her knees—a girl they'd never entirely understood, he thought, and not nearly enough loved until it was too late.

'Are you going to be happy, living in Spain?' he asked abruptly.

A strange smile touched her mouth before she answered him. 'I've no idea...I shall have to find out!'

He turned back once to look at her, but she was still sitting there, Jasper's rabbit holes apparently forgotten.

The start of a new term withdrew Richard and Josh to the fastnesses of Trinity College, except for weekend visits, and Luis began to study in earnest with his professor. He found the Russian language engrossing, but even more to his taste were their long discussions on the theory and practice of communism, the ideal society, and Bakunin versus Karl Marx. Phoebe, watching anxiously, reported to Hugo that some invisible point of danger had been navigated round without shipwreck.

'Luis has decided to be happy here for the time being, which means that Holly can stop worrying about him and concentrate on her own work. Dear George Harkness wants to exhibit some pieces in New York and Paris...did she tell you?' She frowned, aware of having strayed into a different anxiety. 'There's nothing we can do to stop her going back to Spain when Luis goes, except pray that she will be safe and happy.' Phoebe looked at her husband and almost smiled as she thought of something else. 'You're much kinder than my sister—she would certainly remind me that Holly wouldn't have met Luis at all if I hadn't insisted on our Spanish connection!'

'I expect I love you even more than Lydia does,' Hugo explained generously. He kissed the end of his wife's nose, and tucked her hand in his as they made their usual evening stroll round the garden. 'I don't think you need worry about Holly's safety in Spain—Luis has promised me that he will protect her with his own life if need be.'

'And much good *that* will be if he gets himself shot first,' Phoebe pointed out with unaccustomed tartness.

'In that case, we should have to rely on Juan,' Hugo agreed, '...more reliable altogether, being half a Maynard!'

Her mouth twitched, but she tried to sound severe. 'I know you're trying to cheer me up, but I can't help feeling *low* about her, Hugo.'

'Sweetheart, nor can I,' he confessed unexpectedly, 'but there's nothing you or I can do to make her change her mind. I hinted one day with my well-known delicacy and tact that she would be giving up a home, a family, and an

352

important career here. She agreed, rather sadly I thought, but explained that it was scarcely a matter of choice...she was going because it was part of the inevitable pattern of her life. If you think I should have been able to argue her out of *that*, I can only admit that I failed.'

Phoebe gave the hand that held hers a little pat, and walked for a few moments in silence. 'I suppose Francis will marry them before they leave England,' she murmured at last. 'At least...I suppose anarchists *do* marry?' she asked in sudden doubt.

'As a rule *not*, my love, but I'm also assured by Luis that he's prepared to waive his prejudice for Holly!'

Phoebe smiled because he wanted her to, but felt nearer to bursting into tears. 'I begin to hate the very sound of Luis's friends, and their narrow, stupid ideology.'

'It's not entirely stupid, and some of it's even rather grand,' Hugo pointed out thoughtfully, 'but I've never had the heart to tell him that the anarchist vision of society is about as reachable as the Holy Grail.'

They walked in silence after that and returned to the house at last to find that Lydia had just arrived. She didn't normally pay them late-evening calls, and it was immediately obvious from her pale and rigid face that something was seriously wrong. Almost before they were settled in the library she fired her opening shot, and Phoebe was made aware that shipwreck hadn't been avoided after all.

21

'Wedding arranged, invitations all out, presents flowing in, and *now* my daughter informs me that she'd rather not get married after all,' Lydia said bitterly.

Phoebe tried to pour a little oil on troubled waters. 'She's overwrought, dearest...missing Ned. It was thoughtless of George to send him away again, just before the wedding. She'll be herself the moment he gets back.'

On the spur of the moment it was the best she could do, but Lydia waved the explanation aside. 'Helena is *never* not herself, only occasionally aware that she regrets having made a wrong choice. This time even Francis couldn't persuade her that the choice *wasn't* wrong, and she's written to Ned in Spain to tell him so.' Lydia shot an angry glance at Phoebe's face, saw only sadness there, and spoke in a calmer tone of voice. 'I expect you'd like to remind me that I didn't want Ned for a son-in-law—it's true; but only because I couldn't see Helena accepting a constant stream of advice from Cecily Harkness. Afterwards I realized that Ned could be trusted to *deal* with his mother.'

Phoebe nodded, but her mind went back to the afternoon of Ned's return from New York. Every instinct he possessed must have urged him to rush out on to the croquet-lawn and catch

354

Helena up in his arms. The expression on his face had said as much, but he'd schooled himself to patience instead. Phoebe could remember thinking it admirable at the time; now she understood that Helena would have seen it as a deadly lack of passion.

She looked at Hugo and he obligingly put into words the question she was reluctant to ask herself.

'What's the reason given for her change of heart?'

'Oh, she looks beautifully sad and full of remorse, and whispers that it was all a dreadful mistake...because she loves Ned like a brother! Francis, of course, believes her, not having the slightest conception of the deviousness of women.'

Phoebe frowned over this and finally un-ravelled her sister's own true meaning. 'You think it's Luis's fault, don't you, because until *he* arrived Helena was quite enough in love with Ned to marry him. Well, that is cruelly unfair, Lydia. Luis has given *Kate* more encouragement to think he's fond of her than Helena, and no-one but a blind woman could have failed to see that he *came* adoring Holly.'

For once Phoebe's usually serene face was flushed with indignation. Injustice was never forgivable, and here she was quite sure of her ground. 'You've never liked Luis, or approved of him being here. But if you must blame someone, blame *me*—it's my fault that he's at Hindleford.'

'I'm not in any doubt about *that*,' Lydia

snapped. 'I've said all along that your infatuation with the Rodriguez family was unnecessary and absurd. It now turns out to have been rather tragic as well.' Then she swept out of the room leaving silence behind.

Hugo glanced at his wife's face, and knew the extent of her distress, but he smiled at her encouragingly. 'No need to look so heart-broken, sweetheart. Helena will rather enjoy her reputation as a dashing jilt, Ned will recover—as young men do—from a painful dent in his heart, and Lydia will find some way of dealing with an outraged Cecily Harkness. Then life will go on, remarkably much as before!'

Phoebe tucked her hand in his, but still looked sombre. 'What you say is true, but I'm afraid that what Lydia said about me might also be true. It's a facer when I *meant* so well, but I expect you'll be kind enough not to point out that the road to hell is paved with good intentions!'

Hugo kissed his wife's sad mouth. 'We should never have let Luis ignore Helena,' he suggested solemnly. 'A modicum of the attention she takes for granted and no challenge would have been thrown down; a few lectures on the theory and practice of revolutionary socialism and she'd have been blind to a charming smile and the sort of exotic grace that our dear Ned can't lay claim to!'

He managed to make it sound, Phoebe thought, like an absurd illness that Helena would soon recover from, and she tried to believe him. Holly could have told her that for once he might be wrong. Rather to her surprise, Helena continued to visit the pottery, and was candid about her reason for doing so.

'I'm in such disgrace at home that even my twin disapproves of me, which is *much* worse than having Mama's coals of fire heaped on my head. Perhaps *you* think I'm a heartless cow as well, and would rather I didn't come, but at least Arnold still smiles as if he's pleased to see me.' She tried to sound bright, and even managed to smile when she caught Holly staring at her.

'I'm sorry...for you *and* for Ned,' Holly mumbled. It was scarcely adequate, but the rest of what she was thinking seemed better not said at all.

'Kind of you not to crow when the beautiful Miss Fanshawe finally discovers that the world isn't her private oyster!' Helena's voice trembled, but she went on doggedly with her confession. 'I'm in rather a mess, as a matter of fact.'

'Well, better to admit now rather than later that you can't face Burslem after all.'

'Better still to admit to you, at least, that I can't marry Ned when the only man I can see is Luis. I have to say it to *someone* or go mad, although I think you knew already.' She saw the sadness in Holly's face and made another attempt to smile. 'It's all right—I know *he* doesn't notice anyone but you...poetic justice, d-don't they c-call it?'

Holly gravely offered a paint-stained hand-kerchief and waited for Helena to wipe away the tears that now trickled down her pale face.

'This is where I ought to recommend a curative visit to Spain,' she said next, 'apparently it never fails, but at the moment I doubt if Uncle Francis would agree. You need to do *something*, though. If Miss Carlton managed to teach you any French at all, what about a visit to Paris?'

'Miss Carlton failed,' Helena said definitely, 'and in any case I'd rather not look as if I'm running away.' She took a deep breath and hurried on. 'I was hoping you'd let me be more useful here. It *isn't* so that I can throw myself in the way of Luis—he never comes to the pottery. I can't make pots like you and Arnold, but even Father admits that I'm quite deedy when I put my mind to something. I'd be far better at luring in desirable rich patrons than you are, and fending off the hopeless ones; then when...when you and Luis go back to Spain, I could still go on doing it for Arnold.'

She waited for Holly to answer, and had to wait so long that she finally lifted her hands in a little gesture of defeat. 'You don't like the idea...I suppose I guessed you wouldn't.'

'I like it very much, as it happens,' Holly said slowly. 'Only it's against all the rules. Loving Luis, you ought to be *hating* me, not wanting to help us here.'

Helena looked down the beautiful straight nose inherited from her Maynard grandfather. 'So *boring*, rules...don't you think?'

It seemed to settle the arrangement, but even Phoebe looked doubtful about it when it was explained to her, and Holly bluntly asked why.

'I suppose because I don't think Helena's enthusiasm will last,' Phoebe admitted. 'At the moment she feels guilty about poor Ned and apart from sending back innumerable wedding presents, hasn't anything else to do.' She nibbled her lower lip, a sure sign that what she had to say next was troubling her. Then she plunged, as usual, into the heart of the problem.

'Dearest, shall we ignore Helena's sad muddle about who she loves, and talk about you? I know it's difficult at the moment with Luis an exile from his own country, but wouldn't it be simpler to let Francis marry you and live here, while you have to, as man and wife?' She saw the little frown that pulled Holly's dark brows together, and embarked nervously on her next proposition. 'If...if it's so *very* against his principles to marry, why not live as man and wife anyway? We wouldn't mind...I mean, I dare say we'd get used to it.'

Holly's frown was chased away by a smile that lit her face. 'Oh, my dear Aunt Phee, there's a clanker if ever I heard one—*you'd* hate us to be living in sin, and Aunt Lydia would never hold her head up in the neighbourhood again!' Then she grew serious over what needed to be explained. 'Luis would like us to be living together, but while his friends are being persecuted in Spain it's a matter of pride to forego his own pleasures.' Her clear eyes examined the expression on Phoebe's face. 'Does it sound silly to you? It's important to Luis...a kind of test of himself to be worthy of the crusade that is coming; *nothing* must be allowed to matter more than that.'

'It's also a test of you, but perhaps that mustn't be allowed to matter either.'

The unaccustomed tartness in her friend's voice made Holly smile, but she answered firmly. 'Well, it doesn't matter very much, and *my* real test is to have everything running smoothly at Brightwell by the time we're able to leave.'

Phoebe hoped to ease her irritation by reporting the conversation to Hugo, but for once he made matters worse by suggesting a reason for her agitation that she hadn't wanted to face: she couldn't decide whether she wanted Holly and Luis to marry or not.

'His "crusade", by the way, has already begun,' he added. 'He made a speech at last night's Union debate that had the under-graduates cheering in the aisles...he's a born orator, apparently, who can hold an audience spellbound.'

'Well, there's nothing wrong with that, is there?'

'Nothing at all, except that from the Authorities' point of view the message was decidedly inflammatory, and Richard and Josh were responsible for getting him invited there. We shall certainly receive another broadside from Lydia when she knows about that!'

Phoebe gave a little nod. 'That settles it...I shall write to Asunción today and ask her to let Marilar come for a long visit; then Luis will *have* to forget his wretched politics and look after his sister. It will soon be the Long

Vac, too—Oxford undergraduates will be safe from inflammatory speeches, and if Richard has a grain of common sense left he'll teach Luis to play cricket instead.'

Hugo smiled at this masterly arrangement, but entered a small caveat. 'I hate to be a wet blanket, my love, but Marilar is *not* our independent Holly. I can't see Asunción letting her daughter embark on a journey across Spain and France alone.'

'Nor can I, but she doesn't have to,' Phoebe said serenely. 'Ned will be coming home and I shall promise her that she can entrust Marilar to his care with *every* confidence.'

Phoebe's invitation was sent, but almost turned down out of hand; then because Asunción was ashamed of a reaction that seemed entirely selfish, she showed it to Juan. He handed the letter back to his mother without saying anything.

'I'm to refuse, of course,' she said impatiently. 'You think it so obvious that it's not worth discussing?'

'I think you shouldn't have asked me if you'd already made up your mind,' he suggested with a faint smile.

'That's no answer, Juan. Put aside courtroom tactics for a moment and be plain with me, please.' He saw the anxiety expressed in her face and restless hands, and thought he understood what troubled her.

'You're afraid Marilar will come back changed—less obedient, less content to accept

361

our way of life—but we might have feared that Holly's coming *here* would teach her different habits. It never did as far as I could see.'

'Marilar has never stopped missing her, and nor have I,' Asunción said slowly. 'Perhaps nor have you,' she might have added, suddenly certain that it was true, even though Juan's face had become expressionless. It was a condition hard for a true Spaniard to achieve, but more often now than when he'd been a child, she saw in him distinct traces of his English father. She would have liked to say so, but never did for fear of hurting him. He smiled as if he knew what she was thinking, but only reminded her of Phoebe's invitation.

'You must decide, but if you *are* asking me, I think Marilar should be allowed to go—for her own sake, and perhaps for Luis's as well. It would be good for him to have her there.'

Asunción nodded, accepting what she'd known all along. 'Yes, she must go to England, if only to be happy and carefree for a little while, instead of living in *this* poisoned atmosphere. My father tries to convince me every time I see him that sheer violence and disorder are justified because it's the only weapon the downtrodden have to use; he knows it's no good trying to convince you.'

'And I can't convince *him* or Luis that violence on the left merely provokes bloodshed on the right, and thus this country goes spirally down into hell itself.' Juan's deep voice was suddenly rough with despair, but when he saw the anguish in his mother's face, he leaned over to hold her hands in his own warm ones.

'Shall I pack you off to England as well, Madre? It occurs to me that Phoebe would like that very well!'

Asunción shook her head and managed to smile. 'Foolish one, of course I shall stay here with you,' she said firmly, 'but tomorrow we must ask Señor Harkness if he will take Marilar with him on his journey home. If Phoebe says he is to be trusted, we may be sure that it is so.'

Ned was already aware of the task he was to be saddled with, and he thought that for once his dear Aunt Phee was being devious. She wanted him to be obliged to take Marilar to Hindleford, in the hope that Helena would have changed her mind again by the time they got there. For himself he had no such hope. Since her letter had arrived he'd swung between pain, anger, and even something that felt curiously like relief, but he hadn't been tempted to think his love didn't mean what she'd said. Now, at least, he wouldn't have to watch her beating irridescent wings against the narrow mould of Potteries life. Yet still a dozen times a day he thought...'Oh Christ, if only I hadn't come to Spain'.

But now the memory of Helena had to be pushed aside; he was in Asunción's house and Marilar Rodriguez was smiling at him—shyly, because her mother was there. She tried hard to seem composed, but excitement shone in her dark eyes, and hummed in her like electricity running through a wire. She expected God knew what, Ned thought, from the adventure ahead, and he was suddenly afraid that she would be bitterly disappointed. He gestured to the cobalt-blue sky above the courtyard where they sat.

'It's different in England—quite often cold and wet even when we're *supposed* to be enjoying summer.'

'I know, Señor—Juan has told me.' The lilt in her voice dismissed a little rain as being of no account. 'But Holly will be there...Luis too, of course. Have you met him?'

'Briefly,' he admitted, aware that although her other brother was silent, he was listening to the conversation. The brilliant sunlight fell on Juan's dark head, finally pinning down for Ned what he hadn't been able to identify until now—a tantalizing likeness to Lydia Fanshawe. But Marilar waited too and he realized that he had sounded curt. She had no way of knowing that his only memory of meeting Luis was painful.

'Your brother was being taught to play a game we call croquet. It's a silly business of knocking balls through hoops, but he seemed to be enjoying it.'

'It doesn't sound at all like Luis,' Marilar said doubtfully.

'Perhaps not, *cara*,' Juan put in with a little touch of malice, 'but you have to allow something for the softening effect on him of England!'

'*Something*,' Ned repeated his own word; 'but not much. I'm bound to say we didn't see quite eye to eye on how to solve Spain's problems.'

'I don't imagine for a moment that you did. Compromise wouldn't strike my brother as a virtue!'

'Nor any other Spaniard that I've met.' The words were bitten off before they left his mouth, but apparently still visible in his expression, because Juan's smile was suddenly full of understanding.

'I expect you wish you didn't own a pottery in Spain at the moment. Now isn't the time to discuss such things, but we could meet before you leave, if that would help.'

Aware that he'd been warned to change the subject, Ned agreed, and hastily complimented Asunción on the beauty of her courtyard.

'I always think of Holly out here,' she said with her serene smile. 'She loved to sit and listen to the fountain.'

'She liked talking to the flowers, too.' It was Juan offering the strange information matter-of-factly, but Asunción thought the words had spoken themselves without his permission, and taken him by surprise.

Marilar, returned from some errand of her own, broke the silence. 'Look, Señor, I've brought these animals for you to see...Holly made them for the crib.' Her fingers stroked a smiling, long-eared donkey. 'Are they not beautiful?'

Ned agreed, seeing not the little clay figures in front of him but a picture of the girl who'd made them—her thin brown face and hands absorbed in the task of creation. When he spoke again he addressed himself to Juan.

'No compromises for Luis, you said, but I know of *one*. Anarchist principles notwithstanding, he is going to *marry* Holly!'

Juan didn't answer for a moment, then gave a little shrug. 'Hard to avoid, I suppose, if his choice is an English girl with a priest for an uncle.'

It was the end of the conversation except to fix the date of their departure for England, and although Ned saw Juan again, Holly and Luis weren't mentioned between them.

When the time came to board the Madrid-Paris express, Marilar's excitement suddenly evaporated. Once Juan's tall figure could no longer be seen waving goodbye, she became so silent that Ned was made aware of the terror she was struggling to hide. She was going to England—a mist-shrouded, distant island where, Juan had said, women sometimes wore men's clothes and where, the dear convent nuns had warned her, the Blessed Virgin Mary wasn't truly loved; it now seemed no adventure at all, but a penance to be endured until Luis agreed to take her home. She wouldn't allow herself to weep, but her white face was pitiful as Ned showed her where she was to spend the night.

'There's nothing for you to worry about,' he said gently. 'My sleeper's just next door. Look...tap on that wall in a moment or two and you'll hear me tap back. Then you can be sure we shan't mislay each other!'

Comforted by his kindness, she survived the loneliness of the night, and agreed to go with him to the restaurant-car the following morning—mainly so as not to lose sight of him, he thought. As the slow hours passed he found her the antithesis of what Helena would have been as a travelling companion—undemanding, but rather dull. Marilar seemed to confirm the truth of something he'd heard Hugo once say: Spaniards preferred not to leave their own country and, even when they did, took it with them, being almost totally incurious about anywhere else. It wasn't until he ushered her on to the channel-steamer's deck to watch England solidify out of the summer-morning haze, that she did more than respond politely to whatever he said.

'Juan is different from Luis and me,' she observed suddenly. Ned looked at her and she blushed a little, because voicing opinions of her own was a new experience that needed practising. 'Grandfather Vargas says that *we* think with our hearts, Juan with his head. People *here* do that, it seems, so perhaps I shall understand him better now.' Her serious face shone for a moment with Asunción's smile. 'But I love him dearly, even when I can't understand him.'

By the time the end of the journey was in sight Marilar had been, persuaded to stop calling Ned 'Señor', and her confidence in him was so complete that it was disturbing to be told he wasn't going to stay in Hindleford. But she caught sight of Holly's tall, slender figure before the train hissed and snorted to a stop in Oxford station and nothing else mattered...not even the fact that it wasn't Luis waiting beside her, but a stranger—a huge young man whose red-gold hair gleamed in the sunlight. Marilar saw him wave to Ned, and then he was walking beside the train as it slowed down, ready to help her alight. They were her first impressions of this stranger—strength and gentleness—never needing to be corrected afterwards. Then Holly was there as well, smiling and holding out her arms; the adventure was back in place again, and excitement bathed Oxford station in a glow of exotic golden light. Marilar wept for the happiness of seeing her friend but, hugged and kissed, she was able to listen to what Holly was saying.

'*Cara*, Luis won't be here until tomorrow evening. He offered *not* to go to a big political meeting, until I assured him that you and I have a great deal of talking to do—eighteen months to catch up on! But you can meet the first of my numerous cousins instead...Aunt Lydia's son, Richard.'

The large young man stepped forward again, to bow awkwardly over her hand. When he spoke his voice, like his face, was very pleasant. 'I asked your brother to teach me how to do this, Spanish-style. He was rather rude about my performance, but I shall persevere. Welcome to England, Señorita!'

Holly watched the little scene with the faintly unsettling feeling that for Richard and Marilar time had been suspended while they stared at one another. He wasn't to know, as Holly did,

368

that Asunción's daughter was behaving strangely out of character. She seemed to have forgotten that her hand was still lost in Richard's large one, and that by Spanish standards it was much too soon in their acquaintance to offer him her soft, slow smile.

Then Ned reappeared from the direction of the luggage-van, and the spell was broken. He kissed Holly's cheek and gripped his cousin's hand, but awkwardness seized them while they searched for something to say about his broken engagement.

'Dear Ned, it's nice to have you home,' Holly murmured at last. 'We're all so *very* sorry about...about what's happened. Helena is, too, but she didn't know what else to do.'

Richard came out of his abstraction frowning at the thought of his sister, but Ned shook his head. 'No point in talking about it here...or anywhere else; it's over now.' He noticed that Marilar sensed something was wrong, and forced himself to smile at her cheerfully. 'You must be on your way—Aunt Phee will be longing for you to arrive at Hindleford. I'm not stopping here, only changing trains.' Holly's face said that she was about to argue, but he gave her no time. 'Less embarrassing this way, my dear, and the truth is that I shall be glad to get home. There's a lot to talk about with my father.'

'Yes...yes, of course. Well, *muchas gracias*, Ned, for looking after Marilar so beautifully.' She reached up to kiss his cheek, and then frowned at him. 'Of all things, Aunt Phee insists on a party to celebrate my twenty-first birthday. I won't badger you to come, but we shall miss you very much if you aren't there.'

He smiled wholeheartedly at last because she was lovely and kind and dear. 'Of course I shall be there...you can't possibly come of age without me!' Then he bowed over Marilar's hand to show Richard how it should be done, and thanked her gravely for a pleasant journey home. Holly watched, and thought with an ache of sadness that Helena had been an awful fool. But they could only leave him standing there, now cut off from what had been his second home since childhood. The sadness wasn't Luis's fault, but she couldn't pretend to herself that he hadn't been its cause.

By the time her brother reappeared Marilar already felt at home in Hindleford. She loved Phoebe Taverner at sight, and felt no strangeness in the company of her large, quietly-spoken husband because he reminded her of Juan—someone else, clearly, who thought with his head. But best of all there was her friend, to be talked to and laughed with as she hadn't talked or laughed since Holly had left Seville. She had also met the family next door; but three blonde and beautiful sisters seemed not to need a stranger, and there'd been time enough to remember how her mother would expect her to behave towards Richard Fanshawe. She still blushed when she thought about their encounter at the railway-station; but then she couldn't help smiling as well.

They were eating the cold supper that permitted Mrs Jim an evening off on Sundays when Luis walked in. He apologized to Phoebe for being late, seemed delighted that his sister had arrived, and kissed both the hands that Holly held out to him.

'A successful meeting...I can see it in your face,' she said smiling at him.

'We trounced the opposition, *tesoro*, but it was almost too easy—they made such stupid speeches.' Elation shone in his dark eyes and in the movements of his beautiful, expressive hands. She knew that he was relishing his English visit unexpectedly—in their more serious discussions he admitted that Oxford's priceless gift was a centuries-old tradition of intellectual freedom: no Inquisition, no index of forbidden books, no government censorship. He enjoyed his Russian studies as well, but they and Oxford were a temporary diversion from the real purpose of his life. His heart was warm—he loved his family, even Juan; Holly knew that he certainly loved *her*. But Spain came first...it always would until its poor, downtrodden people had won their victory.

'Did Josh enjoy himself at the meeting?' Hugo asked curiously.

It had been one of the more fascinating, if worrying, aspects of Luis's stay—to watch the change in Cecily and George's youngest son. He'd been a frequent visitor to the Rectory...a close friend of Richard's ever since schooldays at Rugby. Now they were in the same year at Trinity, where Richard was a steady, plodding student of Modern Languages, and Josh an intermittently brilliant history scholar—much given to wasting time, in the opinion of his tutor. Hugo's impression was that both young men had begun by disliking Phoebe's Spanish guest, but Josh, especially, had given in without a struggle, intoxicated by the glamour of *Hispanidad,* and Luis's dream of a perfect society that would rule itself for the good of all. Hugo had tried to explain to Phoebe that most undergraduates went through a phase when some extreme and pure ideology entranced them, but she had sounded, for once, only very cross.

'Don't try to convince me of the purity of barbarians who regularly assassinate their opponents, and burn down glorious churches! What is more, Hugo, I'm beginning to wish that Luis would *forget* about his wretched crusade. Why can't he just enjoy being alive, like any normal young man?'

'Because he's a Spaniard, my darling, and because the upheaval predicted by Nathaniel Harkness more than a century ago may be almost on top of us at last.'

She had shivered at the thought, but reverted to the beginning of the conversation.

'Richard and Josh guess the real reason for Helena's broken engagement. Why don't they blame Luis? I suppose you're going to point out in a very irritating male way that she's fallen in love with him without the slightest encouragement.'

Hugo smiled at her as unprovocatively as he could. 'Then I won't say what you already know. But *Lydia* certainly blames Luis, and if she thinks he's leading Richard and Josh into the dangerous game of politics she'll dislike him still more.'

It was that same thought that had prompted Hugo's question to Luis now. Trying to break up a fascist meeting organized by Sir Oswald Mosley's Blackshirts might have been exciting, but it was undeniably dangerous as well. Luis smiled as if he guessed what was in Hugo's mind.

'I think Josh enjoyed himself,' he answered truthfully, 'and we discovered something interesting in London...did you know that his aunt Jane and her husband, Professor Larkin, were founder-members of the British Communist Party? They differ from *us*, of course, but...'

It was as far as he got before Holly held up her hands, in rueful protest.

'Dear Luis, before we hear another word about mad Aunt Jane, promise me you'll try to remember that Marilar has *just* arrived, and she hasn't seen you for months. For the moment you're required to be *brotherly!*'

Hugo observed the little scene, aware that under Holly's playful manner lay a growing sadness. It was as if she watched someone dearly loved becoming day by day more addicted to a craving that might eventually prove fatal. But although Luis might agree with Saint Augustine that 'total abstinence was easier than perfect moderation', for the moment he was still able to moderate the compulsion that drove him. He registered the reprimand Holly hadn't put into words, and went to stand apologetically beside Phoebe.

'Forgive me...a shameful lack of *cortesía,* my mother would say! Now I am entirely at your service, Señora Phoebe—yours and Holly's and Marilar's.'

She smiled because it was difficult not to forgive him when he looked so charmingly full of remorse. 'Well, if I have your *undivided* attention, dear Luis, let us talk about Holly's birthday party. Apart from wanting Hugo and Anne Maynard to sing and play for us, *she* refuses to show the slightest interest in it!'

The birthday celebration took place a fortnight later, and even the weather—a perfect August evening—conspired to make it memorable. But when the last guest had finally said goodbye, and Holly, Marilar and Luis had agreed to go to bed, Phoebe wandered through the dishevelled rooms and out into the pre-dawn silence of the garden. The world was silver-lit by an almost full moon, but for once she was blind to its beauty. Huddled in an old coat of Hugo's, because the air was fresh and cool, she thought about the night just past. The images that filled her mind should have given nothing but pleasure...Holly, cool and lovely as a wood-nymph in pleated jade-green chiffon, dancing with Luis; Marilar's dark head close to Richard's fair one, and the white ruffles of her dress blown like spray against his black jacket as they drifted round the floor; Helena in a cloud of blue tulle as fragile as butterfly wings flitting from one admirer to the

374

next...all so beautiful to watch, and all for some reason so deeply worrying.

'Sweetheart, you must be very tired,' said Hugo's voice behind her. He came to stand beside her, with his arm round her shoulders, and saw the trouble in her moonlit face. 'It was a wonderful party everyone agreed, so why are you out here, alone and palely loitering?'

'I think I was staring at the future, and not liking the look of it very much,' Phoebe admitted. 'They all *seemed* joyous enough—even dear Ned, smiling and going out of his way to give little Annie Blake an enjoyable evening—so why do I have this lowering feeling about them—that they're all threatened, and dreadfully vulnerable?'

'Because we live in an increasingly threatening world, I expect,' Hugo said quietly.

'It's not only the impersonal dangers they can do nothing about. Beneath all tonight's music and gaiety there were different undertones—Ned deeply unhappy, Helena feverishly determined to be gay, Richard bewitched by a girl who probably *can't* be transplanted here from Spain, and even little Rosalind trying to hide the grief of knowing that Josh scarcely noticed her. It's as if they're all *wilfully* making the choices that will hurt them most...' Her voice died into silence, but Hugo broke it after a moment or two.

'You haven't mentioned Holly...and Luis.'

'No, because they trouble me most of all. Luis *wants* danger...seeks it like a *torero* longing for the moment of truth. He wants Holly as well, and because she knows that he needs her she will go with him and love him as best she can...but be so *very* unhappy in the end, I think.' She turned to smile tremulously at Hugo. 'I may yet have to confess to Lydia that *she* was right all along...I should have forgotten about that damnably beautiful and harsh peninsula!'

22

Twenty-one...fully adult in the eyes of the law, her own woman at last, Holly reckoned; but as the summer died in a blaze of autumn glory she found her new state unexpectedly disappointing. It seemed unfair to feel less certain now of what had once been simple and clear. She loved Luis, was loved by him, and knew that when the great events he was caught up in had been accomplished, there would be time for *them* to build a life together.

Having settled this yet again in her mind, she could smile at Phoebe, and listen attentively as Luis argued with Hugo about what *was*, as opposed to what *seemed*, to be happening in Spain. But he was so brilliantly talkative and abstracted by turns that she knew the day was coming when he would decide that he must return to Spain. She and Marilar would go with him...that was understood...the very thing she'd been waiting for ever since Brian Starkie's death had brought her back to England. Like any woman promised to a Spaniard, she must be content to wait for life to be arranged for her. She thought she *was* content...until their first argument erupted without warning.

Marilar had gone with Phoebe on a shopping expedition to Oxford. Like her brother, now reluctantly helping to rake leaves together for a bonfire, she found it hard to understand that her friend positively enjoyed hard manual toil in the garden. Happy to be out in a soft, grey day that smelled of wood-smoke and chrysanthemums and river-water, Holly leaned on her rake and smiled at Luis.

'I'm afraid you're not as content doing this as I am!...are you thinking that it's Jim Wilkins's job?'

Instead of smiling back, he stared at her with melancholy dark eyes. 'I think I'm wishing that you weren't so happy here. You seemed to *belong* in Spain...it was even difficult to believe you hadn't been *born* a Sevillana. Here, I have to keep remembering that you're English after all.'

'Does it matter very much?' she asked gently. 'I shall belong again when we go back, but it's useless to ask me not to love England while we're still here.' She watched him for a moment, thinking that however long *he* stayed at Hindleford, he would never be able to seem less Spanish, even if he wanted to. The shining blackness of his hair, the gleam of very white teeth in a brown face when he smiled, the faint air of hauteur that said proudly to the world he was *hidalgo*—all insisted on his foreignness.

'You want to go back, don't you?' she

asked suddenly, '...can't bear not to be there a moment longer, however dangerous it may be for you.'

He gave a little shrug that brushed danger aside as being scarcely worth the mentioning; to an anarchist it was a part of life. 'I *should* be there—not here, trying to counter fascist lies and make the smug English bourgeoisie see the truth of our struggle. The great moment is coming, and I'm needed in Spain. You've always understood how important it is...it's one of the things I love about you. But we shall go together, *tesoro*...we must *always* be together.' He smiled then, and his hand touched her cheek in a tender caress, but in the midst of an unsettling mixture of other emotions, she was aware of a little spurt of anger that she knew he wouldn't understand. He saw the shadow in her eyes and thought he knew its cause.

'It's not *still* that wretched pottery? Darling, *give* it to the Blakes—*anything* as long as you forget about it.'

She took a deep breath and reminded herself that he'd been very uncomplaining about the long hours she'd worked at Brightwell. 'It's not the pottery. Arnold can manage now, with Helena helping, and Uncle Hu to keep an eye on him.'

Luis's face was suddenly brilliant with happiness, but before he could do more than stretch out his arms, she stepped away from him, frowning a little.

'There's someone else to consider. When *we* leave Marilar must come with us. You're usually too busy to pay much attention to her, but I can promise you that she'll hate being dragged away from Hindleford.' She saw the blankness in his face, gave anger its head and shouted at him.

'Luis, forget you're an anarchist for a moment, with a mission to save Spain! Think in *human* terms for a change—Marilar's deeply happy here, and she'll be deeply *unhappy* if she's suddenly told that she's going home. Your *friend*, Richard Fanshawe, will be bereft too, but if sisters don't count in your scheme of things, friends certainly won't either.'

Luis folded his arms against the temptation to sink pride and forget everything but the simple fact that the girl in front of him was beautiful and almost dearer than anything else on earth. It was part of the danger he lived with—that he loved her too much, when *she* might believe that he didn't love her enough.

'Marilar is eighteen, imagining herself in love for the first time, in a country where behaviour is much freer than it is at home,' he said stiffly. 'Back in Seville, without Richard to hold her hand when they walk by the river, and dance with her to the gramophone, she'll become a Spanish *señorita* again, content when the time comes to have a good, suitable marriage arranged for her. Richard will miss her for a little while, and then remember that he knows a lot of other pretty girls who, more conveniently, *aren't* Catholics strictly reared to give themselves only in marriage.'

It sounded more or less reasonable, Holly thought, if you ignored what you knew of the people concerned; but equable, undemonstrative Richard Fanshawe was quietly and completely in love for the first time and perhaps the only time in his life. She had no doubt about that, even though he might have perceived enough difficulties ahead not to tell Marilar so. Holly knew that Marilar would go uncomplainingly—she'd been brought up to do what her menfolk ordained for her; but to marry her off to some 'suitable' Spanish husband would surely be to extinguish the joy that now shone out of her.

'I think you're wrong, about both of them,' Holly said at last, 'but time will tell which of us is right. I'm sorry I shouted at you, by the way—I expect it comes of being in this country where our habits are so free!'

Luis abandoned pride, and cupped her flushed face in his hands. 'You had a right to shout...I made you angry. I may do that again, *tesoro*, when I forget that there are other things that matter besides fighting for Spain. But will you always remember that I love you?...*promise* me that, please.'

She offered her mouth for his kiss, and the quarrel was abandoned, even though she remembered afterwards that the question of when they were to leave had been left unsettled. It still hadn't been discussed a week later when she went over to the Rectory with a list of ceramic exhibitions, and found only her aunt there instead. She asked for Helena and was told that she'd been taken to Oxford to have an aching tooth attended to.

'Well, I just wanted her to see this leaflet, Aunt Lydia—Brightwell gets a good mention! She's very helpful there now...worth much more than the small fee the pottery pays her.'

'I find the whole business rather absurd,' Lydia Fanshawe said coldly. 'She should find something more worthwhile to do.'

Holly stared at her aunt's still-beautiful, set face, and knew again the feelings that had been familiar since childhood—reluctant admiration for a woman so different from herself, and always the knowledge that admiration wasn't enough because they'd never learned to love one another.

'Helena seems to enjoy what she does,' she suggested diffidently. 'She isn't a potter, but Uncle Francis is right to say that under that disguise she likes to wear of being as beautiful and brainless as a butterfly she has a very good head for business!'

Still Helena's mother didn't smile, and Holly suddenly guessed what was coming next.

'She ought to be safely married to Ned Harkness by now—*would* have been but for your Spanish friend dazzling her with his flamboyant good looks and Latin charm. He has ingratiating ways, no doubt, but I very much wish he would go back to Spain, and take his demure little sister with him. There, that's speaking bluntly, Holly, but I'm tired of pretending that I share your and Phoebe's infatuation for the Rodriguez family. Juan isn't even our half-brother in *name*.'

It was blunt indeed, but it wasn't what made

381

Holly catch her breath. Somewhere on the margin of her mind there hovered a truth conjured up by what her aunt had just said. It was still too indistinct to be recognized, but one day she would be obliged to face it. Now, there was only Aunt Lydia to be dealt with, and the long-running skirmish that seemed suddenly to have become open war.

'He is your half-brother in *blood*,' she pointed out coolly, 'but perhaps what really upsets you is the fact that Richard seems to share *our* high opinion of Juan's sister. Dear Aunt, she is a Catholic, which perhaps you don't like, but I defy you to find anything else about her to object to. I'm sorry if that sounds impertinent, but I can't let you sneer at someone as sweet and good as Marilar.'

Lydia stared at the girl in front of her— slender, erect, and very angry. Just so had they confronted one another time and time again from the moment when Francis had first brought his niece home from Tilbury. She'd never given in, never changed her stubborn, independent mind once it was made up. But a sense of infuriated helplessness made her aunt pursue surrender now, even at the cost of painfully digging up the past.

'Marilar is very much like her mother,' she said at last. 'Asunción was *more* beautiful perhaps, but she had the same engaging ways and desire to please. She pleased my father certainly, with the result that our family life was destroyed. He came back from Spain withdrawn into some lonely world of his own, my mother became a confirmed, unhappy invalid. I had small reason then to like the Rodriguez family; I have less now. Luis has been the cause of making Helena and Ned unhappy, and when Marilar goes back to Spain, as I've no doubt she will, Richard will be unhappy. If that weren't enough, he and Josh Harkness now neglect their studies to listen to your wretched friend, and the intoxicating rubbish he's continually preaching. Richard is going to be a diplomat, not a wild-eyed revolutionary.'

Holly listened to the long passionate speech in silence, aware at the end of it that anger had melted into the most aching sadness, even for the woman in front of her.

'Luis talks only about Spain,' she felt obliged to say, and what he dreams of *there* isn't rubbish. I'm sorry for all the unhappiness, Aunt—yours as well—but Asunción has known grief too, and so will Marilar when the time comes to leave. If it makes you feel any better, we *shall* go soon, even though it's madness for Luis to return to Spain at all. I'm afraid he hankers after something a little more dangerous than breaking up fascist meetings here!'

Her smile wavered and went out, and Lydia was moved by sudden pity. She asked the very question that Holly had once listened to from Ned Harkness...a long time ago, it seemed now.

'Will you be happy in Spain?'

This time it seemed necessary to be firm. '*Very* happy,' she insisted. 'I belong there, you see...with Luis.'

Lydia smiled with unexpected warmth, and the discovery that Holly still couldn't bring into focus was again a shadow on the margin of her mind. There was no hurry, it seemed to say; but one day the moment of truth would come. For now, all she need do was walk away from the Rectory with one firm decision taken—she would tell Luis that the sooner they left Hindleford, the better. Think of *that*, she told herself, and forget about Aunt Lydia's smile. Henry Maynard had bequeathed it to his daughter, but just as certainly he'd bequeathed it to his son, Juan.

Holly selected their departure date carefully, but when she tried it out first on Hugo his answering smile was full of understanding.

'I'd say it's about right, sweetheart, much as *we* shall hate to see you go—not precipitate, but on the other hand not keeping our dear, disruptive guests here for too much longer, either!'

His shrewdness no longer surprised her, nor his kindness. Since living at the Manor she'd become aware of the strange diversity of people who now depended on 'the Captain' to settle their problems for them. He was the rock on which Hindleford life was built, even though Aunt Phee still remembered with a smile a time when he'd been reckoned a difficult, unsympathetic man. Holly dragged her mind away from this fascinating byway of past history and smiled at him rather sadly.

'Given the choice, I'd stay a long while yet,

384

but it's no good dodging the truth. Luis doesn't *mean* to switch people off the nice, safe rails they were travelling on to something much more risky, but that's the effect he seems to have.'

'They could always refuse to be switched.' Hugo was tempted to add that she might even refuse herself, and then decided against it. 'Your Aunt Lydia may put all the blame on Luis, but *we* don't have to.'

Holly stared at him with her clear, level gaze. 'She puts the blame on the Rodriguez *family*—Asunción most of all, I think. It seems a long time to remember an old grief with such passionate resentment.'

'Well yes, but it's something you don't realize when you're young—like poor old King Charles, the past is sometimes an unconscionable time a-dying!'

Holly nodded thoughtfully, then put the past aside with a little sigh. 'Uncle Hu, will you keep an eye on the pottery for me? I don't think Helena and Annie between them will let Arnold get in a muddle, but he's a *little* bit dreamy. Ned will exhibit for him in the Harkness showrooms if necessary, and I shall send an irritating, interfering stream of suggestions from Spain!'

Hugo smiled at the idea, then grew serious again. 'What about Miss Carteret...potter of unique and precious distinction? Is she going to idle away her time in Spain or, even worse, get entangled in its damnable political squabbles?'

'Certainly not,' Holly said firmly. 'She's going back to work at the Harkness pottery—it's already fixed with Sir George.'

It was also settled that they were to leave at the beginning of December. Marilar accepted the news in silence, but managed to say after a moment or two that her mother had been lonely long enough without them. Then she went to her own room, and didn't reappear until it was time to go down to dinner. Holly thought it likely that the hour in between had been spent on her knees in front of the little ivory carving that had been Asunción's gift to her before she left Spain. The Queen of Heaven was, for Marilar, the source of all strength and grace. She might bring herself to accept the rest of the creed Luis and his friends believed in, but she would die clinging to her own faith as well.

It wasn't obvious that Marilar avoided a weekend visit to the Rectory, when Richard was likely to be at home. But it seemed that he wasn't there at all, being too busy to leave Oxford, Helena reported.

'It's his and Josh's final year,' Holly tried to explain casually, when what she really longed to do was hug her stricken friend. 'Richard wants to join our foreign service...to be a diplomat, I mean, and it's very important for him to get a good degree. That's why he must work hard now.'

'Yes...yes, I understand,' Marilar agreed quietly, and then called upon her last ounce of womanly Spanish pride to produce a smile. 'Men are different from us...they must go out into the world and...and *do* things.' But the little gesture with which she suddenly touched Holly's cheek confided all her sadness. 'I couldn't bear to leave without *you*...and nor could Luis.'

She didn't refer to Richard again, and even made herself believe that she hoped *not* to see him before they left. She'd been in mortal danger of forgetting how she was expected to behave—it was very mortifying, but perhaps the fault of this soft, green landscape so different from her own; even Luis had been affected by it, she'd noticed.

The Saturday of their last weekend in Hindleford came and she was careful to stay close to Phoebe, leaving Holly and Luis to embark on a round of farewell visits in the neighbourhood. Breakfast was over, and the morning was looming long and empty in front of her when Richard suddenly walked in. He glanced briefly at Marilar, but spoke pointedly to his aunt.

'There's a rather splendid horse fair at Banbury this morning. I saw Hugo drive off with Smithers, so I've borrowed Father's car in case you'd like to go.'

Phoebe thought of several things, the most obvious of them being her nephew's sure knowledge that she hadn't the smallest interest in seeing horses being sold. She smiled at his strained face and said what was expected of her.

'Dear Richard, what a *very* kind thought, and what a pity I'm so busy this morning. But that needn't stop you taking Marilar.' She looked kindly at her guest. 'Working horses...not the beautiful, aristocratic creatures you have at the Seville Feria, but perhaps you won't mind that?'

Marilar merely shook her head, being unable to speak, and ten minutes later a silent pair were driving out of the village northwards. The route to Oxford was familiar to her now, but she wasn't aware that, once past St Giles, they weren't on the Banbury Road at all. At Woodstock Richard turned the car off the main road into the bare, winter parklands of Blenheim.

'A horse fair, you said,' Marilar reminded him, at last sure of her voice. 'I see no horses.'

'I know, but I suddenly lost interest in our four-footed friends. Will you settle for a glimpse of one of England's most bombastic architectural piles instead? We can come and go here because the agent is an old friend of Uncle Hu's.' She hesitated, scarcely understanding what he said, and he had to ask again. '*Please*, Marilar...I can't talk to you properly in here.'

She got out of the car quickly, to prevent him helping her, and stuffed both hands into the pockets of her coat. It was a habit caught from Holly, useful now when her hands were trembling. Richard started to talk about the house in front of them, looked at her pale face under its coronet of glossy black hair, and forgot all he'd ever known about a family called Marlborough.

'I wasn't going to see you again,' he said abruptly. 'That's why I've been sticking to Trinity.' He held out a hand and she put hers into it, because it needed to be there, not in her pocket after all. But she thought of Asunción and the dear nuns and was able to speak bravely.

'A week from now we shall be arriving in Seville. I long to see Mama and Juan again, naturally, but I shall remember my...my kind friends in England.' She turned her head away, apparently engrossed in another walker on the skyline. Then Richard's other hand gripped her shoulder, forcing her to look at him, and he saw that her eyes were full of tears.

'I know I shouldn't say how dearly I love you,' he said simply. 'There isn't any point when I can't say anything else. I'm not twenty-one yet—just a student who'll do his damnedest to pass the Foreign Office exams, but I might still fluff *those*. Even if I get in I shan't be earning much for years, and the nature of the job is to be moved around a lot. You see, just when you're getting useful somewhere, they like to shove you off somewhere else.'

He stopped talking to shake his head at her. 'Sweetheart, you're supposed to say it's all quite hopeless, not *smile* at me...too young, shaky prospects, wrong religion—nothing at all for your family to approve of.'

'How will I know what they shall approve,' Marilar murmured, English grammar going haywire, 'unless you ask them?' Her huge eyes, soft as dark pansies, searched his face to be sure that he was serious. '*Will* you ask them one day, Richard, when we're older...though perhaps not *very* much older?'

Tears trickled down her face but her mouth

was smiling because she was certain of the answer now. He forgot all Holly had ever told him about the way Spanish maidens were reared, and enfolded her in his arms. He kissed her mouth, her wet cheeks and closed eyes, and then her mouth again, while time stood still and the world contained only themselves.

'I love you more than I know how to say,' he said at last, 'and I shall love you until I die. That being so, perhaps it doesn't matter very much if we have to wait a year or two.'

She nodded, then shook her head, not sure which was required.

'Shall I be allowed to write...perhaps come and see you?'

Marilar stared at his face, grave and blue-eyed and different from the faces of the men she saw at home. A year or even two without him...it seemed an unbearably long time, and men were known to be less patient, less enduringly faithful than women; they couldn't help it—nature had arranged it so. She pushed aside the pain of that thought to smile at him.

'Come for the Feria, Richard...Seville is so beautiful then.'

'I will if I can, my blessed one, but I'm having to sit Finals then, I'll come straight afterwards. It's you I shall want to see, not Aunt Phee's aristocratic horses.'

They suddenly held each other close again, because parting was so near and it was going to be so hard; but there was a little while yet to wander hand in hand, remembering the moment when time had stopped for them on a platform at Oxford's railway station.

Three days later she stood there on a different platform, with Holly and Luis, waiting for the London train. She smiled at Phoebe and Hugo, but heard nothing of the conversation. One hand was in her pocket again, clutching a small jeweller's box that had been delivered from Oxford the day before. It contained Richard's parting gift—a fire-opal set in filigree and mounted on a little gold ring.

Luis was a kind, attentive companion. He took great care of them and did his best to keep them entertained; but it was surface chatter—his heart and mind were full of the knowledge that they were journeying towards Spain. Marilar knew that it didn't matter if *she* scarcely listened to what he said. But when he left them to smoke a cigarette in the corridor, she heard Holly's faint sigh of relief...*two* of them hadn't been listening, it seemed. Self-discipline could be relaxed for a moment because Luis wasn't there. Holly's face was desolately sad, and when they looked at one another there was no need to say anything at all.

23

The rainy autumn season was over in Seville—the air was soft, the sky a delicate, December blue. There were late roses blooming in the sheltered courtyard, and in the middle of the little pool a laughing, bronze boy still rode his dolphin. Everything seemed as it had been when Phoebe's telegram had arrived two years before...Holly thought she might never have gone away at all. But the impression wasn't true. A second glance at Asunción's face revealed the anxieties that had had to be endured. And now, happy though she was to see Luis again, his mother was sharply aware that the future was still perilous.

When they were alone, Holly smiled at her friend. 'I'm sorry...England *didn't* cure him of the conviction that he must help to save the world; in fact, he infected my cousins with the same disease. Instead of scarcely knowing one "-ism" from another, they're now almost as concerned as Luis to fight the good fight against the enemies of the people!'

'The people are not winning,' Asunción said with sadness. 'My father would have been thrown into prison—at *his* age—for some rash speech if Juan hadn't fought to get the sentence changed.' She lifted her hands in a little gesture of despair, then hid them again because they trembled. 'We live in terrible times, *tesoro,* and I *ought* to wish that you had all stayed safely in England.'

Holly wrapped her in a warm hug, then smoothed the dark hair that she had disarranged. It was beautiful still, but meshed with silver now. 'Well, I'm *very* glad we came. I expect Juan is still often away, and you've been alone too much.'

'Everything is bearable when he's here,'

Asunción admitted, then hesitated before deciding what to say next. 'He didn't want you to come back with Luis. Don't be hurt if he says so, *cara*...he means it for your own good.'

Asunción's pleading face and the charming room around them receded, and were blotted out. 'I hope you never come back to Spain'—the words hammered in her brain, and she was back on the river-path at home, staring at Juan Rodriguez. She hadn't seen him since then, and some certain knowledge buried deep in her mind said that there would have been more chance of happiness and peace of mind if she never saw him again. *Luis* was the reason she was there, but the truth was that one casual, contemptuous kiss from someone else had had the power to sear itself on her memory.

'Holly dearest...are you not well?' Asunción's voice, sharp with anxiety, made itself heard. She ducked her head until the threat of faintness passed, and then straightened up again.

'I'm quite all right—a bit light-headed, I expect, at being back in Spain.' She clutched desperately at something else to talk about. 'Aunt Phee and Hugo send their love. I was to tell you that they both adored your daughter!'

'Something has happened to her in England—something happy *and* sad, I think. If it's too important to tell me about I shall know it's very important indeed.' Asunción considered Holly's pale face, and wondered what else had happened in England.

'I hoped that you'd come back *married* to

393

Luis,' she said a little wistfully. 'I should love you for a daughter.'

With a huge effort of will Holly smiled a little but shook her head.

'It's for Luis to choose the time; he must be allowed to finish his work first if he wants to.' Her smile grew steadier. 'It doesn't matter...I *feel* like a daughter, anyway.'

Asunción touched her cheek with gentle fingers. 'Still pale, *tesoro*...no more talking until you're rested after that long journey. Juan is in Madrid on some government business as usual; I'm never sure when I shall see him, but I pray to God every day that when he comes home he hasn't been made a judge.'

Holly had no need to be told what she meant. Judges were obliged to pass sentences on the guilty and, like politicians, they made popular targets for anyone with vengeance in mind. This was Spain, where people now had their own cruel ways of settling vendettas. She closed her eyes for a moment against a world that seemed to be disintegrating into chaos, and clung to the one certain fact she knew.

'I'm going to start work at the pottery again—on Monday. I shall need something to do.'

Asunción nodded, kissed her, and went away repeating that she was to stay quiet until the sound of train wheels no longer reverberated in her head. Holly started to unpack, discovered that she was emptying a drawer of underclothes she'd just put away, and sat down abruptly with her face in her hands.

For a moment or two panic paralysed her entire body; then, like a climber on some perilously exposed peak, she began to inch her way back towards safety. She was in Spain where she was happy to belong, with work to do and people who needed her. Soon she and Luis would marry, and they would find a home of their own—near Asunción and Marilar, of course, but not shared with another man whose too-powerful magnetic field sent other people's frailer little compasses out of true. Juan Rodriguez didn't want her in Spain at all, but once away from his mother's house it needn't matter to her or Luis *what* an autocratic relative decided was best for the rest of them.

More or less calm at last, Holly finished her unpacking and went downstairs to assure Asunción that she was herself again—restored, and happy to be home in Spain.

She went back to the Harkness Pottery after the weekend and found that nothing had changed there in her absence. Her old friends still worked clay as their ancestors had done before them; still fired the lovely, traditional shapes of Andalucían earthenware, and painted it in the colours they saw around them. She returned contentedly to the house after her first morning's work, let herself into the courtyard, and found that Juan was not only back but locked in the middle of a violent quarrel with Luis.

It seemed that her heart stopped beating for a moment; in fact her whole body was clamped in stillness. Only her eyes continued to function, informing her that he looked drawn and tired, and formidably angry. Against his height and breadth, Luis appeared rapier-thin and younger than the gap of five years that separated them. Danger was alive in the air between them but she could only stand there, waiting for something that would release her from paralysis. Luis provided it by coming to stand beside her, with his arm round her shoulders. But she could feel him trembling and knew that they were needing to support each other.

'In a moment, *tesoro*, my dear brother may remember that it's time he greeted you. He hasn't exactly made *me*, welcome, but perhaps he'll do better for you.' Luis spoke in Spanish, the language they'd been arguing in, and she automatically followed suit.

'*Buenos días, Juan...Cómo está usted?*' The formal phrase was automatic too, because—a few shattering moments on an English river-bank apart—formal was what they'd always been with each other.

He answered in English, and the switch was deliberate she thought, to deny that she was included in their Spanish family life.

'I'm unable to welcome you,' he said in a deep, rough voice, 'because I've just been belabouring my brother for bringing you back at all.' He saw Luis about to speak and turned to him, giving him no chance. 'You'd like to remind me that this is my mother's house and that *she* will welcome whom she pleases. Quite right, she will; but I'll remind *you* of something. For as long as you are here you'll do *nothing* to endanger her or Marilar. If you've come back simply to live in Spain, this is your refuge, and I can find work for you. If you've come to rejoin what remains of your friends, you must live elsewhere—or I shall turn you over to the authorities.'

His face might have been carved out of stone; only his eyes seemed alive, and full of pain. Holly felt Luis flinch, and then stand erect about to issue some challenge of his own. But Asunción's maid, Caterina, swung open a door and bustled out into the courtyard.

'*Teléfono, Don Luis*—muy *urgente, ha dicho el señor.*'

Holly expected him to ignore the summons but, after a muttered sound she couldn't identify, he kissed her hand to apologize for leaving her there with Juan, and followed Caterina into the house. She was on the point of deciding to do the same thing herself when Juan spoke again.

'Don't go, please. Listen to what I have to say.'

'You've made yourself very clear already... brutally clear.' Her voice didn't shake—she was dimly aware of being surprised about that. And if she strolled casually enough to one of the courtyard chairs, he wouldn't know that she needed it to lean against.

'We live in brutal times,' Juan said harshly. 'Let me tell *you* what my brother already knows. You shouldn't be here, because sooner or later—probably sooner—this country is going to explode into civil war. Luis's friends now live entirely outside the law, and they provoke their enemies to do the same. Before long *everyone* will be forced to choose one side or the other.'

'You blame only Luis's side,' Holly protested passionately. 'Their methods may be cruel, but life has *made* them cruel. What about the millions of peasants who have to work themselves into the dust to stop their families from starving? What about the punishment meted out by General Franco's Army of Africa when the miners finally rose? Unspeakable things were done at the *invitation* of the Government by Moors to Spanish women who had *no* stick of dynamite in their hands.'

In the silence that followed she listened to the tinkle of the fountain in the little pool—and remembered that the magical use of water was something else the Moors long ago had brought to Spain. She felt angry no longer, only unutterably sad because *nothing* was simple about the situation they were trapped in. Then, because she had to, she looked at Juan and saw the same sadness in *his* face.

'I know what Luis and his friends want, Holly—a new heaven and a new earth; but those things won't come by way of murder and arson and the raping of nuns. Ends *never* justify the means, and the tragedy is that there are people on the other side, like my friend José Antonio, who know it too.' Heart-break made Juan's voice ragged, and suddenly she wanted more than she had wanted anything else in life to enfold him in her arms, and to offer *him* what comfort she could. Her hands were even stretched out towards him before she remembered that *this* Rodriguez didn't need her. She let them fall to her sides, and without speaking again walked away from him up the stone staircase to the verandah above.

Juan stayed there, apparently staring at the fountain; seeing instead a slender, valiant girl, whose beauty threatened to destroy him because she belonged now, as she had always done, to Luis.

Marilar's first letter from England seemed not unexpected—a response, Asunción thought, to her daughter's messages of gratitude very properly sent to Hindleford. But a third envelope to arrive, addressed in the same decided hand, was *not* what might have been expected and she was bound to comment on it.

'A faithful correspondent, *tesoro*,' she observed, passing over the letter, and only her tone of voice indicated that it was time some explanation was offered. Flushed but not flustered, Marilar did her best.

'It's Señora Fanshawe's son, Richard, Mama. He was...was very kind to me. Well, they *all* were but...Richard taught me to ride a bicycle. It was necessary to learn, you see, because in Oxford everybody uses one.' She smiled seraphically, confident of having spoken nothing but the truth, then went away to read her letter in private. Having considered this and other important facts, Asunción took the problem to her friend.

'*Cara*, since I seem to be excluded from

Marilar's confidence—for the second time—I need *you* to tell me about your cousin Richard. What kind of young man is he, apart from being well able to ride bicycles, I understand?'

Holly's vivid grin appeared because Asunción made it sound like a circus accomplishment, but she understood the anxiety behind the question and tried to answer it.

'Richard is Helena's twin brother, not very like her except that he has fairish hair and blue eyes. He's reading Modern Languages at Oxford and hopes to join our foreign service...he's also large and kind and *very* dependable.' But the trouble in Asunción's eyes didn't lessen and made her add, 'I'm afraid you still don't like the friendship.'

'I don't like it at all. From the little Juan has allowed himself to say of Lydia, she is a woman different from Phoebe, with no compassion for *any* of the Rodriguez family. I understand the reason of course, but this Richard is her son. Even if he means no unkindness, what does he understand of a girl like Marilar brought up to give her heart only to one man? What does he know of our Spanish ways?'

'I can't swear to what he understands or knows,' Holly was obliged to admit. 'All I'm sure of is that he'd never knowingly hurt her. He's Uncle Francis's son too and, though not at all saintly, *very* like his father in most things.'

Asunción was not to be comforted. 'I am to be content with that, knowing nothing of the Reverend Fanshawe? Very well, my dear, we must wait and see whether the letters Marilar lives for continue to arrive. But that visit to England changed my daughter; she would have talked to me before.'

'You spoke of another exclusion,' Holly suggested gently, although she thought she already knew what it was.

'Marilar informs me that she is going to be useful—like *you*. There is a small orphanage attached to the convent where she went to school. She is going every day to help wash and feed the babies. It is all arranged, apparently.' Asunción's hurt was unmistakable. Holly would have eased it if she could, but not at the cost of betraying Marilar.

'She loves children, and she needs something to do—the orphanage seems a lovely idea to me. I didn't *encourage* her to be so independent, by the way, but I'm quite sure Juan thinks I did.'

Asunción gave a little nod. It was true that he had blamed Holly and England, in that order, for influencing a girl who, had once wanted only to be docile. It was a typically male attitude, irritating because *he* had been the one to urge her to send Marilar to Hindleford. He was altogether difficult nowadays, but Asunción easily forgave him. He lived under the kind of pressure that made a man short-tempered and unreasonable. The hours he worked were killingly long, and all the time he trod a tightrope between one side and the other—defending anyone he thought innocent, no matter what cause they fought for.

'He's very abrupt with you,' she said sadly. 'I'm sorry, my dear—it's only because he's overworked, and always anxious.'

Holly smiled cheerfully, spoke cheerfully; she was becoming quite practised at it now. 'No, it's *mostly* because he'd rather I wasn't here at all. I try not to be when he's around...I scuttle round corners and hide in cupboards, so as not to risk the great man's displeasure!'

Asunción's face lightened at last. 'Bad one, I know now when you're teasing me. But you have all the love a girl could need from Luis, from Marilar, and me—does that make up for Juan?'

Holly caught her breath on a sudden stab of pain and kept nodding her head, like an automaton that hadn't been told when to stop. 'You'd make up for anything,' she said, and then firmly moved the conversation away from a subject that was becoming unbearable.

'Luis is being *very* good, don't you think—working so hard, and doing nothing to alarm us?'

Asunción could thankfully agree. It was true he continued to visit Manolo, but surely a young man was permitted to pay some attention to his grandfather? She knew that all around them the situation went from bad to worse, but Juan was careful not to discuss politics in front of them, and seemed to have wrung a promise from his brother not to do so either. Within her home, therefore, life seemed comparatively peaceful; they could prepare for the festival of Christmas pretending that the Prince of Peace might be allowed to work his miracle.

It wasn't to be expected, of course, that

Luis would go with them to Midnight Mass on Christmas Eve. But as Holly set out with Asunción and Marilar, they were suddenly joined by Juan. It was a jolt under her heart because she hadn't known he was even back in the house after one of his regular visits to Madrid. He had an apartment there, and Marilar had informed her delicately that he didn't live in it alone. 'A lady's voice sometimes answers when Mama telephones,' she'd said. 'I'm very glad...he'd be lonely there otherwise.' Holly doubted this about him. Dependence on other people would never be his weakness; but it was easy enough to believe that if he wanted women's company he need never go short of it.

She pushed the thought away as they joined the stream of people making for the Cathedral and, once inside, was caught up as always in the unfolding of the story, timeless and joyful. The soft blaze of a thousand candles lit the great, dark spaces of the church, and for the moment her only grief was that Luis had cut himself off from so much heart-easing beauty. They walked home afterwards scarcely talking, still wrapped in the mystery of the mass. It was already another Christmas Day.

She got ready for bed, donned nightgown and slippers, brushed her hair again, and admitted to herself that she had never been more wide awake. She opened her long window on to the verandah and crept down the outer staircase. The moon hadn't yet risen, but the purple-blackness of the sky was sewn with stars...larger and brighter than the ones at home.

A little night-light burned beside Marilar's crib in the corner of the courtyard, and in its soft glow Wise Men, shepherds, and animals grouped themselves around the manger. She knelt down to look at the little figures...a great deal seemed to have happened to her since she'd fashioned them, and it was harder now than it had been in the Cathedral to cling to the belief that individual joy or sadness mattered very little in the scheme of things.

'You're homesick...is that why you're out here, instead of sleeping as all good children are supposed to be?' Juan's voice, pitched low to disturb no-one else, sounded almost beside her. She turned to find him there, still fully dressed, a presence felt rather than seen in the dimness of the night. He held out his hand to pull her to her feet, then released it immediately, and in order to move away from him she went to stand by the pool. The bronze boy no longer piped sparkling drops of music into it, but a star lay reflected in the still water.

'The crib animals reminded me of childhood,' she murmured. 'I always longed to know whether it was true that all the animals in fields and stables knelt down at midnight to celebrate the moment when Christ was born. Each year I thought I'd find out one way or the other, and each year I never did, because the story seemed too beautiful to need proving.'

'You didn't answer my question...homesick, or not?'

'Perhaps, a little, for my uncle's church, which is even older than Seville's Cathedral.

404

It's minute by comparison, with nothing much in it of *worldly* value; just centuries of prayer.' Juan had come to stand beside her and she couldn't move away again; it was necessary now to turn and face him. 'But remembering such things doesn't make me unhappy; I feel that I belong *here* now.'

'I don't know why you should want to,' Juan said slowly. 'Spain is nobody's idea of a perfect place to live in.'

Holly gave the little shrug learned from Asunción. 'Aunt Phee repeated for me something her father once said to *her*—everyone has two countries; their own and one other. *His* second country was Spain, and it happens to be mine as well.'

'If you're reminding me that Henry Maynard was *my* father as well, let me tell you that he was wrong about me. One country is enough for me, and I've chosen poor, troubled Spain, *not* England.'

She smiled in the faint starlight—a slender figure in a white gown delicately frilled at neck and wrists like a choirboy's surplice; only she was nothing on God's earth in the least like a choirboy, standing there in front of him. He could smell the soft flower perfume she used, almost feel the warmth of her body beneath the thin robe.

'Your father forgot something,' she said, almost as if he hadn't spoken. 'Love is yet another country that most of us have to wander into, with no maps or signposts to stop us getting lost. But perhaps you'll deny that, too? There'll be no getting lost for Don Juan Rodriguez, because he's a man who always knows exactly where he is!' Her low voice, half-mocking, half-hoarse, stopped abruptly because her throat was clogged with tears. There was a silence that Juan broke at last.

'He knows he's going to bed, and so are you, before...before the rest of this household is entirely roused.' His hands gripped her shoulders, biting through the thin cotton material. 'Remember that *I'm* not the man who shares your third country, Señorita, and then excuse me if *I* don't see you to your bedroom door!'

She pulled herself away from him, feeling scorched by the contemptuous flame of anger in his voice, and humiliated by her own stupidity. Her gown was thin to the point of transparency, and he could scarcely be blamed for thinking that she'd come down deliberately in the hope of flaunting herself in front of her fiancé's brother. It was already Christmas Day, but instead of feeling joyful and serene she must somehow climb the staircase without weeping her pain out loud.

When it was time to go downstairs again she was pale but calm enough to be able to lay claim to a peaceful night. Luis suggested a walk alone after breakfast and she was glad to go, but it was unfortunate that his first question should almost echo Juan's in the courtyard.

'You're very quiet, *querida*...homesick for Hindleford?'

She stopped to lean on the parapet of the

406

river quietly flowing beside them down to the Atlantic...not a bit like the backwater at home, nothing to make tears prick her eyelids with the ache of memories.

'Not homesick, just wishing we could get on with our lives.' She turned towards him and he saw the anguish in her face. 'Luis...*couldn't* we get married and be somewhere on our own? I *know* Spain's important, but so are *we.*'

He wrapped his arms about her because sobs suddenly began to rack her body; other people walked along the path and stared at them before moving on, but neither of them noticed.

'My dearest one, listen to me,' he said when she was calm at last. 'I love you more than life, and one of these days soon we shall be happy together. Only a little more patience is needed and then I shan't have to pretend that I'm invisible whenever a soldier or a Guardia Civil appears. This wretched government is collapsing, and a new election is inevitable. For *once* we shall be ready for it—all of us, anarchists, socialists, communists, at *last* united to fight as the Popular Front for the people of Spain. We shall win this time—even our wretched opponents know that. No more hiding then, and no more fear, *tesoro.*'

His eyes shone with such tender joy that it seemed possible to take heart and hope again. Together they *would* find contentment, and all her night-time terrors would die away. At last she managed to smile. 'All right...this time we're going to win—so why can't we get married now?'

'Because, dear heart, I have to be *certain* that nothing is going to go wrong. Until then, I want to know that you're still one of his Britannic Majesty's subjects with a passport to prove it, not the wife of a known anarchist.' His face was grave now, and she was aware that it had changed in recent months—boyish no longer, it was a man's face, resolute and disciplined.

'Nothing will go wrong, my dear,' she said quietly, 'and I won't badger you again. But it *is* Christmas Day, and perhaps even a famous anarchist may be allowed to forget Mikhail Bakunin and welcome Jesus Christ.'

24

Luis was proved right in his prediction. The Spanish government finally fell early in the new year of 1936, and the elections on which his hopes were pinned were bound to follow. The campaigns conducted by both sides were memorable for their general viciousness, but largely overlooked by an English press absorbed by events at home. Less than a year after the rejoicing at his Silver Jubilee, King George V was dead. The throne would now be occupied by a young and dashing bachelor monarch—to be called the eighth Edward.

'The old King's funeral was a great State occasion attended by the crowned heads of Europe. Spain, having now no king, sent a general instead as its official representative, and Hugo Taverner's attention lingered on the photograph of General Francisco Franco y Bahamonde, marching in the funeral procession. Hugo had followed the General's career with interest, and was privately of the opinion that it might yet prove a good deal more remarkable still, but it was an opinion he was careful not to air in front of Phoebe. She was anxious enough about Holly as it was. Still, he found himself obliged to answer the questions that Richard Fanshawe plied him with whenever he was at home. Hugo teased him one day about his new-found interest in Spain, but kindly offered him an excuse for it as well.

'Memories of our firebrand Luis, or a budding diplomat's thirst for knowledge about a fascinating country he might find himself working in one day?'

'Scarcely even budding, when I don't even know if the FO will have me,' Richard pointed out. His fair skin flushed a little; but even if it hadn't given him away, he had no taste for subterfuge. 'My interest in Spain is entirely personal, Uncle Hu...Josh and I both want to know what's happening for Luis's sake, but there's much more to it than that for me. My girl is there, you see. Holly is too, of course, but it's Luis's privilege to make sure that *she* doesn't come to any harm.'

Hugo filled his pipe with the laborious technique a one-handed man was obliged to use while he pondered what to say.

'Silly to pretend I don't know who you're

409

talking about,' he answered at last. 'Asunción's daughter is lovely and sweet and good, and it would have been clear to anyone not totally blind that the two of you were very taken with each other.'

Richard didn't protest at this dreadfully prosaic way of describing it—even the best of men, as Hugo Taverner was, probably forgot in middle age what it was like to be young.

'She's *everything* that's lovely, but you don't congratulate me on finding such a pearl. Why not, I wonder?' His steady blue gaze was fastened on Hugo's face, requiring an honest answer.

'Because you're an ambitious young man with his way to make. For years after you get started you'll be a very small fish in a big pool, sent from one God-forsaken posting to another while you learn your *métier*. Marilar is the product of a sheltered Spanish upbringing, which fits her to be the perfect wife and mother in a sheltered household of her own. Try as I will, I can't see your future life matching what *she* needs in any way.' He tried to read the expression on his nephew's face and failed. 'I'm sorry, but you did ask,' he added apologetically.

Richard's tight-lipped mouth relaxed into a pleasant smile. 'So I did...a mistake, I'm afraid! Well, now tell me something else. Is Luis right in thinking his side is going to win the election? His letters to Josh sound as if the bright proletarian day is about to dawn at last.'

'His side, being united for once, will almost certainly win, I think,' Hugo said slowly, 'but God knows what that actually means for Spain. The Right has temporarily sunk its differences, too—Monarchists, Carlists, Catholics, José Antonio's Falange, all marching under the National Front banner. I find it very ominous that *both* sides describe themselves in such military terms, as if a war had started already.'

Richard took so long to answer that Hugo finally prompted him. 'You haven't told me what you think.'

He was rewarded with a singularly sweet smile. 'I think that as soon as Finals are over I ought to nip down to Seville and get Marilar out of that ghastly place! She'll be much better off here.' Richard nodded to confirm what he'd just said, and then loped away, leaving Hugo to return thoughtfully to his own fireside.

Phoebe put down her husband's copy of *The Times* as he came into the room, wondering why she continued to read its pessimistic leading articles. Anyone with a grain of common sense would refuse to be told that Mussolini was carving out a new Roman Empire by hurling down bombs on Abyssinian tribesmen still only armed with spears; anyone who wanted to stay calm about the prospects of future peace in Europe would ignore Germany's reoccupation of the Rhineland, expressly forbidden under the terms of the Treaty of Versailles. She smiled resolutely at Hugo, and tried to sound cheerful.

'*The Times* predicts a win for the Popular Front in Spain. For Luis's sake we ought to

411

be pleased, but I can't help feeling sorry for Juan's friend as well. In the end I don't know *what* I want, except for none of them to come to any harm.'

'It's as good a wish as any, sweetheart,' her husband agreed, and decided not to report for the moment what it was that Richard wanted.

Within a week or two the election results were known. The Popular Front *had* won, and the Spanish Republic was now certain to veer sharply left again—the turn of the long-suffering people had come.

It had come with a vengeance, as the following weeks of spring made clear. Political prisoners were freed or brought back from exile; hungry peasants in Andalusia were encouraged to help themselves to the estates of absentee landlords; anyone who wanted to show true revolutionary zeal in Catalonia could simply set fire to a hated church, or pillory the people who still dared attend it. It *was* the glorious new dawn...or the end of a unique country—whichever way you chose to look at it, Hugo confessed to his brother-in-law.

'I think I know which way *you* look at it,' Francis Fanshawe observed, '...old evils merely replaced by others no less dreadful?'

'Yes, and I can prove it to you. I asked Juan to keep in touch with me, and his letter this morning reports that his friend José Antonio—charming and patriotic though he is—has been thrown into prison on some entirely trumped-up charge of treason against the Republic.'

'Well, dreadful indeed,' Francis agreed sadly, 'but success always goes to people's heads to begin with. Surely things will settle down in time?'

'There won't *be* time,' Hugo almost shouted, 'because the generals are waiting in the wings! Luis's anarchist friends see themselves as the saviours of the Spanish people, but the Army knows that it has a mission to save *Spain;* it doesn't give a damn about the people.'

Francis looked miserable. 'I keep remembering something I now wish I had forgotten. Years ago, long before you married Phoebe, she came across an old journal upstairs, written by a Harkness ancestor who had not only travelled through Spain just after the Napoleonic Wars, but survived to tell his tale. Even *then* he predicted some cataclysmic upheaval. Unfortunately the journal had to be returned to Burslem because I could think of no moral justification for keeping it here!' Francis smiled ruefully at the memory and then returned to the matter in hand. 'It's strange how closely we seem to have been associated since then with that poor, wretched country.'

'All thanks to our late friend, Lydia would say,' Hugo pointed out. 'But for Henry Maynard, Holly would be living safely here, Helena would be contentedly married to Ned Harkness, and Richard and Josh would have remained in happy ignorance of the murderous fascination of Spanish politics!'

'There are moments when I rather agree with my wife,' Francis was obliged to admit. 'Certainly if it hadn't been for Henry we should never have met Luis Rodriguez, and I'm bound to consider *him* a charming but dangerous young man.'

Hugo wished he could have said that the memory of even the most charming young man would fade in time, but the truth was that Luis's impact on them looked like being stubbornly persistent.

'Luis is an atheist, you know,' Francis commented with a faint sigh. 'To that extent he's not the husband I could have wished for Holly. And even if it brands me as a dyed-in-the-wool Victorian, there was quite a lot to be said for being able to *tell* your children whom they were to marry.'

Hugo grinned at the wistful suggestion and diverted his brother-in-law's attention to a happier subject. 'Are they all going to be on Magdalen Bridge as usual for the May Morning singing?'

'Some back-sliding *was* creeping in, I fear. Helena seemed to think she was past the age of putting flowers in her hair and rising early enough to listen to unearthly dawn music. But Kate didn't argue for once; she merely *looked* so heartbroken that Helena changed her mind. I sometimes wonder how we managed to beget our youngest daughter; she puts me more in mind of old Joshua Harkness—all intelligence and will-power!'

Reluctant or not, Helena *was* part of the May

414

morning crowd, but afterwards she left Josh to entertain Rosalind and Kate to breakfast while she and Richard sat by the river and munched the bacon sandwiches cajoled out of Mrs Briggs at home.

'Like old times,' Helena murmured, 'just you and me, friends again. I thought you were never going to forgive me for splitting up with Ned.'

Richard turned to look at her, but she was watching the water eddying past—little sparkling rings that spread, and broke, and then reformed again. Her face had lost its roundness recently and its quick gaiety. He thought they were *both* feeling too old for the revels they had just attended.

'I understand better now,' he said through a mouthful of sandwich, 'having a few problems of my own.'

She smiled at him then, and looked herself again. 'Marilar being one of them?'

He nodded but didn't answer, and after a moment she went on. 'Ma won't be very pleased, but Father *will* be. She's just the sort of girl he wishes *we* all were—biddable and sweet and gentle.'

'I haven't spoken about her to anyone but Hugo. He tried not to say it in so many words, but the message was clear: I'd do much better to travel alone for years to come, and even when I *can* afford a wife, Marilar would hate the wandering life I'd have to offer her.' Richard stared at his sister frowningly. 'That's the bit that worries me *most*—perhaps she's too young and inexperienced to understand that she'd have

415

only me to rely on for happiness.'

Helena thought it so very likely to be true that she found it difficult to produce a comment even halfway encouraging. 'Could you wait and see what happens? If it's all written in the stars that you and she belong together, it'll come about eventually...no need to plunge in *now*, boots and all?'

He didn't answer, but threw bread to a passing swan that had suddenly decided to loiter instead. 'What about you, twin? Are you going to go on toiling away at Brightwell for Holly, and eating your heart out for our Spanish friend?'

She smiled again, but the amusement in her face was rueful and against herself. 'Quite a come-down for the all-conquering Miss Fanshawe! It's not quite as bad as it sounds, though. I actually enjoy the business side of the pottery and—with dear Uncle Hu's help—I flatter myself I make a good job of it. I doubt if I shall ever forget Luis, but that mad fever in the blood has gone—it's like slowly recovering from some unforeseen illness.' She lifted her hands in a little gesture that said the subject of Luis Rodriguez was closed. 'Ned appears occasionally at Brightwell but only, I think, because he promised Holly he would. It's strange how eager we all are not to disappoint her! He's very sweet to Annie...and dauntingly polite to me.' Her voice trembled for an instant and then recovered itself. 'Ma's right, you know—we should all have done better *not* knowing the Rodriguez family.'

She scrambled to her feet and smiled at her brother. 'It's time I pedalled home and left you to do some work. I didn't want to come this morning, but now I'm glad we were all here together.'

'Because it might be for the last time?... because life seems less certain than it did, and the future not very certain at all?'

'Something like that,' Helena agreed, and climbed onto her bicycle.

Richard returned to his studies, and all too soon afterwards, it seemed, he was one of the hundreds of candidates, looking unnaturally neat in regulation sub fusc, gown, and white bow tie, heading daily towards Examination Schools in the High. But when the ordeal was over at last Josh, already set free, was waiting for him outside.

'There are various celebrations going on,' Josh said. 'Which shall we give our custom to?'

'None for me, thanks—I'm off to Trinity to clear the stuff out of my room and say a few goodbyes.'

'If that's how you feel it must have been a swine of a paper today—but the last one always is. Don't take it to heart, dear soul—you'll have done all right. We could take a punt out if you don't feel like mingling with the crowd.' Josh looked serious for a moment. 'It's odd—I used to think I couldn't wait for this day to come; now that it has, I hate the thought of leaving Oxford.'

'I know; I'd feel the same except that I'm in a hurry to get down to Spain. According to

Hugo, things are coming to the boil there, so I haven't got much time.'

'You might have mentioned it before,' said Josh. His thin, bright face frowned over some mental calculation. 'Say we leave next Tuesday? That gives me the weekend to nip up to Staffordshire and explain that I've got a little continental bear-leading to do.' He grinned at the expression on his friend's face. 'You'll *need* me to keep an eye on you, and in any case it's time I found out what Luis is up to.'

25

In the Harkness Pottery in Seville, Holly was painting a last swirl of vine-leaves on a wide earthenware bowl when the message was brought—a Señor Harkness was in the yard outside, asking for her. She put down her brush and hurried outside, expecting to see Ned. But waiting for her was the only one of the Harkness children to have inherited Cecily's dark hair and bright, pale blue eyes.

'*Josh*...how in the world do *you* come to be here, all alone?' she asked when she was released from his hug.

'I'm not alone—Richard's out in the street. We weren't sure if anyone without the magic name of Harkness would be let inside.'

'It's a pottery, not a prison.' She beckoned to a young apprentice and asked him to find

418

an English *señor* waiting outside, and smiled as they reappeared—the boy's head scarcely reaching her large cousin's shoulder.

'All right, *not* a prison, but a pretty ramshackle place,' said Josh, glancing around. 'Why doesn't Ned get it cleaned up a bit?'

'Because this is what a working pottery looks like.' She smiled wholeheartedly at them both, suddenly aware that she might as easily have burst into tears. Too much was happening in Spain that was ugly and frightening—her English cousins seemed, just by being there, to lessen the little tremors of apprehension that nowadays always kept her company.

'It's lovely to see you both,' she admitted, 'but if you're celebrating the end of student life, Spain isn't exactly a carefree place to come to at the moment.'

'That's been made clear,' Richard said bluntly. 'In fact it seems a God-awful country if you want my honest opinion. Holly...I didn't write to say we were coming...couldn't make up my mind whether it would be better to or not. What should I do now—write to Señora Rodriguez, asking permission to call? I've come to see Marilar, of course, but I want to behave according to *costumbre,* not make things more difficult for her.'

Holly gave the matter some thought, being well aware that things were certain to be difficult anyway. 'Perhaps it would be better if I talked first to Asunción,' she said at last, 'Marilar, too, if she doesn't know you're here. I expect you'll be invited to dinner, but a formal note will be brought round. Where are you staying—at the Alfonso Xlll?'

'Far above our touch, by the look of it. Hugo recommended the Hosteriá Internacional as being a pension we could afford!'

Holly nodded, then smiled again. 'Dinner will be late, I should remind you—Asunción's invitation will probably say come at 9p.m.! You'll have plenty of time before that to climb the Giralda Tower—very Moorish—and to make a start on the Cathedral—immensely Gothic! As for me, I'd better go and finish what I was doing—*hasta luego, señores!*' She gave them a little bow and walked away—a slender, graceful figure perfectly at home in her surroundings, and yet inescapably different from the people she worked among. Richard thought she looked tired and fine-drawn, but it wasn't to be wondered at in present-day Seville.

'What now?' Josh asked when they were outside the gate again.

'Find something to eat to keep body and soul together until nightfall and then go and look at that bloody tower, I suppose,' said Richard. 'We've told the Guardia Civil we're here as tourists.'

Holly went back to the studio and made herself finish the painting of her bowl, but for once concentration had to be forced. Afterwards, walking home, she couldn't help feeling that it would have been better for Richard not to have come at all. His letters had become less frequent, but she'd been careful to explain to Marilar that it was only to be expected—the

420

culmination of three long years of study was bound to absorb his time. Marilar had merely nodded and looked thoughtful. She was less confiding now than in the past, and Holly was left to assume that, although she missed her English sweetheart, she was content for the time being with her home and family and new-found work at the orphanage.

When Holly got back to the house and explained that her English cousins were in Seville, Asunción stared at her suddenly white-faced daughter, but said that of course they must be invited to dinner. Marilar immediately disappeared to her own room, and didn't emerge until the guests arrived. She blushed when Richard circumspectly bowed over her hand, but her mother's salon was not Blenheim Park and he understood the gentle formality of her welcome. Luis was delighted to be reunited with his Oxford friends, Asunción was a charming hostess, and Marilar eventually grew calm again. A dinner-party that might have been rather difficult, Holly thought, was going well after all, and dear Richard was behaving with just the right degree of shy attentiveness towards Asunción.

Whilst the others reminisced about past summer days at Hindleford, the Señora eventually broached the subject of her daughter with a smiling directness that he hadn't expected.

'Marilar enjoyed her stay in England so much that she found it hard to settle down again to Spanish ways. Now that she *is* content, it would be unkind to distress her merely to prove to *yourself* that holiday friendships don't last!'

'It would be exceedingly cruel,' Richard agreed steadily. Faint colour had run up under his fair skin, but his eyes—blue as his grandfather's had been, Asunción remembered—held hers.

'I'm sure for myself what will last, Señora, but I can't speak for Marilar. I would ask her to marry me now if I could, but it will be a year or two before I'm able to support her. I love her dearly, but I can't think of a single reason why you or she should think I'm worth waiting for that long.'

Asunción remembered what Holly had said about him, and thought that it was true. He would take Marilar far away, but he would make her a good husband; and unacknowledged but helping his cause was Asunción's sense of a certain rightness about it all. How strange but satisfying it would be if he and her daughter should complete what she had begun herself with Henry Maynard.

'I can't speak for Marilar either,' she said quietly. 'It still isn't customary here for unmarried girls to be left alone with male friends, or even with their *novios,* but such a rule would be unreasonable in your case. You are welcome to come here and talk to her.'

Richard thanked her gravely, knowing that she was being kinder than she need have been, and that Holly must have done her best for him. He sent her a grateful glance across the table, and saw her smile. She still looked tired, and he noticed that she took no part in Luis's excited account of what had been happening since the

422

elections. He thought he wasn't mistaken in sensing that she struggled to conceal some sadness of her own, but then Marilar raised her eyes to look at him and he could think only of her again.

The following day he and Josh tried to behave like tourists, pretending to ignore an atmosphere of suppressed but threatening tension in the city. It was hard, now, to visualize Seville dressed in the fairy-tale glitter of the Feria, and they were both relieved when it was time to reappear at the house in Santa Cruz. Richard was also getting impatient to see Marilar alone, but immediately it was clear that their pre-arranged plans were going to go awry.

Instead of being left alone with her while the others sipped ice-cold *manzanilla* in the evening freshness of the courtyard, Richard found himself being introduced to a man who seemed almost, but not quite, a stranger. His face was grey with exhaustion and strain, scarcely explained by the fact that he'd just returned from a visit to Madrid. Still, there was no mistaking the fact that *he* was in charge of Asunción's household. His family's eyes were on *him*, and even Josh—no respecter of authority as a rule—was looking serious for once. Only Holly seemed not to be looking at Juan Rodriguez, but Richard remembered Aunt Phee saying that the two of them didn't get on. She'd also explained sadly that her half-brother preferred to ignore his link with England, and it didn't seem to suggest that he'd welcome an English fiancé for his young sister. Richard had got to this depressing point in his reflections when Juan addressed him directly.

'Forgive me if I'm blunt, Señor, but the truth is that you should never have come to Spain. I think you ought to leave immediately.'

Asunción gave a little gasp, but it was Luis who jumped to his feet in a flame of anger.

'Richard and Josh are my *friends*, they're Holly's cousins, and Marilar and I were *welcomed* by them in England! Take no notice,' he insisted, turning to them; 'my brother is quite *mad.*'

Watching intently, aware that something much more than this man's known dislike of England and the English was involved, Richard waited for what Juan would say next.

'I'm sorry...no discourtesy was intended, but there's no time to pick and choose my words. What I'm about to tell you must remain a confidence between us; otherwise we shall *all* be in danger of being shot as conspirators. Three days ago a Spanish journalist in London was instructed to charter an English aeroplane to fly to Las Palmas in the Canaries, where General Franco has been to all intents and purposes exiled by this government. The aeroplane will take him to Morocco, to resume command of the Army of Africa. *That* will be the signal for the Army on the mainland to rise against the Republic—the beginning, in other words, of an atrocious, full-scale civil war.'

Even knowing Luis as well as he did, only *his* reaction took Richard slightly by surprise. No look of white-faced horror...instead, an

424

expression of pure, exalted happiness trans-figured him.

'At *last*...oh God, at last we can fight and win. Do you hear, my dearest love?' Holly nodded her head, but couldn't smile at him. Luis stared at her for a moment, then went to kneel beside his mother's chair. 'It was bound to happen, *cara,*' he said more gently. 'Nothing could *stop* it happening, but this is the best way of all, with the generals having to be responsible for starting it.'

'There is *no* "best way" of starting a war,' Asunción cried out. 'Can't you understand that?' Holly took hold of her trembling hands for comfort, but Juan gave Luis no chance to argue.

'The blame for starting it scarcely concerns us,' he said wearily, 'and God knows who will win.' Then, for the first time, he stared at Holly's chalk-white face. 'I was going to ask *you* to take Marilar to England, trusting that Phoebe and Hugo Taverner would be kind enough to make her welcome. Now, it seems that your cousins can be responsible for you both. So, contrary to my first remark, I'm deeply thankful to see them here.' He turned to smile at them, and Richard caught a startling glimpse then of his charm, as well as the rock-like strength of his personality.

'Aunt Phee would ask nothing better than to see Marilar back,' Holly said quietly. 'You too, my dear,' she murmured to Luis, 'if only *you* will leave as well?'

He came to stand in front of her, holding

her hands. 'Don't ask me, *amore;* if there is to be a war, I *must* be in it on the side of the people.' She had known the answer before he spoke...thought that she had *always* known that this was how matters would end.

Juan now looked at Richard. 'Could you leave tomorrow? The rising is timed for July the eighteenth, and you must be safely in Portugal by then, not still trying to cross Spain itself into France. There is a Madrid to Lisbon train calling at Badajoz that you ought to be able to catch.'

Richard leaned forward in his chair, large hands gripped together between his knees, because he still hadn't said a word alone to Marilar, and it was an agonizing thing to have to bare his heart so publicly. But first, he spoke to Juan.

'This wasn't an accidental visit. I came *hoping* to take Marilar away from Spain—Holly, too, if she would come—and I'll get them safely to England, *somehow.* But you and the Señora must understand that I should want to *keep* Marilar there as my future wife.' Then he smiled at *her,* with loving tenderness. 'Sweetheart, I tried to explain before...it will be a longish wait before I can ask you to marry me...but there'll be nothing for you to worry about, because I love you more than I can say.'

Holly looked from his eloquent eyes to the white-faced girl who stared at him. But she seemed to find nothing to say, and finally it was Juan who spoke again.

'Well, then, the four of you will leave

tomorrow? I'll have the rail tickets delivered to your pension. The connecting train leaves Seville at noon.'

There was silence in the courtyard, broken at last by Marilar's voice, sounding harsh and unlike itself. 'No...*no!* Mama, tell Richard, please...I *can't...won't*...go. I must stay here. I don't want to go to England.'

Asunción's face was full of pain, but she shook her head gently. '*Tesoro,* Juan knows best. If he says you and Holly must leave...'

'Holly can go...I shall stay. Not even Juan can *make* me go if I don't want to.'

Richard looked at his cousin and thought he knew what was coming next. 'I must stay too,' Holly said, as calmly as she could. 'My place is here, with Luis, and his family.' She tried to smile at Richard. 'Forgive us for seeming ungrateful—it was so...so lovely of you to come.'

He nodded at her, but walked across the courtyard to Marilar. 'Tell me what it is you're saying no to—leaving your family at a terrible time, or coming to England as the girl I'm going to marry?'

'B-both,' Marilar sobbed. 'I can't live always in strange places, and have to send my children away to be loved by other women, and have none of the life I am used to.' Her huge eyes pleaded with him to understand. 'I am *española,* Richard...not like...like Holly, or other English girls.'

He wondered what would have happened if he'd seen her alone...had a chance to hold her

427

in his arms and remind her of a few moments in a deserted park when they'd been sure of loving each other. Perhaps she'd have been persuaded to come with him, only to spend the rest of her life regretting it. Feeling cold and very sad, he faced Juan again.

'It seems that I misunderstood,' he said stiffly. 'I still want to take the girls to England, but Marilar will be free to come back as soon as she can.' He doubted if she even heard what he said. An intoxicating mixture of excitement, fear and regret was mingling with the novel discovery that she could decide her future for herself.

'You can't make me go...nor can Juan. I shall say goodbye now, Richard.' She turned away from him, stopped, and withdrew his little fire-opal ring from her pocket. 'It was wrong of me to accept this.' Then, with tears beginning to trickle down her face, she ran into the house.

Richard picked up the ring and stared at it for a moment; then he crossed to where Asunción was standing.

'*Adiós Señora*. Josh and I won't trouble you by staying for dinner after all...thank you for...for receiving us so kindly.' He gave Holly a quick hug, and tried to smile at her. 'Sorry I couldn't persuade *you*, at least, love; Aunt Phee worries about you here.'

'Wait...I'll come with you now, *amigos*,' Luis said quickly. 'You'll need to find somewhere to eat.' He kissed his mother's cheek, and a moment later the heavy door closed behind the three of them. Juan gave a tired shrug,

428

announced to Asunción that he would eat a sandwich while he worked in his room, and left her and Holly staring at one another.

'My dear, you should have gone with them,' Asunción said slowly. '*Our* world is coming to an end.' Her control broke at last, and tears began to brim over her eyelids. Holly stretched out her arms, and the two of them stood there, holding each other while the evening shadows gathering around them seemed to foretell the dreadful darkness ahead.

They made a pretence afterwards of eating supper, but it was a relief when they could agree that the day had come to an end, and say goodnight. Luis hadn't returned, but Holly knew that he was capable of keeping Richard and Josh out of their beds for hours while he persuaded them of the rightness of the people's cause. The servants had retired, and the house was quiet, but someone else, like herself, wasn't sleeping. She could see a square of light thrown on the stone flags downstairs from an unshuttered window. It was like a magnet, dragging her down the outer staircase and along the verandah to a room where Juan still sat at his desk; but his dark head was pillowed on his arms—a strong man for the moment beaten by exhaustion, or despair.

She made a little sound and he lifted his head at once—angered, she thought, that she should have observed him in a moment of weakness.

'I'm sorry...you're very tired,' she said quietly, 'and I shouldn't be here.'

'Quite right,' he muttered without looking at

her. 'If *you'd* agreed to leave with your cousin, Marilar might have been persuaded to go as well.' He looked up suddenly and she saw the pain and utter weariness in his face. 'Don't tell me again that your place is with Luis—I'm well aware that you think that's where you belong.'

And in *that* moment she knew the truth at last—knew finally where she *did* belong. The words were almost torn from her mouth that her true place was beside a different man. But he had no need of her, and she was long promised to Luis. Then Juan spoke again and she struggled to make sense of what he said above the raging turmoil of her mind.

'We don't need you here at all. Haven't you realized yet that Luis will enlist immediately on the Republican side, and go to an obscenely evil war as joyfully as if it's some kind of crusade?'

'Yes, I do realize that,' Holly said with difficulty. 'It's partly why I insisted on staying. You're often away yourself—I have the right to try to help Asunción by being here. And you're wrong about Marilar. She *wouldn't* have agreed to leave. She's had time to realize what marrying Richard would mean—it seems too frightening a life for her, always separated from everything that she holds dear here.'

Juan dragged himself to his feet and came to stand in front of her. 'For God's sake understand what it will *mean* to stay. Whichever side wins, there'll be nothing to choose between Franco's Moors and Republican militiamen on a mindless rampage. A soldier drunk on victory

430

isn't going to stop enjoying himself because you beg him to remember that you're the proud owner of a British passport. You'd be just another girl to be used and flung aside so that his friends could take *their* turn.'

Holly pushed the dark wings of hair away from her face with trembling hands. It was a gesture he'd often seen her make...graceful, as all her movements were, as much a part of her as the perfume of her skin, and her rare, transfiguring smile.

'Marilar has made her choice, I've made mine,' she said at last. 'But whatever happens I'm not your responsibility. You can go back to Madrid with a clear conscience...in fact, with no conscience at all. You *did* once warn me not to come back to Spain.' Her eyes met his, challenging him not to remember the only time he'd kissed her. She knew that he did remember—because for this little moment of time there was nothing left in the world but their shared knowledge of what would happen if he touched her again. But his hands were clamped to the edge of the desk in front of him, and at last she gave a little sigh, admitting defeat. She spoke again, with a thread of voice he scarcely heard.

'Did you mean what you just said...about not wanting me here? It's important for me to know.'

'Yes...I meant it,' he finally got out. 'Now leave, please...I've still work to do.'

She'd got as far as the door when his hoarse voice made her spin round again.

431

'Holly, remember this is Spain, not law-abiding England. Rather than see you at the mercy of a pack of drunken soldiers, I'd shoot you myself.'

The faintest of smiles touched her pale mouth. 'Dear Juan...*most* comforting!' Then she walked out of the room.

26

She was very tired but sleep was fitful, broken by the sound of voices and of slamming doors that she wasn't sure whether she dreamed or not. Sunlit images of the past haunted her brain, mocking the choice she'd made. Soon Richard and Josh would be leaving a country about to be plunged in nightmare; she might have gone too, but the only service she could render Luis was not to desert him or Asunción.

With that accepted once and for all, she went downstairs early in search of him. He always rose before the rest of the house was astir; she would find him in the courtyard as usual, drinking coffee and reading the journals that he'd been out for. But this morning only Caterina was there, washing the stone floor. She smiled at Holly, wiped wet hands on her apron, and fumbled in her pocket for a letter. 'From Don Luis, Señorita,' she said handing it over.

Holly read it sitting by the pool, while the

clove carnations Caterina had watered scented the air.

My dearest girl,
   The moment comes to say goodbye. *I* have work to do, *you* must go back to England—for once Juan is right.
   By the time you read this I shall be on my way to Barcelona to join the Anarchist Militia...the great adventure finally begins. Justice says that we *must* win, but nothing is certain even now; we've been so often cheated before.
   You've tried very hard, my dear one, to pretend to believe what I believe, but in your heart I don't think you managed it—another way of saying, perhaps, that this isn't your country after all...these aren't your people.
   So now I must let you go, even though I shall love you until the day I die. Go back to England; I now break the promises we made. But pray for Spain sometimes to that God you *do* believe in.

Adiós,
Luis

Holly read it a second time, with her breath caught on something that was half sob, half hysterical choke of laughter. The letter was so entirely typical of Luis Rodriguez—tenderness and truth and heroic panache all mixed together to weave the spell that made him enchanting to anyone he met. She was certain that he

433

loved her but, like the Muslim women obliged to walk behind while their menfolk rode on donkeys, she would always have come behind the visions in his head. He would ride blithely to a cruel, sordid war and she would fear for him and always love him. But she was conscious of a huge sense of reprieve as well because her promise to him had become nearly unbearable.

Caterina had disappeared and the sun was beginning to lay a bar of light across the courtyard floor, but it was still too early to disturb Asunción. Holly stayed where she was, back turned to Juan's window. She wouldn't think of him there, lost at last in the sleep of exhaustion...wouldn't remember Luis, or Richard sadly getting ready to leave without Marilar. It was enough to breathe in the scent of the carnations, feel the freshness of the morning air on her skin, and know that all they could do was wait for some cataclysmic event to happen.

She opened her eyes, sensing that she was no longer alone. Marilar was there, still dressed in the white cotton robe that made her seem like a child again. But she looked tired, as if her night had been sleepless too, and for once the expression on her face was sullen.

'You're up early, *cara*,' Holly said quietly. 'Couldn't you sleep, either?'

Marilar shrugged the question aside. 'I saw you out here—that's why I came down.'

Because she was lonely...afraid...regretted sending Richard away? For the first time in their friendship Holly was unable to read her face, and uncertain how much to say.

'I'm afraid we shan't see Luis for a little while. He left me a note to say that he's going to Barcelona.'

'I know...I was in Mama's room last night when he came to say goodbye. He said he's not betrothed to you any more, so there's no reason for you not to go back to England.'

It wasn't tiredness or fear making her sound cold. A girl who'd never been anything but gentle and affectionate had suddenly crossed some invisible boundary into open hostility. 'He said your engagement had been a mistake,' Marilar went on in the same hard, stranger's voice, 'but I could have told *him* that.'

Feeling faintly sick, Holly had the certainty that it would be a mistake to ask her what she meant; and yet the jeer couldn't be left lying there between them, unattended to.

'*How* could you have told him?'

Marilar's pale face was flushed now. 'Because you're in love with Juan...I've known that about you ever since we came back to Spain.'

Holly couldn't stop herself turning round. All this nightmare conversation needed now was the discovery that Juan was at his open window, listening to it. But Marilar had still more information to share.

'He's not there—he left after Luis did, during the night. His friend, José Antonio, has been moved to a prison in Alicante. Juan has gone to see him, but he promised Mama he'd come straight back before...before the f-fighting

435

begins.' Her voice suddenly wavered and broke, and Holly understood. The girl in front of her had been transformed by fear, and who on earth could blame her?

'If he promised, he'll keep his word,' she said gently. 'He'll be here when we need him.' It gave away her own reliance on him as well, but that scarcely mattered now; the only important thing was to help Marilar. 'Cara, are you sure you don't want to go to England? It isn't too late to...'

'No...you go,' Marilar cried. 'We don't want you here any more. Juan belongs here with us...he doesn't want you, or any of his English relatives. I saw you, last night, creeping down to his room, to persuade him into something that will hurt us.'

Her wild, sobbing voice rose to a climax that echoed round the courtyard and brought Asunción running from her bedroom. Marilar was wrapped in her mother's arms and comforted, and gradually the storm of weeping subsided. At last Asunción led her back inside the house, but Holly stayed where she was, sick and shivering, and unable to decide what to do next.

She was still crouched there when Asunción returned, followed by Caterina with a tray of coffee. The Señora's hands sketched a little gesture of apology but she was calm and unsmiling.

'Drink, my dear...then we'll talk. Marilar is asleep, now.'

Holly did as she was told, grateful for the hot,

436

fragrant coffee, but she was the first to speak.

'I upset her by suggesting that there was still time to change her mind about going to England.'

Asunción gave a little shrug. 'I'm sorry for your cousin, but the life he is bound to lead would never have made Marilar happy.'

The coffee wasn't helping after all; Holly began to have the impression that nothing that was happening was real, when even Asunción had withdrawn her loving friendship.

'She could have gone to England without marrying my cousin, and she is very frightened of staying here,' she said bluntly.

'Of course—how can she *not* be frightened? But her worse fear is to be separated from her family and her home.'

Holly accepted it as true and went on to something that was more difficult to talk about. 'I believe Luis told you before he left that *our* engagement is over?'

It was Asunción's turn to nod, almost carelessly. 'I'm sorry if that hurts, my dear, but in the long run you will be thankful. Young men who dream dreams and see visions, as my son does, make *very* bad husbands.'

Holly stared at the bronze boy in the middle of the pool, thinking how strange it was that he would still be laughing on the dolphin's back, belonging here, when it seemed now that she did not. She took a deep breath but tried to speak lightly. 'Juan has told me several times that I'm not needed here, Luis's farewell note said go home, and even Marilar just now seemed afraid that I'd remind Juan of his English relatives, regardless of the fact that he scarcely spares them a thought! I wanted to *help* by staying, but now *you* must tell me the truth: should I go or stay?'

'There is nothing for you to stay *for*, now,' Asunción said steadily. 'Once we knew your betrothal to Luis was over I promised Juan not to let your cousins leave without you. A message has gone to the *hostería*, asking them to collect you on their way to the station.'

Holly glanced automatically at her watch again—noon was still nearly four hours away; all the time she needed to pack the pieces of her Spanish life neatly away and close the box. The time for feeling pain would come afterwards. She looked at Asunción but, like Marilar, this dearly-loved friend had become a stranger. The *coup de grâce* had been delivered if not brutally, at least with a finality there was no arguing with. She put down her coffee-cup carefully, and stood up.

'Then I must go and start packing. Perhaps you'll say goodbye to Marilar for me when she wakes up; I don't think I need leave any message for Juan.' Then she walked away and climbed the staircase to her own room.

Asunción watched her go, wondering how much more pain would have to be endured before the gods above decided they'd all suffered enough. She hid her face in her hands to shut out the bright, mocking sun, but by the time Carlos reported that the taxi-cab of the English *señores* was at the door she was calm

438

and composed again.

Holly said an affectionate goodbye to the servants, then thanked Asunción in the formal Spanish phrases she might have used to a stranger. Marilar didn't appear at all, but that was something to be thankful for.

'I'm *very* glad you changed your mind,' Richard said, as they drove away from the house.

'It was changed for me,' Holly said distinctly. 'If you want to know the truth, I feel like an under-housemaid being dismissed, for not quite coming up to scratch!' She smiled as she spoke, but he almost winced at the anguish in her huge, dark eyes. Defeated for the moment by so much pain, he said nothing else but merely sat holding her hand until they reached the station.

There, as in the rest of the city, an undercurrent of menacing excitement seemed to run through the crowds like an electric current. What no-one knew for certain, all anticipated. Seville scarcely dared breathe, and the miasma of some unknown but violent threat hung in the hot summer air.

'I suppose Josh is struggling to buy the tickets,' Holly said, suddenly aware that there was no sign of him waiting for them. 'Hadn't I better go and help him?'

'We don't need tickets—a minion came round with them this morning. He'd been given money to bring, too, in case we should have to hang about in Lisbon, waiting for a ship. Thinks of everything, does Juan Rodriguez.'

'He wants to make sure we leave.' Holly

blinked away the tears that suddenly stung her eyes, and pretended to be still looking round for Josh.

'It's just the two of us travelling,' Richard said abruptly. 'I tried to argue Josh out of it but he decided to stay in Spain.'

Holly stared at her cousin's troubled face and guessed the rest of it. 'Luis's "great adventure", I suppose?'

'Yes, he reckoned that Burslem could wait a little longer—said he'd got a lifetime of it ahead of him. I told him he was being a bloody fool, but Luis pipes a tune he can't resist dancing to.'

Anger was added now to the ferment of the day's emotions. Holly felt weak for a moment with the longing to rage against Josh's foolhardiness and Luis's blind disregard of everything except the vision he could dazzle other people with. But no amount of rage would do a particle of good.

'Cecily Harkness won't be pleased,' she said quietly instead, and saw Richard suddenly grin at the heroic understatement.

'She'll skin me alive for bringing him to Spain at all, but I'll meet that problem when I come to it. There are one or two others to be going on with! Pray God, for a start, that this train leaves more or less on time, or we shall miss the connection at Badajoz.'

It left half an hour late, but Holly assured him that, by Spanish standards, that meant it was almost early. Their journey lay northwards, into the desolate province of Extremadura, but

Richard stared out of the window without seeing it, thinking about the girl who'd had courage enough to stay behind but not enough to come with him. She hadn't even troubled to wave them goodbye. He frowned over that, and remembered Holly's bitter little comment when she got into the taxi. Now that there was time to think about it, he realized that he still didn't know why he wasn't making the journey home alone.

'I've had to come without Marilar,' he said suddenly, 'but it's worse for you. Luis has gone to war, and you actually seemed to *like* living here.'

She registered the disbelief in his voice, and had to admit that the sun-bleached wastes they were travelling through bore little resemblance to the usual travel posters of Spain. 'This is not lush Andalusia, and you can see why so many of the *conquistadores* who hacked their way through Mexico and Peru came from here—there wasn't much to stay at home for.'

'But you didn't want to leave, all the same,' Richard pointed out, 'and it wasn't only because of Luis. What changed things overnight?'

'Luis decided that our engagement was a mistake, and I discovered that the rest of the Rodriguez family didn't want me there either, for a variety of reasons.' Holly tried to smile, unaware that her eyes looked stricken still. 'I hadn't quite believed in the streak of cruelty that's said to hide behind the Spaniard's charm—until this morning! The people here are like their landscape and their

441

climate—very extreme. They don't deal in our gentle compromises, which is why they're about to tear themselves to pieces in a civil war.'

She turned to stare out of the window and Richard returned to his own anxious train of thought. July the eighteenth, Juan had said. It was still two days away—more than time to see them safely into Portugal as long as nothing went awry with the generals' plans. He'd read enough of Spain's past hundred years of history to bank on no such miracle, but in what Holly admitted was an extraordinary country anything was possible—perhaps even an efficiently-conducted uprising for the first time.

It happened, more or less, while they waited in Lisbon for the sherry boat the British Consul had promised them was due from Sanlucar. Suddenly the Portuguese newspapers were full of the drama that had begun to unfold in the rest of the peninsula. General Franco *had,* as Juan had foretold, been flown to Morocco; the Army there had risen against the Republic, followed by the rebel generals on the mainland. Seville was one of the cities almost immediately in their hands, defended for the Government only by workers starved of weapons.

Holly struggled to decipher the Portuguese reports and make sense of them.

'The fighting has all been on the other bank of the river...away from the district of Santa Cruz. But Luis was right to leave when he did—he wouldn't have been allowed to escape once the Nationalists were in charge.'

442

'Do you hate Juan for being on the opposing side? I suppose you must do,' Richard said gently.

He saw but didn't understand the sad smile that touched Holly's mouth and then faded again. 'No, I don't hate him, and he doesn't even *have* a side. He marches down the middle, on some lonely, quixotically foolish campaign of his own, to make Spain reasonable! He's not quite Spanish enough, you see.'

'But you seem to understand him very well,' Richard suggested with a hint of surprise.

'Perhaps because *I'm* not entirely English!' Holly's voice caught on a sob, but she went back to the task of translating the Portuguese newspaper. The uprising hadn't been successful enough; and nor had the Government stamped it out strongly enough. The stalemate meant a long and bitter war.

The Consul hadn't misled them. The sherry boat, homeward-bound, arrived and accepted them as passengers. A fortnight after leaving Seville they were steaming into Southampton Water, to find that England looked green and peaceful and almost ridiculously normal. They might have dreamed the recent feverish weeks except for Hugo's calm explanation when he brought them home from Oxford of what was happening in Spain.

'It's reasonably clear now,' he said. 'Imagine a line drawn diagonally across the country, north-east to south-west; roughly speaking, the Nationalists are on one side of it, the

Republicans on the other. Madrid is still in the hands of the Government, but only just.'

Richard waited until Holly had been kissed and taken indoors by Phoebe before he asked the question that was troubling him now. 'Have you heard from Staffordshire? Josh swore he'd telephone his parents, or write; but if he didn't I shall have to go and see them, I'm afraid.'

'No need...they know already. Cecily not unnaturally blames *us*...for the Rodriguez connection! She's not what you'd call a temperate woman at the best of times, so God help us if anything happens to Josh.' Hugo ran his hand through untidy hair that was sprinkled with silver now, but the gesture itself was familiar to Richard from childhood. 'I didn't want to say so in front of Phoebe and Holly but it's going to be a long, bloody and atrocious war. Russia is aiding its anarchist and communist friends; Germany and Italy are meddling for the Nationalists. What better opportunity will *they* have to train their troops and airmen for a quite different war?'

'Is *that* how you see it?' Richard asked sombrely, '...the fascists hell-bent on taking over Europe?' He saw Hugo nod, and gave a little shrug. 'Why bother with the Foreign Office, then? I might as well join the Territorials now, and be done with it.'

'Nonsense—*one* lunatic firebrand in the family is quite enough! Diplomacy may save our bacon yet, and in any case you've got a career to think of.' Hugo's rare smile warmed his face. 'We're *very* obliged to you for bringing Holly back...I

444

was afraid she'd sit tight and refuse to leave.'

'So was I—in fact she was certainly minded to, but things changed,' Richard said vaguely. 'She'll explain them to you.' He frowned over a confession of his own, and finally offered it. 'Marilar refused to leave her family even when Juan wanted her to come here. Diplomatic life makes no appeal, apparently.' His troubled blue eyes met Hugo's. 'You were right about that.'

'I'm sorry,' his uncle said gently, and left the subject there.

Inside the house Phoebe smiled contentedly at Holly. 'Dearest, I couldn't possibly wish a war on anyone, but still it's lovely to have you home again—I thought we'd lost you for good to Spain.'

'You haven't lost me at all, Aunt Phee; I've been jilted! Luis has finally decided that Destiny requires him to think only of Spain, not of me.' She sounded cheerful...even smiled as she spoke...but Phoebe sensed behind the bright façade loneliness and an aching sense of rejection.

'Then Destiny is uncommonly stupid,' she said with a rare flash of anger. 'But I'm more inclined to blame Luis. He should have had time to learn by now that happiness only comes from being loved by other people.'

'He's not much concerned with happiness,' Holly pointed out gently. '*Don't* blame him, please. He *does* truly love us all, even his brother, I think; but Spain comes first. And some of it's my fault, anyway. He didn't come first with me. I never meant him to know but

445

perhaps he guessed.' She kissed Phoebe by way of apologizing for the fact that it was all that she meant to say on the subject, and then began to talk about Brightwell.

'I can't take over the running of it again—Helena's been doing that far too well; but there are all sorts of experiments I want to make, with Arnold's help.'

Phoebe hesitated, then offered a warning. 'Don't be surprised if Helena decides to leave now that you're back. She's very unhappy I think, and would be thankful to get away from Hindleford. Lydia and Francis pretend not to notice that she's either feverishly bright or wrapped in despair, but I feel very sorry for her.'

Holly reflected for a moment, before making up her mind. 'I'll leave going over until tomorrow, I think; otherwise it looks as if I can't wait to interfere again.'

Had she known that Ned Harkness would be there, making one of his regular calls at the pottery, she might have decided to go after all, but as it was he found only Arnold hard at work as usual, and Annie mowing the lawn in a garden that Brian Starkie would scarcely have recognized. Ned stopped to listen to her for a moment, because she sang as she walked up and down in a contralto voice that seemed too deep and rich for her thin body. When Brian had found her in the covered market in Oxford she'd been reduced to singing for the coins that passers-by sometimes threw into her hat; now she sang because her frail brother was safe, and

446

she was content, making the garden beautiful in memory of their dead friend. Ned recognized in Annie Blake someone as nearly selfless as a woman could be; it didn't once occur to him that she treasured his visits, and smiled a little more joyously when he was there.

'Morning, Annie...Helena not about today?'

'A puncture on the way over this morning. She's taken her bicycle down to the forge to get it mended.'

'I'll go and meet her, then. I can't stay long, and there's an exhibition we need to talk about.'

'Helena says Holly's due home...did you know?'

Ned nodded, suddenly looking grim. 'She and Richard couldn't persuade my brother not to stay behind, unfortunately. I wish they'd never gone to that benighted country.' He waved and walked away, in no danger of not finding Helena. There wasn't enough of Brightwell for that—just a cluster of cottages straggling along the curving street, a farm or two, the smithy, and a village pub where the men gathered to play darts on winter evenings when darkness drove them indoors. Horse power was still used locally for ploughing, and pulling the heavy farm wagons, but more and more deliveries came by van, the village people went to Oxford on the weekly motor-bus, and few of the local gentry now made their calls in horse-drawn traps or carriages. Ned saw changes each time he came to Hindleford, and regretted them all with the fervour of a city man who deeply loved the countryside.

Helena was sitting outside the forge, sunlight gleaming on her bright head, a cigarette between her fingers sending a thread of smoke into the still air. She didn't see him come, being deep in some reflection of her own; so for once there was no flashing smile and no cool, impersonal greeting that denied the slightest memory of a time when they'd been necessary to one another. Helena Fanshawe didn't need *anyone* nowadays, it seemed. Young men and old watched when she went by, eager to make her smile. Ned had seen her charm play over them often enough until she grew tired of the game and walked away. It hurt, now, to remember a small, warm creature who had used to wind her arms round his neck and insist breathily that she would love him 'for ever n'*ever*'.

'Annie said you'd be here,' he murmured now, dropping down on the bench beside her.

She let the stub of her cigarette fall, ground it out with the heel of her shoe, and scuffed dusty earth over the remains.

'Caught smoking in public *again!* What a pity Mrs Drew-Smythe didn't drive by—it would've been something else to mention after Church on Sunday. "My dear Mrs Fanshawe, don't you think Helena is becoming just a *trifle* too naughtily modern? Ancilla does admire her so, but I should *hate* for my little girl to be led astray."! She's a smiling, venomous cow of a woman, is Mrs Drew-Smythe, and one of these days I shall have to tell her that not even Circe, Delilah, and all the sirens combined could make Ancilla remotely strayable.' Helena

448

turned to glance at Ned, certain that he would be frowning and remote because, as usual, she had embarked on the sort of conversation he enjoyed least. 'You didn't follow me down here to talk about our charming neighbour,' she said abruptly.

'No...I wanted to know what you're sending to the London exhibition. It will be an important one for Arnold.'

Helena gave a little shrug. 'Don't ask *me*—Holly is probably back at Hindleford by now; I imagine *she'll* want to decide. In fact she'll have to, because I shan't be here...it doesn't need two of us to run the pottery, and I'm getting rather bored with it.' A bright smile lifted the corners of her mouth but left her eyes unamused. 'In fact I'm rather bored altogether...with Hindleford, and vicarage life as well.'

'No flicker of excitement provided by any of your numerous admirers?' Ned enquired coolly.

She seemed to pass them under brief review. 'None at all, I'm sorry to admit...I think I shall accept your Aunt Jane's kind invitation to go and stay with her in London. Even dyed-in-the-wool communists must have their lighter moments, wouldn't you say?'

She jumped up as the smith's huge son appeared, wheeling the mended bicycle. Her real smile this time sent him blinking happily back inside the forge, but Helena's intention of riding away was thwarted by Ned making a sudden grab at the machine. They confronted one another over the handle-bars—tall, stern-faced man and a girl who for once wasn't entirely mistress of the situation.

'We'll *both* walk; I'll push,' he said briefly. 'What's the attraction of going to Aunt Jane and her mad husband—because your Spanish friend was impressed by them? Isn't it enough that Josh seems ready to dance to any murderous tune Luis pipes...must *you* still be besotted with him too?'

She could have laughed or wept, even done both together, so far was Ned from guessing the truth, instead she shouted at him.

'Josh is nearly twenty-one, not a child who can only do what other people tell him. Why not blame Richard for leaving him there, or Aunt Phee for inviting Luis to England at all? If Josh wants to share in what's happening and be a soldier for the poor people of Spain, why *shouldn't* he?'

'Because he's *English*, God-dammit,' roared Ned, '...because he's got a job waiting for him at home...and because this isn't some childish game—he stands a bloody good chance of getting himself killed...for Spain's poor people, of course.'

She was halted on the brink of another tirade by the roughness in his voice that said he loved young Josh, and wanted nothing more than to go out to Spain and drag him home. Her anger suddenly became sad despair for the tangle they all seemed to have made of their lives.

'Josh *chose* to make his own mistake, if that's what it is,' she said quietly. 'We're

450

all responsible for ourselves now, with no-one else to blame if we come unstuck.' She kicked a pebble underfoot, straight and true as he'd taught her to years and years ago. The memory of it was a knife-twist in her heart that drove her into another blunder. 'You'll be able to forget about the pottery now...quite a bore it must have been for *you*, having to keep turning up at Brightwell.'

'I don't find life nearly as boring as you seem to,' Ned commented, 'and I shall certainly continue to visit the pottery.'

'To see Holly, of course.' There'd been a time when he'd come very close to being in love with her. Helena knew that as surely as she knew Holly had loved *him* before Luis danced his way into her heart. Annie Blake was in love with him too, of course, but Helena had been able to observe *her* with pity—Ned treated her with the pleasant courtesy a man offered a woman he had no interest in. It was infinitely more difficult to be generous about her cousin and she was still struggling with herself when Ned spoke again.

'Holly's going to be one of this country's master-potters, if she isn't that already. We want her associated with *us*, not with Wedgwood, or Doulton.'

'Spoken like a true Harkness! Old Joshua would be proud of you,' Helena said brightly.

'And now, spoken like just *me*, I'd say she's feeling very anxious about Luis and his family. You *could* think of staying here to be helpful, instead of racketing about in London with a lot

451

of shady communists.'

'So I could...but you know me—never one to let duty stand in the way of pleasure!' Her lovely mouth smiled, but when she made the mistake of looking at him he saw that her eyes were brilliant with unshed tears.

'I sometimes think I don't know you at all,' he said slowly.

'I'm not sure I know myself—the brilliant and beautiful Miss Fanshawe has come a trifle unstuck if you want to know the truth.' She went on looking at him because she suddenly couldn't do anything else; even if he understood now what he hadn't known before, it didn't seem to matter any more.

Ned stared at her, and spoke at last in a voice she didn't recognize. 'I thought it was still Luis you were unhappy about. Was I wrong...oh Christ, Helena, was I *wrong?*' He flung the bicycle in the hedge so that he could grasp her shoulders instead, forcing her to look at him.

'I love Holly dearly but I don't want to marry her. I put up with the girls my mother invites to Burslem, but even less do I want any of them. Only *you* will do for me, but I'll go lonely all my days rather than be a poor substitute for Luis Rodriguez...now say something, please.'

Tears beaded her lashes but she managed to look at him. 'The truth is shaming. I thought you *were* falling in love with Holly when she was studying in Oxford...I couldn't blame you, she's so...so special, and all I seemed to have was a pretty face. I pretended that I'd asked

452

you to look after her—that's why she rushed off to Spain. Then when Luis arrived here, adoring her too, it became a sort of challenge to get him to notice me. My father said once that Luis was dangerous, and that added spice to the game—I only realized that was all it was when it was too late and I'd mucked up you and me.'

Ned's hands tightened on her painfully, biting through the thin cotton of her summer dress. 'Helena love, there can't be any mistake this time. All I can offer you is a life with me in Staffordshire, and perhaps it still won't be enough. It's...it's actually rather a good place when you g-get used to it, and everyone w-would adore you for sure, but...'

She reached up suddenly to end the stammered speech by kissing his mouth, and then was swept into Ned's arms. There were long months of heartache to be made up for...the day was suddenly golden, and the world could wait while they explored their own private heaven. The leaping desire beneath his tenderness promised that life in Staffordshire would be quite exciting enough, and Helena was flushed and trembling when he finally raised his head to look at her and discovered a ring of interested observers as well—the baker and his bored-looking horse, Constable Wilmot sitting on a bicycle, three small boys, and one large Boxer dog.

'The entertainment's over,' Ned said breathlessly, '...you can all move along now!'

The immortal constabular phrase produced howls of merriment all round, but Constable Wilmot managed to have the last word.

'Mornin', Miss Helena...I reckon the Reverend's goin' to be busy pretty soon!'

The party dispersed regretfully and Ned even remembered to retrieve the bicycle.

'I've got witnesses, dear love,' he said as they walked on towards the pottery. 'You can't back out now.'

Helena smiled with a radiance that made him catch his breath. 'No backing out, but no fuss and delay either, please, Ned. We'll just get married as soon as the "Revrend" can fit us in.'

They had to stop again, of course, along the way, but even so the pottery was reached eventually. Annie registered the entrancement in their faces and quietly blew out her own little candle of hope. Arnold, not given to noticing very much outside the magic world of the studio, remarked after they'd gone that happiness gave off a kind of warmth for other people.

'It's about time those two were happy,' his sister agreed in an expressionless voice. 'They've been meant for each other long enough.'

'It means we shan't have Helena here in future. I'm glad for *her*, Annie, but shall we be able to manage on our own, do you think?'

His thin face was suddenly anxious again— security something he still hadn't learned to take for granted.

Annie smiled at him. 'We don't have to manage, love, and you don't need to worry...Holly's coming back.'

454

It was a beautiful day for a wedding, calm and golden as only October can be. The churchyard path was carpeted with fallen leaves, and a drift of smoke from Will Tomkins's hidden bonfire scented the air. As much of Hindleford as could cram itself into the church was there, but the ceremony was the simple one Helena had wanted. Kate approved of it too, relieved to be spared bridesmaid duties. Rosalind didn't care—with no Josh there to see her looking beautiful, nothing mattered any more.

Given away by Richard because her father was waiting to conduct the service, the bride went to meet Ned in a dress of cream chiffon, and a wide-brimmed straw hat that Holly had trimmed with the garden's last, late roses. Francis watched her walk towards him and felt easy at last about this most difficult of his children. It was sad to see Ned flanked only by James on a day when Josh should have been there as well, but at least Cecily Harkness had finally agreed to come. Phoebe gave George the credit for persuading her to change her mind, but looking at her long-suffering expression during the wedding-breakfast at the Rectory, Holly thought that her husband might have spared himself the trouble. She shared her opinion with Hugo, then flushed a little, feeling suddenly ashamed.

'Sorry! *Not* a very generous thing to say. Of course Lady Harkness must be feeling heartsick about Josh. I don't think weddings agree with me, Uncle Hu.'

He smiled at her reassuringly. 'It doesn't show...you look very festive and beautiful, and perhaps *you're* entitled to be feeling a little heartsick, too.'

Holly stared at him, knowing that he would understand anything she needed to say. 'I feel altogether unreal, as a matter of fact—half of me sitting in this room rejoicing in Helena and Ned's happiness, the rest of heart and mind not *here* at all. It's a very unsettling condition!'

'My dear, I expect Luis and Josh are perfectly safe and sound. Imagination always deals in the heroic, but ask any old soldier what he remembers most and he'll tell you the discomfort and boredom of service life!'

Holly smiled because Hugo wanted her to, and thought she meant not to say that it wasn't an unknown battlefield that imagination clung to. Then the next moment she gave herself away.

'Juan loves Asunción and Marilar very dearly and knows that their safety depends on him. I should think that would make him a *little* bit careful, wouldn't you?' Holly's eyes, huge and dark with anxiety, were fixed on Hugo. 'Otherwise he'd be inclined to try to rescue anyone the Nationalists *most* want to dispose of...it's the sort of thing he *would* do.' Her voice trembled slightly, then recovered itself. 'I'm afraid Uncle Francis is beginning to look desperate—it's time you went and helped him with Cecily Harkness.'

Hugo accepted the suggestion, aware that she'd said all she could trust herself to say on the subject of Juan Rodriguez. But he walked away wondering for how much of the time she'd been promised to Luis she'd known that, heart and soul, she loved his brother.

Helena and Ned took the bold new step of flying in an aeroplane to Paris for their honeymoon. It gave Hindleford something to marvel at for several days, but then the village settled down again. Richard bought his first bowler hat and, though the lowliest of the Foreign Secretary's minions in Whitehall, returned home occasionally wrapped in an aura of affairs of State and the higher diplomacy.

For Holly the condition she had tried to explain to Hugo remained. She was the girl who cycled to Brightwell every day, to be caught up in the endlessly fascinating craft of handling clay; but she had an *alter ego* as well, who still walked the streets of Seville and listened to the music of a fountain in Asunción's flower-filled courtyard, and had ghosts for company. She didn't mention the name of Juan Rodriguez again until Hugo's newspaper reported the execution in his prison at Alicante of the old Dictator's son, José Antonio Primo de Rivera.

'He came once to the house to see Juan while I was in Seville,' she said slowly. 'It was easy

457

to understand why Marilar had been enchanted with him as a schoolgirl.'

'Intelligent and charming,' Hugo agreed, 'and passionately convinced that if Spain didn't jettison all its old values it could become great again. So *exactly* the sort of man the country can't spare that, in the present general madness, it was certain to allow bigoted fools to shoot him.'

Holly put down the newspaper with trembling hands. 'I've often wondered what Juan would do in the end...now I know. He'll have taken a side at last, and be fighting against the people who murdered his friend...poor Asunción, left knowing that her sons must try to kill each other.'

They heard no news directly from Seville as the first winter of the war closed in, but very occasionally scribbled notes arrived from Josh. Written long before they arrived, they'd usually been taken into France and posted there by journalists anxious to experience the fighting at first hand for a little while. Atrocities on one side provoked reprisals on the other. Russia and a volunteer International Brigade supported the Republicans; Germany and Italy sent men, weapons and aeroplanes to help General Franco in his 'holy crusade' against the godless Reds.

It was a dreadful war; but it was happening far away, and there were matters nearer home to be concerned about...a King who chose to abdicate before he had even been crowned, and signs too clear to be ignored that the German Führer's ambitions didn't stop at salvaging the

458

pride of a defeated country. Richard was careful not to broadcast at Hindleford the scraps of intelligence and rumour that came his way in London, but to Hugo and his father one day he confided that the international situation was beginning to look very grim.

'Hitler and Mussolini are as thick as thieves, and they're both building up armies and fleets again to realize their megalomaniac dreams. It's a nightmare prospect that we might have to fight them *both* next time...especially with America determined to look the other way.'

Francis stared miserably at the prospect his son had laid in front of him, but Hugo shrugged it away. 'Don't let's despair. We can still rearm ourselves and call their bluff...*frighten* some sense into them if it can't be done in any other way.'

Richard allowed the conversation to rest there, reluctant to say that the British government seemed ready to outdo the French in not wanting to frighten *anybody*. His next visit to Hindleford came sooner than anticipated. Finding the Rectory empty of everyone except Mrs Briggs, he borrowed his father's old bicycle and pedalled over to find Holly. She looked pleased to see him, but said that he must wait while she finished an urgent piece of work.

'Take as long as you like,' he agreed obligingly. 'It's a privilege to watch the artist at work!'

But he was more inclined to watch the artist herself and wonder whether what had happened in Spain would always keep her trapped in memories she couldn't put aside. A wicked waste if so, he thought, of a girl so different from the heartless and vapid creatures who cluttered the London social scene. Absorbed in the task in front of her, Holly's face was familiar from childhood—still with its fringe and wings of short, dark hair; but they framed features that had become grave and beautifully defined. Strongly-marked black brows drew attention to her eyes, and her skin had never quite lost the silken warmth of colour inherited from her Indian grandmother. She was still the solitary creature she'd always been, keeping hidden from the rest of them whatever anguish she was feeling. At last she set down her brush with a little sigh that said the bowl in front of her was finished...now he was free to talk if he wanted to.

'I've got unexpected leave,' he said abruptly.

'For an unexpected reason?' she asked with a smile.

'Yes...a junior slave in our Embassy in Berlin has fallen sick—through sheer pressure of work, I expect, poor sod. It's hard on him to be shipped home *now* of all times, but it's a chance in a million for me. I reckoned my first foreign posting would be Bogota or Ashanti!'

It *was* incredible luck, but although Holly could feel his excitement, she sensed sadness as well.

'Are you thinking that although Bogota would have been out of the question for Marilar, Berlin might not have been?' she suggested gently.

'I miss her; I think I always shall,' Richard answered with his usual simplicity, 'and I can't

460

help worrying about what's happening to her. But for the first time since you and I came back, I'm thankful that she understood things better than I did. Berlin at the moment is the last place on earth to leave a shy, non-German-speaking girl on her own; but even if I *could* have turned it down, I wouldn't have wanted to, and that's how it would have been for the rest of our lives.' He gave a rueful little smile. 'Pride took a fall as well when she turned me down, but she was right.'

It took no account, Holly thought, of the sort of love that allowed a man and a woman to ignore everything else rather than lose each other. But perhaps Marilar hadn't known that power of the heart, any more than Luis had. Richard watched Holly's face, wondering what was the memory that made it look so sad.

'My pride seems to be mending,' he said suddenly, 'but how is yours? It seemed to me you left Seville feeling rather battered by the Rodriguez family.'

'Yes...but I expect it served me right. I was arrogant enough to think I understood them, just because I loved them. If Josh would only leave Spain to fight its own battles and come home, we could forget what Aunt Lydia calls a "peninsula that reeks of blood and incense"! She forgot to include the scent of orange blossom...but otherwise she's right!' Holly smiled herself to show that it was a chapter of her life almost closed and tidied away, and then consulted her watch.

'Now pray for me. If I've gauged a new

461

copper-oxide glaze and the kiln's air-intake correctly, the pieces that are ready to be taken out should be a beautiful and new *sang de boeuf* red; if I haven't, days of work will have been wasted.'

Richard took the hint and got ready to leave, but dropped a shy kiss on his cousin's cheek before he rode back to Hindleford.

He left for London again, and then Berlin, a week later...with Lydia proud to see him go, but anxious for the well-being of her only son in a capital known to be a sink of depravity and every kind of vice. Fortunately there were other things to think about as well—village celebrations to be organized, marking the coronation of King George VI, the happy news from Burslem that Helena and Ned were expecting their first child, and always the familiar, comforting pattern of Hindleford life. The slow turning of the year absorbed as usual the attention of people not much given to noticing what was happening abroad. The Spanish war dragged on, they knew, in bloodshed and bitterness, but it had long since ceased to be a novelty.

Only with Holly did Hugo ever discuss the subject, knowing that her mind—and probably her heart as well—had found it hard to relinquish Spanish memories. But one blustery November afternoon when they were out walking together, he suggested that she would want to go and see her friends as soon as the war ended, and she answered very firmly.

'No, I shan't ever go again. If there was nothing to stay for—Asunción's actual words!—there's nothing to go back for, either. I shall stay here now.' She shot a glance at the frown on Hugo's face and for once misunderstood it. 'That doesn't have to mean staying with you and Aunt Phee for ever more. It must be more than you both bargained for, having me around for so long.' Suddenly nervous of having taken *their* affection for granted as well, she spoke without thinking, and realized too late that she'd only succeeded in making Hugo Taverner angry. His hand descended heavily on her arm, forcing her to stand still. For once there was no warmth in his face, only the cold disapproval of someone she had deeply disappointed.

'I'm sorry,' she stammered, '...it's not what I meant to say. But I just seem to assume the right to stay with you, and the truth is that I don't have any right at all; strictly speaking, I'm not even your relative.'

'Talk in those terms to Phoebe if you want to break her heart. Don't you realize that you've become the daughter we never had?'

'I'm sorry,' she muttered again, and saw the fierceness fade from his face.

Hugo's fingers touched her cheek in a little gesture of forgiveness. 'Something more happened in Spain, I think, than you can bring yourself to talk about. It isn't only the memory of Asunción, or even Luis, that still haunts you.'

Holly stared at him with candid eyes and knew that it would be a relief to tell this wise, familiar friend the truth. 'I was labelled from the beginning "Luis's girl", and I loved

463

him in a fashion that seemed quite adequate enough until I came to know what loving a man really meant. Unfortunately, my second choice was even worse—no distracting visions, but someone who is about as self-sufficient as a man can be.'

'Juan Rodriguez?' Hugo suggested gently.

Holly smeared away a tear that had begun to trickle down her face and tried to smile. 'Another slap in the face for England! He didn't need *me*, any more than he wanted his father's legacy here.'

'I feel sorry for him on both counts,' Hugo remarked with gravity, then tucked her hand through his arm and went on walking again.

They got back to the house as dusk was falling, in time to see an Oxford taxi-cab turning out of the gravel sweep on to the road. The visitor it had brought was being ushered carefully inside by Nellie, because he could only move slowly, leaning on a stick. Phoebe came into the hall, and ran towards him.

'Oh, my dear, welcome home...' Then she caught sight of her husband in the open doorway. 'Hugo, just look who's here!'

He and Holly were both staring—at a grey-faced, shabbily dressed young man, who seemed almost confused to find himself the centre of so much attention. He was recognizably Josh Harkness, but his dark mop of hair was over-long and unkempt, and the bright, intelligent eyes that had been his most attractive feature were now sunk back in his head, like the eyes of an old man.

464

'Dear Josh...is Luis here as well?' Holly asked.

In the terrible little silence that followed she could guess what he was going to have to say, but it seemed to take a long time before he forced words past the obstruction in his throat. But first he tucked his stick over one arm and gripped both her hands.

'No, my dear...I had to leave Luis in Spain. I was going to write and break the news to you, but then that seemed a cowardly thing to do. He was killed beside me nearly two months ago.' She buried her face against him and he cradled her against his rough jacket as gently as he would have held an injured animal. But she felt his body tremble for the strain on his unsupported leg, and lifted her head to stare at him with huge eyes full of pity.

'*You've* been hurt, too—come, Josh...take my arm.'

The little scene stayed etched in Phoebe's memory afterwards—the gaunt, shabby young man being led by a girl who perhaps had barely taken in what she'd just been told. They moved slowly back into the firelit library, in a little silent procession. Then Josh lowered himself into an armchair with a sigh of relief, and smiled his thanks for the glass of wine that Hugo put into his hands.

'Dear boy...you look so tired. Shall we leave you to rest, and hear about...about everything later?' Phoebe asked.

'Now that I've begun, I think I'd rather get it over—not the entire story of the past

465

eighteen months, just what happened recently.' He stared at Holly's white face, and then at Hugo, who nodded as if to confirm that he should go on.

'We'd been on the Aragon front for months past—there'd be weeks at a time when very little happened; then we or "they" would start an attack—usually futile in the long run, but for a little while it would gain us a few hundred yards of ground. Two months ago we started a bigger offensive to try to relieve some of the terrible Nationalist pressure on Madrid. It was more successful than usual, and we were feeling rather pleased with ourselves until they sent bombers over to push us back.' He fell silent for a moment, staring at the wine in his glass but seeing instead, Holly realized, a scene that he would never forget.

'German bombers, I suppose?' Hugo prompted quietly.

'Of course—much better than anything the Republicans were able to buy from the French, and much better flown, too. They're efficient devils, the Germans.' He took a sip of wine, then put the glass down and linked his hands together.

'There was very little shelter—we hadn't had time to dig ourselves in—and Luis was twenty yards nearer to the explosion than me. He was dying when I crawled over to him, but he...he knew me, and smiled.'

In the quietness of the room Holly remembered exactly how Luis had smiled; for months past she had scarcely been able to remember his face; now it was achingly clear in her mind.

'And...afterwards?' she asked unsteadily.

'I'd been hit in the leg, and eventually got sent down the line to Lérida. I was discharged in Barcelona a month later, as being no more use to the Republican cause, and free to cross into France. I've been slowly making my way home ever since, travelling a bit, resting a bit.' He half-turned to where Holly was sitting, still and pale as a statue carved in stone. 'Nothing really makes his loss bearable, but perhaps this might help. He went to fight for a vision he had of Spain, and for a little while he saw that vision come true. In our sector there were no fancy uniforms, no ranks, and no distinctions; we were all just comrades, fighting for a cause we believed in. In the villages behind the lines all the old evils had gone too—there were no owners of anything, land, food, or even money. Everyone was given according to their need, no-one too much or too little. The anarchists' dream was not only proved workable but realized, and my friend *saw* it before he died.'

Holly found only two thoughts in her mind—the first of them was that Juan should have been there to hear what Josh had said. The second required a question that was difficult to ask.

'Will Asunción have been told?'

She was answered very gently—it wasn't a quality she'd associated with Josh in the past; he'd been sharp and funny and clever, but

467

not gentle. It seemed an unexpected change in someone who'd been entangled in a bloody war.

'There are Red Cross people on each side, exchanging that sort of information. She will know by now,' he said.

Holly nodded, then asked one more question. 'Do you think they're all right in Seville?'

'I'm sure Asunción and Marilar are. Seville fell immediately to Franco's men; since then the fighting has been well to the east of them. I can't tell you about Juan, I'm afraid.' He watched her pale face for a moment, then began to speak again as if he'd forgotten there weren't just the two of them in the room.

'Luis and I did a lot of talking together when things were quiet. He'd come to understand that he should never have expected you to marry him.'

'Because I could never turn myself into a thorough-going revolutionary—I know...his farewell letter said so.' She spoke too carelessly for Josh to be deceived. The rejection had been, and still was, a bitter hurt to her. He shook his head, suddenly certain that she must be told the truth.

'Luis adored you, my dear; revolutionary or not, he didn't care. But there was something else he *did* care about—a conviction he couldn't escape that even if you loved *him*, you loved Juan a great deal more. Believing *that*, he couldn't hold you to a promise he knew you wouldn't break yourself.'

Holly stared blindly at the flames leaping in

the hearth, not seeing them for the tears that had begun to trickle down her face.

'I wanted to stay even so...to take care of them,' she said hoarsely, 'but none of them wanted me—Juan least of all.'

'It nearly broke Asunción's heart to send you away,' Josh insisted quietly, 'but Juan said you'd never agree to leave unless she pretended not to want you there.'

Holly saw once more in her mind's eye a scene she'd gone over time and time again. She'd been tricked into leaving, but Asunción had tricked her only for the sake of affection after all, and Luis had loved her *more* than she deserved. The cold loneliness locked up in her heart began to melt. Sadness remained, but not the hurt of having been spurned all round. She fumbled her way across the room to kiss Josh's tired face and make for the door.

Phoebe released the breath she'd been holding and got up to go as well, murmuring that Josh must be sent to bed as soon as his room was ready. It left only the two men in the quiet room, Josh staring into the flames leaping on the hearth, Hugo remembering another time...another young man whose life had been changed by going to a war.

'Who will win in Spain?' he asked out of the silence that had fallen on them.

'Franco because he's clever enough and ruthless enough to hold his motley crew together until he *does* win. The Republicans are already falling apart.' Josh eased his aching leg and took another sip of wine. 'I couldn't say so in front of Holly and Aunt Phoebe, but I'm thankful Luis died when he did. The glorious vision couldn't have lasted, you see. By the time I was sent back to Barcelona everything had changed. The Stalinists were in charge, and anarchists like Luis—Trotskyists, they were branded by then—who'd fought and died for Spain had become a worse enemy than the Nationalists themselves. So much for solidarity...so much for the brave new dawn! I'm sick to my stomach of ideologies, Uncle Hu.'

'Then thank God you're back here, where ideologies count for very little...too little, some might think.' He saw Josh stare round the firelit room and understood him. 'You can't be certain what's real at the moment—this, or what you remember. It will seem hard to believe, but time deals eventually with pain, I promise you. What will you do now, lad?'

Josh smiled at the boyhood word. 'It depends on Father. I'm hoping he'll agree that he doesn't need me in the firm, as well as Ned and James. I'd like to stay in Oxford—bury my head in some peaceful post-graduate research, perhaps even write about the last eighteen months. They *need* writing about.' Then he spoke in a different tone of voice, putting his own memories aside. 'Tell me what's been happening here. I feel like Rip Van Winkle!'

'The best news is that Ned and Helena finally married after all...they're expecting their first child in the New Year. Richard's got his first foreign posting—in Berlin, lucky young devil! But I'm bound to say that his letters make frightening reading. The "war to end all wars" that my generation thought we'd fought will turn out to be another politician's dream.'

Josh was still considering this when Phoebe came back into the room. Hugo smiled at her, but spoke again to Josh. 'You're about to be cossetted—I recognize the gleam in my beloved's eye!'

'Merely a hot bath, clean sheets and a comfortable bed...the least we can offer a returning hero,' she insisted.

'It sounds like paradise to me, Aunt Phee,' said Josh, and limped with her out of the room.

28

At the Rectory Rosalind learned gradually about the two-edged way in which life made a habit of delivering its gifts. To have Josh back and actually living across the garden had been even more than her nightly prayers had asked for, especially when Helena was no longer at the Rectory to shine down all competition. But as the spring of 1938 went by, she wondered if she hadn't preferred him in Spain—at least then she'd still been free to *imagine* him coming home to fall in love with her at last. *Now*, it was a red-letter day if the Josh who'd returned from that adventure remembered to ask after the well-being of the godson they shared.

She tried to be cheerful—pride insisted on it; but she hated Spain—pride insisted on that as well. Her mother was right; no-one with a grain of common sense would have anything to do with a place so harshly different from England that it always left its mark on those who went there. She was forced to say so one day when Holly found her weeping over the task of polishing the wall-memorials in her father's church. It had seemed safe to let cheerfulness slip for once but her cousin had walked in unexpectedly and found her there in tears.

'Poor Ros...I dare say it's the disgusting smell of brass polish,' Holly suggested. 'I hope the shade of Admiral Monkton knows what you are suffering for his sake. Aunt Phee can remember him as a red-faced gentleman who used to shout at the village children and relive the Battle of Jutland, which we'd fought all wrong, apparently!'

Rosalind brushed aside the well-meant diversion. 'I *like* the smell of Brasso,' she said, sniffing still. 'I was crying about Josh if you want to know...because he isn't the laughing, carefree boy who liked me before he went away; now he'd scarcely notice if I dropped dead at his feet. I'm sure it was dreadful out there, with Luis getting killed and everything, but why can't he *forget* Spain now? Even when he smiles at me he's not seeing *me* at all.' She was weeping again in earnest, because it was a relief to let out some of the misery and resentment bottled up inside her.

Holly led her to the recumbent stone figure

472

of a Maynard who had gone to a much earlier crusade, then sat down beside her.

'It's hard for someone who hasn't been there to understand,' she began to explain patiently, 'but Spain *never* quite lets you forget her; fascination or deep dislike—either will do, as long as you remember!' She looked at Rosalind's tear-wet face and thought how hard it had been for her to grow up—a pretty girl but always overshadowed by Helena's beauty; a bright enough girl, but no match for Kate's beguiling oddity and intelligence...poor little pig in the middle—just like the game they'd used to play.

'Josh *deliberately* remembers,' Rosalind sobbed angrily. 'He thinks of nothing but his wretched book.'

'Of course—he's an historian, and unlike most of *them* he's helped to make the history he's writing about. Apart from that, it's something he wants to do for Luis and the rest of the men he fought with.'

Rosalind dried her tears and stared at her cousin. 'Even when it's done, he won't go back to being the Josh we used to know...will he?'

Holly thought of the quiet, preoccupied man Josh had become, who limped because his injured leg still troubled him, and instead of playing carefree games now studied the news of what was happening on the continent of Europe.

She shook her head. 'No...I'm afraid Spain *did* change him.'

Rosalind gave a little sigh, and then stood up.

At least it wasn't *her* fault...Spain was to blame, and the Rodriguez family, whose lives had got so muddled up with their own. 'I expect I'll get over him now—you can't go on loving someone who refuses to be the person you knew.' She nodded as if it was clear at last, reminding Holly of Aunt Lydia, and then went back to polishing the Admiral's memorial.

Walking home, Holly thought about that conversation. She had seen no point in mentioning that Josh was quite often found over at Brightwell when she emerged from the studio. He explained that the long walk exercised his damaged leg, but Holly was becoming certain that there was more to it than that. Annie Blake's smile and quiet welcome drew him there, and he found unexpectedly in her company the comfort he needed. She'd known grief and hardship of her own and survived both without bitterness. Holly thought Josh valued her for that, and he was right to do so.

Rosalind had said something else that needed thinking about. She would make up her mind to stop loving Josh because he no longer corresponded to the image in her heart. It sounded simple; a little of Aunt Lydia's strong-mindedness and the thing was practically done. Holly envied them both but knew that the system wouldn't work for her. She had an altogether more stubborn heart than that. She wouldn't ever go back to Spain unless Asunción asked her to; but if he survived the war Juan would make sure that his mother didn't ask. It was as difficult to imagine *him* changed as it was to imagine him dead—heart and mind insisted that both were impossible. But one country would always be enough for Juan Rodriguez, and his choice was Spain.

A year later the Republican forces finally admitted that they'd been fought to exhaustion and defeat. The great adventure was over, but Holly was thankful that Luis was dead. The alternatives of exile in France or life in a Nationalist gaol would both have been unbearable. She had given up hope of ever hearing again from Seville but one day a letter from Asunción arrived, soon after the ending of the war. It needed reading several times to make sure that it contained no trace of the warmth and kindness of a woman she had once known. Holly searched it, too, for the smallest reference to the fact that England was finally girding herself to fight the country whose bombers had killed Asunción's son. There was no such reference there. At last she tore the letter up, merely mentioning to Phoebe that she'd heard at last from Spain.

Surprised that she hadn't been offered it to read, Phoebe stared at Holly's unrevealing face.

'Asunción must have said *something* if she wrote at all.'

'Well, let me see—she was briefly very sad about Luis, and the whole tragedy of the war, and less briefly thankful to have Juan safely home. Less briefly still, she seemed delighted that Marilar is to be married—to someone who was a fellow-officer of Juan's in the Nationalist army; a charming man who will make her an excellent husband.' Holly ticked the items off on her fingers. 'That covers it, I think.' Then she tried to smile at Phoebe's expression. 'Dear Aunt Phee, Spaniards *hate* writing letters; those who can't be seen and spoken to are best forgotten in their view! It's time for *us* to forget now, as well—our Spanish connection is over.'

'Yes...yes, I think perhaps it is,' Phoebe slowly agreed. 'For the first time since I was born there forty years ago, the link is finally broken.'

It became only a small private sadness as the next anxious weeks went by. Czechoslovakia followed Austria into the Wehrmacht's hungry maw; and, not to be entirely outdone, Mussolini invaded Albania. Hugo broke his heart over a government seemingly content to hand Hitler and his mad bedfellow the rest of Europe on a plate, and for the first time in her life Phoebe thanked God that she had no sons. But when the German army next poured over the Polish border, she switched off the wireless broadcast of the news and stared fearfully at Hugo.

'War *now*, surely?'

'Why?' her husband shouted. 'We and the French have swallowed every insult so far, every broken promise, every torn-up treaty...why should Poland bother us? Let him grab that as well.'

But it seemed that even Neville Chamberlain had his sticking-point. For Poland the British Empire *was* finally prepared to go to war and

476

so, even more reluctantly, was France. Before they'd had time to forget the lessons so usefully learned in Spain, German soldiers and airmen could begin applying them elsewhere.

By the time the first Christmas of the war came round Phoebe and Mrs Jim acknowledged in the Manor kitchen the extent to which their lives were already transformed.

'Christmas morning and no church bells ringing,' Phoebe said sadly. 'I know there are worse things to bewail, but it seems to sum up all the joy we must do without.'

'Won't be for long,' insisted her comforter. 'Jim was talking to Colonel Wyndham only yesterday. Seems there's some "Line" or other the Germans won't get past this time. Jim's not one to put much faith in the Frenchies, speakin' generally, but he came back quite cheerful-like after seeing the Colonel.'

Phoebe could imagine Archibald Wyndham giving everyone he met the benefit of his expert military opinion; but the dear man was right to keep the villagers in good heart when more and more of its young people were being sucked into one service or another. Richard was back from an Embassy closed down in Berlin, but only to rejoin the Territorials immediately. Josh had surrendered the Junior Research Fellowship his Spanish Civil War thesis had won for him at Balliol, and talked his way into the RAF; James Harkness was already at sea. Instead of any of *them* at the Christmas luncheon-table there would be three London evacuees.

Phoebe gave a little inward sigh over times that made a mother be without her children, then smiled because the kitchen door opened and Holly walked in, still wearing her working clothes. Christmas Day or not, Will Cooper's livestock still had to be fed, and their stalls mucked out, and she was now a member of the Women's Land Army, with corduroy breeches and dark-green sweater to prove it. She carried a little wicker basket filled with brown eggs and decorated with a sprig of mistletoe.

'From Will, Aunt Phee...with the compliments of the season, and not a word to Mrs Drew-Smythe—to whom he's sworn that none of Alice's hens are laying! She tried to bribe him, silly woman.'

Phoebe averted her nostrils from the smell of roasting goose. It had been smuggled over from the same source the day before and her conscience was troubling her, even though it would feed Anne Maynard and the Blakes as well as themselves.

'I shall be firm with him after Christmas... tactful, but firm,' she said quietly. 'We must be treated like everyone else.'

Holly grinned. 'Even though it's Maynard land he farms, and I'm practically his only help, give or take three small Cockneys who are more trouble than they're worth! Can I go to matins dressed like this? I've still got work to do afterwards.'

Phoebe nodded, thinking that regular atten-dance at church was something else her London mudlarks were having to learn about, less willingly. Some of the children had already been taken home when the expected air raids on London didn't materialize; but her trio, white-faced and skinny when they arrived, already looked as robust as the village children, and Phoebe now took a proprietary pride in them.

They went in procession through the frosty whiteness of the garden, collecting Lydia, Rosalind and Kate on their way. Holly walked with Hugo and found that the memory of another Christmas had crept insidiously into her mind. She was almost convinced nowadays that her fight to get over loving Juan Rodriguez was won...memory might keep a place for him, and for the rest of his family, because life was continuous after all, not a film with chunks cut out of it and the remains pasted together again. But already she'd learned to take pleasure in the company of other men; she hadn't been born to be a spinster—she'd find someone else to love when there was time to spare again from milking Will's cows and sowing seed and lifting potatoes. But for the moment memory had her by the throat, and she was walking along a starlit street in Seville with Juan to Midnight Mass.

'Come back from wherever you are,' Hugo suggested beside her.

She turned to look at him but for once answered not quite honestly. 'I was thinking about the past—remembering a time when Luis was here. He crossed swords with Ned, who's since turned out to be right. The Oxford Union vote not to fight for King and Country looks pretty silly now. Richard was the peace-maker then, trying to make Luis understand that we often say what we don't mean.'

'Perfidious Albion! We certainly convinced Hitler that we wouldn't fight. It might turn out to be what saves us in the end. He could have gobbled up Europe a year ago, when we hadn't the faintest hope of stopping him.'

He had to halt in his tracks because Holly had stopped to stare at him. 'You don't believe it's just a phoney war, Uncle Hu?'

'No, sweetheart, I'm afraid I don't...but I'm about to listen to my brother-in-law's tidings of great joy, and I shall try to look suitably receptive.'

It was the end of the conversation because they were almost at the church door, and there were friends and neighbours to be greeted. But it lodged itself in Holly's mind, and only a few months into the New Year Hugo was proved right—it wasn't a phoney war at all. German armies occupied Denmark and Norway, then overran Holland and Belgium. Before May was out they were driving into France itself. Colonel Wyndham's famous 'Line' proved no obstacle at all, and Jim Wilkins recalled bitterly to his wife that he'd survived the first war trusting the judgement of his own Staff officers no more than he'd trusted the French.

On a hot afternoon towards the end of May Hugo sat in his Oxford office pretending to

480

read the papers under his hand. But his mind was on a desperate army that included Richard Fanshawe, fighting its way to the French coast. The Belgian King had surrendered, a new French government was asking for armistice terms, and the British Expeditionary Force faced the prospect of being annihilated. The sea and the Navy might save it, if it could only reach them in time. Hugo's work was still lying neglected when his elderly clerk, called out of retirement, opened the door.

'A visitor asking for you, Mr Taverner. No appointment...shall I send him away? He says the name's Rodriguez.'

There was a moment of silence in the room before Hugo spoke. 'No, show him in.'

He thought back to their last meeting—four years since Juan had come to Hindleford, asking them to offer Luis a refuge...unforgettable years for any Spaniard, and they were written on the face of the man who walked into the room. But his voice hadn't changed, nor the smile that softened the stern planes of his face into sudden pleasantness.

'I'm afraid I've taken *you* by surprise and discomposed your clerk!'

Hugo stood up, holding out his hand. 'Hubert is easily discomposed at the age of seventy-one—he was my uncle's clerk, and this is his war service!'

Juan stared round the room, then again at the man who watched him. 'The smell is familiar—leather, old files, and the dust of generations of hopes and fears! I suppose all lawyers' offices are the same the world over.'

'I dare say, but that isn't what you came all this way to talk about. With so much to say it's hard to know where to start...with Luis, I suppose. Josh Harkness first brought us the news of his death...we were all so very sorry.'

He spoke with his usual directness, but Juan registered and understood the touch of formality as well. Hugo Taverner was aware that Luis's brother had fought on Franco's side, and his expression suggested that he'd disapproved even though he wouldn't allow himself to say so.

'Young men like Josh...thousands of them... distinguished themselves in a cause that died on them in the end,' Juan said quietly.

'I know...he was aware of that even before he was shipped home from Barcelona. But how does the *Nationalist* cause look now...don't tell me *you're* still content with that?'

A grim smile touched Juan's face for a moment. 'I should have remembered that you would know a lot about Spain—you always did! I hated the Republicans because I saw them destroying my country, and because they murdered my friend. But how *can* I be content with a régime that now means to control the very minds of its people, and eliminate anyone who made the mistake of fighting on the losing side?'

Hugo heard the note of anguish in Juan's deep voice, and felt the need to apologize. 'I'm sorry if I seemed to be judging you—God knows *we*

482

don't have the right to do that. Our government hasn't exactly distinguished itself in the past few years—hence the bloody mess we're in now. I don't know yet how you got here, or why you came, but you might soon regret your choice. It looks as if we're next on the list to receive the Wehrmacht's attentions, and as the officer in charge of our Local Defence Volunteers I can tell you that we're anything but ready for them.'

'Legally I'm not here at all, but I have a lot of friends scattered around the peninsula, including the British Consul in Cadiz! The papers I arrived with don't bear much inspection—certainly not enough to get me accepted in the British Army; but that's why I've come for your help, Hugo. Now it's time to help *fight* the Fascists. Even setting aside the fact that they killed Luis, they *can't* be allowed to take over the whole of Europe.'

Hugo suddenly smiled at him. 'For years Lydia wanted to hide your existence from the neighbourhood. Perhaps at last she's going to have to admit that Henry Maynard fathered a son! Shall we go home? Phoebe will fall on your neck, I warn you.'

'Are...are all the rest of the family still here?'

'No...only Holly, but you'll be lucky if you get a glimpse of her; we rarely do.' He smiled and said no more on the subject, merely recommending Hubert on the way out to tell callers that Messrs Taverner & Taverner were closed for the rest of the afternoon.

29

Juan's 'glimpse' came that same evening, long after their frugal supper was over. They'd listened to a news broadcast almost too sombre to talk about and plunged instead into the exchange of family news. He spoke briefly of the tragedy of the Spanish war.

'Foreigners were involved too, of course, but the true horror came from Spaniard killing Spaniard with a ruthlessness that took us back to medieval wars. Even so, life begins again...the human race insists on that,' he finished up, with a reassuring smile for Phoebe. 'And there's good news to give you—Marilar is safely, happily, married to a man who can take care of her because he wore the blue beret, not the red, during the war.'

Phoebe saw a little picture in her mind's eye of Marilar laughing at Richard as he taught her the art of balancing on a bicycle—now *she* was married to a Francoist, because that was where safety lay, and Richard was perhaps already dead in northern France. That remembered picture could be forgotten now; it belonged to a time that had gone for ever.

The evening was warm and still, and they sat talking in the dusk—long windows open to the terrace, no lamps lit that needed hiding for the blackout. An almost full moon was rising, and by its light Juan saw the slender figure of a girl walking slowly across the garden, as if she were very tired. Conscious of being watched, she lifted her head and waved. Phoebe stood up and called to her.

'Dearest, what a time to finish work!'

'I know, but Will wanted to finish getting the hay in—old Curly's aching bones predict that the weather's going to break. Alice gave me something to eat. Now I'll wash and fall into bed, I think.'

'Say hello to a visitor first.'

She came towards the little group clustered round the open window, and dimly saw a tall man rise from his chair in the shadows.

'Buenas noches, Holly,' said the remembered voice of Juan Rodriguez.

She didn't faint, but it was necessary to make a grab at the open window-frame.

'A—a *Spanish* visitor, no less,' she managed to get out. 'Did you drop from the sky? Perhaps the Germans taught you the trick—*they* seem to be very good at it.'

'I came in a British merchant ship, without benefit of the Germans.'

'Well, if you haven't disappeared again by the morning perhaps I'll see you then. Right now I'm tired and smelling strongly of hay and horses.' She let go of the window and forced trembling legs to carry her along the path to the kitchen courtyard. The Wilkins had already gone to bed, and she could bow her head on the kitchen table for a moment before making the huge effort of climbing the stairs.

'She's a farm-girl now,' Hugo said un-necessarily in the silence that followed her departure, 'and like everybody else, she works far too hard.'

Juan brushed the explanation aside. 'You were kind enough to say this afternoon that you had no right to judge us. My impression is that Holly *does* judge, and finds me wanting!'

Holly also meant, if possible, to avoid seeing Juan again. It ought to be easy enough when her working day began at 5 a.m. and she was away from the house almost until nightfall. But after a hot morning's work among the vegetables that Will was also growing intensively now, he told her to go and cool down by the river with her lunchbox. 'Alice's instructions, maid, and you know we've *both* to do as she bids! You can be back for milking at five.'

It was a respite she was grateful for after a broken night. Whatever had brought Juan to Hindleford, he was certain not to stay long; but when she examined her state of mind it was a great relief to discover that anger had taken charge. He had no right to drift back into their lives, *now* of all times. The past was dead and buried, and all that mattered was the dangerous, exhausting present. She couldn't, wouldn't, be trapped again in an illusion of longing that had nearly destroyed her once before. There were *real* agonies all around them now—like the sight of Aunt Lydia going to call on another woman in the village with a son in France. Holly offered up a little prayer for Richard, shared

486

Alice's sandwiches with a friendly moorhen, and then, hypnotized by the water sliding past her, suddenly fell asleep. The sun, moving round, woke her by shining on her face, but when she opened her eyes Juan was sitting there, patiently watching her. Hot and dishevelled, she felt at a disadvantage, and it was necessary to make a quick grab at saving anger.

'You didn't make the journey to England just to sit and watch a Thames backwater going nowhere in particular...isn't there something more important you ought to be doing?'

'Yes...but I can't start doing it until Hugo has worked out how my new life here is to begin. Your authorities are rightly nervous about anyone arriving from a pro-fascist country, and Juan Rodriguez may seem a trifle suspect.'

'Why *have* you come?' Holly asked coolly. 'You were very definite once before that Spain was your choice, not England.'

'Yes, I was...but then the Germans hadn't killed my brother, and England wasn't fighting for her life.'

She wouldn't look at his face, but it seemed safe to watch his long, brown hands stripping the bark off a piece of hazel twig he'd picked up.

'I don't imagine that my being here is going to make the slightest difference, but I had to come all the same. My mother understood that...I think she would have liked to come too,' Juan finished up quietly.

Holly stared now at her own scratched, work-roughened hands, and remembered Asunción. 'She wrote me one letter after your war ended. I

487

tore it up rather than hurt Aunt Phee by showing it to her. Luis was scarcely mentioned, but there was a lot about Marilar marrying the *right* kind of Spaniard—I use the word advisedly!'

She wasn't aware of Juan moving, but suddenly he was near enough to seize her hands in a crushing grip.

'Tell me what *you'd* have written in my mother's place,' he said harshly. 'She's the daughter of a known anarchist, the mother of another one, even though the Rodriguez name gives her a little protection. Of course she's careful what she writes, and thankful to have Marilar taken out of the danger that Luis's reputation left behind.'

Holly had no option now but to look at him—couldn't help but see in the clear afternoon light the lines of suffering etched on his face and the sprinkling of silver in his dark hair. He was ten years older than herself, therefore thirty-five now, but he looked much more; he'd surely been surfeited with horrors, without coming to fight in another war. Anger, never to be relied upon, abandoned her, leaving only aching sadness behind. But she dragged her hands free and buried them in the pockets of her slacks.

'I'm sorry I didn't understand how things were,' she muttered. 'It's been my mistake all along...not knowing nearly as much as I thought I did.'

'You thought my mother would want you to stay, but it was she who drove you away. Was *that* one of your mistakes?'

'It was for a long time; then Josh came back

488

and told me what Luis had said. It was a cruel, Spanish way to get me to leave.'

'Would you have gone in any other way?'

'Perhaps not, but I'm not used to having choices made for me.' Holly edged further away from him, and picked up a handful of little stones to send skimming into the river because it helped to have something to do with her hands. 'I keep forgetting Spanish *costumbre* of course; nothing has changed since the Dark Ages and your women are still required to wait and be told what to do.'

'The system works quite well,' Juan pointed out, 'and but for the war, you'd have been part of it yourself, married to Luis.'

'Now *you're* mistaken,' Holly said gently. 'I even got to the point once of begging him to marry me, but there was always a reason for another delay. I didn't understand at the time, but I do now. He was like a medieval knight, needing a lady to sing his dreams to and to give him her favour to wear when he went into battle. What he *didn't* need was a flesh and blood woman to distract him with the earthy joys and pains of real-life marriage.'

She saw Juan frown and hurried on before he could say that she was talking nonsense. 'I wasn't the only one to misunderstand. My beautiful cousin Helena nearly wrecked her own chance of happiness for the Spanish fire and passion she imagined she saw in Luis. The passion was there, but it was for Spain, not us. Richard made the same mistake with Marilar, and when the moment of truth came and a choice had to be made, he lost *her*.'

'It sounds as if the Rodriguez family has done you all quite a lot of harm,' Juan said after a moment's silence.

Holly managed to smile. 'Well, Aunt Lydia always did maintain that we should have nothing to do with you...but the most valuable experience is bought painfully!'

She scrambled to her feet, pleased with herself for having survived a huge ordeal. Anger and grief had both been dealt with, and the heart-stopping shock of seeing him again was over.

'Now duty calls,' she said cheerfully. 'Will's herd will be bellowing their heads off to be milked if I don't go...a Land Girl's life is *nothing* if not earthy!' She nodded goodbye and walked away from him, slender and erect and graceful...just as memory had always held her in his mind's eye. There was nothing very alluring about her working rig of cotton shirt and rolled-up trousers; her dark hair was cut shorter than before, and her thin, brown hands were scratched. He'd warned himself that he *and* she would certainly have changed in four, long, desperate years; they'd become different people, and the current of awareness that had run between them since the day he'd met a long-legged schoolgirl on this same river-bank was certain to have left them sparkless and at peace now.

He buried his head in his hands, struggling to shut out the image of her tired, sleeping face before the sun had woken her. The memory of her greeting the night before still stung; without it he would have picked her up in his arms, so that she might sleep more comfortably. She'd made it clear enough that the connection between them was broken, but what an aching, intolerable grief it was that only *one* of them should have changed after all.

He lifted his head at last and looked around him at the peaceful, tree-lined stretch of river—nothing spectacular about it, nothing very special...except to the people whose land it was. But it had been his father's land, and for as long as it was threatened these had become *his* people. He didn't regret coming to share in a seemingly hopeless battle, any more than he regretted the knowledge that he would love Holly for as long as there was life in his body—he knew now that life had always had these things in store for him.

That evening after supper Francis and Lydia Fanshawe appeared, warned by Phoebe of her unexpected visitor. They looked drawn with anxiety for their son, but spoke kindly to Juan of Luis and tactfully concealed their surprise that he should have found his way to England. At nine o'clock as they gathered round the wireless for the news broadcast Holly arrived just as it was about to begin. Showered and changed, she still looked tired, but coolly beautiful now in a cream linen dress, and a green sweater pulled round her shoulders.

Tonight there was news to hear. British troops had managed to reach Dunkirk and they were being evacuated. The Royal Navy was there, as close as it could get to the bombarded, treacherously shallow waters of the port. But an armada of little craft was steaming across the Channel as well—tugs, motor-launches, pleasure boats, anything that would float—to ferry the waiting men out to the Navy's ships...the stuff of a legend was on its way. When the announcement was over Lydia hid her face against her husband's shoulder, and his eyes were full of tears.

Unable to share in the conversation afterwards, Holly stepped out into the coolness of the garden. The gradual northern dusk was falling, but when Juan followed he could easily make out the pale shimmer of her dress. He caught up with her but she didn't acknowledge that he was there, and they walked in silence for a while. A moth blundered past them in the thickening darkness, and a late blackbird rehearsed a phrase of tomorrow's morning song.

'Peaceful England, but for how much longer I wonder,' Holly murmured at last. She was very conscious of the man beside her, but everything was experienced vividly now; he was simply part of the terrifying, uplifting, emotional days they were living through. If she remembered *that* she could go on walking with him in the cool darkness without bursting into tears.

'May we put the war aside, just for a moment, and talk about ourselves?' Juan asked quietly.

'If...if there's anything important to say, but I doubt that very much.'

His hand on her bare arm seemed to burn the skin, and she stood still immediately so that he had no excuse not to let go of her.

'It's not important to anyone but me in the present desperate scheme of things, but blame a lawyer's training, Holly—we can't help tidying up loose ends. I should like you to know the truth at last, and there may never be another chance to tell you. I had to accept that you were going to marry Luis—*he'd* found you first, and you were promised to him. Any other man I might have tried to displace, but not my brother. If I'd known what you told me this afternoon I hope I should *still* have had the strength of mind to make sure you were got safely out of Spain. Then Luis was killed, but the war dragged on and on, and it became even more impossible to imagine myself coming to suggest that you might now like to forget about Luis and think of me instead.'

The darkness was complete but the rising moon showed him her face—a combination of light and shadow, dramatically, heartbreakingly beautiful. 'For *you* there were years of peaceful life in England, a world away from our chaotic, bitterly divided country. I imagined you loved by every man who clapped eyes on you, and I learned to live with the idea that I would never see you again. I should never have done so except for another war that I knew I had to take part in.'

His deep voice stopped, and there was silence, because the blackbird had given up too. It took Holly a long time to find something to say, and when she found it, it wasn't about themselves. 'We spoke of countries once. One was all you needed then, but I'm glad you've changed your

493

mind. Phoebe always kept the sadness hidden, but she longed for you to acknowledge your true father, and so *wanted* to share Hindleford with you.'

'I'm not going to share it now. If the skies don't fall in on us in the very near future and some divine intervention helps this country to perform a miracle, I shall go back to Spain eventually. I promised Asunción I would. It's an unhappy place to live in at the moment, but it won't always be so and I still belong there.'

Holly let out a little sigh, as if she had been holding her breath. 'Then nothing is changed, after all. You *don't* need us...you never will.'

Both his hands fastened on her this time, forcing her to turn and face him.

'You haven't mentioned the third country you once warned me about. I pretended to ignore that too, but I knew more about it than you did. I'd been hopelessly lost in it from the moment you arrived in Spain.'

Hope, forbidden, and fragile as the first green shoot of spring, wanted to open in her heart, but she trod it down fiercely. The touch of his hands was such comfort that she yearned to rest her head against him and weep away the bitter loneliness of years; but hope was a liar, and dupes were fools, and she'd learned to make her life without him.

'I dare say you've forgotten another loose end in Madrid,' she heard a cool, polite voice mention. It must belong to her, although she scarcely recognized it. The woman who shared his life in the capital was the last person on earth she'd intended ever referring to, but a mental picture of her was suddenly clear and insistent—she'd be beautiful for sure, as Asunción had been, smiling, and gently docile as all good Spanish women were.

'I suppose Marilar talked to you,' Juan said evenly. 'Teresa Quiñones is the sister of a friend of mine—a kind and generous woman whom I might have married if *you* hadn't come to Spain. She's known since then that I shall never be able to marry anyone else.'

The little green shoot, not quite dead, lifted a trampled head, but Holly disregarded it. She would remember instead that streak of cruelty that seemed to run through every Spaniard.

'I'm not quite sure what you're offering *me*...the chance to be equally kind and generous for as long as the war keeps you here? I don't think so, thank you.'

She pulled herself away from him and began to march towards the house, but his voice halted her.

'I didn't come prepared to offer you *anything*... I thought I should be years too late, even if I *hadn't* imagined the pull between us in the past that made it seem such an agony to have you in Spain at all. Your greeting last night confirmed that there was nothing to hope for, but still I insist that you know the truth—I've loved you for a long time. God willing, I shall eventually go back to Spain, but I shall go *still* loving you.'

She had spun round, and now the moonlight fell on *his* face. How many times she'd conjured it up in dreams, only to wake alone and lonely.

But the *truth,* he'd said...well, she would be truthful too.

'I was going to marry Luis because I'd promised I would. I knew when it was much too late what I felt about *you,* but I thought you understood as well and just despised me for it. It's taken me all these last, long years to put myself together again and prove that I can manage on my own. When the war ends...if it ever ends...I shall go back to being a potter—*that's* what I'm good at. I shouldn't be any good at all at being an obedient Spanish wife.'

She stared at him, and saw his face change.

'You...you couldn't consider being both potter *and* wife in Spain...as disobedient as you liked?'

The yearning tenderness in his voice brought her to the edge of tears, but she said hoarsely, 'Times like these confuse people...they make it seem right to grab at a little temporary happiness—to defeat the barbarians, Uncle Hu would say. But I want happiness that will *last,* given the chance.'

'So do I...will you marry me, blood of my heart?'

For a moment longer she stared at him, then doubt was beaten at last and she gravely nodded her head. She was pulled into his arms, and the moon was blotted out—with his mouth on hers there was nothing to fear...nothing to be aware of except mutual need, and leaping desire, and an end to loneliness. But at last he lifted his head.

'Now listen, my darling one. A soldier is what

I've been before, and as soon as Hugo has got me properly vouched for I expect I shall be drafted into the British Army. I'd like to ask your uncle to marry us as soon as he can, but it seems cruel to parade our happiness in front of him and Lydia just now.'

Holly shook her head. 'You don't know Francis Fanshawe well enough yet. Even if Richard has been lost to them...no, *especially* if that has happened, I think...my uncle would say that life must never be blotted out by death...that we must cherish every morsel of happiness we can find, not waste a crumb of it.'

'Then let us go and ask him,' said Juan. He left a kiss folded in the palms of her hands to last the night, he said, and led her back to the house.

By the time of their wedding ten days later it seemed still harder but even more necessary to cling to that philosophy. The Dunkirk epic was finally over and more than three hundred thousand exhausted men had been safely brought back to England—a miracle, everyone agreed...but no word had been heard of Richard Fanshawe.

Francis tried to explain that in the chaotic state of things it would take weeks to restore Army records again, but he knew that Lydia didn't believe what he said; in his heart he couldn't blame her—he didn't believe it himself.

On Holly's wedding morning Phoebe walked out into the early June freshness of the garden to pick rosebuds for a posy, because even a wartime bride must have flowers, she insisted to Hugo. But he found her later, sitting on a secluded bench, flowers unpicked, staring at something only she could see.

'More news this morning, my love,' he said quietly. 'The Prime Minister announced to the House of Commons last night that Mussolini now feels brave enough to declare war on us as well.'

She turned her head away so that he shouldn't see her face, but her voice shook. 'What a wedding-present for Holly! Dear God, will there ever be any good news?'

Hugo took her hand in his warm one. 'When we least expect it, mark my words. But while we wait for it to come, we have a wedding to celebrate. I hope that hasn't slipped your memory.'

'How could it? But this isn't the sort of day I would have wanted for Holly, clouded with so much anxiety and grief.'

'Nothing can spoil it for her or Juan. They're transfigured with happiness.'

Phoebe nodded, taking comfort from the fact that what he said was true. 'Nearly half a century ago my father took his wife to Spain and fell in love with Asunción instead. All that sadness and everything that it's led to since seems pardoned by today's ceremony, and at last even Lydia understands that, despite the anguish she's suffering.' Phoebe covered Hugo's hand with her free one. 'Is it *very* bad for us...the news about Italy?'

'According to Mr Churchill, we should look on it as a privilege to be fighting the Duce. His voice chews every syllable of the man's name and spits them out with a heart-lifting snort of disgust! I think he's right, and in any case it's a sound maxim in war to *know* who your enemies are.'

Phoebe smiled almost naturally. 'With you and Winston Churchill, why should I despair? I feel strong enough to pick Holly's roses!'

It was to have been a very private occasion, but Hindleford took a different view. A pity, they couldn't help thinking, that a lovely maid of theirs should go to someone who'd take her away from the village when he got the chance...still, she'd got a real man by the look of Juan Rodriguez.

It was Helena's opinion too, when she could spare a moment from remembering her own wedding day. She hadn't seen Ned since he'd volunteered for the Royal Army Medical Corps; a short-sighted orderly was better, he'd argued, than no orderly at all, and the Army had agreed with him. James was also missing from the congregation, being somewhere in the Atlantic on a destroyer, but Josh had managed to get leave from his fighter squadron in Kent. Standing beside him, Helena saw the smile he beamed across the aisle at Annie Blake. It was so open a declaration of love that his muttered confession came as no surprise.

'I'm a poor risk, matrimonially-speaking, but one of these days I'm going to ask that girl to take me on.'

Helena nodded, approving his choice, but hoping he understood that *he* would have to take on Arnold and the pottery as well.

'Nothing like a war for allowing you to see things clearly,' she agreed. 'Look at me...lost in admiration nowadays for her ladyship; it hasn't always been like that!'

Believing it, Josh grinned. His mother was a valiant forceful woman; but she couldn't have made an easy mother-in-law. Then he grew serious again. 'I haven't said this to Holly, but I can say it to you. At last I can remember Luis without rage—that score is going to be settled one day soon.'

Helena found herself clutching his hand. 'No needless heroics, Josh, please...' She couldn't bring herself to mention Richard, but got out something else. 'Remember Annie—she'd rather have a husband than a hero.' Then it was time to get to their feet because Anne Maynard's organ voluntary was announcing the arrival of the bride with Hugo.

Half an hour later they emerged from the dimness of the church into brilliant morning sunlight. Standing with a knot of people who'd arrived too late to go inside was a tall, fair-haired man dressed in hospital blues. He was supported by a crutch, and flanked by Mrs Briggs, bathed in happy tears.

The bride saw him, released Juan's hand and stepped aside, leaving the way clear for the woman behind her, but Lydia Fanshawe faltered and went very white. Richard smiled at his mother.

'Dear Mum...I got a bang on the head...it took me a little while to remember who I was!'

Then Lydia moved at last, ran the last few steps, and enfolded him in her arms.

It became after that, as everybody agreed, an even more joyously emotional wedding than most. Juan watched the company assembled on the Manor lawn...a sprinkling of uniformed men and women, no lavish wedding-feast, or extravagant clothes, but otherwise who would have guessed that these people were facing the imminent invasion of their small, dear island, with a shattered army and no allies left to help them?

He found Hugo Taverner beside him and made an expressive gesture with his hands.

'I dare say you're thinking that you've married into a mad race of people,' Hugo suggested cheerfully.

Juan shook his head, watching Kate Fanshawe and Jim Wilkins perform a triumphant dance on the lawn around her brother, who had been lost and was found again.

'I was remembering the German troops that Hitler sent to help General Franco in Spain—unimaginative, efficient men who always did what they were told, unlike some of our Spanish fighters! But for the first time I begin to understand why they may be going to lose again in the end. They will simply be baffled by people who don't even know that they are beaten.'

'Exactly,' said Hugo, pleased with him.

'Therein lies our salvation, coupled with an outside miracle or two that God in His infinite goodness will be required to send us.'

He and Juan smiled at each other, and thus Holly found them. She tucked a hand in her husband's arm, and said wistfully, 'I wish Asunción were here; I'm certain that today would make her very happy.'

Juan bent down to kiss her sad mouth. 'Dear heart, I think she may even guess what's happening. I was given to understand when I left Spain that I shouldn't be welcome if I reappeared without you! Now, have we been polite long enough? Do you suppose anyone will notice if we slip away? A weekend doesn't allow us much of a honeymoon.'

'Go with God, my dears,' Hugo said gently, and to the echo of that loveliest of farewells, they went away together, hand in hand.

The publishers hope that this book has given you enjoyable reading. Large Print Books are especially designed to be as easy to see and hold as possible. If you wish a complete list of our books, please ask at your local library or write directly to: Magna Large Print Books, Long Preston, North Yorkshire, BD23 4ND, England.

Other MAGNA General Fiction Titles In Large Print

FRANCES ANNE BOND
Return Of The Swallow

JUDY GARDINER
All On A Summer's Day

IRIS GOWER
The Sins Of Eden

HELENE MANSFIELD
Some Women Dream

ELISABETH McNEILL
The Shanghai Emerald

ELIZABETH MURPHY
To Give And To Take

JUDITH SAXTON
This Royal Breed

Other MAGNA General Fiction Titles In Large Print

ELVI RHODES
Summer Promise

SALLY STEWART
The Women of Providence

ELISABETH McNEILL
Perseverance Place

NICHOLAS RHEA
Constable Among The Heather

JUDY TURNER
The Arcade

MISS READ
Village Affairs

PERFICK
The Darling Buds Of May